Brenda Harlen is a
Boon True Love wh
the company.

USA Today bestselle
than forty books for Mills & Boon. You can usually find her in
her office with her laptop loving the fact that she gets to work
in her pyjamas.

Michelle loves to hear from her readers! Visit Michelle on
Facebook at Michelle Celmer Author, or email at
michelle@michellecelmer.com

Scarlet Wilson wrote her first story aged eight and has never
stopped. She's worked in the health service for twenty years,
trained as a nurse and a health visitor. Scarlet now works in
public health and lives on the West Coast of Scotland with her
fiance and their two sons. Writing medical romances and
contemporary romances is a dream come true for her.

Tempted by
the Royal

BRENDA HARLEN
MICHELLE CELMER
SCARLET WILSON

MILLS & BOON

First Published in Great Britain 2019
by Mills & Boon, an imprint of HarperCollins*Publishers*
1 London Bridge Street, London, SE1 9GF

TEMPTED BY THE ROYAL © 2019 Harlequin Books S. A.

The Prince's Holiday Baby © 2008 Brenda Harlen
Christmas with the Prince © 2009 Michelle Celmer
The Prince She Never Forgot © 2015 Scarlet Wilson

ISBN: 978-0-263-27938-2

1019

Printed and bound in Spain
by CPI, Barcelona

THE PRINCE'S HOLIDAY BABY

BRENDA HARLEN

In memory of Tom Torrance—
January 28, 1951–March 6, 2008

A teacher and mentor and friend;
a genuine prince among men.

Prologue

"You didn't need to come over here, Grandma. I told you on the phone that I was fine."

Theresa Shea plunked her purse on the bar and narrowed her gaze on her granddaughter behind the counter at Shea's Bar & Grill. Yes, she certainly looked fine. But Molly had always been one to keep her chin up no matter how much her heart was breaking inside. And she'd had a lot of heartbreak to deal with over the past six months.

"Maybe I needed to see for myself."

"And now you have."

"And now that I'm here, maybe I'd like a cup of coffee."

Molly poured her a cup of coffee, pushed it across the counter.

She'd been working there for so many years now, she didn't even have to think about the tasks anymore. Everything was automatic, routine, and not at all what James Shea wanted for his daughter.

"What are you doing here?" Theresa asked softly.

"Right now? Trying to figure out the produce order for next week."

"He wanted you to go to college, to do something more."

Her granddaughter's fingers tightened around the pencil in her hand, but there was no other outward sign of the emotions that were churning inside her. Molly didn't talk about her father but Theresa knew he was in her thoughts almost constantly, especially here, at the restaurant that had been his livelihood and his life. And she knew that Molly was so determined to hold on to Shea's because it was the only part of her father she had left.

"I'm happy here," Molly finally said.

"Are you?"

Molly continued punching numbers into the calculator, frowned.

Theresa tried a different tack. "Do you ever write anymore?"

"I write checks to pay the bills."

"You know that's not what I meant."

"It's all I have time for right now."

"You have to learn to take time for the things that are more enoyable than necessary."

"I will," Molly promised. "After all the necessary things are done."

Theresa picked up her purse. She knew when she was banging her head against a wall and her granddaughter's stubbornness was a brick wall.

"All right, I'll go. But if you need anything—"

Molly leaned across the counter to kiss her grandmother's cheek. "I won't. I'll be fine."

Which was exactly why Theresa was worried.

The phone rang as she turned away, and Molly reached for it. Theresa didn't hear the words she spoke, but the tone gave her pause. When Molly hung up, she said only one word, "Abbey."

Molly's sister, Theresa's youngest granddaughter, had disappeared a few days earlier after leaving a note that said only "don't worry—I'll be home in a few days" and absolutely nothing about where she was going or who she was with.

"Where is she?"

"Las Vegas." Molly swallowed. "With Jason."

Theresa didn't want to ask, was certain she already knew, and her granddaughter's next words confirmed it.

"She just married my fiancé."

Chapter One

Nine years later—

Prince Eric Santiago lied when he told his best friend that he had a plane to catch. The truth was, his pilot wasn't coming to pick him up for the return trip to Tesoro del Mar until the following morning, but after almost two weeks with Scott Delsey and his soon-to-be-wife, Eric needed some space. Spending so much time with the blissful couple and seeing how in love they were only made him more aware of what was missing from his own life.

When he'd accepted the invitation to visit Scott's ranch in Texas, he'd thought his friend might want to offer him a job at DELconnex, his communications company. On more than one occasion in the past, Scott had mentioned that he could use someone with Eric's education and experience, though they both knew Eric had no intention of leaving the Tesorian navy.

Now, of course, the situation had changed, and Eric was willing to consider any possibilities his friend presented. It turned out one of those possibilities was to stand up as the best man at Scott's wedding.

It seemed that everywhere around him people were getting married and having babies. First it was his eldest brother, Rowan, who had been forced by tragedy and tradition to the altar. Luckily for him, he'd managed to fall in love along the way. After six years of marriage, he and Lara were happier than the day they'd exchanged their vows, even with—or maybe because of—the two active young sons who did their best to run their parents ragged.

Three years after Rowan pledged "till death do us part," their youngest brother, Marcus, had found a woman who inspired him to do the same. Recently, he and Jewel had welcomed their first child into the world—a beautiful baby girl who looked just like her mother and already exhibited the legendary charm of her father.

Both of his brothers had lucked out, and Eric was genuinely happy for them. But the only mistress Eric had ever been committed to was the sea—and she'd tossed him aside, carelessly discarding everything he'd given her and taking away everything he was.

As he drove his rented Mercedes northeast toward San Antonio, he forced himself to acknowledge the truth he'd been avoiding for too long—he wasn't just alone, he was lonely.

He envied what Rowan had with Lara, what Marcus had with Jewel, what Scott had with Fiona. And he wondered why he'd never met a woman who made him think in terms of marriage and forever. Okay, having spent the better part of the last twelve years on board a ship might have something to do with it. Add to that the uncertainty of never knowing if the women he'd been with were genuinely interested in him or only attracted to his title or his uniform, and it probably wasn't surprising that he'd reached the age of thirty-six without ever having been in a long-term, committed relationship. Still, the realization wasn't going to fill his life or keep him warm in bed at night.

The rumble of his stomach finally broke through his intro-spection and a neon sign announcing Shea's Bar & Grill snagged his attention.

Despite the fact that the building was smack in the middle of nowhere, there were several vehicles—mostly dust-covered pick-up trucks—in the parking lot. His empty stomach again protested his decision to leave his friend's ranch before dinner and he flicked on his indicator to make the turn.

He parked his shiny rental between an ancient red pickup and a mud-splattered Jeep and sat for a moment, wondering if he would look as out of place in the bar as his vehicle did in the parking lot. A man who'd grown up in the public eye wouldn't usually worry about such things, but Eric had become more sen-sitive to the attention—and the speculation that surrounded him—since the accident.

He pushed out of the car, slowly limped toward the entrance. The deliberate, unhurried movements helped ease the stiffness from his hip so that he was walking almost normally by the time he reached the door. His therapist had warned that he might al-ways have the limp and the discomfort—at the time, he'd thought it was a small price to pay for being alive. When he'd had to leave the navy, he'd realized the physical scars weren't the biggest price.

A sign inside the door invited him to seat himself. He by-passed several empty tables around the perimeter of the dance floor and made his way to the bar. As he slid onto a vacant stool, he forgot about his hip and everything else as he glimpsed a vision that was more impressive than anything he'd seen while sightseeing in Texas.

Hermoso…espectacular…perfecto.

Her hair was as dark as midnight and tumbled over her shoulders like a silky waterfall. She was wearing a deep, V-neck shirt that revealed just a hint of cleavage and was tucked into slim-fitting jeans that molded to narrow hips and long legs.

His gaze skimmed upward again and locked with hers.

He felt a sharp tug of attraction deep in his belly, an almost painful yearning, and he could tell by the sudden widening and darkening of eyes the color of a clear summer sky that she was experiencing the same sensation. Instantaneous, raw and powerful.

But then she tossed her hair over her shoulder and smiled easily.

"Hey, handsome." The slow Texas drawl made him think of lazy Sunday mornings spent lounging in bed—and wasn't *that* an unexpectedly intriguing image? "What can I get for you?"

She smiled again, and suddenly he was wanting a lot more than he'd come in for, but he forced himself to respond just as casually. "A beer would be good."

She grabbed a clean mug from the shelf behind her. "Any particular kind?"

He tore his gaze from the stunning face to glance at the labels on the taps. He noted the familiar Amstel, Heineken and Beck's brands, but opted for one that he guessed would have a more local flavor. "Lone Star."

She tipped the glass beneath the nozzle to catch the amber-colored liquid that flowed out. "You're a long way from home, aren't you?"

"Am I?"

She slid the beer across the bar to him. "Well, you don't sound like a local, and if you were, I would have seen you before now."

He didn't think she was flirting with him exactly. But she seemed, if not interested, at least curious, and he couldn't resist testing the waters.

"You don't remember?" he asked, his tone intended to convey both disbelief and disappointment.

She made change for the ten he gave her and leaned across the bar in a way that greatly enhanced his view of her cleavage. "If I don't remember, *you* obviously didn't make much of an impression."

He grinned at her quick response and lifted his glass to his lips as she moved down the bar to serve another customer.

He'd struck out with the sexy bartender, but it was his first time at bat after a long absence from the plate and, the way he figured it, it was only the top of the first inning. There was a lot of the game still to be played.

Eric ordered a barbecued pork sandwich with a side of spicy fries and washed it down with another draft as he watched the woman who'd eventually introduced herself as Molly Shea check on her customers at the bar. She took a moment to chat with each one as if they were all old friends, and he knew some of them probably were.

"How long have you been a bartender?" he asked her.

She poured a glass of water and squeezed a wedge of lime into it. "Forever."

"Has it always been your ambition?"

"It's honest work," she said.

"I wasn't implying otherwise," he told her. "You just seem like a woman who could do so much more."

"I can make all the fanciest drinks," she said, deliberately misunderstanding him. "But we don't have much call for them here."

"You're determined not to give away anything about yourself, aren't you?"

"Bartenders don't make confessions, they listen to them."

"I thought that was just a stereotype."

"I used to think so, too. But I learned quickly that a sympathetic ear and a shot of Scotch whiskey is a lot more successful at loosening tongues than a long couch and a fifty-minute clock."

His gaze skimmed over her face. "The ears are nice," he agreed. "But I'll bet it has a lot more to do with your soft voice and warm smile." And the idea of this woman on a long couch—minus the fifty-minute clock—was more than a little intriguing.

"Is that why you're here?" she asked. "Are you looking to unburden your soul?"

"My soul isn't burdened."

Her only response was to raise her eyebrows.

"No more than most," he clarified.

She smiled at that, and he felt a funny little kick in his belly. It was lust, he was certain of it. Certain that what he was feeling for this intriguing bartender couldn't be any more than that.

Eric picked up his cup and frowned when he found it empty. He'd switched to coffee after his second draft, and he'd already had one refill, making him wonder just how long he'd been sitting at the bar.

"It's almost eleven," Molly told him, somehow anticipating his question as she brought the pot over to refill his cup again. "Isn't there somewhere else you should be?"

"Not anymore," he told her.

Her eyes were unexpectedly sympathetic as she asked, "Did she kick you out?"

"Who?"

"Whoever's responsible for that lost look in your eyes."

"No one kicked me out." Then he smiled at her. "Not yet, anyway."

She laughed. "You've got another hour."

* * *

He was still there at the end of the hour.

And Molly was still as conscious of his presence as she'd been from the minute he walked in the door. Conscious of his attention focused on her as she began tidying up her workspace and wiping down the counters after last call.

She was flattered, of course. The man was sinfully good looking with that dark hair and those smoldering eyes, a mouth that made her think of long, slow kisses and shoulders that looked as if they could carry the weight of the world.

But he didn't belong there. She'd recognized that fact even before he'd opened his mouth and started speaking in that smoothly cultured voice that spoke of private schools and a wealth of other privileges.

And she wondered what he was doing in Texas or, more particularly, what he was doing in her bar.

She did know that every time she caught him looking at her, her pulse spiked. And when he smiled, her heart pounded and her blood heated. Though her experience with men was limited, she recognized her reaction for what it was: lust, pure and simple. And when a man looked like the one sitting at her bar, she was certain he had more than enough experience being the object of women's desires.

The stirring of her own desire, however, was unexpected.

She wasn't the type of woman to fantasize about having sex with a man she didn't even know. Of course, her lackluster experience with Trevor had pretty much nixed her fantasies about sex—and the few brief relationships she'd had since then hadn't given her reason to hope for anything different.

But she poured herself a single glass of wine—part of her usual closing up routine—and slid onto the stool beside his. "Are you really waiting for me to kick you out?"

"I'm not in a hurry to go anywhere else."

"If I'm going to let you stay while I close up, I'll need to know more about you."

"Such as?"

"Where you're from—because we both know it's not Texas."

"Tesoro del Mar," he told her.

"Treasure of the Sea," she translated.

"You speak Spanish?"

"A little." She sipped her wine. "And is it—a treasure of the sea, that is?"

"Absolutely."

"What brought you from there to here?"

"I was visiting a friend."

"A girlfriend?" she guessed.

"No," he said, then, "yes, there was a woman."

She lifted a brow. "Only one?"

He smiled. "My best friend is getting married. His fiancée is the only woman I've seen since I've been here."

"How long has that been?"

"Almost two weeks."

"And why is it that you're alone in a bar at quarter after twelve on a Sunday night?"

He made a point of looking her over. "I'm not exactly alone now, am I?"

"Alone *except* for the bartender," she clarified.

"I would say alone *with* an incredibly beautiful woman."

The heat in his gaze added weight to his words, but Molly wasn't going to let herself get all tongue-tied and weak-kneed just because a handsome man paid her a compliment.

"I'm flattered," she said. "But you're going to be disappointed if you think a few smooth words will convince me to go home with you."

"Since I don't even have a hotel room booked, I was hoping

you would invite me to go home with you." There was something in his tone that told her he was only half joking.

"Not going to happen," she told him.

"Is there anyone special in your life?"

She smiled. "There are a lot of special people in my life."

"I meant a boyfriend," he clarified. "Since you're not wearing a ring, I'm guessing there's not a husband or fiancé."

She shook her head. "I don't really have time to date. Too many other things going on."

"That might be a valid excuse for neglecting to return a phone call," he noted, "but it hardly explains not dating."

"Does a broken engagement explain it better for you?"

He nodded. "Broken heart, too?"

She hesitated a moment, then shook her head. "No, and maybe that's one of the reasons I haven't been dating. I realized how close I'd come to making a very big mistake, and I needed some time to figure out what I really wanted."

"And have you?"

"I'm still working on it."

"Me, too," he admitted.

"I would have figured you for the type of man who knew exactly what he wanted."

"I used to be." His eyes held hers for a long moment, then his gaze dropped to her mouth. "Not only did I know what I wanted, but I knew how to get it."

Then he leaned down and kissed her.

And she kissed him back.

She, Molly Shea, who didn't do anything spontaneous or impulsive, was kissing a stranger in a bar—and thoroughly enjoying every second of it.

Because—WOW—he knew how to kiss.

Her brain scrambled to find an explanation for this inexplicable turn of events. She wanted to blame the wine, though she'd only had half a glass. She might consider the lateness of the hour, except that she was accustomed to working nights and wasn't at all tired. Or maybe it was just the strength of a purely physical attraction that she hadn't felt in a very long time.

His tongue slid between her lips and the random thoughts and desperate explanations faded into nothingness as her brain seemed to stop functioning altogether.

His hands slid up her back, drawing her close, closer. Her breasts grazed the solid wall of his chest. Her nipples tightened, her belly quivered. He drew her to her feet, and she pressed herself against him, shocked—and aroused—to feel the hard ridge of his erection against her belly.

He wanted her.

Of course, he was a man and the state of his arousal might have more to do with that fact than the identity of the woman in his arms, but she wasn't going to worry about that now. She was just going to bask in the knowledge that she was wanted, revel in this affirmation of her feminine power. At least for another minute.

Had she ever been kissed so thoroughly? Until her blood felt like molten lava pulsing through her veins and her knees went weak and everything inside her started to quiver? Never.

Not even Trevor's kisses had made her feel like this. He was the first man she'd ever been intimate with, and she'd never responded to him the way she was responding now. Of course, her relationship with Trevor had come on the heels of the break-up of her engagement, when she'd been desperate to feel wanted by someone. But even then, she'd never wanted to be with him as desperately as she wanted to be with Eric now.

And the wanting terrified her.

She forced herself to ease away from him and when she spoke, she kept her voice light, careful to give no hint of the churning inside. "You know what? You're as sexy as sin and when you kiss me, it makes my heart pound like you wouldn't believe, but I don't do one night stands with strangers."

"I don't, either…as a rule." He slid his hands up her back, and she shivered as his fingers traced lazily along the ridges of her spine. "But there's an exception to every rule."

"And you think you should be mine?" she asked skeptically.

"I think *you* could be *mine*."

She pushed his arms down, stepped away from him and temptation. "I might be a small-town girl, but even I can recognize a big-time con."

He winced. "Okay, it did sound like a line."

"You think?" What was even worse than the obvious script was how much she still wanted to give in to the desire thrumming between them.

"What I think is that, for the first time in a long time, I've met an interesting woman and I'm not ready to say goodbye to her yet."

He sounded sincere, but if she'd learned nothing else from her failed relationships, she'd learned that she didn't have a clue when it came to understanding the motivations of men. "Do you mean that?"

"Yes, I do."

His voice was sure, his gaze steady, and despite the doubts and insecurities that swirled inside her, she wasn't ready to say goodbye yet, either.

"I'm not working tomorrow," she finally said. "If you wanted to meet me back here around ten, maybe we could spend the day together."

"I'd really like that," he said. "But I won't be here tomorrow."

Disappointment weighed heavily in her belly. "You won't?"

"My plane's scheduled to leave at 8:00 a.m."

"You're going back to Tesoro del Mar?"

He nodded, and though she regretted that it was true, she knew his leaving wasn't any reason to throw caution to the wind and do something completely crazy.

"I guess this is goodbye then," she said.

"I guess it is," he agreed.

Then he tipped her chin up with his finger and brushed his lips against hers. It was a gentle kiss this time, as fleeting as their time together had been.

"Goodbye, Molly."

"Goodbye." She watched him cross the room. She watched as he flipped the lock and pushed on the door, and she felt all of her reason and common sense sweep through the open portal and into the night.

"Wait." The word sprang from her lips without conscious thought.

He turned back. Waiting.

She could let him go—and always wonder what might have been. Or she could be wildly spontaneous and spend the night with a man whose kiss had singed her right down to her toes.

She'd always believed it was better to regret something she'd done than something she'd left undone, and while it was possible she'd wake up with regrets in the morning, she knew she would regret it more if she let him walk away.

Eric sensed the battle waging inside Molly and it took every ounce of willpower he possessed to keep his hand clamped around the handle of the door to keep from reaching for her again. If they were going to spend the night together—as he very much wanted them to do—it would need to be her decision. And he knew it wasn't one she would make lightly.

She'd admitted that she didn't date much, and he knew a

woman as beautiful and warm and friendly as Molly didn't sleep alone unless it was what she wanted. So what made him think that she would break her self-imposed rules to spend the night with him?

Chemistry.

It had crackled between them from the first moment their eyes had locked across the bar and had been building and deepening ever since. The sizzling kiss they'd shared was further proof of it.

His body was still humming from the after-effects of that kiss, or maybe it was almost three years of self-imposed celibacy that had everything inside him churned up. Whatever the reason, he knew what he wanted. He was just waiting for Molly to reach the same conclusion.

She looked at him now, her eyes locked with his, and she said only one more word.

"Stay."

He flipped the lock on the door and moved back to her.

She met him halfway—her arms lifting to circle his neck, her body pressing against his, her mouth opening for his kiss.

His hands moved over her, hotly, hungrily. She gasped and sighed in response to his touch, and those sexy little sounds nearly snapped the last of his control. She was so eager and passionate, as hungry for him as he was for her, and it was an effort not to tear away her clothes where they stood and bury himself inside her.

The woman had him tied up in knots, desperate and aching with desire.

He cupped her breasts and felt her nipples pebble in response to the brush of his thumbs. She arched against him, a silent plea for more. Even through the layers of their clothing, the erotic friction of her hips pushing against his was almost too much.

She was sexy and sweet, giving and demanding.

And she was his.

The thought came from out of nowhere, the sudden drive to take and claim and possess both unfamiliar and undeniable.

He was leaving in the morning. They both knew they wouldn't have anything more than this one night together. But he was determined to make it a night neither of them would ever forget.

This was crazy.

Even as Molly led Eric up the stairs to her apartment over the bar, she knew it was outrageously insane to even consider having sex with a man she'd never laid eyes on a few hours before, who would be leaving again in another few hours and whom she would probably never see again after that.

She didn't care.

Right now all she cared about was getting naked with him.

And he wanted the same thing, if the trail of clothes they left in the hall on their way to her room was any indication. She led him unerringly through the dark to the bed, then pushed him back onto the mattress and tumbled down with him.

She reached for the small lamp on the night table, but he caught her hand and brought it to his lips. He kissed her palm, nibbled on her fingers, and sent sparks of heat zinging through her system.

Oh, yes, there was heat. And Molly gloried in this confirmation that she wasn't unresponsive or dispassionate, she'd just needed a man who knew how to touch her the right way. And Eric definitely knew how to touch a woman the right way.

She wanted to touch him—was desperate to touch him—too. With limited experience to fall back on, she allowed her instincts to guide her. She ran her hands up his chest, over his shoulders, down his arms. She reveled in the feel of all those hard, tight muscles bunching and flexing in response to her eager touch. His skin was warm and smooth and taut; his body exquisitely carved and sculpted. Everywhere she touched, he was hard and strong, so completely and perfectly male. And for now—for the next few hours that remained of the night—he was hers.

Her fingertips paused in their exploration, hovering over the puckered ridge of skin she'd discovered beneath his lowest rib.

She felt him tense as she slowly traced the diagonal line of the scar toward his hip bone. Her fingers moved lower, finding a wider, longer scar on his upper thigh, and she instinctively knew this was the reason he hadn't wanted the light.

His perfect body wasn't quite perfect after all. And yet, the physical scars on his body somehow enhanced rather than detracted from his appeal.

"A recent injury?" she asked softly.

"Not so recent," he said, but offered nothing more.

She traced her fingertips over the scars again, as if her touch could ease the strain she heard in his voice, the tension in his muscles. "What happened?"

"A naval training exercise went wrong."

His simplistic explanation was a clear indication that this wasn't something he wanted to talk about. But his response had given her another valuable insight about this man. "So you're a sailor."

"Was," he corrected.

"With a woman in every port?" she teased to lighten the moment.

"Never more than one at a time."

"Good to know." She kissed him then, deeply, hungrily.

She kissed his lips, his throat, his chest. Her hair spilled over his shoulders, providing a curtain behind which she continued her exploration. She'd never been so aroused, so tempted, so bold. But she let her instincts, and his throaty groans of appreciation, guide her. She nibbled her way down his belly, savored the salty masculine flavor of his skin. Then her lips found the ridge of scar tissue her fingers had recently discovered, and her avid mouth gently feathered soft kisses along the puckered skin.

"If you're trying to kiss away the pain, where I'm really hurting is just a little bit lower," he told her huskily.

She chuckled, letting her tongue taste, tempt, tease. She heard the sharp intake of his breath, and knew her bold acceptance of his challenge had surprised and aroused him.

She heard the crinkle of plastic as he unwrapped the condom he'd snagged from his pocket before discarding his pants somewhere in the hall, and was grateful he'd had the foresight to think of protection. She let him sheath himself, then kissed her way back up his body, her taut nipples grazing his chest, her hips rocking against his. His hands skimmed over her thighs, his fingers curled around her buttocks, pressing her closer.

She waited for him to press into her, to take control in search of his own pleasure. But he didn't seem to be in any big rush to the finish line. In fact, he seemed more than content just to touch her, tease her, taste her.

Molly endured the exquisite torture for as long as she could, then she straddled his hips, positioning herself so that the tip of his erection was at the juncture of her thighs.

Slowly she lowered herself, moving just the tiniest bit, taking only a fraction of an inch inside of her. Then a little more.

His hands were on her hips, his fingers biting into her flesh. She could feel the tension in him and knew he was fighting against the instinct to drive into her. He was bigger than her, stronger, and they both knew she was only in control at the moment because he wanted her to be, but still, the sense of power was exhilarating.

She continued to tease him, taking him a little bit deeper inside, then drawing back again. His eyes were so dark they were almost black, and they were intently focused on her. Watching her as she watched him.

Watching her as his hands skimmed up her sides to her breasts, as his fingers toyed with her nipples, circling, stroking, squeezing.

Desire curled like a fist deep in her belly, tight, tighter, until she cried out with her release.

It was the signal he'd been waiting for, and his hips jerked off the mattress and he buried himself deep inside of her in one powerful thrust that had her crying out again at the shock of the next climax that ripped through her, leaving her weak and breathless and shattered.

But Eric wasn't finished with her. He held himself perfectly still until her body had stopped shuddering, then he flipped her over, so that she was on her back and he was stretched out on top of her, pressing deep inside of her.

He whispered to her, speaking softly in Spanish. She didn't understand all of the words, but his tone was as sensual as a caress, and just as arousing. He began to move. Slow and deep strokes that touched her very core. Then hard and fast thrusts. Harder. Faster.

She'd thought she was sated. He'd made certain she was satisfied before he'd pursued his own pleasure, and yet, she could feel the desperate, achy need building inside of her again. Her heels dug into the mattress, her nails bit into his shoulders, and her hips matched his frantic rhythm as her desire escalated again until the world dropped away and there was nothing to hold on to but each other.

He collapsed with his head on her pillow, his arm wrapped around her, and his heart beating against hers.

They made love twice more before exhaustion finally overrode passion, and Molly fell into a deep and blissful sleep in the warm comfort of his arms.

She woke up in the morning, cold and alone, and found herself regretting not the hours she'd spent with Eric but that he was already gone.

Chapter Two

"Pregnant?"

Molly stared at the doctor for a minute, then laughed as she shook her head.

"I think you're going to want to run that test again."

Dr. Morgan looked at her with both understanding and compassion in her deep green eyes. She'd been Molly's doctor for more than twenty years, long before her dark hair had become so liberally streaked with grey and the faint lines around her eyes and mouth had multiplied.

"I'll rerun the test," she told her. "If you can look me in the eye and honestly tell me that you haven't had sex in the past two months."

Molly's fingers curled around the edge of the examining table, her damp palms sticking to the paper. "Not unprotected sex."

"Well, I'm glad to hear that," Dr. Morgan said. "But you know there isn't any method of contraception that is one hundred percent effective."

She could only stare at her as the reality of what the doctor was saying began to sink in and her heart began to hammer out its panic against her ribs.

"It was one night," she whispered.

One night after four years of going to bed alone.

"That's all it takes," the doctor said gently.

Molly shook her head, still unwilling to believe what the doctor was saying. "But I don't feel pregnant. I don't feel any different—just tired."

"That's often one of the first signs."

"I haven't been sick."

"Not every woman experiences morning sickness. You might be one of the lucky ones."

Lucky? Molly was too stunned to really know how she was feeling, but she was pretty sure it wasn't lucky.

"That's assuming you want to continue with this pregnancy," Dr. Morgan continued gently. "It is still early and—"

Molly shook her head again. She knew what the doctor was going to say—she was going to tell her there were options. She knew what those options were. She also knew there was only one choice for her—and it was the same choice her own mother had made thirty-one years earlier.

"I'm going to have the baby," she said.

"Do you know the father?" Dr. Morgan asked gently.

Her cheeks burned with shame as Molly realized she probably should have kept her "one night" comment to herself, but she managed to choke out the lie, "Of course."

She knew his name—his first name, anyway. And she knew he was from a country called Tesoro del Mar. And she knew that he kissed like there was no tomorrow and made her feel as no man had ever made her feel before. Beyond that, she knew almost nothing at all.

"If you're going to have this baby, the father should be told," Dr. Morgan said. "This isn't something you should have to go through on your own."

She nodded, because she knew it was true. She also knew that if she somehow managed to track him down, Eric wasn't likely to be thrilled to learn that he'd knocked up some woman he picked up in a bar. And that was the tawdry truth of what had happened between them, even if, at the time, it hadn't seemed tawdry at all.

But the soul-deep connection she'd been certain she'd felt in the darkest hours of the night had been illuminated as to what it really was in the bright light of day—a good healthy dose of lust that temporarily overrode common sense—and a passion that was apparently stronger than latex condoms.

Molly walked from the doctor's office to Celebrations by Fiona. The exclusive boutique was ten blocks from the medical arts building and she was more than halfway there before she questioned the wisdom of undertaking such a stroll in low-heeled sling-backs and ninety-degree heat. But she'd needed some time to think about the news she'd been given and she knew that when she got to Fiona's, she wouldn't have a minute to do so.

Her cousin had established a reputation as one of the premier event planners in Texas and her services were sought by everyone who was anyone in the state. She'd planned the island nuptials of a Cowboys' quarterback, personally oversaw every detail of the small garden wedding for an Oscar-winning actress and co-ordinated the renewal of vows to celebrate the fiftieth anniversary of the governor and his wife.

But it turned out that her most challenging assignment and most demanding client wasn't a celebrity or politician, it was herself. And her mistake, in Molly's opinion, was in not hiring someone else to oversee the details of her own wedding—a wedding at which Molly would be the maid of honor the following month.

It seemed like a lifetime ago that Molly had been shopping for dresses and bouquets of flowers, dreaming of "happily ever after." She'd been so full of hope for her future, eager to marry the man she loved, looking forward to raising a family together.

Though that engagement had fallen apart, she'd still believed that someday she would find someone special to share her life and build a family with. Now she'd skipped over the marriage part and was going straight to motherhood—definitely not her childhood dream but a reality that she would have to deal with it.

First, however, she had to tackle the issue of a bridesmaid dress.

Fiona was hovering just inside the door, waiting for her, when she finally arrived.

"Goodness," she said, noting her cousin's flushed cheeks. "You look like you just finished running a marathon."

"Even a short walk feels like a marathon in this heat," she said, not wanting to admit how far she'd walked or where she'd come from.

Fiona scooped a bottle of water out of the minifridge in her office and handed it to her.

"Thanks." Molly took the bottle and sank into an empty chair. "Have you finally picked a dress for me?"

"Sort of."

Molly arched a brow as she uncapped the water.

Fiona gestured to a garment rack that was crowded with gowns.

Molly stared. "There must be a dozen dresses there."

"Sixteen," her cousin admitted.

"I realize the layered look is in, but sixteen might be a bit excessive."

"I couldn't decide," Fiona said, a trifle defensively.

"Couldn't you at least have narrowed it down?"

"That is narrowed down."

Molly shouldn't have been surprised. Even with all of Fiona's contacts in the industry, it had taken her cousin three weeks and trips to both New York City and San Francisco to finally decide on her own gown—from a local boutique.

"I know that pastels are all the rage for summer weddings," Fiona was explaining now, "but I think jewel tones work better with your coloring and, since you're my only attendant, you can pick whatever you want."

Whatever she wanted so long as it was sapphire, emerald or ruby, Molly noted, and rose from her chair for a closer examination of the gowns.

But as she sorted through the collection, her mind slipped back to another examination, to her conversation with Dr. Morgan and the one word that continued to reverberate inside her head.

Pregnant.

"Any thoughts?" Fiona asked.

I thought I would regret it more if I didn't spend the night with him.

Of course, that thought was immediately followed by a wave of guilt. As much as she hadn't planned to get pregnant at this point in her life, she wouldn't regret the child that she would have. The baby growing inside of her probably wasn't the size of a pea yet, but Molly loved her already.

"Molly?" The prompt drew her attention back to the rack of dresses.

"They all look great," she said, forcing enthusiasm into her voice.

"That's what I thought, too," Fiona told her.

Molly went with her instincts and grabbed a strapless floor-length gown of deep blue silk and slipped through the door. She stripped away her clothes, careful not to look at her refection in any of the mirrors that surrounded her. She didn't want to look at her body, to think about the changes that were happening inside of her—changes that she knew were invisible to the outside world but essential to the tiny life inside her.

She tugged the zipper up, straightened the skirt and stepped back outside to show her friend.

"Oh. Wow." Fiona grinned. "That's it—it's perfect."

Molly exhaled a silent sigh of relief that she would be spared having to model the other fifteen dresses.

"You are going to knock his socks off in that dress," her cousin said.

"Whose socks am I knocking off?" she asked warily.

"The best man's."

Molly wasn't so sure that she wanted to be near any man even taking his socks off, because the last time that happened she'd ended up pregnant. Well, at least she'd had the chance to experience the most amazing sex of her life first. Yeah, it was good to know that she'd discovered a sex drive just in time to put it on the back burner for the next several years while she raised the illegitimate child of a man whose last name she didn't even know.

"I can't wait for you to meet him," Fiona said, for the millionth time since she'd first met her fiancé's childhood best friend. "If I wasn't so in love with Scott…" She deliberately let her words trail off, then grinned. "But I am in love with Scott, so it would be really great if you managed to hook up with him."

"I'm not looking to hook up with anyone," Molly said firmly.

Fiona forged ahead, as if she hadn't even heard her. "I really wished you'd met him when he was here, then you'd know what I'm talking about."

"I'll meet him at the rehearsal," Molly reminded her.

"Are you bringing anyone to the wedding?"

"You know I'm not."

"Because he's not bringing a date, either."

"Fiona," she warned her cousin.

"I'm just saying."

"I know what you're saying. And I know you just want me to find someone as wonderful as Scott, but I'm really not looking to get involved with anyone right now." And probably not for a long time. "There's just too much going on in my life right now to even think about adding the complication of a relationship."

Fiona's eyes narrowed. "What aren't you telling me?"

And that, Molly knew, was the problem of having a cousin who was also her best friend and who knew her better than any-one else in the world. But she shook her head, not ready to share the news with anyone just yet.

"Your wedding is less than a month away," she reminded Fiona. "You should have enough to think about without worry-ing about my love life."

Her statement succeeded in deflecting her cousin's attention, as she knew it would, and they talked about flowers and music and other details until Fiona's next appointment arrived and Molly was able to escape.

He couldn't get her out of his mind.

Almost two months after he'd returned to Tesoro del Mar, Eric still couldn't stop thinking about Molly Shea. At first, he'd been certain it was just the memories of spectacular sex that haunted his dreams. He'd wanted to believe it was nothing more than that. But as six weeks turned into seven and he still couldn't forget her, he finally admitted it was more than the incredible sensation of her body wrapped around his that kept him awake at night—it was the sparkle in her eyes, the way she smiled, the sound of her laughter.

It was all those memories that plagued his thoughts and made him wonder if he shouldn't have stayed in her bed instead of worrying about his flight home the next morning. But really, what difference would another day or two have made, except maybe to make him even more reluctant to leave the haven of her arms?

Still, he was a prince. He most certainly wasn't going to let himself get tied up in knots over any woman, and especially not an American bartender. But with each day that passed, the memories he'd expected to dim only grew sharper, and the need inside him grew stronger.

Or maybe he just had too much time on his hands.

He'd been at loose ends since the accident that had prematurely ended his naval career, and without any direction or focus. He'd assumed some duties back home, but as important as he knew the royal family was to the country, he wasn't sure he could imagine making a career out of public appearances and shaking hands with foreign diplomats.

His recent conversation with Scott hovered in the back of his mind, but he knew the offer to work at DELconnex wasn't the answer. Or not the whole answer. He wanted something more than a new career. He wanted a wife—a family.

He frowned at that thought. Not that it was unusual for a thirty-six-year-old man to think about settling down, but it was unusual for *him*. On the other hand, nothing had been "usual" for Eric since he'd left the navy, and maybe it was time he gave serious consideration to the thought of marriage.

His brother Rowan hadn't been given the luxury of time before he'd been pressured to find a wife. Hundreds, maybe thousands, of women had put themselves forward as bridal candidates when it became known that the prince regent was required to marry. Rowan had surprised everyone when he'd proposed to the royal nanny rather than a woman with recognizable title and ancestry.

Marcus, his younger brother, had also balked at tradition in choosing his bride, marrying a woman who was a foreigner and a successful business owner. And while there was no doubt that both of his brothers were blissfully happy with their respective wives, Eric had always thought that when the time came for him to marry, he would choose a more traditional kind of wife— someone who understood the role of a royal spouse and would be both suitable and content to fulfill it.

But somehow it was thoughts of a sweet and sexy bartender that hovered in the back of his mind and invaded his dreams. And—seven weeks after a single night together—these thoughts began to cause him serious worry. Never before had he been so preoccupied by a woman. Never before had he yearned so deeply for what he couldn't have.

Being born a prince meant there were few things beyond his grasp, but Molly was one of them. They'd both agreed there would be nothing between them after that night. At the time, it had seemed like a perfect arrangement—one night, no strings. But even as the sun had begun to rise in the morning, Eric had regretted their bargain.

One night hadn't been nearly enough to sate the passion that burned so hotly and fiercely between them. Not when, seven weeks later, just thinking of Molly was enough to make him ache with longing.

He wanted to go back to Texas to see her again, and his friend's upcoming wedding gave him the perfect excuse to do so. Of course, he would have to check in with Rowan first, to ensure there were no pressing matters that required his presence in Tesoro del Mar over the next few weeks.

Having decided he should discuss the matter with his brother, he wasn't surprised when he received a call requesting his presence in the prince regent's office. He was surprised to see Cameron Leandres leaving as he was entering.

"Who's going to get fired for letting our cousin through the front gates?" he asked Rowan.

"No one."

Eric took a seat across from his brother's desk and raised his brows.

"I invited Cameron here to discuss the environmental concerns to be addressed at the summit in Berne next month."

"The summit I'm attending?"

"The summit you were going to attend," Rowan corrected. "I've asked Cameron to take your place."

Eric was genuinely perplexed by this turn of events. "Why?"

"Because you're going to be too busy overseeing the expansion of DELconnex U.S.A. into Europe to give this matter the attention it deserves."

Eric scowled. "I haven't told Scott I'd take the job."

"But you want to."

"How do you even know that he offered it to me?"

"I had to call to decline, with sincere regret, the invitation to Scott and Fiona's wedding because it coincides with the opening of the new youth center in Rio Medio that I've already committed to attending. And while I was talking to him, I asked him what kind of offer he'd made to you this time."

Everyone in the family knew that his friend had been trying to entice Eric to join his company since he first launched DELconnex nearly a decade earlier.

Eric and Scott had been friends since two decades before that, when six-year-old Scott Delsey had come with his family to Tesoro del Mar when his father was appointed U.S. ambassador to the small Mediterranean nation. As ambassador, Thomas

Delsey had spent a lot of time at the palace, frequently with his wife and son. Scott had become friends with all of the princes but had developed a particularly close bond with Eric, who was also six at the time. It was a bond as strong as any of blood, and that had endured even after the ambassador had finished his ten-year term and returned with his family to the United States. Eric and Scott had gone to the same college and though they'd later gone their separate ways in life, they'd always remained in touch.

"It's a tempting offer," Rowan said now.

"I've resisted temptation before," Eric told him, even as memories of his trip to Texas taunted him with the knowledge that he'd also succumbed to temptation—and quite happily.

"Why are you thinking of resisting?" his brother asked, and it took Eric a moment to haul his mind out of Molly's bed and back to their conversation.

"Because you need me here."

"I need a minister of international relations, and I think Cameron is well-suited to the position."

"There was a time when he thought he was well-suited to your position, and tried to take it from you," Eric felt compelled to remind him.

"That was six years ago."

"Do you really think he's changed?"

"I think I'd rather know what he's doing than have to guess at it."

Which Eric thought was a valid point. But he was still uneasy about his brother's decision to give any real authority to their cousin—or maybe he was just feeling guilty that Rowan's plan would allow him to do what he wanted when Rowan hadn't been given the same choice.

"I've neglected my duties to this family for too many years already," he protested.

"I probably can't count the number of diplomatic dinners and political photo ops you skipped over the past dozen years," the prince regent admitted. "But those were more than balanced out by the fact that you were serving your country."

Eric was uncomfortable with the admiration and pride he heard in Rowan's voice because he knew his service hadn't been any greater than that of any of his brothers. "Which is no more than you did by giving up your life in London when Julian died, and coming home to run the country and raise his children. And you still do the diplomatic dinners and political photo ops, and more than anyone probably even knows."

"It hasn't all been a hardship," Rowan said, with a smile that told Eric his brother was thinking of his wife and their family.

Eric lowered himself into the chair facing his brother's. "How did you know Lara was the right woman for you?"

"I didn't at first," he admitted. "Or maybe I did but refused to admit it, because I knew getting involved with the royal nanny would create a situation fraught with complications. And it wasn't so much that she was the right woman as she was the *only* woman—the only one I couldn't get out of my mind, the only one I wanted to be with for the rest of my life."

"The only one who would put up with him, more likely," Lara said from behind him.

Eric glanced at his sister-in-law, who was standing in the doorway with a ten-month-old baby tucked under one arm and a three-and-a-half-year-old holding her other hand. Her strawberry-blond hair looked a little more tousled than usual, and there was a stain on the shoulder of her blouse that he knew was courtesy of the baby, but despite the lateness of the hour and the obvious busyness of her day, her smile was still vibrant and beautiful.

Rowan had definitely lucked out when he'd fallen in love with Lara Brennan, Eric thought, with just the slightest twinge of envy. As Marcus had also done when he'd stopped by a little café in West Virginia and met—and eventually fallen in love with—Jewel Callahan. As Eric hoped he might luck out someday and find his own soul mate.

Unbidden, thoughts of Molly again nudged at his mind, but he pushed them aside.

"And I will forever be grateful for that," Rowan said, smiling back at his wife.

"You can prove it by tackling the bedtime routine with a stubborn three-year-old," she told him.

"It would be my pleasure," Rowan said, holding out his arms to the little boy, who went rushing into them.

Eric had to smile at the obvious bond between father and son. It was hard to believe that when Rowan had taken on the responsibility for Julian and Catherine's three children he had almost no experience with—and even less knowledge about—raising kids. Now Christian was seventeen and about to start college in the fall, Lexi was thirteen with a maturity well beyond her years and Damon was nine and still reveling in the joys of childhood and wreaking havoc on the household. Since their marriage, Lara and Rowan had added two of their own, and Rowan had not only embraced fatherhood but managed to juggle his various responsibilities to reflect his commitment to his family.

Eric wasn't really surprised by the apparent ease of his older brother's transition from footloose financier to responsible prince regent. Rowan had always taken his obligations seriously. More surprising to Eric was that his younger brother had willingly made similar changes in his life. He'd never seen Marcus look happier than when he was with Jewel and their baby daughter.

It was at the baptism for young Princess Isabella that Eric was first confronted by the emptiness of his life. Up until then, he'd never thought about what was missing. Or maybe it was more accurate to say that nothing seemed to be missing because his career had fulfilled him so completely.

Over the past three years, he'd had too much time to think, too much time to wonder if there should be something more, although he hadn't really thought about his restless yearning for more in terms of a relationship until he'd met Molly.

"Bath time and story?" Rowan's question to his son drew Eric's attention back to the scene in the library.

"Story!" Matthew repeated with enthusiasm.

"*After* the bath," his mother interjected firmly.

Matthew scowled as Rowan rose with him in his arms.

Eric chuckled. "What is it about little boys that makes them inherently allergic to bathwater?"

"I was hoping you could tell me," Lara said, crossing the room to settle into the chair her husband had vacated. The baby rubbed his face on his mother's shoulder, then popped his thumb in his mouth and snuggled in with a sigh.

Eric felt an unexpected pang as he watched Lara cuddle her infant son. Children were something else he hadn't thought much about because he'd never been in a position to be a father, but spending time with his brothers' children had changed that, too. He wanted a family of his own—a wife and children to come home to at the end of the day, to make plans and share dreams with and to simply *be* with.

Dios, that sounded pathetic, as if he couldn't endure his own company. Or maybe he'd just been enduring his own company for too long. After unsuccessful romances, it had seemed easier to accept solitude than yet another relationship failure. But maybe it was finally time to reconsider that position.

"You and Rowan sure do make beautiful babies," he commented to his sister-in-law now.

Lara smiled. "As much as I want to take credit, the dark hair and eyes are trademark Santiago."

"But Matthew has your mouth and your smile, and William's bone structure is just like yours."

"Do you think so?" She seemed pleased that he would notice such details.

"As I said, you make beautiful babies."

"And you're a flatterer as much as both of your brothers," she mused. "So what deep conversation between you and Rowan did I interrupt?"

"Nothing deep," he assured her.

"You've met a woman," she guessed.

He stared at her, baffled.

She laughed, and automatically rubbed the baby's back when he started to stir. "I heard you ask your brother how he knew I was the right woman for him—it wasn't much of a stretch to think that you've met someone who has you thinking in those terms."

"I've just been thinking a lot about my life and my future," he hedged. "And I wanted to tell Rowan about my plan to go back to Texas. It occurred to me that, as the best man, I should be available to help Scott with anything that needs to be done in the last few weeks before the wedding."

Lara's smile was just a little smug. "She's in Texas, isn't she?"

"Whatever you want to believe," he said, knowing it was pointless to deny it.

The widening of her smile only proved she knew she was right. "When are you leaving?"

Chapter Three

Molly pulled a brush through her hair and wrapped an elastic band around it to hold the heavy mass off of her neck. It was only the end of May, not even officially summer yet, but even three days of almost steady rain had done little to alleviate the humidity and forecasters were warning that the season was going to be a brutal one.

As she stripped out of her shorts and T-shirt to change for work, she thought she could use a change of scenery and a break from the oppressive heat—a week or two away from the never-ending problems at home. And she found herself wondering what the weather was like in Tesoro del Mar, if the summers were hot or if there were cool ocean breezes to regulate the temperature.

She wondered if Eric lived somewhere on the coast or in a crowded apartment in the city—or even if there were cities in Tesoro del Mar. She didn't really know anything about the country, or even how big it was, and she didn't know—if she decided to take a trip to the island, as she'd been thinking she might do—if there was any chance her path would cross with his.

It was a crazy idea—almost as crazy as spending the night with a man she didn't know—and yet it was an idea that refused to be discarded.

She'd thought about him a lot since that single night they'd spent together, and not just since she'd learned that she was carrying his child.

But five days after her appointment with Dr. Morgan, she'd still made no effort to find her baby's father and she knew it was past time she did so. She had plenty of legitimate excuses for the delay—including the hundred-and-one daily tasks that kept her at the restaurant for ten or more hours a day.

But the truth was, not one of those things had made her forget about the child she carried or the obligation she had to notify her baby's father. She just didn't know how she was going to track him down.

She booted up the computer and considered what she knew about Eric. Beyond his name, she knew that he lived in a country called Tesoro del Mar and that he'd been in the navy. It wasn't much, but at least it was a start.

A swarm of butterflies winged around in her stomach as she logged onto the Internet and typed the words *"Tesoro del Mar," "Eric"* and *"naval accident"* into the search engine.

She'd barely clicked Enter when the results filled the page.

Tesorian Navy News. Coast Guard Newsletter. Navy News—International Edition. MedSeaSecurityReport. Royal Watch. Naval Briefs. The Spanish Sailor.

She clicked on the first result, scanned the headline.

Prince Eric Injured in Naval Training Accident.

Prince Eric?

Definitely not the right Eric, she decided, and started to close the document when she noted the photo a little bit farther down on the page.

Her breath caught and her brow furrowed as she leaned closer to the screen for a better look.

It *was* him.

Her heart started to beat harder, faster.

She skimmed the article, barely noting any details of the accident that had resulted in the end of his career. Nothing seemed to matter beyond the title that jumped out at her from beneath his picture. "First Officer Prince Eric Santiago."

It occurred to her that maybe "prince" wasn't a royal title but a naval title. It certainly seemed a more feasible explanation than a member of a royal family wandering into her restaurant—and ending up in her bed.

She tried a different search this type, entering only *"prince eric"* and *"tesoro del mar."*

Again, the results were almost instantaneous, and her hand trembled as she clicked on "theroyalhouseofsantiago."

The site opened to a home page that showed a stunning castle of gleaming white stone in front of a backdrop of brilliant blue sky. She clicked on a link labeled "Members of the Royal Family," which popped up a row of photos with names and links beneath them—one of which was Eric, "Principe de la Ciudad del Norte."

She stared at the image, stunned by this confirmation that Eric wasn't just a guy in a bar—he was a member of the royal family of Tesoro del Mar.

She'd slept with a prince.

And now she was pregnant with his child.

She had to tell him—the logical, rational part of her brain wouldn't let her consider anything else. And now she knew where to find him, though she couldn't imagine that she'd simply be permitted to walk up to the front door of the royal palace and announce that she was carrying the prince's baby.

She couldn't think about this right now—just the thought made her head spin.

Pushing away from the desk, she grabbed her cell phone before heading downstairs to make sure the restaurant was set up for dinner. She noticed the voice mail icon on the display and sighed as she dialed into her mailbox, determined to ignore whatever crisis had her sister tracking her down now. But it wasn't Abbey's number on the display, it was Fiona's, and her cousin's voice was quiet and muffled, as if she was trying not to cry.

Fiona wasn't prone to dramatics, so her brief and teary "the wedding's off" message had Molly detouring through the restaurant only long enough to make sure that Karen could stay behind the bar until she returned. As she drove the familiar route to her cousin's ranch, it occurred to her that whatever had Fiona in a panic, it had succeeded in taking Molly's mind off of Prince Eric Santiago.

At least for the moment.

When Eric contacted Scott's fiancée to let her know that he was coming back to San Antonio, Fiona promised that a room would be ready for him and chatted excitedly about the final preparations for the wedding. But something happened between the time of his phone call and his arrival at the door so that she was no longer bubbling over with happiness but with tears.

Having spent most of his adult life in the navy, Eric felt completely out of his element when confronted by a weeping woman. Not that it was his job to comfort his friend's fiancée— and thank God Scott was there to do that—but he still felt helpless. And clueless.

"We got a call from the manager of Harcourt Castle," Scott

explained, when Fiona's sobs had quieted enough that conversation was possible.

"That's where the wedding's going to be, right?"

His friend gave a small shake of his head as he continued to pat Fiona's back consolingly. "We've had a lot of rain over the past couple of days and some of the lower lying areas experienced flooding, including Harcourt."

Eric knew a flood indicated water damage, which meant the venue was likely out of commission for several months—definitely past the date of the wedding.

"Maybe it's a sign," Fiona sniffed.

"It's not a sign," Scott soothed his bereft fiancée. "Except for the fact that we'll need to find another location for the wedding."

She brushed her tears away and looked up at him, incredulous. "Less than a month before the date?"

For the first time since Eric had arrived on the scene, Scott looked uncertain. "Does that seem unlikely?"

"Not unlikely—" the tears began falling again, her words barely comprehensible "—impossible. And—" she gulped in a breath "—you know why I wanted the castle."

"We met at Harcourt," Scott explained to Eric.

"And he took me back there to ask me to marry him," Fiona said, suddenly sobbing harder.

Yeah, Eric was definitely out of his element, and desperately wracked his brain for a solution—any solution—to stop the tears.

"Okay, so we'll postpone the wedding for a few months," Scott suggested.

"We've already sent out the invitations, ordered the cake, the flowers and—"

"I said postpone," her fiancé interjected, "not cancel."

She sighed. "It seems like we've been waiting so long already, and I just want to be married to you."

"Then let's do it," Scott said impulsively. "Let's forget all the chaos and crises, hop onto a plane to Vegas and get married."

Fiona's nose wrinkled. "Vegas?"

"I know it's not what we'd planned, but we can have a big, blowout reception back here in a few months, when Harcourt Castle is reopened."

His fiancée still hesitated.

Eric had never been to Vegas, but he'd seen enough movies to form an impression of the city and he could understand Fiona's reluctance. She wanted ambience and elegance, and what Scott was offering was loud and garish. Okay, maybe that wasn't an entirely fair assessment considering that he'd never stepped foot in the town, but he thought he'd gotten to know his friend's fiancée well enough during his last visit to be certain it wasn't what she'd envisioned.

"Vegas," she said again, more contemplative than critical this time.

He figured it was a testament to how much Fiona loved Scott that she was even considering it.

"Or you could hop on a plane to a picturesque island in the Mediterranean and have a quiet ceremony on the beach and an intimate reception at the royal palace," Eric offered as an alternative.

The future bride and groom swiveled their heads in his direction.

"Could we?" Scott asked.

"You said it was a small wedding?"

"Fifty-two guests," his friend confirmed.

"We'd need to charter a plane but otherwise, there shouldn't be any problem. So long as there's nothing going on at the palace on that date, we could fly everyone in a few days early for a brief vacation on the island, then have the wedding as planned on Saturday."

Fiona glanced from Eric to Scott and back again. "That sounds awfully expensive," she said, but the sparkle was back in her eyes, revealing her enthusiasm.

"It would be my wedding gift to you," Eric told her.

"A Crock-Pot is a wedding gift," she said. "What you're offering is…a dream."

He shrugged. "You make my best friend happy. If this makes you happy, it's a fair trade."

Her smile was radiant. "Then I'll say 'thank you.' But we'll stick with Scott's plan to hold a formal reception back here in a few months and just have immediate family for the ceremony in Tesoro del Mar. And Molly, my maid of honor, of course."

When Molly arrived at the ranch, she was both surprised and immensely relieved to learn that the crisis had already been diverted.

"I didn't think anything could be more romantic than being married at Harcourt House," Fiona gushed, all smiles instead of tears now. "But a wedding at a royal palace might just top everything else."

Molly sank down onto the arm of a chair. "A royal palace?"

"Scott's in the other room with Eric now, confirming the arrangements."

The butterflies were swarming again.

Eric. The best man. The friend of Scott's that Fiona had been talking about for months who somehow had access to a royal palace. Could it be—

No. It wasn't possible. She'd just been so unnerved by the realization that her baby's father was a prince that she was jumping to conclusions. Because as much as her cousin had talked about the best man, Fiona had never mentioned that he was royalty. Molly *definitely* would have remembered that.

She managed to smile. "So where is this royal palace?"

"It's on an island in the Mediterranean called Tesoro del Mar. I'd never even heard of it before I met Eric, and I didn't even know he was a prince until a few days ago. Scott said they've been friends for so long he doesn't think about the fact that Eric is in line for the throne, but I nearly fainted when I found out. Can you believe the best man at my wedding is a prince?"

"Unbelievable," Molly agreed, as thoughts and questions whipped around in her mind like dry leaves in a hurricane. And before she could grasp hold of even one of them, he was there.

He was standing in front of her—okay, across the room, but the distance did nothing to dilute the effect of his presence. His legs were as long as she remembered, his shoulders as broad, his jaw as strong, his eyes as dark.

Yes, she remembered all of the details—the thickness of his hair, the curve of his lips, the skill of his hands. But she hadn't quite remembered—maybe hadn't let herself remember—how completely fascinating he was as a whole.

He smiled at Fiona. "Everything's confirmed."

She threw her arms around his neck. "Oh, thank you, Eric. You're the best."

"That's why he's the best man," Scott said, unconcerned by the fact that his fiancée was embracing another man. Eric chuckled.

The sound of that laugh, warm and rich and familiar, sent shivers down her spine, tingles to her center.

It was Scott who spotted Molly first, and he smiled. "Hey, Molly."

Eric's head turned. His gaze locked on hers, and widened in shock.

Molly thought she had some idea just how he felt.

"Eric—" Scott turned to his friend "—you haven't met Molly yet, have you?"

"No, we haven't," Molly answered before he could, rising to her feet and praying that her wobbly legs would support her.

"But I've certainly heard a lot about her," Eric said, his eyes never leaving Molly's face.

She definitely hadn't remembered everything—like how one look could make her pulse race and her knees quiver, as her pulse was racing and her knees were quivering now.

"And here she is," Scott said. And to Molly, "This is His Royal Highness, Prince Eric Santiago of Tesoro del Mar."

"Should I curtsy?" she asked lightly.

"No need," he said.

She didn't actually remember offering her hand, but she found it engulfed in his, cradled in his warmth. It was a simple handshake—there was nothing at all inappropriate about it. And yet she felt her cheeks heat, her skin burn, as memories of his hands on her body assaulted her mind from every direction.

The heat in his eyes told her that he was also remembering, and though her mind warned her to back away, her body yearned to shift close, closer.

"It's a pleasure to see you, Molly," he said in that low, sexy voice that had whispered much more intimately and explicitly in her ear as they'd rolled around on her bed together.

"Oh, we're going to have so much fun together in Tesoro del Mar," Fiona said, then to Molly, "You will come, won't you?"

A wedding on a Mediterranean island sounded romantic enough, throw in a royal palace, and Molly could understand why her cousin was glowing with excitement and anticipation. And no matter how much Molly's brain warned that going to Tesoro del Mar was a very bad idea—that going anywhere with Eric Santiago was a very bad idea—she couldn't refuse something that meant so much to Fiona.

So she ignored the knots in her stomach and forced a bright

smile. "Of course I'll be there. You can hardly get married without your maid of honor."

Fiona threw her arms around Molly, just as she'd done with Eric, and hugged her tight. "Oh, thank you, thank you, thank you."

Molly hugged her back. "I just want your wedding to be perfect for you."

"It will be now," her cousin said confidently.

Molly was pleased that Fiona's problems were solved, but couldn't help but think her own had just multiplied.

It had been unsettling enough to accept that she was pregnant with a stranger's baby, but learning that the stranger was her cousin's fiancé's best friend added a whole other layer of complications. And she couldn't help but wonder how differently everything might have played out if she'd known two months ago what she knew now about *Prince* Eric Santiago.

"Okay, now that the crisis has been resolved, I should get back to work," Molly said, eager to make her escape.

But she felt the heat of Eric's gaze on her as she made her way to the door, and acknowledged that this new information might not have changed anything. Because even now, she wanted him as much as she'd wanted him then.

This time, however, she was determined to prove stronger than the desire he stirred inside of her.

At least, she hoped she would.

Chapter Four

Molly *knew* Eric would show up at her door the next morning. She only hoped to have a cup of coffee in her system before she had to face him again—a hope that was obliterated when the knock sounded just as she was measuring grinds into the filter. She set the basket into place, pressed the button and went to respond to his knock.

He was dressed casually in a pair of jeans and a collared T-shirt, much as he'd been the first night he walked into the bar. And though he looked better than any man had a right to look, there certainly wasn't anything about his appearance or his attire that warned he was a prince. And even now, even knowing all the details she'd learned from the Internet, she found it difficult to think of him as royalty. She could only remember that he was a man—a man she'd taken to her bed and with whom she'd shared intimacies and pleasures she'd never before imagined.

"Good morning," he said.

To which she responded with a barely civil, "Come in."

"A little out of sorts this morning?"

"I work nights," she reminded him. "The hours before noon aren't my best time."

"Should I come back?"

She shook her head. "We might as well just get this over with."

His lips quirked. "What, exactly, are we getting over?"

"The awkward morning-after conversation that we managed to avoid the morning after." She reached into the cupboard for two mugs, filled both with coffee, then slid one across the table to him.

He'd drank black coffee at the bar that night, she remembered, which was good because she didn't have any cream. She dumped a generous spoonful of sugar into her own cup and stirred. She planned to make the switch to decaf soon, but the doctor had assured her a couple of cups a day wouldn't hurt the baby and she needed the caffeine right now.

"Well, you could explain why you didn't want Scott and Fiona to know we'd met before."

"Because they would have had questions about how and when, and I wasn't sure how to answer." She sipped her coffee, felt it churn uneasily in her stomach.

"How about the truth?"

"The whole truth?"

"I'm not ashamed of what happened between us. We're both adults, we were attracted to one another, we acted upon that attraction."

"I don't do one night stands with strangers," she told him.

"I seem to recall you telling me that already—right before you invited me back to your apartment."

She felt her cheeks flush at the reminder—or maybe it was the heat in his gaze that was causing her own body temperature to rise. She wasn't in the habit of having sex with men she barely knew, and she'd *never* had sex with a man she'd met only a few hours earlier. But she'd let herself give in to the yearning because she never expected to see him again.

It was supposed to be a crazy, once-in-a-lifetime impulse, a chance to prove to herself that she could be wild and spontaneous and not tie herself up in knots about it forever after. Except that it turned out to be a crazy, once-in-a-lifetime impulse that was going to have some major, long-term repercussions.

Repercussions Prince Eric still didn't know about.

"Just because I slept with you once doesn't mean I'll do so again just because circumstances have thrown us together and it's convenient."

He smiled at her across the table—a smile that made all of her bones turn to jelly and made her grateful she was sitting down.

"I wasn't thinking about the convenience factor so much as the it-was-really-great-sex factor."

"The only reason I made an exception to my rule was because I didn't expect to ever see you again."

"I didn't think I'd ever see you again, either," he admitted. "And yet, you've been on my mind almost constantly over the past few weeks, and it was always my plan upon returning to Texas to find you."

"That wasn't our agreement," she reminded him.

"So let's make a new agreement."

"What do you propose—lots of hot sex in the few weeks leading up to Scott and Fiona's wedding, after which I go back to serving drinks and you go back to doing whatever it is a royal does?"

Something in her tone must have given her away, because his brows lifted. "You're annoyed that I didn't tell you I'm a prince," he guessed.

"Do you think?"

"Why don't I remember your affinity for sarcasm?"

"Maybe because we really didn't know one another at all before we fell into bed together."

"Are you saying your decision to sleep with me would have been different if you'd know I was a prince?"

"Yes," she asserted vehemently.

"Why?"

"Because then I would have known that I meant nothing more to you than another conquest in another town."

Even as she spoke the words, she realized how hypocritical they sounded. After all, she was the one who'd insisted that a one night stand was all she wanted.

But he didn't point out this fact. Instead he said, "You were never a conquest. You were a beautiful woman who intrigued me as no woman has done in a very long time."

She wanted to believe him, but she couldn't get past the fact that he was a prince and she'd been rejected by too many average guys to believe that she could have captured the attention of someone so extraordinary.

"I'm not going to sleep with you again."

He lifted his cup to his lips, drank. "I got the impression, when Fiona asked you about coming to Tesoro del Mar, that you wanted to refuse."

"It's not that I wanted to," she denied. "It's just not a great time for me to be leaving the country."

"Is that the truth? Or is it that you didn't want to be with me?"

"You weren't a factor in my decision," she lied.

"No?" he challenged softly and, reaching across the table, brushed his knuckles down her cheek.

The gentle caress sent tingles down her spine, and when she responded with another no, it sounded almost like a sigh.

He smiled. "Well, I'm glad you are coming. Tesoro del Mar is a beautiful country, and I will look forward to showing it to you."

"I'm going for Fiona, not for a vacation."

"There's no reason you can't do both."

She shook her head. "I really can't be away from my business for too long."

"You don't have a manager?"

"*I'm* the manager."

"But you don't work every single shift," he guessed.

"No," she admitted. Karen had shared the managerial duties for a few years now, usually covering the dinner shift so that Molly had a break between lunch and evening duties and could take the occasional day off. "But I'm never too far away if there's a problem."

"Is it that you don't trust your manager to take care of things in your absence?" he wondered. "Or that you don't trust yourself to be alone with me?"

"There's nothing wrong with your ego, is there?"

He only grinned. "I don't recall you having complaints about my ego—or any of my other parts—when we were together."

No—there had definitely been no reason to complain and no ability to do so when she was writhing and moaning with pleasure.

"Are we finished here?" she asked, deliberately ignoring his comment. "Because I have to be downstairs for a delivery in about ten minutes."

He pushed his chair away from the table. "Fiona will let you know the travel arrangements."

"Thanks." She followed him to the door.

He stepped out onto the landing, then pivoted back to face her again. "And the answer to your question is no—we're not even close to being finished here."

* * *

Molly was in a mood when she went down to the bar and she knew it. She was tired and she was cranky and it was all Eric's fault. As if it wasn't enough to find out that the man she'd picked up in her own bar was a prince, now he'd suddenly reappeared in her life, wanting to pick up right where they left off.

Of course, he didn't know that the last time they'd gotten naked and horizontal together, they'd made a baby. She was certain that little bit of information would make him reconsider his pursuit of her, but she definitely wasn't ready to share.

You have to tell him.

She sighed even as she cursed the nagging voice of her conscience. She *knew* she had to tell him. She *would* tell him. Just not yet. Not until she was feeling a little less flustered and emotional about everything.

Okay—that might take a little longer than the seven months remaining before her due date, so maybe that wasn't a reasonable guideline.

After the wedding, she decided. She would be close to the end of the first trimester by then and there wouldn't be any reason for them to remain in contact afterward if he didn't want to.

She nodded, satisfied with that reasoning. "After the wedding."

"What wedding?"

She hadn't realized she'd spoken the thought out loud until Dave, the delivery man from the local liquor store responded with the question.

She scrawled her name on the bill he presented to her and shook her head. "I'm babbling to myself. Obviously I've got too much on my mind."

"My brother talks to himself all the time," Dave told her. "My mother thinks he's a genius. My dad just thinks he's nuts."

"There's probably a fine line there," Molly said.

"Which side do you fall on?" he asked curiously.

"Nuts," she said. "Definitely certifiably insane."

She had to be if she was still attracted to a man who'd messed up every single aspect of her life.

"Admitting a problem is the first step toward getting help," he said, and winked at her.

She restocked the shelf behind the bar, then carried the extra inventory to the storage room. The boxes were heavy, and though the weight wasn't anything she couldn't handle right now, she knew there would come a time when she would have to stop that kind of lifting. She wouldn't do anything that would jeopardize the well-being of her child.

But, as she stifled another yawn, she found herself worrying that she might already be jeopardizing her baby's well-being. She was tired—physically and mentally exhausted. Was that normal in the first few months of pregnancy? Or were the erratic hours at the restaurant taking an additional toll on her body?

She'd had to drag herself out of bed this morning, and she'd turned the shower spray to cool to jolt herself awake. What she'd told Eric was true—she'd never been at her best in the mornings, but she wasn't usually so grumpy.

Even when she'd been in high school and had to get up for classes in the morning, she often worked late to help her dad. When she was a teen, he'd been strict about keeping her away from the bar, but when the last customer was gone and the door was locked at the end of the night, she would come out of the kitchen to help him with the clean-up of the restaurant and the close-out of the register and anything else that needed to be done.

She'd loved that time of night, the quiet camaraderie they'd shared. Just thinking about it now, she felt an aching emptiness inside. Her father had been gone for almost ten years now, but there still wasn't a day that went by that she didn't think about him and how much she missed him.

He'd been in her thoughts even more than usual recently, and she wondered if that was because she so desperately wanted to tell someone about the baby she carried. She knew her father would have been disappointed about the circumstances of her pregnancy, but he would have been thrilled about the child. Family had always been the most important part of life to James Shea, with even the bar running a distance second.

When his wife bailed on him after fifteen years of marriage, he'd raised his daughters alone, and he'd raised them with love and compassion. If he'd had one regret, it was that Maureen had cut all ties when she'd walked out. He felt it was important for children to have the love of both parents, and he always lamented the fact that he couldn't give that to his daughters.

He wouldn't approve of Molly's decision not to tell Eric about her pregnancy, of that she had no doubt. Not that she wasn't ever going to tell him, she reminded that nagging voice in the back of her mind, just that she needed some more time to assimilate what she'd learned about her baby's father before she told him he was going to be a father.

She thought about how her dad would react to that bit of information.

"You always were my princess," he would have said with a smile. "And now you'll have the title to prove it."

Because he would also assume that, being pregnant with Eric's baby, she would marry him—whether or not it was what either of them wanted. Yes, family was important to James Shea, and so was responsibility, as he'd proven when he married Molly's mother after learning that she was carrying his child.

But that was thirty-one years ago, and even if Eric offered marriage as a solution, she knew it wasn't one she could accept. It certainly wasn't a solution that had worked for her parents. Not that they hadn't tried—at least for a while. But in the end,

Maureen Shea had woke up one morning and, looking around, decided she didn't like what her life had become and walked away from everything.

Molly didn't think she would ever understand how a woman could walk away from her child like that—cutting all ties and never looking back. Instinctively, her hand went to her still-flat tummy. Though her baby was just starting to be, she was already overwhelmed with love for her child and she vowed silently but vehemently to always be there for her baby.

Which meant that she had to start giving serious consideration to the day-to-day practicalities of parenthood. In particular, she needed to consider what was she going to do when she had a child of her own—could she continue to serve customers with a playpen behind the bar? And even if that worked for the first several months, she couldn't keep a toddler confined to a mesh-cage for a six-hour shift any more than she could allow him free rein to crawl around the restaurant.

But what other option did she have?

Sell.

The answer popped into her head from nowhere—or maybe it had been lurking in the back of her mind since Abbey had first spoken of the possibility after their father died.

Her sister had broached the subject a few more times since then, but Molly had always balked. Shea's was their legacy, the only thing they had left that was their father's.

And even if they sold the bar, even if they found a buyer, what would she do after? Who would hire her? She had no real skills, no experience, and now she had a baby on the way.

You could write.

This time the voice in head sounded suspiciously like her grandmother's, and the words were a familiar refrain.

Even as a child, she'd had stories in her head. Her father had enjoyed the fanciful tales she'd spun and appreciated that her narratives entertained his customers; her grandmother had always insisted that Molly was a born storyteller. Molly only knew that there were characters and scenes constantly spinning around in her mind and she had a drawerful of notebooks in which she'd jotted down those ideas in an attempt to clear them from her mind.

But while she might occasionally fantasize about being a writer, she didn't have any illusions that she could simply decide to make that kind of career change and expect to pay the bills. So what could she do?

She felt the sting of tears in her eyes as the questions came at her from all directions. Questions without apparent answers. Problems without any solutions.

She sat on a stool and pressed the heels of her hands to her eyes and wished again that her father was here. Since he'd passed away, she'd been the mature and responsible one—the one everyone else turned to for help, the shoulder that others cried on. For once— just once—she wanted a shoulder to cry on, strong arms to wrap around her, someone she could count on and believe in and—

She shook her head, furiously pushing aside the image of Eric Santiago that managed to steal into her mind. How could she even think about leaning on him when he was the one who'd started her world spinning out of control? She couldn't. No way, no how.

Molly would handle this current predicament as she'd handled everything else in her life since her father died—on her own.

Eric managed to stay away from the restaurant and the temptation of Molly for three days. On day four, he decided he wanted to go out for lunch, and found himself driving toward Shea's. She was right in saying that they didn't know one another very well, but what he found more interesting than this assertion was her determination to keep him at a distance so that she wouldn't get to know him.

This time when he entered the restaurant, he saw Molly not standing behind the bar but seated at it, talking to another woman beside her. He wasn't going to interrupt, but it was almost as if she was as attuned to his presence as he was to hers, because she looked up and her eyes met his.

He smiled, and she smiled back, albeit tentatively.

As if cluing in to the silent exchange, the woman seated beside Molly looked up. The two women looked enough alike that he would have guessed they were sisters, though he hadn't known that she had a sister, which again proved her point that there was a lot they didn't know about one another.

Molly was wearing slim-fitting jeans and a sleeveless blouse with tiny little flowers embroidered on the collar. Practical yet feminine, he thought, and so perfectly suited to Molly. Her sister was wearing a dress with a criss-cross tie down the back that drew attention to her curves and strappy sandals with pencil-thin heels. Her hair wasn't as long or as dark as Molly's and was streaked with lighter strands.

His gaze moved back to Molly, noting the hair that was pulled away from her face in a ponytail, the deep blue eyes surrounded by thick dark lashes, full lips that were slicked with clear gloss, and he felt the now-familiar stir of desire low in his belly.

"Just in the neighborhood?" Molly asked.

"Just hungry," he said. "And I heard they serve a pretty good lunch in here."

"You heard right," Molly said. Then, at the nudge from her sister, she made the introductions.

"This is my sister, Abbey," she told him. Then to Abbey, "Meet Prince Eric Santiago."

"*Prince* Eric?"

"Scott's best friend," Molly explained to her sister.

"The best man," Abbey said, and lifted a brow. "And are you? The best, I mean."

Eric looked at Molly, who rolled her eyes.

"You're married," she reminded her sister.

"Separated," Abbey said.

"And Eric came in for a meal, not an interrogation." Molly stood and, grabbing a menu from the counter, led him to a booth in the corner.

"I wouldn't mind some company," he said, sliding into the booth.

"You want me to send my sister over?"

"I meant *your* company," he clarified.

"Sorry, I have to finish up next week's schedule."

He hadn't really expected that she would accept his invitation.

For reasons he couldn't even begin to fathom, she was edgy around him, almost antagonistic. Instead of dissuading him, her attitude only made him all the more determined to break through her barriers and rediscover the warm, wonderful woman he knew was inside.

"You could do that here—unless you think I'm too much of a distraction."

"You're just too much."

He grinned. "I'll take that as a compliment."

"You would." She dropped the menu on the table, then with a sigh, she slid into the seat across from him. "You have a way of irritating me so that I forget I'm trying to be nice."

"Why does it take such an effort?"

"Because you rub me the wrong way."

He let his eyes rake over her, in a slow and very hot perusal, before he said, "That's not how I remember it."

She huffed out a breath. "You see? That's exactly what I'm talking about. I'm attempting to have a normal conversation and you keep throwing out these little references to a night I'm trying to forget."

"Why are you trying to forget?"

"Because it's over and done and it's not going to happen again."

"It seems to me that if forgetting is such an effort, it's not nearly as over and done as you want to believe."

She drew in a deep breath, expelled it slowly, deliberately.

"I wanted to say that hosting the wedding in Tesoro del Mar is an incredibly kind and generous thing to do."

"And you're surprised that I can be kind and generous?" he couldn't resist teasing.

"No," she said. "I'm just trying to thank you for turning what could have been a disaster into a celebration."

"My motives aren't entirely noble."

"No?"

"I want to spend time with you, Molly, and you'll have a lot fewer excuses to avoid me when we're in Tesoro del Mar."

"You made the offer before you even knew I was Fiona's maid of honor," she pointed out.

"Guilty," he admitted. "But that doesn't mean I'm not willing to take advantage of the fact."

"I'm flattered by your interest, Eric, really. But I'm not looking for a relationship right now."

"Why not?"

"My reasons aside, I can't believe you're looking to get involved with a bartender."

"I'm not a snob, Molly."

"But you're a prince, and I can't imagine a foreigner with neither a title nor a fortune would ever be a suitable companion—even temporarily—for a royal."

He couldn't help but smile at that. "Both of my sisters-in-law used to think the same way. Lara was an Irish nanny. Jewel was an American horse trainer."

"And your point?"

"Well, I'm not asking you to marry me."

She responded to his assurance with a small smile, and he felt another tug inside. It was warmer and softer than desire, but somehow stronger, too. And he realized he would do almost anything to earn another one of those smiles, for more quiet moments like this one.

"But when we get to the island," he continued, "I might ask to show you around."

She studied him for a moment, those deep blue eyes considering, before she said, "And if you ask nicely, I just might say yes." Then she slid out of the booth. "Enjoy your lunch."

As Eric watched her walk away, appreciating the way worn denim molded to a nicely toned derriere, he was pleased with her response. It was a small step forward, but after so many in retreat, at least it was progress.

Chapter Five

Abbey came into the kitchen the next day and sat by the prep counter to watch Molly chop carrots and celery into sticks. For her sister to show up at the restaurant two days in a row was unusual, and Molly found herself wondering if Abbey had come in to see her or hoping to see Eric again—a question that was answered when Abbey said, "Jason came home last night."

Molly stopped chopping to look at her sister, trying to decide if this was good news, trying not to resent the fact that her sister didn't see anything wrong with asking for advice about her marriage to the man she'd stolen from Molly.

"Do you want to reconcile?" she asked.

Abbey nodded. "I just want everything back the way it was before he left."

"So what's the problem?"

"He said there are changes that need to be made." Abbey pouted. "What kind of changes?"

"For starters, he wants me to get a job."

And the only job Abbey had ever wanted was to be a wife and mother—and Molly suspected it was the unrealized latter part of that desire that was the cause of most of her sister's marital problems.

"It's not that I'm opposed to working," Abbey said. "I've just never been really good at anything."

"You've never *tried* to be good at anything," Molly corrected. "Except shopping."

Her sister brightened at that. "I could get a job as a personal shopper."

"At least then you'd be spending other people's money."

"Do you really think I'm qualified?"

"I have no doubt you're qualified, but I'm not sure there's much demand for personal shoppers outside the big cities."

Abbey sighed. "You're probably right."

Another few minutes passed, during which Molly tried to discard the thought that popped into her mind, but it refused to go away until finally, with more resignation than enthusiasm, she said, "You could work here."

Abbey stared at her as if she'd suggested that she dance naked on the tables instead of serve meals to the customers seated at them.

"Work?" she echoed. "Here?"

"I know it's an odd concept, but there are several of us who actually do so. The pay's not great," Molly admitted. "But the tips are pretty good." And after the abrupt and unexpected departure of one of her waitresses, Molly was desperate for another pair of hands to work the dinner shift. She'd been doing everything she could to help out herself, but she was already feeling the effects of the extra hours on her feet, and knew that couldn't continue.

"Tips?"

"Of course, you'd have to learn to smile instead of scowl if you wanted to earn any."

Abbey sighed. "When can I start?"

"Four o'clock."

Molly wasn't surprised that Abbey showed up less than five minutes before her shift was scheduled to begin, but she was pleased that her sister apparently remembered the routine from when she'd waited tables through high school. Abbey caught on to the routine quickly and managed to take orders and deliver meals with little mishap. She finished her first shift with sore feet and a pocketful of tips that, when added up, elicited a weary smile.

Abbey worked again the next afternoon, and the day after that, and by the end of the week, Molly was actually starting to think the arrangement might work out.

Though there hadn't been an empty table during the midday rush, the restaurant was now mostly empty and Molly poured herself a cup of decaf and took a seat at the bar. There was a table with three men in suits who were finishing up a business meeting along with their lunches, another at which was seated a couple of older women who seemed more interested in conversation than their meals, and at a booth in the back, a young couple lingering over coffee.

Molly was proud that her business appealed to such an eclectic group, and pleased that the additional funds she'd spent on advertising over the past twelve months was proving to be a good investment. Shea's had once been "the little roadside bar just past the sharp curve in the highway," now it was "that fabulous little restaurant just past the sharp curve in the highway."

She hadn't taken the first sip of her coffee when her brother-in-law came in.

"If you're looking for your wife, she just left."

"I'm not," Jason said, then walked behind the bar, poured himself a cup of coffee and sat down beside her.

It was the first time she'd seen him in the restaurant since he and Abbey separated a few months earlier, and she was as curious as she was wary about his reasons for being here now. Because he, too, didn't seem to think there was anything wrong with dumping his problems in Molly's lap, despite having dumped her to marry her sister.

"I have a business proposition to discuss with you."

Now she was *really* curious, but she just sipped her decaf and waited for him to explain.

Instead of speaking, he set a cashier's check beside her cup.

Her eyes popped open wide as she took in the numbers.

"Where did you get that kind of cash?"

"My severance package from Raycroft Industries."

She'd read about the proposed merger of the local manufacturing plant with a multinational corporation several months earlier and had wondered how it might affect her brother-in-law, who had worked there for the past half-dozen years.

"I'd like to buy into a partnership," he said.

For the amount of the check he was offering, he could buy the whole restaurant, and Molly was almost tempted to let him do so. She'd certainly feel more comfortable selling out than going into partnership with a man who had betrayed her once already. "Why?" she asked instead.

"I have managerial experience and I think I'd enjoy working here—and working with Abbey might give both of us something to focus on other than the baby she wants so badly and can't have."

Which led Molly to suspect that Abbey had decided she'd rather own the restaurant than simply work in it—and, like everything else she'd ever wanted, there was a man willing to give it to her.

"Is this what Abbey wants?" she asked him.

"If she had her way, we'd spend the whole amount on fertility treatments. But I think she could be convinced to agree to this."

Molly felt an instinctive tug of sympathy for what her sister and brother-in-law had been through, and a twinge of guilt that what they'd struggled for so desperately had happened so easily for her. And then a surge of annoyance at letting herself experience even that momentary twinge when it was Abbey and Jason together who had destroyed her own dreams.

"Have you really thought about this, or is it an impulse?"

"You know I don't do anything on impulse," Jason said.

"Weddings in Las Vegas aside?"

"It was one wedding, and it was because Abbey and I didn't know how to tell you that we'd fallen in love."

Molly sighed, because she knew it was true and because— nine years later—she was over it, or at least she felt that she should be. Was it the depth of the hurt that made her heart still ache? Or was it something lacking inside herself that made her unable to truly forgive their betrayal?

In either case, she knew it was time she got over her resentment and got on with her life, and maybe Jason was offering her the chance to finally do just that.

"Speaking of weddings," she said, "I'm going to Tesoro del Mar for Fiona and Scott's."

Although Abbey was the bride's cousin, too, she'd never been as close to Fiona as Molly was. And Fiona had never forgiven her for stealing Molly's fiancé, holding so tightly to her grudge against Abbey that she hadn't even wanted to invite her youngest cousin to the wedding. It was their grandmother who had insisted that she do the right thing, and while Abbey and Jason would be invited to attend the rescheduled reception in a few months, Fiona refused to extend the close circle who had been invited to the island ceremony to include them.

"I was going to ask Karen and Sam to cover my night shifts," Molly continued, "but if you wanted to take them instead, it would give you a chance to see if this is what you really want, before making a final decision."

He reached for her hand as she pushed her stool back. "Thanks, Molly. I know you don't owe me anything, but I appreciate this opportunity."

"Don't screw it up."

"I won't," he promised.

When Eric walked into Shea's, he saw Molly holding hands with another man and felt the churn of dark and unfamiliar emotions in his belly. He had no claim to her. One night of sex, no matter how spectacular, gave him no proprietary right, but that knowledge didn't negate the fact that when he'd seen the other man reach for her, he'd felt his own hands curl into fists and heard only one thought in his mind—*mine.*

She was on her way to the door when she saw him a minute later. She smiled easily, as if she hadn't just been cozied up with some other guy.

"You're a little late for lunch today, aren't you?" she asked him.

"I had lunch with Fiona and Scott today," he told her, responding in a similarly casual tone.

"And you're early for dinner," she prompted.

He managed to smile. "I actually came to see you, if you've got a few minutes."

"Can we take those minutes upstairs? I've been here since eight and I want a change of scenery and popcorn." She started up to her apartment without waiting to see if he agreed.

He followed.

She unlocked the door, kicked off her shoes and moved into the kitchen. Snagging a box of Orville Redenbacher's from the cupboard, she unwrapped the cellophane from a package and pressed a couple of buttons on the microwave.

He frowned, remembering what she'd said about having been at the restaurant since eight. "That isn't your lunch, is it?"

"Not really. I snacked on some cheese balls and potato skins in the kitchen, but I was suddenly craving popcorn." She frowned at that.

"Vegetables are one of the food groups, too," he pointed out.

The popcorn had mostly stopped popping, and she smiled as she opened the door of the microwave and pulled the bag out. "And corn is a vegetable."

She tore open the top of the bag and a puff of steam and rich, buttery scent escaped. "Why did you want to see me?"

"You mean, other than the fact that I really like looking at you?" he couldn't help but tease, and had the pleasure of watching her cheeks flush.

"Other than that," she agreed dryly.

"I wanted to let you know that I finalized the travel arrangements. Scott and Fiona are coming with me tomorrow, but you can fly in with Scott's parents next Wednesday, if that works better for you."

"My grandparents aren't coming at all?" she asked.

He shook his head. "Fiona didn't seem surprised."

"I'm not really, either," she admitted. "I was just hoping… Neither of us have our parents anymore. My mom walked out, my dad died, and Fiona's mom and dad were both killed in a car accident a few years back, so aside from each other and Abbey, our grandparents are the only real family we have."

"Do you want me to talk to them, see if I could change their minds?"

She smiled. "Thanks, but no one changes my grandmother's mind about anything once she's made it up and she refuses to go anywhere near an airplane."

"So do you want to come tomorrow or next week?" Eric asked her.

She hesitated, then said, "I think tomorrow could work."

He was both pleased and surprised by her response. "I thought you didn't want to be away from the restaurant for too long."

"I didn't," she admitted. "But I had an interesting conversation with someone before you showed up and I'm starting to think that this is something I have to do."

"An interesting conversation with the guy at the bar?" He shouldn't have asked—he knew it was none of his business. But the question had been eating away at him since he'd seen them together, noted the obvious familiarity in their interactions with one another.

"Jason," she said, and nodded.

"And who is Jason?"

"My ex-fiancé."

He scowled. "You were engaged to that guy?"

"A long time ago," she said.

Which made him feel marginally better until he remembered that the guy had been holding her hand not such a long time ago.

"What time tomorrow?" she asked, in what seemed to him an obvious attempt to change the topic but might simply have been a desire to know the specifics of their travel plans.

"Six-thirty," he told her.

"A.M.?"

"Yeah."

Molly crumpled up the now empty popcorn bag and tossed it into the garbage. "Then I'm going to kick you out now so I can pack because I have to be back downstairs in an hour."

As usual, Molly worked until closing that night. Jason came in at ten and stayed behind the bar with his sister-in-law, shadowing her every movement. Usually Molly could close every-thing up and be cashed out within half an hour of locking the door behind the last customer, but having to explain every step to Jason meant the routine took more than twice as long.

Still, she was awake and ready when the knock came at the door at precisely 6:30 a.m. the next morning—if not exactly alert.

She was surprised that Eric had come up instead of sending his driver, and more than a little disconcerted when he swore softly in Spanish and reached out to her.

"Mi Dios." He brushed a thumb gently beneath her eye, trac-ing the purple shadows she hadn't even tried to cover with make-up. "You don't look as if you've slept."

"I got a few hours," she said, shifting away, as much from the casual intimacy of the gesture as the surge of warmth evoked by his tender touch, to reach for her suitcase.

He immediately pried the handle from her fingers. "I've got it."

She lifted a brow. "You take control quite easily for a man who's probably had servants picking up after him his whole life."

"No one waits on anyone else in the navy, regardless of title or rank," he told her.

The statement reminded her not just that he'd served his country but of the scars on his body that had been earned in that service. But instead of thinking of the injury that had ended his career, she found herself thinking of his taut, hard muscles and warm, smooth skin and the heat of his body moving against hers. Just the memories were enough to make her body tingle all over, stirring up yearnings that had been long dormant until the first night he'd walked into the bar.

Over the past several weeks, she'd managed—with effort— to keep those memories at bay. Mostly, anyway. But her tired brain was no match for the rising heat in her blood evoked by his nearness. She'd read about the enhanced sensual awareness that many women experienced during pregnancy and knew that she was one of them.

"Damn hormones," she muttered under her breath.

He turned. "Did you say something?"

She just shook her head and followed him down the stairs.

While Scott and Fiona were cuddled close together, talking about the wedding or the future or whatever else soon-to-be-marrieds talked about, Eric watched Molly sleep.

He'd watched her sleep the night they'd spent together in her bed, when exhaustion had finally overwhelmed the passion that brought them together. He wanted her now as much as he'd wanted her then. The only thing that had prevented him from waking her and slipping into the wet heat of her sexy little body was the realization that they'd depleted the store of condoms he'd bought from the vending machine in the men's room.

As he watched her now, he wondered what it was about this one woman that had taken hold of him. And he was baffled that the woman who had once been so warm and willing in his arms was so determined to keep him at arm's length now.

He knew his reappearance in her life had thrown her for a loop, but he suspected that there was more going on than that. It was as if, in the few weeks that he'd been gone, her entire life had been turned upside down. He wasn't egotistical enough to believe that he was responsible for that. As spectacular as their night together had been, neither of them had expected it would be any more than that.

But he got the impression there was something going on in her life that weighed on her mind, that was responsible for the shadows beneath her eyes and the wariness in her gaze. Or maybe he was making a big deal out of nothing. Maybe her exhaustion was simply the result of having been up too late last night and needing to be up again early this morning. Knowing the hours that she worked, he was glad she'd managed to shut down and rest for a few hours during their journey.

He was also glad she'd agreed to come to Tesoro del Mar in advance of the wedding. Not that there was a lot of planning to do—the palace staff would take care of most of the details without blinking an eye, as they'd done for the prince regent's wedding six years earlier and the celebration of Marcus's nuptials three years after that.

One of the perks of being a royal, as Marcus liked to say, was having staff to whom to delegate. Ironic, considering that Marcus had met his wife while traveling in the United States under their mother's maiden name so as to keep his royal status hidden, and had spent several months having tasks—such as mucking out stalls at his wife's Thoroughbred training facility—delegated to him. Of course, she hadn't been his wife at the time, and she hadn't been thrilled to learn the true identity of her stable hand, but once again, their feelings for one another had proven stronger than any of the obstacles between them—one of which had been the accident that ended Eric's naval career.

He felt a twinge in his hip and shifted in his seat. A phantom pain was brought on by even the most fleeting flashback of the moment that had changed his life. He was getting more adept at pushing the memories—and the accompanying panic—aside. He did so now, focusing his thoughts again on his friend's imminent wedding.

No one outside of the family had ever been married at the palace, but Rowan and Marcus had both agreed that Scott was part of their family even if it wasn't Santiago blood in his veins.

After Marcus and Jewel married, there had been a lot of speculation throughout the media that Eric would be next—which he had to agree was likely since he was the last unmarried Santiago brother and his oldest nephew was still just a teen-ager. And he certainly had no philosophical or personal objec-tions to marriage—he'd just never met a woman who made him think in terms of forever. He'd never even met a woman who lingered in his mind after he'd left her bed…until Molly.

He turned away from the window to confirm that she was still sleeping. She was, and in sleep, her worries seemed to finally— if only temporarily—be forgotten. Her features were relaxed, the dark fan of her lashes casting a shadow against her pale cheek. He knew her skin was soft, and smoother even than the finest silk. And hidden beneath her lashes were eyes of the most startling and vivid shade of blue, eyes that had darkened and clouded in the throes of passion, the color shifting and changing not unlike the moods of a turbulent sea.

Mi Dios, he was getting turned on just by watching her sleep. Watching her sleep and remembering, and remembering—wanting.

Sexual frustration was a new—and not at all pleasant— experience for him. In the past, whenever he'd wanted the com-panionship of a woman, it had been easy enough to come by. But after the accident he'd turned his attention to rehabilitation. He'd been so intensely focused on healing his body that he hadn't al-lowed anything to distract him from the task. Not until the night he'd walked into Shea's Bar & Grill and spotted Molly working the tap.

Almost three years of abstinence seemed a reasonable expla-nation for the extent of his reaction to her, and his response to the experience of making love with her. Afterward, he managed to convince himself that the sex hadn't really been as spectacu-lar as he remembered, that it was just so long since he'd had sex that the experience only seemed heightened.

And yet, back in Tesoro del Mar, where the women were plentiful and beautiful and willing, there hadn't been one who had tempted him into her bed. Not one who tempted him to forget about Molly.

She shifted, her head rolling from one side to the other. She hadn't reclined her seat—probably because she hadn't intended to fall asleep, but exhaustion had won out. A slight furrow creased her brow as she shifted again, still asleep but obviously not very comfortable. She drew up one knee and leaned back so that her head fell against his shoulder.

Her hair tickled his cheek, the scent of her shampoo teased his nostrils, and he held his breath while he waited for her to wake. She didn't, but snuggled in, apparently finding a position that was finally comfortable—at least for her. Because while he didn't mind having her close, he was suddenly uncomfortably aware of her nearness, her softness, her femininity—and *everything* that was male within him responded.

He glanced over at Scott and Fiona, saw that they were still cuddled close together, talking quietly, so he just shifted his seat back and settled in, while Molly's scent—and his desire—continued to torment him.

Chapter Six

Molly woke just as the wheels touched down on land. But even when she felt the plane make contact with the runway, it took a moment for that fact to penetrate her consciousness. She'd been so tired lately—physically and mentally exhausted. Even when she slept, her sleep had been restless, unsettled. But this time, she awoke feeling rested and refreshed—at least until she realized that she'd been using Eric as a pillow.

She jolted upright, her face flaming. "I…um…sorry," was the best apology she could manage to stammer out.

His smile was slow, easy. "No need to be embarrassed," he said, speaking softly so that Scott and Fiona, seated across from them, wouldn't hear his words. "After all, it isn't the first time you've fallen asleep in my arms."

"But it will be the last," she muttered in response.

"Your choice, of course," he assured her, unbuckling his seat belt. Molly fumbled with hers, unfamiliar with the mechanism.

Eric watched her struggle for a moment before reaching over to release the clasp.

She held her breath as the backs of his knuckles brushed against her middle. Through the soft cotton of her T-shirt, her stomach quivered in response to the brief contact that reminded her not just of the baby that was nestled deep in her womb, but that it was *his* baby.

And in that moment, she really wanted to tell him. She wanted to share the joy and excitement of every minute of her pregnancy with him. But aside from the fact that an airplane probably wasn't the most appropriate place to share the news, especially with their friends seated across from them, there was the fear that he might not share her joy and excitement.

And if his reception of the news was less than enthusiastic, she shouldn't be surprised. Even she'd been more shocked than pleased when Dr. Morgan had advised her of the pregnancy, and though she already loved her baby more than she would ever have thought was possible, she knew she couldn't expect that Eric would feel the same. Which was why she knew it was important to choose the right time and place—and then to give him time and space to absorb the news and consider all of the implications.

No, it was definitely not the-airplane-has-just-landed-and-he's-so-close-that-I-can't-even-think-straight-because-my-hormones-are-running-riot kind of news.

Instead, she only said, "Thank you."

He released the ends of her seat belt. "You're welcome."

The warmth of his breath caressed her cheek, and a wave of heat washed over her, leaving her weak and flushed.

It was as if every nerve ending in her body was attuned to him, sending tingles of awareness and wanting through her system every time he even glanced in her direction. She'd never responded to anyone as she responded to him.

She wanted to blame it on the pregnancy, all those hormones running amok through her system, but she knew it was Eric.

Because the fact was, she wouldn't *be* pregnant if she hadn't had the same instinctive response to him from the very beginning.

The limo driver took them along the coast, so that they were flanked by rolling green hills on one side and powdery sand and crystal blue waters on the other. It was all so peaceful now, but Molly imagined that could change in the blink of an eye, that a storm could churn up the water so that the waves lashed against the rocks like angry sea monsters.

A fanciful thought, she knew, encouraged by the inherent beauty and mystery of this land that could make her imagination run as wild as it had when she was a child. Or maybe it wasn't so surprising that she was remembering childhood dreams—after all, she was riding with a prince on the way to his castle. She just had to remember that this wasn't a magical enchantment and she wasn't looking for a "happily ever after" ending.

Still, there were thoughts and ideas swirling through her mind that she vowed to jot down at the earliest opportunity. And when she caught her first glimpse of the royal palace, she couldn't entirely stifle her gasp of surprised pleasure.

It stood high atop a jutting cliff, a stunning structure of towers and turrets that was both more imposing and impressive than she could have imagined. She'd been curious enough to do some reading about the Santiago family and knew they had ruled long and ruled well, and she sensed that this castle, standing strong and proud on the hill, wasn't just a symbol to the people of Tesoro del Mar but a promise.

Another fanciful thought, perhaps, and while she'd been prepared for a fairy tale—something reminiscent of a little girl's misty-edged dreams—the reality was somehow even better.

The driver parked at the bottom of a set of wide stone steps that led up to a pair of imposing wooden doors that looked as if they could withstand the attack of a medieval battering ram. Those massive doors opened into an entranceway that was bigger than Molly's entire apartment, with a floor made of marble and walls papered in something that added hints of both shimmer and depth. Sun streamed through the tall arched windows that bracketed the doors, bathing the space in warmth and light, and fresh flowers spilled out of tall vases so that the air was perfumed with their fragrant scent.

They were greeted by a housekeeper who curtsied to the prince before advising that the guests' rooms were ready. Eric thanked and assured her that he would show them the way, then directed them up the curving stairs to the second floor, then the third. He guided them down a wide hallway, where the sound of their steps was muffled by the plush carpet. The walls were hung with pictures and tapestries, and the windows draped with velvet curtains.

Fiona and Scott were delivered to their suite before Eric led Molly a little bit farther down the hall.

"Your rooms overlook the gardens," he told her.

Not a room but *rooms,* she noted, as he opened an ornately carved door and led her into a sitting room that boasted a couple of richly upholstered chairs on either side of a stone fireplace and an antique writing desk and balloon-back chair. Behind the desk was a window, wide and multipaned, with the promised view of gardens that boasted a stunning array of vibrant colors and exotic scents.

Through the sitting room was the bedroom with a tall chest of drawers and matching bedside table of gleaming cherrywood and a wide bed topped with a thick duvet and piled with fluffy pillows. The bathroom was half the size of the bedroom again, with a deep whirlpool tub and separate shower, toilet and pedestal sink.

"If you need anything, you only need to ring for housekeeping," he told her, gesturing to the phone beside the bed.

"You might need a crowbar to pry me out of here after the wedding," she warned.

"Then maybe you'll decide to stay," he said, sounding as if he meant it.

"You know I can't," she told him.

But there was a part of her that already wished she could.

Eric had decided to give Molly space.

As much as he was eager to spend time with her and anxious to show off his homeland, he had sensed a new wariness in her since they'd landed in Tesoro del Mar—as if she knew that he now had the home turf advantage and was waiting to see how he would use it. He decided it couldn't hurt to let her wait—and wonder—a little while longer.

It was Fiona who gave him the opportunity, and the opening, he'd been hoping for. Saturday morning, only their third full day on the island, he found her alone by the pool.

"Lose your fiancé already?" he teased.

"He went down to the stables to take a ride with Rowan and Christian."

"What about Molly?" he asked, with what he thought was casual interest.

"She should be down shortly." But she frowned when she said it.

"You're supposed to be relaxing not worrying," Eric told her, lowering himself onto the edge of the vacant lounger beside hers. "I assure you, all the wedding details are being taken care of."

"I'm not worrying about the wedding," she said.

"But you're worried about something."

She sighed. "Molly."

"Is something wrong?"

"I don't know," she admitted. "I know she argued with her sister before we left Texas, although that's not really unusual. And even before that—for the past several weeks now—she's seemed really distracted. As if she's worried about something but she won't tell me what it is."

"She probably figures you have enough on your mind right now."

"She used to tell me everything," Fiona said. "I don't have any siblings, and although Molly does, we've always been as close as sisters. Closer than Molly and Abbey, that's for sure, especially after the stunt Abbey pulled with Jason."

"Molly's ex-fiancé?"

"How did you know they were engaged?" she asked curiously.

"I saw them talking at the restaurant one day, and she told me."

"That's not usually something she talks about," Fiona mused.

"Bad break-up?" he wondered aloud.

"Obviously she didn't tell you everything."

"What more is there?"

"The fact that he's now Abbey's husband."

"Molly's sister married Molly's former fiancé?"

"He was still current when Abbey seduced him." Fiona winced. "I can't believe I told you that. But I figured if you'd met Jason, you knew he was Abbey's husband."

No, Molly had conveniently neglected to mention that fact, and it didn't take a genius to figure out why. He'd asked about the guy he saw her with. She'd used his status as an ex to remind Eric that she wasn't his—a lightweight reminder if he knew that the ex was married to someone else.

"I know it sounds like something out of a soap opera, but that's exactly what happened. And though Molly keeps insisting that she's over him, I wonder if a person can ever get over that kind of betrayal. I worry that she won't ever open up her heart to anyone else."

"That's not something you can make happen," he told her, knowing—and regretting—that it was true.

"I know," she admitted. "It's just that she's my best friend, and while no one else might have noticed the change, I've seen it. She still smiles and laughs and even dates occasionally, but she's so guarded now, so careful not to get too close to anyone.

"I'd hoped that coming here would be good for her. She needed a change of scenery, a change of pace, but she's been so preoccupied lately, obviously worried about something."

"Give her some time," he suggested. "It's only day three."

"I know." She picked up her bottle of sunscreen, reapplied the lotion to her shoulders and arms. "And you've already done so much—none of this would be possible without you and I know I won't ever be able to repay you, but I really want to ask you for another favor."

"What's that?"

"Would you—if you had some free time—mind showing Molly around the island? It might take her mind off whatever is bothering her."

And Eric realized there were times when opportunity didn't just knock, it threw open the door and tossed out a welcome mat.

"I wouldn't mind at all," he said.

Despite his claim that he wanted to spend time with her when they were on the island, Molly hadn't seen a lot of Eric since they'd arrived in Tesoro del Mar. Though she tried not to dwell on the fact of his title, he was a prince and, as such, obviously had royal duties to fulfill. What those duties were she couldn't even begin to guess, but obviously they took up a lot of his time.

Not that she'd left her own responsibilities behind. She called the restaurant daily for an update, usually talking to Karen rather than Jason because Karen had been at Shea's a long time. Molly trusted that she would tell her if there were any problems with the nighttime shifts. So far, everything was running smoothly, which should have reassured Molly but somehow made her feel extraneous instead—and left her with far too much time to think about Eric.

Aside from being wildly attracted to him, during the past couple of weeks in Texas, she'd actually started to like him and enjoy spending time with him—or she would if she could only forget he was a prince.

Since landing in Tesoro del Mar, she hadn't been able to forget that for a minute.

Upon their arrival at the palace, he'd been bowed and curtsied to more times than she could count. He didn't seem to demand or even expect such deference, but he accepted it. As the second oldest son—no, he was the third born, she remembered now. Fiona had briefed her on the history of the royal family, including the tragic story of how Prince Julian—who had ruled the country prior to Rowan becoming prince regent—and his wife, Princess Catherine, had been killed by a freak explosion on their yacht. As a result, Prince Rowan had inherited not only the throne but custody of his older brother's three children.

He seemed to have adapted to sudden parenthood well, as evidenced by the close bond he shared with Christian, Lexi and Damon, as well as his two children with Lara—the former royal nanny.

Matthew and William were two of the most adorable kids Molly had ever seen. When introduced to Rowan and Lara's children, her first thought had been that they both bore a strong resemblance to their uncle Eric. Then she met Rowan and realized the dark hair and eyes and strong bone structure weren't specific to Eric but were family traits.

In fact, she nearly did a double take the first time she saw the prince regent, which prompted Scott to say, "Marcus and Eric look even more alike. When we were kids, people were constantly getting the two of them confused—which we learned to exploit whenever possible."

Eric had smiled at that. "Remember when the gardener swore he'd seen me running through his freshly planted flowerbeds and Nanny Adele argued, just as vehemently, that I'd been in the pool with you when it happened?"

"Marcus was the one who raced through the dirt," Molly guessed.

"No, it was Eric," Scott admitted now. "But seeing Marcus in the pool—conveniently wearing Eric's bathing suit to confuse everyone further—made the gardener question his conviction, which meant that Prince Eduardo couldn't be sure who should be punished."

"So you got away with trampling the flowers?" she asked Eric.

He shook his head. "No—we all got punished. My father was a big believer in taking responsibility for one's actions, and he personally supervised while Marcus and I replanted the whole garden. And he made Scott water the flowers, because he was an accessory."

She'd smiled as she'd listened to their retelling of the story, amused by their boyhood antics and pleased to hear the respect and affection in his voice when he talked about his father, confident that he would want to develop that same solid relationship with his own child.

But she still didn't know how he would react to the news that he was going to be a father himself, and she still hadn't figured out how to share that news when the wedding was finally over.

Right now, however, she was more concerned about what she was going to wear for dinner with Fiona and Scott and Eric because tonight, for the first time since the night of their arrival of the palace, he was free of whatever obligations had kept him occupied and was taking them all out.

She was scanning the meager contents of her closet when her cousin slipped into her room. Fiona held up the dress she was carrying so that Molly could appreciate the simple sheath style in a silky fabric that was somewhere between blue and green and absolutely stunning.

"How did you know I'd have nothing to wear?"

"Because I know you and you wouldn't have thought to pack much beyond your bridesmaid dress, a bathing suit and a toothbrush."

"I thought *you* were bringing the bridesmaid dress."

Fiona's face actually paled. "You didn't—"

"Kidding," Molly interrupted, and grinned.

Her cousin huffed out a breath. "Not funny."

"It was funny," she countered. "It just wasn't very nice, so I'll apologize and say 'thank you'—not just for knowing me so well but for having excellent taste and wearing the same dress size I do."

"*And* the same shoe size," Fiona said, holding out a pair of low-heeled sandals to go with the dress.

"Thanks," Molly said again.

"You can thank me by putting it on—I'm dying to see it on you."

So Molly stripped out of her robe and slipped into the dress, sighing as the silky fabric floated over her body. "I might not ever give this back."

Fiona sighed. "I don't think I'm going to want it back—it looks so much better on you than it ever did on me."

Molly knew that couldn't be true—she'd never seen her cousin look anything less than stunning—but she appreciated the compliment.

Fiona settled back on the bed and they chatted casually while

Molly finished getting ready. She didn't know if they would be dining inside or out and she didn't want her hair tangling around her face if it was windy, so she fashioned a quick French twist and secured it with a handful of pins.

"Does it work?" she asked, turning to her cousin for approval.

"It works," Fiona agreed. "In fact, it looks fabulous."

"And you look a little underdressed," she suddenly realized.

Fiona looked down at the cover-up she wore over her bikini and smiled as she slid off the bed, already making her way toward the door. "Actually, I'm dressed exactly right for a romantic picnic on the beach."

"We're having a picnic on the beach?"

Her cousin shook her head. "Scott and I are having a picnic. *You're* going out for dinner with Eric."

"Fiona…"

It was all she managed before her cousin slipped out the door, closing it firmly between them.

Chapter Seven

Molly stared at the back of the door for a long minute, considering her options. She knew she'd been set up and even knowing her cousin had the best of intentions, she didn't appreciate it. She was tempted to refuse to go out, just to prove that she wouldn't be manipulated, but that seemed both petty and spiteful and she wasn't, as a rule, either of those things. At the moment, however, she was apprehensive about spending time with Eric.

Her nervousness escalated when she left her room and found him waiting for her at the bottom of the stairs.

She felt her cheeks flush as his gaze skimmed over her, from the top of her head to the tips of her toes and everywhere in between. She trailed a hand down the smoothly polished banister, grateful for its solid support as she descended toward him. When she neared the bottom step, he offered her his hand, and she took it.

"You look…incredible."

"Thank you, Your Highness." Then she curtsied, because it

seemed appropriate. "You look quite like Prince Charming yourself."

"Prince Charming, huh? That's quite a reputation to live up to."

"I have no doubt you'll manage."

He smiled, and the slow, sensual curve of his lips made her pulse leap.

She knew how those lips tasted—their tangy masculine flavor. And she knew how they felt—nibbling her throat, nuzzling her breasts, skimming over her heated skin. Talk about heat—just the memories of the night they'd spent together had her temperature climbing toward the roof.

"I'll do my best," he said, leading her to the door beyond which he promised, "Your chariot awaits."

Her chariot was actually a sleek and sexy sports car unlike anything she had ever seen before.

"It's a Saleen S7 Twin Turbo," he told her, as if that was supposed to mean anything to a woman who drove a perfectly nice but unexceptional Saturn. "It has a seven-hundred-and-fifty horsepower V8 engine and can go from zero to sixty in less than three seconds."

"We're not going to do that, are we?" she asked, more than a little apprehensively.

He chuckled. "No. And it's not actually mine—it belongs to my brother Marcus. He was always into fast cars and fast women—before he met Jewel, anyway. Besides being an attention-getter, it's a heck of a lot of fun to drive."

And it was, she found, fun to ride in.

Maybe he didn't take it from zero to sixty in less than three seconds, but he did go fast, zipping through the streets such that everything was a blur through the window.

He drove into the town of Port Augustine, a seaside village bustling with tourists and commerce. As he navigated his way through the city streets, he proved to be a fabulous tour guide, knowledgeable about the island's history and geography.

He parked in a public lot, but it was only when he donned the baseball cap and mirrored sunglasses that she remembered he was a prince and that this was his country and the disguise—lame though it was—was probably necessary if he didn't want to be recognized.

"Ashamed to be seen with me?" she asked, only half joking. Because while she was confident that she looked her best in her borrowed dress, she didn't doubt that a prince was used to escorting much more beautiful and glamorous women than she would ever be.

"On the contrary," he said. "I am always pleased to have the company of a gorgeous woman. But if you are seen with me, I'm afraid you may be hounded by the local paparazzi for the rest of your stay in Tesoro del Mar."

"So the disguise is for my benefit?" she asked skeptically.

"And mine," he admitted. "Because I don't want to share a single minute of the time we have together with anyone else."

"If you wanted to blend in, you might have chosen a less conspicuous vehicle," she pointed out.

"But I wanted to impress you, too."

She couldn't help but smile at that.

"Do I look like an American tourist?" he asked her now.

She noted the Texas Rangers logo on the cap and figured it had been a gift from Scott—or perhaps he'd just borrowed it from his friend. But if his intention was to blend in, she didn't think he would ever manage that. Even with the hat pushed down over his thick, dark hair and those deep, compelling eyes covered with the reflective lenses, he wasn't a man who could walk around without attracting attention. He was too tall, too compelling and far too sexy for Molly's peace of mind. Not that she intended to admit any of those thoughts to the prince.

"Maybe from a distance," she said. "And only so long as you don't say anything, because no one hearing you speak would ever mistake you for a Texan."

"I'll let you do all the talking," he promised, slinging a companionable arm across her shoulders.

"My high school Spanish is more than a little rusty," she warned.

"Everyone here speaks English. Though Tesoro del Mar is officially a bilingual country—with Spanish and French as its two official languages—English is just as common and is taught in all of the schools."

He was proud of his homeland, she could hear it in his voice when he talked about the country and its people. He was a man who would have felt it was an honor and a privilege to serve in the navy, to do his part to keep his country safe, and she could only imagine how devastated he'd been to have that opportunity taken away.

The more she got to know him, the more facets she saw. He was a prince, a soldier, a hero. But mostly he was a good man, a man her baby would be proud to know was its father.

They walked along the streets of Port Augustine, browsed in the shops, drank espresso at an outdoor café, then walked some more before returning to the car.

"Getting hungry yet?" Eric asked as he drove toward the north coast.

"I am," she admitted. "I didn't think I'd want to eat for a week after the lunch Fiona and I had by the pool, but all that walking changed my mind."

"All part of my plan," he told her, "so that you can fully appreciate the experience of Tradewinds Ristorante. I promise you, Genevieve is a culinary genius."

"You must be a frequent customer if you're on a first-name basis with the chef."

"She used to work at the palace," he explained. "Her father still does. In fact, Marcel is the one who put together the sample menu for Fiona and Scott's wedding."

"So why did his daughter leave?"

"She wanted to succeed on the basis of her own work, build her own reputation."

"Obviously she has," Molly said, noting that the line of customers waiting to be seated extended outside of the door. "Do you have a reservation?"

"Please," he chided. "My title is all the reservation I need."

"I thought you were incognito today."

"Not while my stomach is rumbling." But instead of leading her to the front of the line, he guided her around to the back of the building and through an unmarked door.

She recognized the sounds of a busy kitchen—the clang of pots being shifted from prep area to burner to service counter, the rhythmic thunk of a blade chopping and dicing, the whir of a blender pulverizing. And the scents—mmm...the air was rich with flavors that were tangy and spicy and tart and sweet.

"What are you doing with that?" A woman's voice rang with authority through the din, silencing all other murmurs of conversation.

The junior cook to whom the question had been directed flinched as he turned to face his boss's wrath. "I was adding the béarnaise sauce."

"Those potatoes are charred," she pointed out in a cool voice, lifting the plate from the counter to inspect the offending spuds more closely. "And if you thought you could cover that up with the sauce, you were wrong."

"But the order is for Prince Cameron and he does not like to be kept waiting."

"He would like it even less if something came out of this

kitchen that was not prepared to my exacting specifications." And with that, she dumped the contents of the plate into the garbage.

The young apprentice flushed. "Of course, Mademoiselle."

"You will apologize to His Highness for the wait and offer a round of complimentary drinks to his table while I prepare his meal properly."

This directive was met with a brief nod before he hurried out of the kitchen to do his boss's bidding, while the dark-haired woman set to work, muttering under her breath in French.

"The only thing missing is the crack of a whip," Eric commented, loudly enough to ensure that he would be heard.

The tiny chef spun around, her brows drawn together in a scowl that immediately smoothed out when she identified the speaker. "Your Highness," she said, her lips curving into a wide smile.

The words and quick curtsy might have been formal, the embrace they shared after was not. Eric kissed both of the woman's cheeks, as Molly had learned was the European fashion, though with more enthusiasm than she thought was typical.

When he drew back, the chef's cheeks were flushed—whether from the heat of the kitchen or the pleasure of Eric's attention—Molly didn't want to guess.

"There must be a full moon tonight—the royals are all coming out of the woodwork," she teased.

"Please do not place me in the same category as my cousin."

"My apologies, Your Highness."

Her apology sounded more teasing than contrite and, judging from the way Eric's eyes narrowed, he knew it. But he only drew Molly forward. "Genevieve, I'd like you to meet Molly Shea. Molly, this is the incomparable Mademoiselle Fleury, chef *extraordinaire* and proprietor of Tradewinds."

Molly shook the proffered hand, and though the other

woman's smile was warm, she sensed that she was being as carefully measured as the ingredients for a soufflé.

"It's always a pleasure to meet a friend of a friend," Genevieve said.

"Likewise," Molly murmured.

She felt Eric's hand on her waist, his fingers curling over her
hip. "Do you have a table for us?" he asked.

Genevieve rolled her eyes and turned to Molly. "He comes
in at seven o'clock on a Saturday night and expects that I will
have a table?"

Molly shrugged apologetically.

The chef shook her head. "You take too much for granted,
Your Highness."

"Because I know you would never disappoint me," Eric said.

Genevieve sighed. "Paolo will make up the table on the balcony, so that you can have some privacy."

He smiled and kissed both of her cheeks again. *"Merci, mon
ami."*

"C'est toujours mon plaisir."

A few minutes later, Molly and Eric were escorted up a carved
stone staircase. The restaurant was in a prime location overlooking the sparkling turquoise waters of the Mediterranean. The
atmosphere on Genevieve's private balcony was enhanced by the
soft music floating up from the dining room below and the scents
of jasmine and vanilla emanating from the pots of flowers set
around the ledge.

The table was covered with a neatly pressed linen cloth that
was as blue as the sea; the crystal sparkled and the silver gleamed
in the flickering light of a trio of candles.

Molly couldn't help but be impressed by the hastily assembled
scene—and a little wary about the romantic ambience. They were
casual acquaintances who had been one-time lovers and she

hoped, for the sake of their child, that they might develop a friendship of sorts, but she wasn't looking for anything more than that.

There was no doubt, however, that this scene had been set for romance, and it made her wonder how many other women he had brought here—how many dates he'd impressed with a replica of this very same setting. It shouldn't matter; she told herself it didn't matter. This—whatever this was between them—wasn't a date.

But she couldn't help but ask, "Come here often?"

"I enjoy my privacy as much as a good meal, and Genevieve is kind enough to accommodate me in both respects."

"And is obviously discreet enough not to blink when you introduce her to your…friends."

He grinned. "I do trust Genevieve. I wouldn't have brought you here otherwise. But if you think this is part of my usual seduction routine, you'd be wrong. Because the truth is, I haven't dated enough since the accident to even have a routine."

"And before?" she queried.

"As both of my brothers can attest, there has never been a shortage of women eager to be seen on the arm of a prince. So yes, I dated, and probably more than my fair share. But finding a woman willing to stand by a man who was at sea more than on land was difficult. I can't even remember how many relationships sank when I shipped out, but it was enough that I gave up even trying to make anything work beyond the period of my leave.

"And after I resigned my commission, I didn't meet anyone who made me even think beyond the short-term. Until you."

"We didn't even have short-term," she reminded him. "We had one night."

"We could have more."

Molly shook her head, with sincere regret. "But I appreciate the tour," she said.

She wasn't sure if she was relieved or disappointed that he let the matter drop, as he seemed to do, because he only said, "Then you're pleased with what you've seen of the country so far?"

"I think it would be more appropriate to say I'm both amazed and dazzled."

He smiled. "As I said before, you are welcome to stay on after the wedding to enjoy a real vacation."

She shook her head regretfully. "As tempting as that sounds, I'm afraid nothing here seems real. It's like a postcard-perfect world and a zillion miles away from the realities of my life."

"Has your absence from the restaurant been a problem?" he asked.

"Not at all."

"And it annoys you, at least a little, that all the gears are continuing to turn with the most important cog removed from the machine."

She laughed at his analogy—and because it was true. "It's silly, I know, but you're right."

"It's not silly at all," he denied. "We all like to feel as if we have a purpose in life, a reason for being, and it can be difficult to accept that we aren't as essential as we believed."

She knew he was referring to his own life now, to the career that had abruptly been ended by his injury.

"Do you ever accept it?" she asked, aware that she was prying but unable to stop herself. "Can you ever find another purpose?"

There was more than a touch of wryness in his smile this time. "I'll have to get back to you on that one."

They continued to talk while they ate. The meal began with some kind of chilled soup that was a little bit spicy, followed by a main course of grilled sea bass—apparently one of Genevieve's personal specialties—served with garlic lemon green beans and wild rice, and finished with an assortment of pastries, including slices of a baklava unlike anything Molly had ever tasted.

Through it all, Eric made her feel so comfortable and at ease that when he asked if she wanted to take a walk on the beach after dinner, she didn't even consider refusing.

He left a pile of bills on the table that she guessed more than paid for the meal they'd shared. Then, after a quick stop in the kitchen to thank Genevieve for the incredible meal, they walked toward the water. The sun was only starting to set and the sky was a riot of glorious color. Eric took her hand to help her down the narrow steps that were a public access to the beach, and he didn't let go when they reached the bottom. She didn't protest or tug her hand away. It seemed silly to even consider doing so when they'd shared much deeper intimacies.

They hadn't gone far, however, before she realized that Fiona's sandals weren't very practical on sand, so Molly kicked them off and was pleased when Eric discarded his shoes and socks to walk barefoot with her. They strolled along the water's edge, sometimes talking, sometimes not, but he never let go of her hand.

They were almost back at the stairs when he stopped abruptly.

"Look," he whispered close to her ear.

And her breath caught as she watched the sun complete its descent beyond the horizon.

"I have never seen a sunset like that," she breathed the words quietly, almost reverently.

"And I have never seen anything like you framed by the sunset," he said.

Then his mouth covered hers.

Just like the first time he'd kissed her, his lips were warm and firm, confident in their mastery. There was no tentativeness, no hesitant searching for the right angle, no questioning of her response.

And like the first time, there was no hesitation in her response.

It had been weeks—and yet, it somehow felt as if it was only yesterday. The warm strength of his arms around her wasn't just familiar, it was right. And the explosion of sensations made her mind spin, her heart pound and her body yearn.

He found the pins that held her French twist in place and slipped them free so that her hair spilled into his hands. His fingers sifted through the tresses, caught the ends to tip her head back, changing the angle and deepening the kiss.

She sighed; he groaned.

She wanted him—there was no denying that fact. But she couldn't let herself get caught up in the moment, the romance, the fantasy. There was too much at stake now.

Her system jangled with unacknowledged wants, unsatisfied desires, but she forced herself to take a step back.

"I want to go back to the palace now," she said, though she knew the words were a lie.

What she really wanted was for him to kiss her again, until reality faded away and there was nothing but the two of them. She wanted to make love with him again, to experience the fulfillment she'd only ever known in his arms. But she knew that couldn't happen, not while there was such a huge—and growing—secret between them.

Eric clenched his hands into fists to resist the urge to grab hold of Molly and shake some sense into her. What was it about this woman that she was so determined to deny what was between them?

"Don't you think we should talk about this?"

"It was just a kiss, Eric. I hardly think we need to dissect and analyze every insignificant little detail of it."

His nails dug into his palms. "Maybe it's not necessary," he allowed, somehow managing to match her casual tone despite the fury in his blood, "but I'm curious as to which part you think is most insignificant—your tongue in my mouth, your breasts plastered against my chest or your hips rocking against mine."

Her eyes narrowed even as her cheeks flushed with color. "So I responded to you physically. That doesn't mean I want to fall back into bed with you."

"Oh, you want to," he said, confident it was true. "But for some reason, you're afraid to give in to the chemistry between us."

"I just don't want to make a big deal out of something that isn't," she insisted. "And right now, I really want to go back to the palace so I can go to bed *alone.*"

There was more going on, something beneath the surface but he was damned if he could figure it out.

He pulled on his socks and shoved his feet into his shoes, not caring that both were full of sand. The only thing that mattered now was getting Molly back to the palace so he could get away from the woman who was slowly driving him insane.

"Let's go," he said.

She followed silently.

Not a word was spoken as they walked back to the car. As he pulled out of the parking lot, Eric thought that if he lived to be a hundred, he would never understand women.

He knew that was a standard complaint of men around the world, but never had he understood it as he did now. Never had he known a woman like Molly who seemed to delight in sending out mixed signals. One minute she was in his arms, her lips soft and warm beneath his, her body yielding to his, and the next she was pushing him away as if she couldn't stand his touch.

Mi Dios.

His fingers tightened around the steering wheel as he guided the little sports car around the steeply winding curves of Oceanview Drive. Below, the waves crashed against the rocks, but

Eric's own mood was too dark to allow him to pay heed to the vagaries of the sea.

He kept his gaze focused on the road, but he was conscious of Molly seated beside him. He was conscious of the tension in every inch of her body, of the quiet intake of every breath she took, of her subtle and unique scent. And mostly he was conscious of the desire that still thrummed in his blood.

He wanted her—more now even than the first time because he knew how incredible they could be together. And while she'd been kissing him on the beach, he'd been certain she wanted the same thing.

Until she said, "I'm ready to go back to the palace now," in a tone that made it clear she didn't mean to the privacy of his rooms.

And he could respect that. He had no intention of forcing his attentions on a woman who made it clear that she wasn't interested. Except that Molly hadn't made *anything* clear—she'd only made his head spin in circles and his body ache with wanting.

Still, he wasn't going to waste any more time chasing after this woman. She knew what he wanted and he would just have to trust that she would let him know if she ever decided she wanted the same thing.

The touch of her hand on his arm made him jolt.

The fierce grip of cool, clammy fingers eradicated any illusions that she was giving him a signal to do anything but pull over to the side of the road. *Now.*

His gaze swung over, noting the pallor of her skin, the panic in her eyes.

He whipped the car onto the soft shoulder, the tires spitting up gravel.

She flung open the door before he'd completely stopped and raced over to the guardrail. Eric was right behind her, wrapping an arm around her waist and lifting her up so that she could heave over the barrier. And she did—tossing her grilled sea bass back into the ocean.

"Okay?" he asked, when the spasms in her stomach had finally stopped.

She nodded.

Now that the crisis had passed, he was suddenly aware of his arm banded around her ribs, just below the soft curves of her breasts. Of her cute little derriere pressed against his groin. Of her hair, swirling in the wind, tickling his throat, teasing him with the scent of her shampoo. And the sudden stillness of her body that alerted him to the fact that she was just as acutely aware of the intimacy of their positions.

He lowered her feet back to the ground and loosened his hold.

Her fingers curled around the top of the guardrail, gripping the metal barrier as she continued to look out at the sea, looking—he suspected—anywhere but at him.

He returned to the car to retrieve a bottle of water from the first aid kit he habitually carried. "It's not cold but it's wet," he said, twisting off the cap and offering it to her.

She accepted it with a quietly murmured thanks and tipped it to her lips to rinse her mouth, then swallowed a few tentative sips.

"I'm sorry," she said, still not meeting his gaze.

"There's no need to apologize," he told her. "Though you might have warned me you have a tendency toward motion sickness."

"I don't usually," she said, sounding more than a little defensive.

He frowned. "Are you blaming my driving?"

"No," she said. "Maybe it was the fish."

Except that Eric had eaten the same thing she had for dinner, and he knew there was nothing wrong with the way it had been prepared.

"I don't mean that it wasn't cooked properly," she said, knowing Genevieve wouldn't have let the plates out of her kitchen otherwise. "But maybe there was some kind of spice or seasoning that doesn't sit well with me.

"Or maybe I just had too much sun today," she suggested as an alternative. "I spent a few hours by the pool with Fiona earlier."

Which he already knew, of course. He had a clear view of the pool from his windows, and he'd found his gaze straying outside all too frequently because she was there. He also knew she'd spent more time in the shade than the sun and that she'd been wearing a hat.

Yeah, she had all kinds of excuses, as if she was desperate for him to pick one—any one—to believe. And Eric had a sudden, sinking feeling that he knew the real reason for her bout of illness.

And though the possibility made *him* feel a little queasy, it wasn't anything he was prepared to ignore.

"Or maybe you're pregnant."

Chapter Eight

Molly wanted to laugh.

Her sister was always complaining about the cluelessness of men in general and of her husband in particular. No one could accuse Eric Santiago of being clueless—she'd gotten sick once, and he assumed he had all the answers.

Unfortunately for Molly, they were the right answers.

"You're not denying it," he said.

She'd considered doing just that, if only to erase the smug certainty from his tone. But the truth would be only too obvious in a few more months and, ultimately, he had a right to know. She might be annoyed that the decision of when and where to tell him had been taken out of her hands, but she was also relieved that he finally knew.

"No," she finally said. "But it's way too early to be making any big announcement about it, so I'd appreciate it if we could keep this between us."

"It's not that early," he said, obviously having already done some quick mental calculations.

She shook her head. "You're making a lot of assumptions."

"You expect me to believe that the baby's not mine?"

No, but she hadn't expected *him* to assume that it was. She'd still been trying to figure out the best way to tell him about the baby, and to prepare herself for the likelihood that he might deny paternity in the absence of proof. It was what almost any man would do when confronted with the news of an unplanned pregnancy, especially by a woman with whom he'd spent only one night. But she was starting to realize that Eric Santiago rarely did what she expected him to do.

"I'm not ready to have this conversation right now," she said.

"Then when?" he demanded.

"Look, Eric, I know this has caught you off guard, but I want to assure you that I made the decision to have this baby and I will assume full responsibility for him or her."

"*¡Cómo infierno!*"

She blinked, startled by his vehement outburst—and the fleeting hurt in his eyes.

"We made that baby together, we will be responsible for that baby together."

"You've got to be joking."

"I assure you that I am not."

The calm, unyielding tone worried her. Whatever she'd anticipated when she finally got around to telling him about their baby, it wasn't this.

"Did you really think I was the type of man who would abandon my responsibilities?" he challenged her.

"I didn't think *anything*," she denied. "But we spent one night together, and at the time, I didn't know what type of man you were at all."

"You should know me a lot better now."

"Not well enough to anticipate how you might respond to the news of an unexpected pregnancy."

"Then I'll tell you—I have no intention of denying paternity. My child will be acknowledged and accepted as mine and he will take his rightful place in line to the throne."

She'd been stunned to learn that the father of her child was a prince, apparently so stunned that she'd somehow failed to reach the logical conclusion that his status meant that his child would be royalty, as well.

But she wasn't so stunned now that she failed to notice that he'd used both the terms *"he"* and *"his."* She'd found herself thinking of the baby in male gender terms, too, but only because she couldn't think of her child as "it." She wondered if it was the same for Eric or if he was hoping the baby was a boy because a male child was more important in the royal family hierarchy.

"And what if it's a girl?" she asked.

He frowned. "It makes no difference to me whether the child is a boy or a girl."

"Would it make any difference with respect to succession?"

"No. When Alexandria was born, Julian persuaded parliament to change the law to allow for equal primogeniture so that she wouldn't lose her place in line to the throne, which she would have done when Damon was born.

"Which means," he continued, "regardless of the child's gender, he or she will come directly after me in the line of succession."

"And where are you in the line?" she asked, starting to feel a little weak in the knees at the thought that her unborn child could someday rule a Mediterranean country.

"Seventh," he answered her question.

The response helped her to breathe again because she knew,

realistically, that while her child's place in line to the throne meant he *could* someday rule the country, it was unlikely he would ever be called upon do so.

Still—a mother who was a bartender and a father who was a prince? If that wasn't a recipe for disaster for the poor kid, she didn't know what was.

Molly was quiet during the rest of the drive back to the palace. Too quiet, Eric thought, as he maneuvered the vehicle slowly along the winding coastal road, casting frequent glances in her direction to make sure she was okay.

He felt guilty for coming on so strong, but it had seriously irritated him that she could believe—for even half a second—he might not want his child.

As for the paternity issue, he knew there would be some who'd expect him to demand proof before accepting that the child Molly carried was his. He didn't need proof because he knew Molly—obviously a lot better than she knew him.

She hadn't been a virgin when they'd made love, but it had been readily apparent to Eric that her experience was limited. She'd responded to every brush of his lips and touch of his hands with soft sighs and quiet gasps that were filled with wonder. She had been both shy and eager, hesitant and willing, and the contradiction between her obvious desire and innocence had been incredibly arousing.

Glancing at her now, he saw that her hands were folded in her lap, her gaze locked upon them, and he remembered what Fiona had told him about Molly's reluctance to let anyone get close. He was going to have to tread more carefully than he'd done so far if she was going to open up to him.

"I know you aren't ready to make any big decisions right now," he said. "But we are going to have to talk about this sometime."

She nibbled on her bottom lip. "Can it wait until after the wedding?"

He frowned, thinking of her intention to return to Texas right after Scott and Fiona were married, and conscious of the clock that was ticking.

"Will you agree to stay for a while after the wedding?" he asked again.

"For what purpose?"

"To give us a chance to figure this out and make plans for our own."

She turned her head to look at him. "Our own what?"

"Wedding."

"What? No. No way."

"You might want to give the idea some thought before you discard it out of hand."

"*You* need to give it some thought," she told him. "Because if you did, you'd realize the idea is crazy."

As far as proposals went, he realized this one left a lot to be desired. But he felt it was important to communicate what he wanted, and in that first moment when he'd realized Molly was carrying his child, he'd known.

He wanted Molly and the baby.

Their baby.

The rush of fierce possessiveness that swept through him drowned everything else.

"I want to be a father to this child," he said, in case he hadn't already made that point perfectly clear. "And the best way to ensure that is for us to get married."

"Marriage doesn't ensure anything."

"I'm not asking for an answer right now. I'm just asking you to think about it."

"The answer is no. I don't want my child growing up in a fishbowl, and your need to don a disguise when we went into town this afternoon made me realize that the child of a prince—"

"Whether or not we marry," he interrupted, "our child will be a member of the royal family."

"We are not going to marry," she said firmly.

Eric knew that if he pushed her any further right now, she'd only dig in her heels, so he let the subject drop, confident that she would eventually come around to his way of thinking.

When they'd left the palace a few hours earlier, he'd been looking forward to a pleasant afternoon and some time alone with Molly. He hadn't been expected to be hit with the knowledge that he was going to be a father—or to already be thinking of marriage to the mother of his child. And while this situation was definitely outside the realm of his experience, he didn't feel overwhelmed or trapped or panicked. Maybe it was because so much of his life had been turned upside down in the past few years that he was able to take these new developments in stride, but whatever the reason, marrying Molly just seemed…right.

Marcus would probably say he was still suffering the lingering effects of the concussion he'd sustained three years earlier. Of course, Marcus had always been quick with the jokes, and quicker to extricate himself from any relationship with a woman who had even hinted at long-term—at least until he met Jewel.

Unlike his younger brother, Eric had never been opposed to the idea of marriage. He'd just never had reason to consider it. But he was going to do more than consider it now.

There was going to be another royal wedding in Tesoro del Mar—just as soon as he could convince the woman he wished to become his bride.

Molly was relieved when she woke up the next morning and found a note from her cousin telling her that Fiona and Scott had borrowed a car and were taking a drive to the other side of the island. She was grateful for the reprieve, temporary though she knew it would be. Having succeeded in sending Molly and Eric off together the day before, Fiona would want to hear all the details of their outing, and Molly wasn't quite sure how she would answer her questions.

She imagined Eric would give her a wide berth today. Not just because of the friction between them but because he would need some time to figure out what he really wanted with respect to a relationship with his child.

In the light of day, Molly realized she shouldn't have been so surprised by his impulsive proposal the night before. She knew he was an honorable man who took his responsibilities seriously. It would be natural for him to want to assume responsibility for his child. But she was equally convinced that, having had an opportunity to think it through, he would be grateful she hadn't accepted his offer of marriage.

She went down to the dining room for breakfast, helping herself to a bowl of fresh fruit and a muffin. It seemed that everyone else had already been and gone and though she didn't mind the solitude, she was conscious of the fact that she'd slept late every morning since arriving on the island and worried that she would become accustomed to this life of leisure. Long stretches of time in which she was required to do absolutely nothing were beyond her realm of experience, so she was pleased when she wandered into the garden and found Princess Lara there with her sons.

Matthew had a butterfly net in one hand and a bug box in the other and was bent at the waist, peering intently at the grass. William toddled around behind his brother, his steps a little unsteady on the grass. Occasionally he'd land on his diaper-clad bottom, but he'd just push himself up again and keep going, though he frequently looked back to make sure his mother was still there and never ventured too far away from her.

"We're looking for frogs," the three-year-old young prince informed Molly when she joined them. "Would you like to help?"

"Frogs?" Molly squatted down so that she was at eye level with him. "What kind—brown ones or green ones?"

His little brow furrowed and he looked to his mother for help.

"Whichever ones we can find," she told him, before lowering her voice so that only Molly could hear and adding, "which I'm hoping is none."

Molly smiled at the princess, then turned back to the little boy and asked, "Are there any purple ones around here?"

"There's no such thing as purple frogs," he said authoritatively.

"How do you know?"

"'Cause Damon's caught lotsa frogs and he's never caught a purple one."

"And I've told you," Lara reminded her son, "just because you haven't seen something doesn't mean it doesn't exist."

"So there are purple frogs?"

Lara shrugged. "I've never seen one, but who knows?"

He turned to Molly. "Are there purple ones?"

"I can't say for sure, either," she admitted. "But I've heard about them and that they're magical frogs."

His eyes lit up. "Magical?"

Molly nodded. "If you're lucky enough to find one, you pick it up—very gently, of course—and hold it in the palm of your hand for the count of ten. Can you count to ten?"

His head bobbed up and down enthusiastically.

"Okay, so you count slowly and out loud and when you get to ten, it will roll over onto its back so you can see its belly—which is actually more pink than purple—and make a wish as you tickle his belly."

"What kind of wish?"

"Any kind of wish you want."

"And my wish will come true?"

"That's what they say. But," she cautioned, "it only works if you haven't touched any other frogs that day—not green ones or brown ones and especially not blue ones."

His eyes grew wide. "There's blue ones, too?"

Molly nodded.

"Wow." He turned to his mom. "I'm goin' huntin' for purple frogs," he said, and raced off again, lugging both the butterfly net and the bug box.

"Why especially not the blue ones?" Lara wondered, her voice tinged with both admiration and amusement.

"Because the blue ones are poison to the purple ones and when the purple ones get sick, they can't grant anyone's wishes."

Lara laughed and dropped down onto the grass beside Molly. "You certainly piqued my son's interest."

Molly shrugged. "Kids are always a great audience."

"I'd say you're a great storyteller. Ever put any of your ideas on paper?"

She shook her head.

"Why not?" the princess asked.

"Because I'm a bartender, not a writer."

"You have a gift," Lara insisted. "It would be a shame not to see what you could do with it."

Molly's grandmother had said the same thing to her more than once, but she'd thought she was just encouraging her because that's what grandmothers did—and because hers in particular thought she should be doing anything other than serving drinks in a bar. But Molly had never really thought seriously of doing anything else, so she was relieved when William crawled over and drew Lara's attention.

The baby climbed into his mother's lap and laid his head against her breast, rubbing his eyes with hands that were stained with dirt and grass. Lara just sighed and snuggled him closer. "You're getting sleepy, aren't you, dirty boy?"

His only response was a yawn.

Molly felt a strange tug inside her as she realized it wouldn't be too much longer before she would have her own baby to cuddle in her arms.

"They're all such stunning children," she murmured.

"The Santiago genes are strong," Lara said, then smiled. "And exceptional."

Molly nodded. "I met Prince Damon first," she said. "And I was stunned by how beautiful he is. I know he's a boy, but there isn't any other word to do him justice. I thought the same thing when I saw his brother and then Prince Matthew and Prince William, too. And then Princess Alexandria walked into the room and somehow managed to outshine them all."

Lara laughed. "She does, doesn't she? And Isabella, Marcus and Jewel's baby, is just the same. You'll get to meet her when they fly in for the wedding."

"They're coming here for Scott and Fiona's wedding?"

"Yeah, Marcus grumbled, of course, because San Antonio is a lot closer to West Virginia than Tesoro del Mar is, but I don't think he would miss it for the world."

"I didn't realize, until recently, that Scott had grown up here," Molly said. "I'm not sure Fiona did, either, or knew that his best friend was a prince. I mean, Scott had talked about Eric and Marcus and Rowan, but he certainly didn't make a big deal out of the fact that they were royalty."

"Titles shouldn't matter between friends," the princess said simply. "Which is why I'd really like it if you'd call me 'Lara' instead of 'Your Highness'."

"Thank you," Molly said.

Lara rose to her feet with the half asleep baby on her shoulder and grinned. "And as your friend," she said. "I expect to be kept apprised of whatever is going on between you and Eric—because I know there's something."

Molly couldn't deny it, but she could clarify to ensure the princess didn't anticipate any new romantic developments. "Was."

The smile never wavered. "We'll see about that."

And before Molly could think of an appropriate response, Lara had excused herself to round up Matthew, and take both kids inside, to clean them up before they went for their naps.

Despite the hints about Molly's relationship with Eric, she'd enjoyed the time she'd spent with the princess and her children and was disappointed when they left.

Left to her own devices once again, she changed into her bathing suit, slathered on a generous amount of sunscreen and headed down to the pool. She'd forgotten to pack a book and considered detouring past the library on the main level to borrow one, but decided that she wasn't feeling that ambitious. She didn't want to read or think…she just wanted to be.

She laid her towel over the back of the lounge chair, adjusted the tilt and settled in. Then she remembered Fiona's warning about raccoon eyes and tan lines, so she removed her sunglasses and, double-checking to make sure no one else was around, she untied the strings of the halter from around her neck and tucked them into the keyhole between her breasts.

She promised herself that she would clear her mind, that she wouldn't let herself think about Eric or her pregnancy or anything else that would give her worry lines. And she managed to keep that promise—until a shadow fell over her, blocking the sun.

She knew, even before she opened her eyes, that it was Eric. Somehow, instinctively, she just knew.

"How long have you been out here?" he asked her.

She shrugged, then realized her mistake when the top of her bathing suit slipped a little lower.

His gaze dropped, lingered.

"The dress I'm wearing for the wedding is strapless," she explained. "Fiona would have a fit if I had tan lines."

"I imagine she would." He reached for the bottle of sunscreen beside her chair, squirted some on his palm, then rubbed his hands together to spread it over both. "She would be even more upset if you burned."

Molly swallowed as he shifted closer, his intent obvious. "I covered up pretty good before I came out."

"But you don't even know how long you've been out," he said, sliding his hands over the curve of her shoulders.

She had to bite down on her lip so that she wouldn't moan out loud because, oh my, he had such talented hands. Such wickedly, wonderfully, talented hands.

No—she wouldn't moan. But she would, and did, close her eyes, as he smoothed lotion down her arms, then up again. Across her collarbone. And—oh my—over the swell of her breasts.

Desire, hot and liquid, pulsed through her system as his hands glided over her skin, caressing and lingering long after the lotion had been rubbed into her skin.

"I think that's, um, good," she finally managed. "Thanks."

His lips curved. "My pleasure."

"So…" she held a hand over her eyes, shielding them from the sun as she looked up at him "…is there a reason you came down to the pool? Because it obviously wasn't to swim."

"I sat in on a meeting with the Minister of Economic Development," he said, explaining the dark suit he wore. "I came down to the pool looking for you."

"And now you've found me."

"So I did," he agreed, then grinned. "The question now is, can I keep you?"

"Believe me, you won't want to in a few more months."

"I can't imagine that being true," he said, sitting on the edge of the chair beside hers. "Just thinking about the fact that you're carrying my baby—"

"Eric," she warned.

"There's no one around to overhear."

He was right. They were completely alone. It was just the two of them and all of her rampaging hormones—*not* a good scenario.

"And as I was saying," he continued, "just knowing that you're carrying my child makes me want you even more."

"The wanting is what got us into this predicament," she reminded him.

"Yeah," he agreed, and gave her another one of those slow smiles that made everything inside of her turn to mush.

Molly picked up her glass and drank deeply, but what had been ice water half an hour before was now lukewarm and did nothing to cool the heat in her veins.

As the day of Fiona and Scott's wedding drew nearer, Molly saw less and less of Eric. She knew that all the details for the wedding had been taken care of so there was no reason for him to hang around. No reason except that he'd said they would figure things out together and it was kind of hard to figure things out with somebody who was never around.

She knew he was involved in meetings with the Minister of Economic Development and that those meetings were somehow related to the potential expansion of Scott's business, but to Molly, it was just further proof that she couldn't rely on anyone but herself. And even she wasn't so dependable these days, with the way her mind was spinning in circles contemplating all of the possibilities—go back to Texas/stay in Tesoro del Mar/return to her job/sell the restaurant/buy a time-share in Timbuktu.

Okay, so maybe that last option wasn't a realistic one, but she was so desperate for a solution, she was willing to consider almost anything.

Anything except marriage.

Not that Eric had brought up the subject since the night he'd first learned that she was pregnant, which led her to hope that he'd come to his senses. And she was grateful for that. The last thing she needed or wanted was to be pressured into marriage by a man who was intent on doing "the right thing."

But what did she want?

Unfortunately, that was a question to which she didn't have an answer.

Chapter Nine

Eric sat at a table in the corner, a beer in hand, and watched Molly on the dance floor.

He'd been watching her all night, unable to take his eyes off of her since she'd walked down the aisle ahead of Fiona at the start of the ceremony earlier in the evening. He'd always known she was beautiful, but tonight she was simply stunning.

He'd been forewarned by their conversation by the pool a few days earlier that the dress was strapless, but that had hardly been sufficient information to prepare him for the image she presented in the slim column of sapphire silk that shimmered like blue flame when she moved.

The vibrant color made her skin look even creamier, her eyes even bluer. Her dark hair was swept up off her neck and piled on top of her head in some kind of fancy style that tempted him to pluck the pins free so the silky tresses would spill into his hands.

Yeah, he'd been watching her all night and enjoying every minute—until he saw Cameron Leandres approach. His cousin said a few words, Molly smiled, and the next thing Eric knew, they were on the dance floor together.

"You're going to break that glass if you're not careful," Marcus warned from behind him.

Eric forced his fingers to relax and pushed the drink away as his brother pulled out a chair and joined him.

"What is he even doing here?" Eric demanded.

"Cameron?"

"Yeah, Cameron."

"Scott invited him," Marcus said. "Michael and Samantha are here, too."

Eric knew that and he didn't have any issue with his other cousin and his cousin's wife being there, but Michael's younger brother was a different story.

"And you're okay with this?" he asked Marcus now.

His brother shrugged. "It's not my wedding, is it?"

"But this is our home."

"And Cameron is, as much as we'd sometimes like to pretend otherwise, part of our family."

"Yeah—the part that tried to create a scandal and undermine Rowan's authority as prince regent, and then drive a wedge between you and Jewel by revealing that you'd been working at her training center under an assumed identity."

"*Tried* being the operative word," Marcus reminded him.

"And now he's trying to put the moves on Molly," Eric grumbled.

"Are you worried that she's the type to succumb to his questionable charms?"

"No," he said, and he wasn't. "I just don't want him getting any ideas about my future wife."

Marcus choked on his beer.

Eric thumped him on the back, probably a little harder than was necessary.

"Geez," Marcus grumbled. "You should give a guy some warning before you drop a bomb like that."

"Is it really such a shock?"

"The idea of you wanting to marry a woman you've only known a few weeks?"

Eric picked up his beer again, took a long swallow. "Actually, I've known her a little bit longer than that."

His brother's eyes narrowed. "How much longer?"

"A few months."

"The first time you were out in Texas," Marcus guessed. "Lara said you'd met someone there."

"When did she tell you that?"

"When she called and suggested I drop by to visit you in San Antonio and try to wrangle an introduction."

"Because San Antonio is just around the corner from Alliston," Eric noted dryly.

"But she was right, wasn't she?"

"She was right," he admitted.

"So you've known Molly a few months," Marcus picked up the earlier thread of their conversation. "That's still no reason to rush into talking about marriage, unless…" his voice trailed off as realization dawned "…she's pregnant."

Eric knew Molly wasn't ready to make any announcements about the baby they were expecting, but this was his brother and Eric wasn't going to lie to him.

"Due January seventh," he admitted. "And while I expect to have my ring on her finger long before then, I'd appreciate it if you didn't say anything about the baby to anyone else."

Marcus nodded and lifted his bottle again. As he took another swallow of his beer, Eric knew what he was thinking, and the he was debating the wisdom of speaking those thoughts aloud.

"Yes," he said, before Marcus could piss him off by asking the question. "I'm sure it's mine."

"Well, then—" his brother lifted his glass "—congratulations."

Eric nodded. "Thanks." He finished his drink. "Just one thing?"

"What's that?"

"Don't say anything about my plans to the bride-to-be."

"She doesn't know there's going to be a wedding?" Marcus guessed.

"Not yet."

Marcus lifted his glass again. "Good luck with that."

Eric suspected he was going to need it.

By the time midnight rolled around and the bride and groom were whisked away to the airport, Molly was exhausted. But as she waved to the departing couple in the limousine, she was happy for her cousin, and more uncertain than ever about her own future.

She felt Eric's presence before she turned her head and saw him standing behind her.

The intensity in his gaze made her heart pound a little faster, but she managed a smile and said, "You did it."

His brows lifted. "What did I do?"

"You made sure this was a day that Scott and Fiona will never forget."

"I wish I could take the credit," he said. "But really, I only delegated jobs to those who were much more capable of doing them."

"Then you delegated well."

"Thank you." He offered her his arm, and she took it, and they wandered to the back gardens together.

"Did you want to walk?" he asked her.

"Actually, I would love to just sit for a few minutes," she told him. "I feel as if I've been on my feet all day."

"Then we'll sit," he said, and led her over to the stone bench by the fountain.

The ballroom doors had been thrown open and she could hear the band still playing for the few guests that remained. She imagined the revelry might go on for quite a while yet, but she was more than ready to hang up her dancing shoes for the night.

"I told Marcus about the baby."

"Oh."

The disappointment in her tone was obvious. "You don't sound pleased."

She shrugged. "I thought we agreed we wouldn't tell anyone yet."

"He's not anyone, he's my brother," Eric explained. "And in all fairness, he sort of guessed. Have you really told no one?"

"Only you."

"Not even your sister?"

"*Especially* not my sister."

Eric was surprised by this response. While he understood that she wasn't ready to make a public announcement about her pregnancy, he thought she'd be anxious to share the news with her family.

"Abbey had a miscarriage five months ago," she told him. "Actually, it was her third miscarriage in eight years of trying to have a baby."

He could only imagine how painful each experience must have been for her sister, and he was concerned that there was something in the family history that might affect Molly's pregnancy, as well.

"Do they know why she miscarried?" he asked cautiously.

"They have some theories, none of which are genetic, and my

GP assured me that there's no reason to worry that I can't carry this baby to term."

"You haven't seen a specialist?"

"I had an appointment to see an ob-gyn, but I had to cancel it when Scott and Fiona's wedding plans got changed. I'll reschedule when I get back."

"You could see someone here," he suggested. "I could get the name of Lara's doctor… No, I guess I can't without explaining why I'd need it." And if Eric took Molly to an ob-gyn in Tesoro del Mar, the news of her pregnancy would undoubtedly be headlines the very next morning.

"I'll be home within a week, anyway," she reminded him.

Which was another subject he wanted to discuss with her, but he opted to wait. They were actually having a civil conversation and he didn't want to ruin it by asking for something he knew she wasn't ready to consider.

"How have you been feeling?" he asked.

"I'm fine," she assured him. "I promise."

"No morning sickness?"

"Only that one very memorable incident."

He smiled, but his gaze was serious when he asked, "And if I hadn't figured it out—were you going to tell me?"

She nodded. "I was just trying to work out the how and when."

He reached for her hand, linked their fingers together. "From now on, we'll figure our future out together, okay?"

"I think it's important that we work together for the sake of our child, but I don't see that we have a future beyond that."

"Only because you're not looking," he chided. "I want to marry you, Molly."

"Haven't we been through this already?"

"I know it came as a surprise when I mentioned it the first time, but now that you've had some time to think about it, I'd hoped you would have considered the benefits."

"And I hoped, after you'd had some time to think about it, you'd realize how ridiculous the idea is."

"What's so ridiculous about it?" he demanded.

"For starters, how about the fact that we don't even know one another?"

"We know one another a lot better now than we did a few months ago."

"Not nearly well enough to promise till death do us part'."

"We're going to have a baby together," he reminded her. "We'll have plenty of time to get to know one another."

It occurred to her then that he honestly didn't understand why she wasn't thrilled with his "proposal." She didn't know if it was because he was a prince that he expected to get what he wanted when he wanted it, but she knew they would continue to have the same argument about marriage if she didn't make him understand her feelings on the subject.

"Do you know what made today so perfect for Scott and Fiona?" she finally asked.

He looked at her warily. "I thought it was my exceptional delegating skills."

She managed a smile. "No, your exceptional delegating skills ensured that it will be remembered fondly by all of the guests as a beautiful wedding. But what made it perfect for the bride and groom was the way they looked at each other when they spoke their vows, as if there was no one else around, as if nothing else could ever matter as much as their love for and commitment to one another."

She took his hands, willing him to understand. "If I ever get married, it will be because I feel the same way about someone, not because it's the logical or reasonable thing to do."

"Do you really think love guarantees a successful marriage?"

"No," she admitted. "But at least it gives a solid foundation to build on."

"What about attraction?" he challenged.

"What about it?"

"Do you agree that sexual attraction is important in a relationship?"

"Of course, but—"

He touched his fingers to her mouth, halting her words and making her lips tingle and her heart pound.

"'Of course' is all the answer I need for now." His fingertips traced the curve of her lips, first the top, then the bottom, then across the seam.

She shivered, sighed.

He smiled.

"And we have sexual attraction, don't we?"

She could hardly deny it, not when her blood was pulsing like molten lava through her veins and her knees were actually trembling in response to his nearness.

His fingers dropped away from her lips, skimmed over her chin, down her throat and lower, to the hollow between her breasts.

"Don't we?" he asked again.

She could only nod as his fingers caressed the bare skin above the neckline of her dress, creating little sparks of pleasure everywhere he touched.

"The last time I kissed you, you pushed me away."

She swallowed. "I kissed you back first."

He smiled. "Yeah, you did."

His fingers continued their gentle, torturous stroking.

"If I kiss you now…will you push me away…or kiss me back?"

She lifted her arms to his shoulders, her hands diving into the soft thickness of his hair to pull his head down to her.

"Let's find out."

She whispered the words against his mouth, then sank her teeth into his bottom lip and tugged gently.

The unexpected action surprised him—and aroused him unbearably.

His arms banded around her waist, and he yanked her tight against his body so that her breasts were crushed against his chest, her thighs trapped between his. She moaned, but he knew it wasn't a sound of protest but of yearning, that the heat that had been simmering between them for so long was about to burst into flame.

She tore her lips from his only long enough to say, "Let's go inside."

It was what he wanted more than anything, and he glanced up at the sky to say, *"Gracias, Dios."*

Then he took her hand and they raced down the path, staying in the shadows so no one would see them sneaking in through the garden entrance together.

His rooms had never seemed so far away as they did tonight, and when they finally reached the fourth floor, they were both breathless. He flipped the lock on the door and tugged her into his arms.

His hands slid up her back, finding the pull of the zipper between her shoulder blades, sliding it down. The fabric parted and his fingers dipped inside to caress the skin beneath, skim lightly over the delicate bumps of her spine. The sensual caress made her shiver, an involuntary response that caused the tips of her breasts to rub against his chest so that he felt the nipples pebble even through the taffeta silk.

Unable to resist any longer, he pushed the bodice of her dress down, baring her breasts. He dipped his head to kiss and suckle, enjoying the increased fullness and sensitivity, making her squirm with every tweak and lick and nibble.

He pushed the garment lower, over the flare of her hips, so that it pooled at her feet, leaving her clad in only a tiny pair of panties and pencil-thin heels.

"He muerto y he ido al cielo."

He didn't realize he'd spoken out loud until her lips curved, just a little.

A siren's body and an innocent's smile—he had never known a woman with so many inherent contradictions. He had never wanted a woman as he wanted Molly.

She started unbuttoning his shirt; he yanked it out of his pants and tossed it aside as they moved toward the bedroom, shedding the rest of his clothes along the way.

He tumbled her onto the bed; she pulled him down with her, wrapping her legs around him, anchoring their bodies together.

With a quick tug, he tore away the lace panties. She gasped with shock, then moaned when he cupped her. She was wet and willing and he was desperate to have her.

He automatically reached toward the night table for a condom, the habit so deeply ingrained it didn't occur to him not to until Molly took the packet from his hand and tossed it aside as carelessly as he had her panties.

He got the message—the fact that she was already pregnant nullified at least one of the purposes of protection. And he'd seen so many doctors and had so many tests over the past few years he knew there were no concerns about his health, and he trusted that Molly wouldn't have dispensed with the little square package if there were any issues on her side.

Still, her action gave him pause, making him realize that he had never made love to a woman without a layer of latex separating them. But it was how he wanted Molly—with no barriers of any kind between them.

He grasped her hips and drove into her slick heat. She arched and accepted. They moved together in a perfectly choreographed rhythm until her muscles clamped around him, gripping him like a velvet glove, holding him tight, dragging him over the precipice with her.

* * *

They barely let go of one another through the night. He brought her to climax more times than she could remember, so that even while her body still trembled with the after-effects, she'd quivered with anticipation.

She knew it wasn't just the sexual release that she'd needed. It was Eric in her arms, inside of her, filling and fulfilling her. When he was with her, she felt the link, not just physical but emotional, he filled her body and her heart and her soul.

She arched against him, mindlessly, desperately seeking the completion she knew he could give her. She had never given up control easily, but she gave it up to him now, relinquished it happily.

With every sweep of his hands, every touch of his lips, every brush of his body against hers, he made her sigh and gasp and moan. She thought she should know what to expect by now, but though their bodies came together with an ease and familiarity that spoke of passions already shared, each time was different, each experience added new layers of sensation that were somehow deeper, sharper, sweeter than before.

It was exciting, exhilarating—and terrifying.

In his bed, in his arms, she felt safe, secure, protected. In his arms, she could almost believe that a relationship between them might work.

And what scared her the most was that she didn't want to leave—and that was why she had to go.

Chapter Ten

Eric wasn't surprised when he woke up alone.

He didn't think Molly was ready for anyone to know that they were together, and though he hoped to change her mind about that in the very near future, he was feeling too happy this morning to worry about it right now.

Rowan and Lara were already in the dining room when he went down for breakfast. Lara was feeding oatmeal to William who seemed to enjoy spitting it back at her, inciting Matthew to spit his cereal back into his bowl—until his father caught him in the act, which made Eric smile. It was always chaos when the whole family was together—and he absolutely loved it.

Marcus and Jewel wandered in a few minutes later, his younger brother with his baby daughter tucked in the crook of one arm and his other around his wife. And it occurred to Eric that in a little more than seven months, there would be yet another baby at the table—and hopefully another royal bride before then.

When Maria came in to see what he wanted for breakfast, he said, "Just coffee right now, thanks. I'll eat with Ms. Shea when she comes down."

"Of course, Your Highness." She filled his cup. "I'll wait until she returns."

Eric froze with his cup halfway to his mouth. "Returns?"

But Maria had already gone back into the kitchen.

Eric looked around the table, noting that all other conversations seemed to have stopped so that the only sound was William banging his plastic spoon against the edge of his bowl.

It was Lara who finally broke the silence. "She was up early, with her suitcases packed, and asked for the number of a local taxi service. Luis drove her to the airport."

He set his cup carefully back into the saucer. "What time was that?"

"About half an hour—maybe forty-five minutes—ago." Her eyes were filled with sympathy and compassion. "I'm sorry, I assumed you knew of her plans."

"I didn't," he admitted grimly.

"There seems to be a lot of that going around," Marcus noted, amusement in his tone.

"For your information, I did tell her of my plans last night," he told his brother.

"Apparently that went over well."

Marcus's comment was immediately followed by Rowan asking, "Do you want to fill the rest of us in?"

But Eric was already pushing his chair away from the table. "Not right now."

"Well, I wish someone would," Jewel said. "Because I feel like I walked into the middle of a play in the second act."

"You haven't," he heard her husband console. "In fact, I'd bet the action is just about to begin."

* * *

Molly sat on the end of a row of linked chairs facing the ticket counter. On the vacant seat beside her was a discarded newspaper—*La Noticia, Edición Especial*—with the headline A Palace Wedding.

Curious, she picked up the paper and smiled at the photo of Fiona and Scott standing in front of the minister, their hands linked, their happiness radiating even from the page. She skimmed the brief article about the wedding, which outlined Scott's longtime connection with the royal family and briefly summarized his courtship of the former Miss Texas.

Additional coverage was on page two, but when Molly turned the page, she was stunned by the headline there.

WHO IS MOLLY SHEA?
by Alex Girard

Little is known about the slim, raven-haired woman who stood as maid of honor for her cousin, Fiona Gilmore, when she married communications magnate Scott Delsey in a sunset ceremony at the palace yesterday afternoon. But it was obvious that the Texas beauty had captured the attention of not only one but two members of the royal family—His Royal Highness Eric Santiago and his cousin, Prince Cameron Leandres.

The brother of the prince regent couldn't seem to take his eyes off of the woman in sapphire silk, while the son of the princess royal couldn't wait to get his hands on her (see photos below). Will another heir to the throne choose an American bride? Only time—and *La Noticia*—will tell, because the prospect of another royal romance has definitely caught *our* attention.

* * *

The photos were clear—the first of Molly and Eric flanking the bride and groom respectively as they exchanged their vows, the next of Molly and Cameron dancing. She was more amused than annoyed by the coverage, though she could see how such attention could become tiresome if endured on a daily basis, as she knew it was by members of the royal family. And it was just one more reason she needed to leave Tesoro del Mar.

She stuffed the paper in the side pocket of her carry-on so that no one else could pick it up and possibly identify her as the woman in the photos, but still made no move toward the ticket counter.

The screen displaying travel information confirmed a nine-fifteen flight to Miami with a connection through to San Antonio, and if she booked a ticket, she could be on that flight and home in time for dinner. She *wanted* to be home, where she wouldn't be tempted to give in to her dreams about dark-eyed princes. And yet there was a part of her that already regretted slipping out of Eric's bed without giving him any hint of her intentions.

He'd asked her stay—to give them a chance to build a relationship. And it was her desire to do exactly that, that had scared her away.

She knew he'd be angry when he woke up and found she was gone. She also knew that running away was nothing more than a temporary solution. He would come after her—she didn't doubt that for a minute. He wanted to be part of their child's life and he wouldn't let her shut him out. But she didn't want to shut him out—she just wanted to be wanted, too.

No, that wasn't exactly true, either. If it was, she would be content to stay, because Eric had shown he numerous times throughout the night that she was wanted. What she needed was to be loved, as she was starting to love him.

All of her excuses about having to go back because of the restaurant were just that—excuses. She was leaving Tesoro del Mar because she was afraid to go after what she really wanted, because she was afraid that, once again, she might lose everything that mattered.

And, she realized now, all of her reasons for running were about *her*—her wants and needs, her fears and insecurities. It was time to consider the needs of her child ahead of her own, and didn't she owe it to the baby she carried to give him the best possible relationship with *both* parents?

She kept thinking about her responsibilities at the restaurant, but what about her responsibilities to her child? Shouldn't the most important consideration be what was best for her baby?

The ring of her cell jolted her from her thoughts. Her first thought was *Eric,* and her heart pounded with equal parts anticipation and trepidation as she pulled the phone from her purse. But the number on the display belonged to her sister, which gave her pause.

Throughout her internal debate of whether to stay or go, she'd failed to think of how her decision would affect the other people in her life. She wanted to go home and pick her life up where everything was steady and familiar. But having a baby changed everything—there would be no steady and familiar. And she didn't want to flaunt her pregnancy in the face of her sister, who yearned so desperately for a child of her own.

"Are you up really early or really late?" she asked.

"Early," Abbey admitted. "After being woken up by a long-distance telephone call from a reporter."

Molly wiped her clammy hands down the front of her skirt. "A reporter?"

"You didn't know he was going to call?"

"Why would I?"

"Because he was asking about you."

Her heart sank. "What did you tell him?"

"Nothing, really. At least, I don't think so. I was caught completely off guard by the call."

"What did he ask you?"

"First he wanted to know how long you'd been dating Prince Eric, and, well, I was kind of surprised by the question because I didn't even know you were dating him."

"I'm not."

"Oh, okay," Abbey said, sounding relieved that she hadn't been kept in the dark about something so potentially momentous. "Then he asked about your relationship with someone named Prince Cameron, and I had to admit I'd never even heard of him."

Molly exhaled a sigh of relief at this confirmation that her sister hadn't told the reporter anything, but she was still unnerved that he'd even called to ask about her when she'd done nothing to warrant any interest. Okay, she'd slept with a prince—twice now—but no one besides she and Eric knew about those nights they'd spent together.

"Is there something going on that I should know?" Abbey asked now.

"No," Molly said. Then, to distract her sister, she asked, "How are things at home?"

"Good," Abbey answered without hesitation, more eager to talk about her own life than speculate about her sister's. "I mean *really* good, even though I'm not sure how or why things have changed. Jason says that *I* have—that this getting out and meeting people has been good for me. And maybe he's right, because even after I finished my shift last night, I hung around to help out at the bar and we got to talking—I mean, *really* talking, like we haven't talked in a long time. And I really feel as if we're back on track with our marriage."

"That's great, Abbey."

"I know I was upset when you left. I felt as if you were abandoning me when I really needed you, but now I realize you did me a favor. I wouldn't have learned that I could stand on my own two feet if I was always leaning on you."

"But that's what family's for," Molly said.

"Except somewhere along the way I lost sight of the fact that Jason's my family, too, and that we need to be there for one another. Like he tried to be there for me, after the last miscarriage, when I pushed him away. I just felt like such a failure as a woman and a wife."

"You've been through a lot," Molly said sympathetically.

"It was a really rough patch for me," Abbey agreed. "But I'm okay now, and I'm ready to try again."

"Are you sure that's a good idea?"

Her sister huffed out an impatient breath. "Now you sound like my husband. Of course I'm sure. We're never going to have the baby we want if we don't keep trying."

Molly had accompanied her sister to enough specialist appointments to know it wasn't that simple. The doctors had been honest and up-front with Abbey about that—she just refused to accept that she might never have a baby.

So Molly changed the subject by telling her sister about the ceremony on the beach and dancing in the mirrored ballroom, and Abbey sighed, caught up in the romance of it all.

"It sounds like you're having a great time."

"It was incredible," she admitted.

"I wouldn't blame you if you weren't in a hurry to come home," her sister said. "And if you wanted to stay awhile, take a bit of a vacation, Jason and I can handle everything at Shea's."

Molly smiled at the not-so-subtle hint.

And though there was a part of her that actually ached to be home, to fall back into the comfort and routine of her life before Eric, she accepted that nothing would ever again be the same as it was before, and that going back to Texas might not be the best thing for her or her sister right now.

Because if she went home, she'd have to tell Abbey about her pregnancy, and she wasn't ready to say the words she knew would break her sister's heart. Not when Abbey was doing so well getting her life back on track.

But if she stayed, and any reporters saw her spending time with Eric, it wouldn't take them long to figure out she was carrying Eric's baby when her pregnancy became apparent. And then she would be like a goldfish trapped in a bowl. On the other hand, if she went back to Texas now and Eric followed her, nothing would change except the venue, and she didn't want to play out any kind of drama in front of her family. Despite everything that Abbey had done to hurt her in the past, she wasn't looking for payback and she didn't want the news that she was carrying a royal baby splashed across the headlines.

It was that possibility that convinced her to stay in Tesoro del Mar. At least for a while.

"It's funny you should mention a vacation," she said.

"Because?" Abbey prompted.

"Because…" Her response trailed off as she registered the sound of brisk footsteps with a sudden flurry of excited whispers from the travelers around her. Glancing up, she saw Eric, flanked by the two bodyguards that habitually accompanied him into public venues. She forced herself to focus, even as the butterflies in her tummy were kicking up a serious ruckus. "Because I was planning to call and tell you that I've decided to stay in Tesoro del Mar for a while longer."

She didn't hear Abbey's response. She didn't hear anything over the pounding of her own heart as she tried to read the expression on Eric's face.

He didn't look angry. In fact, she couldn't guess anything of what he was thinking or feeling.

"I'll call you soon," she told Abbey, and closed the phone.

The bodyguards stayed back to afford them some privacy, and though she knew Eric was accustomed to their presence, Molly felt uneasy. She knew security was necessary for all members of the royal family—and would be necessary for her child—but it was for her yet another reminder of their disparate lifestyles.

"You've decided to stay?" Eric asked politely.

She nodded.

He noted the suitcase beside her seat. "You didn't check any luggage?"

"No."

"Do you have a ticket you need to cash in?"

"No," she said again.

He sat down beside her. "Were you planning to go anywhere or did you just come here to watch the planes?"

"I thought I wanted to leave," she admitted. "But when I got here, I realized I couldn't go. Not with so much unresolved between us."

His fingertips stroked down her cheek, making her insides quiver. "Thank you."

"I'm not doing this for you—I'm doing it for our baby."

"I'm sure that's true." His smile was wry as he stood up again and offered his hand to her. "But at this point, I'll take what I can get."

Over the past couple of weeks, Molly had been to various places around the island but she still wasn't familiar enough with any of the landmarks to realize that the limo in which she was riding wasn't taking them back to the palace—until she remembered that it had taken about twenty-five minutes for Luis to get her *to* the airport and now, after forty minutes in the car, they hadn't arrived at their destination.

She looked out the window, but nothing looked familiar to her. "Where are we going?"

"To Estado de las Morales."

"Where?"

"It used to be my family's summer house on the northern coast."

"We're not staying at the palace?"

He shook his head. "We'll have more privacy at the summer house."

Privacy wasn't high on her list of priorities. She wanted—needed—other people around to run interference, to ensure that she didn't end up in Eric's bed. Again.

Because as wonderful as last night had been—and her body was still humming its agreement with *that* assessment—she knew that sex would only complicate the situation, and it was already complicated enough.

"I want us to have a chance to get to know one another," he continued. "And we can't do that with servants in every corner."

"There aren't servants at Estada des—"

"Estado de las Morales," he corrected. "There's a minimal staff to ensure things run smoothly—a housekeeper, chef and chauffeur."

Minimal staff notwithstanding, Molly knew she would have to keep the distance between her and Eric at a maximum.

"They have been at the house for a long time and can be trusted not to disclose your presence," he assured her.

"I hadn't thought about the problems that might be created for you by my decision to stay."

"It's not a problem for me but for you," he corrected. "If the paparazzi get another hint of a romance between us, you won't be able to leave the grounds without them being all over you."

She hadn't considered the potential media circus—just one more side effect of carrying a royal baby, she knew, but while she'd accepted her pregnancy and was looking forward to being a mother, the "royal" part was still a little overwhelming.

"Then we'll just have to make it clear we're just having a baby, not having a romance," she said lightly.

He smiled at her lame attempt at humor, then his attention shifted to the window when the driver made a sharp turn and he only said, "We're here."

He gave her a quick tour of the main level and introduced her to Carla, who smiled when he claimed she was "the woman who terrorizes dust bunnies," Stefan, "who will make sure you never go hungry—and that you'll never be satisfied with ordinary cuisine again," and explained that Tomas, the chauffeur/gardener/handyman had gone into town on errands but would be available if she needed a driver or pretty much anything else.

It was readily apparent to Molly that Eric had spent a lot of time at Estado de las Morales and that his relationship with the help was deeper and more personal than that of master and servant. It was yet another side of him that she hadn't seen before, an incredibly sweet and appealing side that threatened to break through all of the walls she was trying so hard to shore up.

"You would like lunch?" Stefan asked her.

Molly shook her head. "No, thanks. I'm not hungry."

She didn't need to eat—she needed time and space to figure out what she was going to do about this man who already meant far more to her than she'd ever intended for him to.

And—she stifled a yawn—about twelve hours of sleep.

"Tired?" Eric asked, as Stefan slipped back into the kitchen to give them privacy.

She nodded. "I don't think either of us got very much sleep last night."

It was a testament to how tired her brain was that she didn't manage to censor the thought before it sprang from her lips, and Eric's grin told her he knew it.

"No, I guess we didn't."

"Would it be okay...if I lie down for a while?"

"Sure." He slid his arm across her shoulders and steered her toward the staircase. "I'll take you up to your room."

"My room?"

He paused on the bottom tread and smiled at her again. "My room's beside yours, on the other side of a connecting door," he told her. "And while I can assure you I won't be locking it from my side, I'm not going to pressure you to share my bed."

"You're not?"

He chuckled. "I can't tell if that was relief or disappointment I heard in your voice."

"I'm not sure, either," she admitted, and stepped through the door he indicated.

The room wasn't as big or as fancy as the one she'd been given at the palace, but it was still pretty spectacular, with a wide window overlooking the beach that had been left open to let the scent of the sea drift in on the breeze. She was Texan born and bred and though she'd done a little traveling in recent years, she'd never ventured far from home, never yearned to settle anywhere else. But in just two weeks she'd fallen in love with this island, and as she inhaled the salty fragrance of the Mediterranean, she knew that scent would always remind her of her time in Tesoro del Mar—and of Eric.

"There's a bathroom through there," Eric said, pointing to a door on one side of the room and drawing her gaze back to him. "And my room is there." He indicated the other side.

Glancing around, she couldn't help but admire the wide, four-poster bed, the meticulously polished dressers and armoire, the cut crystal vase filled with fresh flowers. But again, it was the window that drew her, and she stepped closer to it now.

"Do you ever get used to a view like this?" she wondered.

"If you do, it takes more than thirty-six years," he told her.

She turned to him. "So that's how old you are?"

He nodded.

"I didn't want to ask—or maybe I didn't want to ask at this stage because it seemed like something I should already know."

"You can ask me whatever you want," he assured her. "I might even answer some of your questions."

She smiled at that, and he put his arms around her.

"We rushed into a lot of things," he said. "Maybe we need to slow things down a little."

"Oh. Yeah. Okay."

He chuckled again. "Honey, you're not making this easy for me."

"Nothing's been easy since you walked into my bar," she told him.

"Of all the gin joints?"

She smiled. "Something like that."

"You need to rest," he said. "And if I don't leave now, I'm not sure I'm going to."

He paused at the door and Molly's breath stalled in her lungs as she waited, wondering if he would kiss her, *wanting* him to kiss her. But he only said, "Sweet dreams," and walked away.

Eric let Molly sleep through the afternoon and tried to keep himself busy so he wouldn't think about her being alone in that big bed upstairs, so he wouldn't remember how she'd looked at him before he'd walked out the door. As if she wanted him to kiss her as much as he wanted to kiss her. But he knew that if he did, he probably wouldn't have been able to stop with one kiss—despite having promised her, not a minute earlier, that they would take things slow.

He did want to take things slow. He wanted to kiss her slowly. Then peel her clothes away slowly. Slowly run his hands over every delectable curve. And slowly sink into the wet heat of her body.

Instead, he took a quick and very cold shower.

He spent the afternoon reviewing the most recent quarterly reports of DELconnex and timeline estimates for its introduction into the European market. What had originally just been the seed of an idea that Eric had tossed out at his last meeting with the Tesorian Minister of Economic Development had quickly sprouted and taken on a life of its own. Not only was the Minister amenable to a branch of DELconnex being located on the island, he believed that branch could become the root of future expansion.

It was bigger than what Scott had proposed and, consequently, riskier. And for both of those reasons, it was also potentially much more lucrative. Eric didn't doubt that Scott would jump at the opportunity once he'd had a chance to present it to him. Except that Scott was on his honeymoon right now so the only jumping he was doing was of his wife, and that was a path Eric's mind didn't need to be traveling right now.

By four o'clock, the cold shower he'd taken hours earlier was nothing more than a distant memory, so he sent Carla upstairs to wake Molly.

She came down half an hour later, her hair still damp from the shower, her skin freshly scrubbed.

"Feel better?" he asked.

She nodded.

"Good. It's a nice night, so I've asked for dinner to be set up on the terrace, if that's okay."

She looked down at the capris and T-shirt she was wearing, then at his dark trousers paired with shirt and tie. "Am I dressed okay for dinner on the terrace?"

"You are more than okay," he told her. "You are beautiful."

"But underdressed," she guessed.

"No, I am probably overdressed."

She eyed him critically. "I don't think I've ever seen you in a pair of shorts and a T-shirt."

"A prince—or princess—is raised from birth to understand there is always the possibility of a photographer lurking around a corner, and so there are certain standards of dress that are adhered to."

She thought again of the picture that had been taken of her at the wedding, and realized he was right, and that she should learn to anticipate the same if she was going to stay on the island. But she asked, "Is that possibility one you need to worry about here?"

He shook his head. "Thankfully, no. Would you like me to see if there is a pair of shorts in my wardrobe so I can prove it to you?"

"I would be satisfied if you lost the tie."

He loosened the knot, tugged it free from the collar of his shirt. "Better?"

"Hmm." She tapped her finger on her lips, considering. Then she stepped forward and unfastened the top button, then the one below it.

"You go much further," he warned, "and I'm going to forget about dinner on the terrace to haul you back upstairs."

Molly felt her cheeks flush with color as she took a hasty step in retreat.

A quick glance at Eric revealed amusement lurking in his eyes, and something darker and edgier that she recognized as desire.

"Dinner," she reminded him. "I'm hungry."

His smile was slow and far too sexy. "So am I."

Chapter Eleven

Her cheeks flushed hotter, but she took the arm he offered and let him lead her out to the terrace.

Dinner started with a ginger carrot soup, then there was a salad of fresh greens tossed in a light vinaigrette dressing, then a blackened chicken breast served with sweet potatoes and asparagus.

"Another week of eating like this and the fact that my clothes won't fit will have nothing to do with the pregnancy," she told him.

"You don't seem to have put on much weight." His gaze skimmed over her leisurely, and she felt hot and tingly everywhere his eyes touched.

He paused at the front of her shirt, and she felt her nipples respond as immediately and obviously as if it had been a physical caress.

"Except…" His gaze lifted to hers, and there was no doubt that what she saw in his eyes now was desire. "Your breasts are fuller."

She swallowed. "Soon you won't even notice my breasts because my stomach will be sticking out so far."

"I'll still notice," he promised her.

"We didn't discuss how long we would be staying here," Molly said, not caring that it was both a desperate and obvious change of topic.

"We can stay for as long as you want."

"Don't you have royal duties or obligations to fulfill?"

"My duties are minimal," he told her. "As prince regent, Rowan bears most of the responsibility, but only until Christian is of age to assume the throne."

"Still, I hope you don't feel as if you have to entertain me for however long I'm here," she said.

"The whole point of you being here is so that we can get to know one another better," he reminded her. "And that's not going to happen if we don't spend time together."

"But we don't have to spend every single minute of every single day together."

"Are you worried that I'm going to hover—make you feel confined?"

"No," she admitted. "I just don't want you to feel as if you can't live your own life."

His lips curved, but she didn't miss the shadows that crossed his eyes. "I haven't been living my life for the past three years, why should anything change now?"

"Because you can't live the rest of your life wishing for something you can't have," she told him. "You need to figure out what you want *now.*"

"I know what I want now," he said. "And it's not very different from what I've always wanted—a family of my own. It never happened while I was in the navy—it was too hard to sustain a relationship when I was gone most of the time, but circumstances have changed. And your pregnancy has clarified that desire, because I no longer want a family in the abstract sense, I want you and our baby."

"What about love?"

He frowned at that, as if the concept was completely foreign to him.

"You say you want a family, but don't you want to fall in love first?"

"I've always thought of marriage as a duty," he admitted. "Something I needed to do for my family and my country, to ensure the continuation of the Santiago line, though that hardly seems in jeopardy with the number of babies born in the past few years."

"Is that what our baby represents to you—a legacy?"

"Our baby is everything to me."

It was the conviction in his tone that worried her more than the words. "I'm excited about becoming a parent, too, but you can't let that role define your entire existence."

"Is that what you think I'm doing?"

"I don't know," she admitted. "But since you found out that I'm pregnant, you've been so focused on this baby that I'm worried you're using it as a substitute for everything you've lost."

"I'm thrilled about being a father," he told her. "But I'm not looking to make it my full-time job."

"So what are you going to do?"

"I'm exploring some options."

"That's a rather cryptic response from a man who said I could ask whatever questions I wanted."

"I'm negotiating terms with the Minister of Economic Development to bring DELconnex here."

"You're going to work for Scott?"

"I'm going to head up the international division of the company."

"I almost forgot that Fiona told me you'd gone to MIT with Scott."

"I was also an information specialist in the navy," he told her.

"Which just reminds me how little I know about you."

Eric heard the frustration in her voice and thought he understood it. They were little more than strangers who, as a result of consequences neither had foreseen, were now tied together for the next eighteen years or more. He hoped it would be more—he wanted to believe that he and Molly could build a future and a family together. But he knew that she was wary, so he reined in his own impatience.

"We don't have to figure everything out in the first day," he told her, and she nodded her agreement.

"Although now that I've answered your questions," he said. "I have some of my own."

"What do you want to know?"

"How did your sister end up married to your fiancé?"

Molly's eyes dropped to her glass as she dragged a finger though the beads of condensation on the outside. Obviously it wasn't a question she'd expected—and probably not one she felt entirely comfortable answering. But despite her claims about wanting love, she kept her heart more heavily guarded than the royal banquet hall during a state dinner, and Eric sensed that her sister's marriage was the reason for that.

"She needed him more than I did."

"Why do I think it wasn't quite as simple as you're making it sound?"

She shrugged. "Jason is the type of guy who needs to be needed. If we ever fought, it was usually because he wanted to do something for me that I was capable of doing for myself. I didn't find out until later that he felt I was undermining his masculinity, but all I was really trying to do was assert my independence.

"Anyway, it was just after my dad died. Jason was at the

funeral home for each visitation, he stood by me at the cemetery, and he didn't understand why I couldn't cry.

"I did cry, of course, but only when I was alone. My grief was too private, too raw, to share with anyone. Jason didn't understand that.

"But Abbey fell apart," she continued her explanation. "She was devastated, although to this day I'm not sure if it was because of the depth of her grief or because she was scared to think about what his death meant for her. What would happen now? Who would take care of her?

"So Jason did. He let her cry on his shoulder and he dried her tears, and she showed her gratitude by taking him to her bed. Then he took her to Vegas and put a ring on her finger."

"At what point did they tell you what was happening?"

"Not until after the fact," she admitted. "I felt like the world's biggest dope—betrayed by both of them. But later, when I'd stopped hurting so much, I was actually kind of relieved.

"I loved Jason, but I wasn't in love with him, and if we'd actually gone through with our plans to marry, we would have made one another miserable because neither one of us could be what the other wanted or needed.

"And, until recently, Abbey and Jason were exactly that for one another. And somehow that made it easier—I could believe it wasn't a betrayal of me so much as a need to be together because they were so perfectly suited. I still believe they're a good match but they've got some pretty big obstacles to overcome if they're going to stay together."

"How is it that you believe they can make their marriage work, but you won't even give us a chance?"

"They've been married for nine years and they love one another."

"And in the nine years they've been married, have you had any serious relationships?"

"No."

"Because your ex-fiancé broke your heart?"

"Because no one I dated was interested in anything more than that."

"I find that hard to believe."

"Which is why," she continued as if he hadn't spoken, "I have to wonder what I'm even doing here."

"Giving us a chance to see that we fit."

"You know we don't. We can't. You're a prince and I'm a bartender."

"That doesn't matter."

"Of course it does," she insisted. "And now it's my turn to ask a question."

He wasn't ready to give up, but he also knew it was going to take time for Molly to see what was already obvious to him, so he only said, "What's your question?"

"What's for dessert?"

As if on cue, Carla brought in fresh fruit and custard, and while they finished up their meal, Eric accepted that he was facing an uphill battle in convincing Molly that they belonged together. Her failed engagement had proven to her that she couldn't count on anyone but herself. He intended to prove otherwise.

Molly tried to pretend that she was on vacation. She was, after all, on a beautiful island in the Mediterranean where the sun always seemed to be shining, the sand was soft and the waves inviting. But no matter how hard she tried, she couldn't relax because every minute of every day, she was conscious of Eric's presence when he was near and his absence when he wasn't.

She'd been at Estado de las Morales for nine days and, aside from that blissfully deep sleep she'd indulged in on the very first afternoon, she'd hardly slept. Every time she crawled into her bed, she was conscious of the fact that Eric was in his own bed on the other side of the adjoining door—a door that he'd assured her would not be locked from his side.

She knew the increased sexual desire she was experiencing wasn't uncommon during pregnancy. That knowledge did nothing to ease the ache inside.

But she knew what would—all she had to do was open that connecting door and walk into his room, Eric would take care of the rest. Except that it seemed they both wanted different things from each other and she worried that getting naked with him again might suggest that she wanted a more intimate relationship than she did. Because really all she wanted was sex.

Liar.

Molly sighed at the return of the nagging voice that she'd thought had been silenced by the revelation of her pregnancy to Eric.

Okay, long-term, she wanted more than sex. She wanted to fall in love with a man who could make her believe in "happily ever after." But right now her options were limited and she would happily settle for the sex.

Yeah, she was definitely suffering from hormone overload which, combined with the proximity of a very attractive man who had got her into this predicament, was an almost irresistible combination.

She heard the patio door slide open and glanced up to see Eric step out onto the deck. And her heart skipped a beat, just as it had the first time she ever saw him, just as it did every time he walked into a room.

Damn hormones.

She closed the cover on her book and set it aside.

"Dinner's going to be a little late tonight," he told her. "Stefan's in a snit."

In her short time at the summer house, she'd learned to appreciate the chef's genius and she hadn't seen any evidence that he was temperamental.

"What did you do?" she couldn't resist asking.

"Actually, *you're* the reason he is in a snit."

"Me? What did I do?"

"He had the menu planned for dinner, including oysters on the half shell with cucumber mignonette, but you are allergic to shellfish."

She had no idea what a mignonette was, but it was the second part of his statement that snagged her attention. "I don't have any food allergies."

"But raw oysters aren't recommended eating for pregnant women," he said, confirming that he'd been reading about pregnancy, too. "So it was either tell Stefan about the baby or tell him about your allergy."

She pouted. "I happen to like oysters."

"Which makes that allergy all the more unfortunate."

"So what is for dinner?"

"Well, since Stefan insisted that I—or rather you—had ruined the entire menu, I suggested that I would take you out for dinner."

"I guess that would require changing my clothes."

"That would require *wearing* some clothes," he said, his voice heavy with regret.

Molly sighed. "Couldn't we just make macaroni and cheese?"

"Macaroni and cheese?"

"I don't imagine it was a staple in the palace kitchen when you were growing up like it was in mine."

"Do you know how to make it?" he asked skeptically.

"It's not difficult."

"Then let's go see if we've got the ingredients."

The recipe Molly usually followed involved dumping the contents out of a box, and of course there was no box of prepackaged mix in Eric's kitchen. But she found some dried pasta tucked in the back of a cupboard—no doubt, Stefan usually made his fresh—and put on a pot of water to boil. While the pasta was cooking, she grated cheese for the sauce, adding a little bit of butter and milk to improve the consistency, then a little bit of flour to thicken it up.

All the while, Eric sat on the edge of the counter, watching her and asking questions about both her culinary skills and the nutritional value of the meal. She pretty much ignored him.

She dug into her bowl, humming her approval as she chewed the first mouthful.

"This is good?"

"This is very good," she told him. "And just what I wanted."

"If Stefan knew about the baby, I suspect he would cater to your every whim."

"I don't have whims."

His brows lifted. "What do you call macaroni and cheese and cookie-dough ice cream?"

She made a face. "Not two foods I would eat together, that's for sure."

"But you made me take you into town for cookie-dough ice cream last week," he reminded her.

"I didn't make you—I asked," she said. "And those are cravings, not whims."

"I stand corrected," he said, amusement dancing in his eyes. "If Stefan knew about the baby, he would indulge your cravings."

"I don't mind if you want to tell Stefan and Carla and Tomas—it's not as if we'll be able to keep it a secret much longer anyway," she told him, then grinned. "And I'm already thinking that Stefan's spicy coconut shrimp with mango salsa would be good for tomorrow."

Eric laughed and stood up to take their empty bowls to the

kitchen. When he came back, he had a leather messenger bag over his shoulder.

"Since you gave me dinner, I thought I should give something to you," he said, and handed her the bag.

"I boiled pasta and added cheese sauce, and I only fed you because you were here. It certainly wasn't a gesture that requires any payment."

"Open the bag anyway."

So she did, unfastening the straps to reveal a slim notebook computer.

"Is this for me?"

He nodded.

"Why?"

"I'm not entirely sure myself," he told her. "But when Lara found out you were staying here for a while, she suggested that you could use a computer."

She remembered the conversation she'd had with the princess in the palace gardens, and Lara's suggestion that she write down her stories. She'd never had the time before. Now she had a lot of time on her hands and no reason not to use it.

"That was very thoughtful," she said. "And generous."

"You're not going to tell me why, either?"

"Not yet." She leaned over and kissed him. "But thank you."

While Eric was busy in meetings with the Minister of Economic Development, finalizing plans to bring DELconnex to Tesoro del Mar, Molly spent a lot of time at the computer. Her typing had been slow and awkward at first, but after she'd been at it awhile, her fingers started to fly over the keyboard though they still couldn't keep up with the flow of ideas through her head.

She was just finishing up a story—one that had turned out to be a lot longer and more complicated than she'd anticipated when she wrote the opening line—when the phone rang. She expected that it would be Eric because no one else ever called, and was surprised to hear a female voice on the other end of the line.

The voice was familiar but it took her a moment to get her head out of the story before recognition—and pleasure—set in.

"Fiona?"

"If you're surprised, imagine how I felt when I stopped in at Shea's to see my best friend after I got back from my honeymoon only to find that she'd left the restaurant under the questionable management of her sister to shack up with a prince."

Molly picked her way carefully through the land mines that were planted throughout Fiona's words and asked, "How was the honeymoon?"

"It was incredible," Fiona admitted. "But that wasn't the part of my statement that I wanted you to focus on."

"And I did *not* leave Abbey in charge of the restaurant—I left Karen in charge of the restaurant. Jason is the new night manager and Abbey is only working there part-time."

"Which is definitely a topic worthy of conversation at another time. Right now, I want to hear about whatever happened between you and Eric to have you moving in with him."

"It's only a temporary arrangement," Molly insisted.

"Okay—but why? Not that I'm not thrilled," Fiona hastened to assure her. "I think Eric is great, but whenever I even tried to mention his name to you, you insisted that you weren't looking to get involved."

"I wasn't. I couldn't." She blew out a breath. "Do you remember me telling you about the guy I met at the bar?"

"How could I forget?" Fiona teased. "It's not every day that you have that kind of reaction to— Oh. My. God. It was *Eric*."

That was the thing about Fiona—give her enough dots, and it usually didn't take her too long to connect them.

"It was Eric," she agreed. "But at the time, I didn't know that you knew him. Then when we met again at your ranch, I was too embarrassed to admit that I knew him because I was afraid you would know he was the one."

"But now you've picked up where you left off?" Fiona asked hopefully.

"It's a little more complicated than that. A lot more complicated, actually." She hesitated. "Fiona, I'm pregnant."

"*What?*"

"You heard me."

"Oh. My. God."

"Yeah," Molly said.

"When are you due?"

"Early January."

"What was Eric's reaction?"

So Molly spent a few minutes filling her cousin in on all of the details of everything that had transpired since Eric had learned of her pregnancy.

"I'll bet he asked you to marry him," Fiona guessed, since Molly had opted to leave that part out.

"I'm not going to."

"Why not?"

"I can't believe you even need to ask me that question."

"He's a prince. He's the father of your baby. And you obviously have great chemistry together."

"And you think that's enough to base a marriage on?"

"There are plenty of marriages based on less," Fiona told her. Then another thought occurred to her and she asked, "Does Abbey know?"

"No." She knew no further explanation was required.

"Grandma and Grandpa?"

"No," she said again.

"Well, I'm glad I'm not the last to know," Fiona said philosophically. "But unless you're planning to stay in Tesoro del Mar forever, you're going to have to tell them."

"I know," Molly admitted.

"So when are you planning to come home?"

"We haven't really talked about that."

"Too busy playing…house?" her cousin teased.

Molly had to laugh. "I've missed you, Fee."

"Me, too. But whatever you decide about marrying Eric—"

"I already told you what I decided."

"—you will come back for my rescheduled wedding reception in October, won't you?"

"Of course," Molly assured her.

She talked to her cousin for a few more minutes and, when she finally hung up the phone, knew she couldn't delay sharing the news with the rest of her family any longer. But she dialed her grandparents' number first.

In the five weeks that Molly had been in Tesoro del Mar, Abbey had usually been the one to initiate telephone contact so she was understandably surprised to hear from her sister now.

It had never been as easy for Molly to talk to Abbey as it was to talk to Fiona. She sometimes wondered if Abbey might not have turned to Jason for comfort after their father's death if Molly had been able to offer the support she'd needed. And while that was water long under the bridge, it certainly hadn't helped the relationship between the sisters.

They made small talk for a few minutes—mostly about the restaurant—but Molly knew the longer she waited the harder it would be, so she finally said, "I called because I have something to tell you."

"News about the hunky prince?" her sister asked.

"Yeah. Kind of."

"So tell," Abbey urged.

Which sounded simple enough, but still the words stuck in her throat. "Well, actually…Eric and I…we…or rather I'm…pregnant."

There was, for half a minute, complete silence on the other end of the line.

Then Abbey gave a short, breathless laugh. "I'm sorry," she said. "The line must have cut out because for a second, I actually thought you said you were pregnant."

"I did," she said softly. "I am."

She heard the sharp intake of breath, and hated knowing that she'd caused her sister pain.

"Pregnant," Abbey said again, the word little more than an agonized whisper that reflected the heartache and disappointment of so many failed attempts to have a child of her own.

"I thought you should hear it from me," Molly said gently.

But neither her tone nor her words consoled her sister.

"When you told me you were staying in Tesoro del Mar," Abbey said, "I figured you were having a fling with Eric, but I didn't expect it was anything more than that. And you probably knew you couldn't hold on to him for very long—you couldn't even hold on to Jason—so you got pregnant. And now Eric will probably feel compelled to marry you and everything will be just perfect."

Molly knew her sister was lashing out because she was hurting so badly, so she was prepared to let her vent. But all she heard after that was a click and a dial tone.

Eric hadn't intended to eavesdrop on Molly's conversation, but he'd been walking past the den when he heard her voice and he'd peeked around the corner just to give a quick wave and let her know he was home. She didn't see him—but what he saw stopped him in his tracks.

She was crying.

Her eyes were drenched with moisture and pain and silent tears tracked slowly down her cheeks. He'd never seen her cry, and the sight of those tears now cut him off at the knees.

He didn't hear her say goodbye, but her hand trembled as she placed the receiver back in the cradle, and somehow he knew.

"Your sister," he guessed.

She nodded and wiped her hands over her cheeks, as if to hide the evidence of her tears.

He pushed back her chair and lifted her into his arms.

Her eyes widened, but she held on as he carried her to the sofa, sitting down to cuddle her in his lap.

"Just let me hold you for a minute," he said.

And she did. She buried her face in his shirt and she cried until there were no more tears inside.

He rubbed his hand over her back and murmured soft, soothing words as he remembered the conversation they'd had just a couple weeks earlier when she'd told him she'd never cried on her ex-fiancé's shoulder. He wasn't sure if it was a testament to how close they'd grown over the past couple of months that she'd let her guard down enough to accept comfort from him now or if he'd just caught her at a weak moment, but he was glad that he'd been there when she'd obviously needed someone.

"I had to tell her," Molly said softly.

"Of course you did."

"I talked to Fiona earlier, and I told her. And she was so excited for us. I knew Abbey wouldn't be happy—I know why she couldn't be—but I didn't want to hurt her."

"I know."

"Fiona and Scott have rescheduled their wedding reception for next month and, of course, she wants us to be there, and I couldn't just show up without giving Abbey—or my grand-parents—warning."

"Does this mean I'll get to meet your grandparents?" he asked, deliberately shifting the focus of the conversation so she wouldn't start crying again.

"Do you want to meet them?"

"Of course."

"They know you're the father of my baby," she warned him.

"Then it might be a good idea to introduce me to them as your fiancé," he suggested.

"Except that we're not engaged."

"We could be."

She sighed and pulled away from him. "Why can't you let this go?"

"Because you're using one bad relationship experience as an excuse to avoid marrying me."

"You don't know what you're talking about."

"I know that you've got legitimate reasons for thinking twice before making a commitment—"

"I'm not opposed to marriage," she interjected. "Just marriage to you."

"What's wrong with me?" he demanded.

"I don't think you really want me to answer that question."

"Actually, I do."

She frowned. "You want me to make a list of all of your character flaws?"

"Let's just stick to the ones that are relevant to your not wanting to marry me."

"Okay—you're sarcastic."

His brows rose. "*I'm* sarcastic?"

"You're demanding."

"I have high expectations," he admitted.

"You're stubborn."

"Because I don't give up when something matters?"

"You think you have an answer for everything."

"I like to consider all possible solutions to a problem."

"You're arrogant—you expect to get what you want when you want it."

"I go after what I want," he clarified.

"You're a prince."

"Why is that a reason to not marry me?"

"Because I don't want my child living his or her life under constant media scrutiny."

"You've met all of my nieces and nephews," he pointed out. "Did you get the impression that any one of them has been scarred as a result of the media attention?"

"Two of them are still in diapers."

"Then I guess there's still hope that your completely irrational argument might someday prove to be valid."

"There's that sarcasm again," she noted.

"And you say I'm stubborn," he muttered.

"Shall I go on?"

"I'd say the only legitimate reason you might have for turning down my proposal is my state of mind—because you, Molly Shea, are driving me crazy."

She could hear the frustration in his tone. Should have known to back down. Instead she said, "By all means, let's add questionable mental health to the list."

And pushed him too far.

He responded by hauling her into his arms and kissing her.

Chapter Twelve

She should have been furious. Instead, she melted into his embrace.

He coaxed her lips apart; she opened for him willingly. Their tongues met, mated. Desire pumped through her system like a drug, making her skin burn, her head spin, her heart pound.

With equal parts determination and regret, she tore her mouth from his and dropped her head to his chest. His heart was racing as fast as hers, his breathing was just as ragged.

"And that's another reason I can't marry you."

"You don't like the way I kiss?"

"You'll do anything to get what you want," she corrected. "And you know I can't think when you kiss me like that."

"I don't want you to think," he said, stroking a hand down her back. "Because then you're conjuring up reasons why we shouldn't be together when it's obvious to me that we should."

"You're a prince," she said again. "And I'm a bartender."

"I'm a man and you're a woman, and we're good together, Molly. You know we are. So what is it that you're really afraid of?"

Falling in love with you.

But she didn't tell him that, of course. If he had the slightest clue about her growing feelings for him, he would find a way to manipulate them to his advantage and she'd find herself walking down the aisle. And she refused to let that happen.

But her emotions were already involved—far more than she was willing to admit to, even to herself. Because she'd started to fall in love with him right from the start, and she'd continued falling ever since. Even when he frustrated and annoyed her, she couldn't seem to stop it from happening, and she knew it was only a matter of time before she hit the ground with a splat.

He talked to her and he listened to her as if he really cared about what she was saying. He made her laugh and he looked at her as if she was the only woman in the world who mattered. And when he kissed her, he made the rest of the world disappear.

She knew that if he made a promise to her, he wouldn't break it. That was the kind of man he was—honest, sincere, steadfast and reliable. The kind of man a woman couldn't help but fall in love with.

But would he ever love her? That was the question that continued to hold her back. It wasn't enough that he was an honorable man, intent on marrying the mother of his child because he believed it was the right thing to do. Emotions, at least so far as he was concerned, didn't really enter into it. And if he could never feel about her the way she felt about him, it would break her heart.

Molly didn't answer his question, but Eric hadn't really expected that she would. Besides, he had a pretty good idea what she was afraid of—getting in too deep, caring too much. Yeah,

Abbey and Jason had really done a number on her, and he didn't blame her for being reluctant to trust anyone else.

And though it frustrated him to think about how little progress they'd made with respect to their relationship in the month and a half that they'd been together at the summer house, he reminded himself every day that they were making progress. The fact that she was still here proved it.

Even more telling, he thought, was that she'd made no mention in recent weeks of going back to Texas and he was beginning to hope that she might someday think of Tesoro del Mar as home. A few months ago, that thought might have surprised him, but now he was a lot more certain about what he wanted.

He'd known Molly only a few months, but he almost couldn't remember what his life had been like before he'd met her, and he sure didn't want to imagine his life without her in it—and only partly because she was carrying his child.

He wanted the baby, no doubt about that. And, if not for the child, he probably wouldn't be thinking in terms of marriage, certainly not this early on in their relationship. But even if she wasn't pregnant, he knew now that he would still want Molly.

"Okay," he said at last. "I won't push. I know how to be patient when the situation warrants it."

Her brows lifted. "So now I'm a situation?"

His lips quirked. "No, you're a source of extreme frustration. Night after night, for the past six weeks, I've been lying awake in my bed, unable to stop thinking about you."

"Thinking about sex," she corrected.

"Thinking about *you,*" he said again. "And I think it's interesting how every time I get a little too close—and not just physically—you withdraw."

"Maybe I don't like you."

He smiled at that. "That's one possibility," he allowed. "Another is that you *do* like me. Maybe more than you want to. And maybe living in close quarters and not sharing a bed is starting to drive you crazy, too."

She eyed him warily. "You're not honestly suggesting that we should have sex to dissipate some of this tension?"

"No, I don't think this tension is going to dissipate. I think this tension is proof of the chemistry that has been there from the start and an attraction that has only strengthened and deepened over the past few months." He smiled again. "But if *you* want to believe it, if that's what will finally convince you to open the damn door between our bedrooms, I'll go along with it."

"A man will go along with anything if it will get a woman naked," she said, but without any real heat.

"That might be true," he acknowledged. "But this isn't about a man and a woman—it's about me and you. And it turns out you're the only woman for me, the woman I think I might be falling in love with."

There was a long silence. Then Molly spoke. "So are you going to talk this to death or are you going to take me to bed?"

Four weeks after Molly had raced him to his bed, the chemistry between them hadn't even begun to fizzle. And as phenomenal as their lovemaking was, what Eric really cherished was the growing closeness with Molly. They were talking, communicating, sharing their hopes and dreams for their child and the future.

She'd been seeing a local obstetrician who allowed them to sneak in through a back door directly into an examining room so that they could avoid being recognized by other patients. They had told no one outside of their immediate families and the servants at Estado de las Morales of her pregnancy, but Molly knew it was only a matter of time before someone somewhere figured it out, so she was enjoying the relative anonymity and privacy while it lasted. And so far, everything was progressing well and on schedule with the baby. Just a few days earlier, she'd had a twenty-week ultrasound that indicated the baby was a girl, so they'd started using *"she"* and *"her"* in reference to the child, and he found that somehow made the baby seem even more real. Of course, the expansion of her waistline was another reminder.

He marveled at the changes in her body and couldn't help but smile every time he felt the tiniest movement of their baby in her womb. The only real source of friction in their relationship was Molly's continuing refusal to marry him. Although she claimed the friction was caused by his refusal to accept her unwillingness to marry him.

"I really think we should schedule our wedding soon to ensure it happens before the baby is born," he suggested for the thousandth time.

"You don't want to marry me," Molly said for the thousandth time. "You want to marry the mother of your child, to ensure her legitimacy and secure her status as your heir. I just happen to be the woman you got pregnant."

"And the woman currently in my bed," he pointed out.

"Keep pushing and you'll push me out of it," she warned.

He responded by tightening his arms around her, and she sighed and relaxed against him.

"Lara told me that Rowan was worried that the people of Tesoro del Mar would be scandalized by his relationship with the royal nanny. Can you imagine how they'd react if they knew you were involved with an American bartender?"

"Neither your nationality nor your occupation are as important as the fact that you're carrying my child."

"My mother ran out on her family, my father liked to drink a little too much and I was once engaged to my sister's husband."

"None of that matters to me."

"It should."

He took her hands. "You are a warm and beautiful woman. You're kind and compassionate and—"

"And you're a prince," she reminded him. "You could have any woman you want."

"I want you," he said simply.

She sighed. "Why are you being so difficult about this?"

"I think the determination of which one of us is being difficult is a matter of perspective."

Her lips curved at that. "Maybe it is. But the fact remains that we've been going around in circles about this issue for weeks now."

"And we'll continue to do so until you agree to marry me and give our baby the family she deserves."

Molly was quiet for a moment. "A long time ago, when I was still young and naive enough to believe in 'happily ever afters,' I expected that I would be married before I ever had a baby. I wanted my children to be born into a traditional family. But even if we married, nothing about our life would be traditional, nothing about our child's life would be normal because she will be royal."

"The child will be royal whether or not we marry," he pointed out. "And I happen to think my family is pretty wonderful despite being royal."

"They are wonderful," she agreed. "But I don't see Rowan picking up pizza on his way home after work or Lara carpooling with other moms at the day care or other normal family-type activities."

"Normal is a matter of interpretation," he insisted.

And another circle was complete without them getting any closer to setting a wedding date.

* * *

The argument with Eric was still on her mind several hours later, so Molly was pleased when Lara stopped by, granting her a reprieve from her own thoughts.

"I had a few hours free and decided to check in and see how your collection of children's stories was coming along."

"It keeps growing," Molly admitted. "Every time I think it's the last one, another one pops into my mind."

"How many do you have so far?"

"Fourteen."

"Wow." Lara laughed. "That's a lot more than I would have guessed."

"Me, too." She smiled at Carla as she brought in a tray of tea and cookies. "Thanks."

"What are you going to do with them now?" Lara asked, accepting the cup of tea that Molly poured for her.

"Lexi's drawing me some pictures to go with the magic frog story so I can have it printed and bound for Matthew."

"He'll love it," Lara assured her. "But I was actually wondering about your plans on a bigger scale."

"I don't have any bigger plans."

"Well, you should start making some because I have a friend—he's a friend of a friend, actually—who wants to see what you've got."

"Someone wants to read my stories?"

Lara smiled. "He's not just 'someone.' He's an editor at a major publishing house in England."

Molly bobbled her cup and had to set it aside for fear she would drop it. "An editor?"

"Did I overstep?" Lara asked cautiously.

"No. I'm just… An editor… I'm stunned. I can't believe it."

Lara grinned. "Good. And while you're basking in that little revelation, I'm going to risk overstepping again and ask you when the heck you're going to put my brother-in-law out of his misery by agreeing to marry him."

Molly sighed. "I can't believe you're taking his side on this."

"It's not about sides," Lara denied. "And if you think I can't understand how difficult this is for you, you're wrong, because I've been exactly where you are."

"Where is it that you think I am?" Molly asked cautiously.

"Involved with a man who seems completely wrong for you."

She didn't bother to deny her feelings. "I'd say the problem is more that I'm completely wrong for him."

"And yet, anyone who knows Eric and has seen the way he looks at you, would dispute that."

"He's attracted to me." She glanced down at her swollen belly. "Or he was, at one time, obviously."

Lara laughed. "I don't think the attraction has faded. If anything, I would guess that Eric's feelings for you have grown and deepened over the past few months, and not just because you're carrying his child."

"None of which changes the fact that I'm wrong for him."

"Isn't that his decision to make?" the princess asked gently.

"Maybe. Except that he's so determined to do the right thing—which he insists is marrying me—that I'm not sure he's considered the long-term consequences."

"And why are you so determined *not* to marry him? What are you afraid of?" Lara echoed the question her brother-in-law had asked the day before. "That you'll fall in love with him? Or that you won't?"

And Molly found herself admitting to Lara a truth that she was only starting to acknowledge herself. "I'm afraid that I already have."

* * *

Molly had never been a nervous flier. Of course, she could count on one hand the number of times she'd been on an airplane, and there was always so much excitement associated with whatever journey she'd been about to embark on that she hadn't worried about any of the details. But as she stood at the security counter and watched the minutes tick away on the clock on the wall, she was definitely starting to worry.

She tucked her hands into her pockets and noted the steady progression of travelers moving through the other lines. Families with children, couples, singles. No one seemed to be subject to anything more than the standard questions and a minimal wait. Why were they concerned about her?

Because she knew there was some concern. When she'd first walked up to the security gate, the guard had asked about her destination and the purpose of her trip in a bored tone that told her he'd asked the exact same questions too many times before. Then he'd scanned her passport and frowned at the computer screen.

"Is there a problem?" she'd asked, confident that there couldn't be. It was the same passport she'd used to enter the country and it didn't expire for another two years.

But the response didn't reassure her. "Wait one minute, please."

Then the guard had left her standing there while he took her passport through a secured, frosted-glass door marked *SEGURIDAD/SÉCURITÉ.*

And she'd been standing and waiting a lot longer than "one minute."

Maybe she should have waited for Eric to return from his business trip so she could fly to San Antonio with him, but after her recent conversation with Fiona, she'd been anxious to get home and see her family. Eric had agreed to meet her in Texas and they would fly back together again after the weekend.

She looked at the clock again, calculated that he'd been gone at least seven minutes, and was grateful that she still had almost an hour before her flight was scheduled to leave. Whatever was going on, she was sure it would be straightened out in time for her to get on the plane.

Her certainty wavered when the same guard stepped out of the office again—followed by three other men. Two were some kind of military, evidenced by their uniforms and the weapons they carried, the third was wearing a suit with a badge clipped on the jacket pocket and an air of authority that made her pulse race.

She'd done nothing wrong. Logically, she knew there was no reason for them to detain her. But the escalating fear was a lot stronger than logic at the moment.

"Miss Shea?" the man in the suit said.

She swallowed, her heart pounding so hard she wondered that he couldn't hear it. "Yes?"

"I'm Aidan Lamontagne, Chief of Airport Security. Would you come into my office for a minute, please?"

She knew it wasn't a question so much as a directive. She nodded anyway and murmured her agreement.

"Is there a problem?" she asked again, not quite certain any more and all too conscious of the military guards posted on either side of the door, no doubt to prevent any attempted escape.

"That's what we're trying to figure out," he admitted. "You're an American citizen, Miss Shea?"

"Yes."

"And you've been in Tesoro del Mar since May twenty-ninth?"

She shifted in her chair and wondered if it was the extension of her visit that was the problem. Though she'd come into the country on the royal family's private plane, she'd still filled out immigration papers indicating her intended date of departure— a date that had passed more than two months earlier.

"Yes," she said again.

"For business or pleasure?"

She shifted in her chair again. "I came for a friend's wedding."

"When is the wedding?"

"It was June tenth."

"And since then?" he prompted.

"I've been on something of an extended vacation."

"Where are you staying?"

"With a friend." She folded her hands in her lap. "I'm not sure I understand the reason for all of these questions."

"The address where you're staying, Miss Shea," he prompted in the same implacable tone.

"3880 Camino Del norte De la Costa."

She saw recognition light in his eyes, knew he was familiar with the address, as no doubt someone employed with national security would be familiar with all of the royal family's properties.

"You are staying at Estado de las Morales?"

She nodded. "Yes."

"As a guest of the royal family?"

"Yes." She felt her cheeks heat up in response to his narrowed gaze. She and Eric had both wanted to ensure her presence at the estate wasn't common knowledge because they wanted time to let their relationship develop without public scrutiny. Now, with this security officer so obviously skeptical about her connection to the royal family, she wondered if that had been a mistake.

"I'm a—" she swallowed "—a friend of Prince Eric Santiago."

"You are aware that His Royal Highness is currently out of the country."

"Of course I am," she said wearily. "He's in Monaco on business. He's scheduled to return on Thursday and was planning to meet me in Texas for my grandparents' anniversary."

He pushed his chair away from the desk. "Excuse me a moment, please."

He walked past the guards and into the outer office. She saw the light on his phone illuminate, confirming that he'd left her to make a private call.

She brushed her hands over the thighs of her jeans, more annoyed than worried now. Obviously there had been some kind of mistake—she just hoped Mr. Lamontagne would clear it up so she could get on the plane. Over the past few months, she'd been too preoccupied trying to figure out her relationship with Eric and making plans for the future of their child to think much about everything—and everyone—she'd left behind in Texas. But since Fiona had contacted her about coming home, she'd been thinking about home a lot.

She knew her cousin didn't need her help with anything so much as she wanted all the details of what was happening with Eric, and though Molly was looking forward to spending time with Fiona, she didn't know how she was going to answer her questions. Because the fact was, almost four months after moving in with Eric, she didn't have any more answers about her future than she did on day one. While there was no doubt they both wanted what was best for their child, they couldn't seem to agree on what that was.

Or maybe it was her own feelings for the prince that were confusing the issue.

Mr. Lamontagne's return pushed these thoughts from her mind and she gave him her full attention, anxious to know the reason she'd been detained and that it had been cleared up.

"I apologize for the confusion," he said, "and can advise that the palace is sending someone to pick you up."

"Pick me up?"

He nodded.

"But I'll miss my flight." She glanced at her watch. "I'm supposed to be on a plane to the United States in twenty minutes."

"I'm sorry, Miss Shea."

That was it—no other explanation was given.

She wanted to kick and scream but she knew it would be no use. He was just doing his job.

"Officer Melas will escort you to the administration area on the second floor to wait for your party there."

Eric was on his way home from Monaco when Rowan contacted him about the incident with Molly at the airport.

"You need to fix this," he said.

"I'll track down Lamontagne as soon as we land."

"I meant that you need to fix this with Molly," Rowan said, confirming that he knew Eric was responsible for what had happened.

And Eric knew that Molly would be more difficult to deal with than the security officer.

He'd made a lot of mistakes in his life, but he was hard-pressed to find one that could top this. Molly was going to be furious when she realized he was responsible for flagging her passport so she couldn't leave the country without him knowing, and he couldn't blame her. His actions had been uncharacteristically impulsive and shortsighted, and he had no doubt he would pay for them now.

She was in the conservatory when he got home, surrounded by flowers and plants and illuminated by the sunlight streaming through the windows. Her computer was perched on her knees and her fingers raced across the keyboard. After a few minutes, she paused and lifted a hand to rub her belly.

"Writer's block or baby kicks?" he asked.

She looked up at him and smiled. "Hi. I didn't think you were coming back until tomorrow."

He crossed the room to give her a long, lingering kiss. "The meetings finished up early and I was missing you."

"But I wasn't supposed to be here," she reminded him.

"I know. I stopped by the security office to see Aidan Lamontagne and straightened that out before I came home."

"So it's fixed?" She set aside her computer and stood up. "You have a quick conversation with the head of airport security, who wouldn't let me on an airplane twelve hours ago, and he's suddenly reassured that I'm not a threat to national security?"

He'd thought she would be pleased that the problem was sorted out. He hadn't anticipated that she'd be suspicious by the ease with which he'd done so.

"If he'd ever believed you were, you would have left the airport in handcuffs."

"Well, I guess I should be grateful for that—but I'd still like to know why I was detained."

And she had a right to know.

Bracing himself for her reaction, he admitted, "You came up on the system as a person of interest with a directive to contact the palace if you attempted to leave the country."

"What? Why?"

"Because I was pissed when I woke up the morning after Scott and Fiona's wedding and found you were gone."

She stared at him, stunned, hurt. "*You* arranged it so I couldn't leave the country? You asked me to stay—you made me think that I had a choice, but I never really did. You were never going to let me leave."

"I wasn't going to let you leave without talking to me about why and where you were planning to go."

"Neither one of those questions should have been a big mystery to you. I was leaving because the wedding was over and I was going home."

"Okay—maybe I overreacted."

"Maybe?" The hurt had quickly turned to fury.

"I did overreact," he admitted. "I just didn't want you going anywhere until we'd had a chance to talk."

"Haven't we done enough talking over the past four months?" The ice in her tone chilled him to the bone.

"I forgot that I'd had your passport flagged."

She looked away, but not before he saw that her eyes had filled with tears. "I hate this."

"I said I was sorry," he told her. "What more can I do?"

"I'm sure you are sorry," she agreed. "Though I'm not sure if you're sorry that you ever did it or just sorry that you forgot to undo it before you got caught. But what I hate is that you have that kind of power. What's going to happen if we disagree on an issue about our child? Am I going to have any say or is everything just going to be your way because you can make it so?"

He was grateful that the chirp of his cell sounded before he could open his mouth, because he had no idea what he could say to diffuse an explosive situation that he knew was entirely of his own making.

He flipped it open, but kept his eyes on Molly. "Yes?"

She'd turned her back to him and folded her arms across her chest in a classically defensive posture. He wanted to take her in his arms, to soothe the hurt even though he knew he'd caused it.

He listened to the voice on the phone, then snapped it shut again and told her, "The plane is ready."

She closed the lid on her computer, tucked it under her arm. "This doesn't make everything okay."

Eric sighed wearily as he watched her storm out of the room—knowing and regretting that it was true.

Chapter Thirteen

Molly's mood hadn't improved much by the time they landed in San Antonio. She was still stunned by the revelation of what Eric had done, and furious there was nowhere she could go to get away from him.

A few months earlier, Molly had agreed to sublet her apartment above the restaurant to a new waitress, so she'd planned to stay with her grandparents to maximize her time with them. When Eric first told her he wanted to stay with her, she'd been pleased by his interest in spending time with her family. Now she had to wonder—did he really want to meet her grandparents, or did he just want to stick close to keep an eye on her?

She'd honestly believed they'd grown close over the past few months, but now Molly wondered if she really knew him at all.

As he drove the rental car through the familiar streets of town, she was both excited and nervous about the reunion with her grandparents. Molly had spoken to them regularly over the

past several months, but after telling them about her pregnancy—
an announcement which had been met, not unexpectedly, with
a lecture about "the lack of morals in young people these
days"—she'd been careful to steer clear of that topic in subse-
quent conversations.

There would be no steering clear of it this weekend, she knew.
Not when the proof of it was now obvious to even an octoge-
narian with bifocals.

But her grandmother made no comment about the belly that
pressed between them when she greeted her at the door with
a warm hug.

"I'm so glad you're finally here," Theresa Shea said, kissing
both of Molly's cheeks. "And look at you—you're glowing."

"I'm hot, Grandma. Hauling around an extra twenty pounds
has thrown off my internal thermostat."

"Nonsense," Theresa chided, turning her attention from her
disgruntled granddaughter to the man standing in the doorway
behind her. "And you must be Molly's prince."

"Please, just call me Eric," he said.

"Hmm," she said, which Molly knew meant she was reserv-
ing judgment. Ordinarily, the presence of royalty would have
flustered her grandmother, but she knew Eric's status was tem-
pered in Theresa's mind by the fact that he'd impregnated her
granddaughter. "You got any luggage? I can call Lawrence to get
it for you."

"Just these," he said, indicating the two small suitcases in his
hands.

"Molly's can go upstairs, the first door on the right. You'll be
sleeping on the pull-out downstairs."

If Eric was surprised by the sleeping arrangements, he didn't
show it and left his bag at the entrance as he took hers up the stairs.

"Where is Grandpa?" Molly asked.

"In the garage, tinkering with some kind of engine with the Walters' boy."

For as long as Molly could remember, her grandfather had always been tinkering with one thing or another. "I'll go out and say hi," she said. After which, she wanted only to kick off her shoes, put her feet up and relax.

"You can say hi later," Theresa told her. "I want to go shopping."

"Shopping?" Molly asked wearily.

"I need a new outfit for the party."

Molly stared at her grandmother. "For Fiona and Scott's wedding celebration?"

Theresa nodded.

"But—it's tomorrow."

"I know that," her grandmother said with just the slightest hint of irritation. "I might be old, but I'm not senile."

So instead of putting her feet up, Molly put a smile on her face and took her grandmother shopping.

Four hours later and still empty-handed, Theresa announced that she'd had enough of the crowds at the mall and was certain she could find something in her closet at home that was appropriate.

But when they passed a little coffee shop, her grandmother steered her inside. "I want a cup of tea," she explained.

"We can have tea at your house," Molly said.

"Yes, but we can't talk with your young man around."

"He's not my young man."

"Which is what we need to talk about."

So it was that Molly was sitting across from her at a little table with a cup of decaf in her hand.

"He should marry you," her grandmother said firmly.

Molly stared into her cup, well aware that the admission she had to make was going to swing the direction of her grandmother's wrath, but knowing she had no choice. If her grandmother started in on Eric about the importance of their child being born legitimate—as, given thirty seconds alone with him, she just might do—he would undoubtedly admit that Molly was the one holding out.

"He thinks so, too," she admitted.

Theresa's cup clattered against her saucer. "He asked you to marry him?"

"It wasn't actually a proposal," Molly said.

"But he wants to do the right thing?"

Molly sighed. "Who says it's the right thing? Why is having a child out of wedlock more scandalous than entering into a marriage for all of the wrong reasons?"

"Giving your baby a family isn't a wrong reason."

"It didn't work for my parents, did it?"

Theresa sighed. "Because your parents weren't willing to work at their marriage."

"Because they both felt trapped by circumstances."

"Is that how you feel?" her grandmother demanded. "Because I might be old-fashioned in a lot of ways, but I know darn well that a young woman who gets pregnant nowadays only stays that way if she wants her baby."

"I do want my baby," she admitted, her hand automatically moving to her rounded belly. "But I'm not sure I would ever have seen Eric again if not for the connection with Fiona and Scott, and even now, I'm not sure he wants to be a husband and a father so much as he feels compelled to do the right thing."

"Wanting to do the right thing proves the boy was raised right," Theresa said approvingly.

Molly couldn't help but smile. "The 'boy' is thirty-six years old and seventh in line to the throne of his country."

Theresa's gaze sharpened. "Is *that* what's bothering you—that he's a prince?"

"We have nothing in common, Grandma. A marriage between us would be doomed to fail even before it began."

"If you have nothing in common, the last four months must have been extremely difficult for you."

Molly felt her cheeks flush. "Okay—so maybe we're not completely incompatible," she admitted.

"Then maybe you need to consider that marrying him isn't a completely unreasonable idea."

Eric was sleeping on a lumpy couch in Molly's grandparents' basement. Correction: he was *trying* to sleep on a lumpy couch in Molly's grandparents' basement, a fact which might have made him smile if he wasn't so damn uncomfortable.

They obviously knew he and Molly had been intimate—she wouldn't be pregnant otherwise. And he knew that their acceptance of the baby she carried didn't translate into approval of that fact.

He also understood that the lumpy couch was punishment for sleeping with their granddaughter outside of the sanctity of marriage. And now that he was on the verge of becoming a father of a baby girl himself, he appreciated that position because there was no way his little girl was going to be unchaperoned with a man until he was her husband.

He didn't sleep well—and while the bed was partly to blame, the recent strain in his relationship with Molly was the bigger problem. He knew it was his own fault; he just didn't know how to fix it.

He felt a little bit better after a breakfast of eggs and bacon and fried potatoes and freshly squeezed juice. It wasn't a fancy meal but it was hot and hearty. The only thing he missed at the table was Molly.

"Is Molly still sleeping?" he finally asked.

Theresa chuckled. "Goodness, no. She was up and gone more than an hour ago. Took some of my homemade cinnamon rolls over to Abbey at the restaurant."

Probably to avoid having breakfast with him, he couldn't help but think, again regretting the distance between them. Had he not bungled things so badly, she might have asked him to go with her, because he guessed that she could use some moral support in facing her sister.

"How is Abbey doing?" he asked cautiously.

"Are you asking if she's accepted that Molly's going to have a baby?"

He nodded.

"She's getting there. It probably wouldn't have come as such a shock if Molly had been married first. That's the usual order of things—wedding and then baby—and a ceremony might have prepared Abbey for the possibility that her sister was going to be a mother."

"Do you really think so?" he asked. "Or is that just your way of asking about my intentions regarding your granddaughter."

"I really think so," she said. "Besides, Molly already told me that you asked her to marry you."

"She did?"

"Thought she'd enjoy watching you on the hot seat, didn't you?"

"Yeah," he admitted, knowing he deserved to be there.

"I love my granddaughter," Theresa said now. "But she's too stubborn for her own good sometimes."

"I can be just as stubborn," he promised her.

She smiled. "I'm counting on that."

Molly's apprehension increased with every mile that brought her closer to Shea's. This would be the first time she'd seen her sister since she'd left San Antonio almost five months earlier and since the conversation in which she'd told Abbey of her pregnancy. Which was why Molly had a box of Grandma's homemade cinnamon buns and jittery nerves as she walked across the parking lot early Friday morning.

She'd thought about asking Eric to go with her. Despite everything that had happened in the last twenty-four hours, she trusted that he would be there for her if she needed him. But Molly wouldn't let herself need him.

The door was unlocked, so she tucked her key back in her pocket and walked in. She set the box of pastries on the counter. "Got any coffee to go with these?"

"Molly!" Abbey's eyes lit up and she immediately came around the bar to embrace her sister.

It was a warmer greeting than Molly had expected. And then they hugged, and Abbey's gaze dropped to her sister's belly and her eyes filled with tears.

Molly held her breath.

"You look good," Abbey said, then smiled at her sister through her tears. "Really good, Molly."

She swallowed. "Thanks."

Abbey moved back to the other side of the bar. "You said something about coffee?"

"Yeah, that would be great. Make mine decaf."

Abbey poured two cups, pushed one across the bar.

Molly slid onto a stool. "Was it really only a few months ago that we were on opposite sides of this counter?"

"Hard to believe isn't it?" Abbey folded her arms on the polished wood. "I'm really glad you came in. I was going to call you, but when I realized you were coming home for Fiona and Scott's reception, I decided it would be better to talk to you in person—to thank you in person."

"Thank me?"

"To apologize *and* to thank you," her sister clarified. "I was kind of nasty to you the last time we spoke."

"I understand why you were upset."

"I *was* upset. And hurt and frustrated and angry. It just seemed so unfair that Jason and I have been trying so hard for so long to have a baby and you spend one night with a guy and end up pregnant."

Molly only nodded.

"And then, I was telling Jason about it—" she managed a smile "—okay, I was complaining to Jason about how unfair it was, and how your baby should have been our baby, and I finally accepted that wanting a child doesn't mean I need to have a baby. There are tons of babies out there in need of families and maybe Jason and I could be that family to one or more of them."

She paused to take a breath and to blink away the moisture from her eyes. "We have an appointment with a couple of adoption agencies next week and another with a caseworker from Family Services. We know it might take a while before we get a child of our own but there are a lot of kids who need a temporary home so we thought we might foster while the adoption process gets underway. Or maybe we could even adopt through Family Services—I didn't realize that could be done but I was talking to Karen about fostering and she told me that was how her sister adopted both of her kids."

As the story spilled out, her words were punctuated by occasional tears and hopeful smiles that reflected her passionate feelings.

And Molly felt her own eyes fill as she realized that Abbey might finally find the happiness and contentment that had eluded her for so long.

The same happiness and contentment that had so recently slipped from her own grasp.

* * *

Harcourt Castle was everything Fiona had wanted for her wedding reception and the night was beautiful—if a little anti-climactic after the celebration at the royal palace in Tesoro del Mar. There were twinkling lights and soft music and waiters dressed in black tie circulating with trays of hot hors d'oeuvres and cold champagne. In the arbor where Fiona and Scott had originally intended to exchange their vows, a screen had been set up so that the guests could watch the video of the ceremony that was performed in Tesoro del Mar.

"It was a truly beautiful ceremony," Theresa said, dabbing her eyes.

"You could have been there," Molly reminded her, to which her grandmother shook her head firmly.

"If God wanted me to fly, he would have given me wings," she said, as she had so many times before.

"He didn't give you wheels, either, but that never stopped you from driving," her husband noted.

It was the only real issue on which Molly had ever heard her grandparents disagree—because Lawrence longed to travel and see the world and Theresa didn't.

"But what was with those vows?" Lawrence asked now. "I never heard anything like that before."

"We wrote our own," Fiona explained.

"What for?" her grandfather demanded. "Something wrong with the usual ones?"

"Times change," Theresa reminded him.

"You're telling me," Lawrence grumbled. "They don't even ask a wife to 'obey' anymore. When we got married, you promised to 'obey'."

"And how long did that last?" Scott asked.

"We've been married sixty-four years," Lawrence told his

newest grandson-in-law. "Because Theresa knows who's the boss."

"I certainly do, dear," his wife agreed, and took his arm to lead him away from the circle of their grandchildren.

"I think we all know who's the boss in that marriage," Jason said.

"Grandma definitely makes the decisions," Abbey said, linking her arm through her husband's. "But she manages to do it in a way that lets Grandpa thinks he's making them."

"Everyone needs some illusions," Scott said.

"And what are yours?" his bride wanted to know.

"Well, everyone but me," he said, wrapping his arms around his wife. "Because I have everything I could ever want right here."

Molly looked away when Scott bent his head to kiss Fiona— and found Eric looking at her.

"Cold?" Eric asked, slipping an arm across her shoulders when she shivered in response to the breeze that blew through the open windows.

She shook her head, because she wasn't anymore. And she was no longer surprised at how attuned he was to her needs, or by his willingness to meet them.

In the distance, Molly saw her grandfather hand a glass of champagne to his wife and brushed his lips against hers, and she knew that her grandparents were proof positive that love could and did last.

Looking around, she noticed that almost everyone was paired up with someone else, and as she stood there in the warmth and comfort of Eric's arms, she wondered if maybe she'd been too hasty in turning her back on the possibility of her own "happily ever after."

Eric thought something had shifted in his relationship with Molly that night, but two days later, on the day that they were scheduled to return to Tesoro del Mar, he wondered if he'd only imagined it. Once again he'd woken up to have breakfast with her grandparents, and once again Molly was already gone.

He knew where she was this time—she'd gone to the restaurant to sign the final papers to turn management of Shea's over to her sister and brother-in-law. He didn't think it had been an easy decision for her to make but, aside from telling him of the decision, she hadn't discussed it with him.

"You seem a little preoccupied this morning," Theresa said to Eric.

"I guess I'm just thinking of everything I'll have to do when I get back tonight," he told her.

"You're anxious to get back, aren't you?"

"I've enjoyed the time we've spent here," he said. "But there are business matters that need to be attended to."

"Can I tell you a story?" Theresa asked, in what seemed to him an abrupt change of topic.

"Okay," he agreed cautiously.

"It happened a long time ago—I can't remember exactly how long ago, although I do remember that Lawrence and I had only been married a few years because we were still living in that little bungalow on Chetwood Street. It wasn't much of a house, but there were some beautiful big trees in the backyard that would be filled with birds every summer.

"Anyway, I was outside one morning, weeding the garden. We used to grow our own vegetables back then, too, and it was my job to tend to them because Lawrence was working almost round-the-clock at the diner. That's all that Shea's was at the time—a twelve-by-twelve diner that served simple meals to simple folks."

She carried the coffeepot to the table and refilled his cup, and Eric settled in to listen. He wasn't yet sure what the point of this story was—or even if Theresa had one—but over the past couple of days, he'd spent a lot of time with Molly's grandmother and found that he genuinely enjoyed her company.

And whatever the topic of conversation, she inevitably had a story. Or she made one up. He was never quite sure whether her tales were fact or fiction, but she spun them so well it didn't really matter. He figured it was a talent she'd passed on to her grand-daughter, as Molly had finally let him see some of the children's stories she'd been writing and told him that Lara had put her in touch with an editor who wanted to take a look at them. He'd been thrilled for her and proud of her, and quite impressed when he'd been given the chance to read what she'd written.

"Are you paying attention to this?" Theresa demanded, her eyes narrowed on him.

"Of course," he said. "You were outside weeding the garden."

"Yes, wrestling with some nasty pricklepoppy that was trying to strangle the roots of my tomato plants," she continued. "And right there in the dirt, I found a baby bird that had fallen out of its nest—or maybe been knocked out by a bigger bird. 'Cause this one was a tiny thing, and helpless. It might have been a sparrow, though I don't remember for sure. I didn't really know what to do with it, but I knew it would die if I just left it there, so I carried it inside. I kept it fed and gave it a little bed to sleep in while its injuries healed.

"Lawrence made me a little cage for it, so that it wouldn't try to fly too soon and hurt itself again. But by the time it was healed and ready to fly, I didn't want to let it go. It started to fight against the cage, demanding to be let free, and then one day it just suddenly stopped fighting, as if it recognized the futility of beating its wings against the walls that held it. And then it stopped singing, too.

"So I took the cage outside and finally released it. I watched it fly farther and farther away until I couldn't see it anymore be-cause of the tears in my eyes.

"It was about a week later—I was in the garden again—when it came back. I wasn't sure it was the same bird at first, until it perched right on the fence where I was working and chirped at me. And I realized then how wrong I'd been to keep that bird inside a cage, to make it stay with me. That it would only ever be able to sing if it was free."

He picked up his cup, surprised to find it empty again. He'd been so caught up in the story he hadn't realized he'd drank it, but not so caught up that he didn't see the point she was trying to make.

"You think Molly feels trapped," he guessed.

"I think she feels that the circumstances have limited her options."

He frowned. "Three days ago, you gave me the impression that you wanted me to marry your granddaughter."

"*I* do want you to marry my granddaughter," she said. "But over the past couple of days, I've finally accepted that might not be what Molly wants."

"Are you suggesting now that I should just give up? That I should let her go?"

"I'm saying that she'll always resent feeling as if she had no choice."

He could understand that, but just the thought of being without Molly left his heart feeling as empty and hollow as he knew his life would be without her.

"I love her," he said, suddenly realizing it was true.

"I know you do," she said, and patted his arm, obviously not as surprised by the revelation as he was. "And that's why I know you'll do the right thing."

"What if I let her go and she doesn't come back?"

"Then it wasn't meant to be," she said simply.

He shook his head. He wouldn't—couldn't—believe that. Nothing in his life had ever seemed as right as being with Molly.

And yet, he knew her grandmother had a point.

You made me think that I had a choice, but I never really did.

If he took Molly back to Tesoro del Mar with him now, he would always wonder if she'd gone because she wanted to be with him or because she felt she had no other options.

He had to open the door and let her fly.

Chapter Fourteen

Molly spent the morning at Shea's finalizing the details of the agreement that would transfer ownership of the restaurant to Abbey and Jason. Though it was difficult to let go of the business that had been her life for so many years, she knew it was time. The restaurant had once seemed so inextricably linked to her father, but now Molly understood that Shea's was just a building on a piece of property. It was the memories that were the true legacy, and she would take those memories with her wherever she went.

And right now, her plan was to start a new life in Tesoro del Mar. Regardless of what arrangement she came to with Eric about their baby, she wanted her daughter to be close to her father and she knew that could only happen if she was living in Tesoro del Mar. It wasn't hard to imagine a life in a country she'd already fallen in love with—it *was* hard to imagine a life without the man she loved.

Maybe you need to consider that marrying him isn't a completely unreasonable idea.

She sighed as her grandmother's words echoed in the back of her mind.

Was it unreasonable to want the man she loved to love her back?

But even if, by some miracle, he did fall in love with her—would love be enough to make a marriage work?

She knew there were no guarantees in life—except that she was guaranteed to live her life alone if she didn't stop hiding behind her fears and go after what she really wanted.

And what she really wanted was Eric.

With her heart lighter than it had been in days, Molly didn't worry about the fact that the rental car wasn't in the driveway when she got back to her grandparents' house. In fact, she didn't think anything of it until she went up to her room and saw the envelope on the dresser with her name on it.

Frowning, she tore open the flap.

Dear Molly,

By the time you find this note, you're probably wondering where I am and why I'm not hovering over you to make sure your bags are packed so we can head back to Tesoro del Mar.

I've made a lot of mistakes in my life, but none that I regret more than the mistakes I've made from the very beginning in my relationship with you. I don't mean our baby—though our child might have been unplanned, I have never regretted her existence. But I do regret everything that's happened since I found out you were pregnant and every attempt I made to manipulate or coerce you into doing things my way. Parenting should be a joint venture. Marriage should be a true partnership.

Anton has filed a flight plan and we are scheduled to leave at four o'clock. I figured this would give you enough time after you got back from your meeting at the restaurant to pack and get to the airport if you want to come back to Tesoro del Mar with me.

If you're surprised that I'm giving you a choice, you might be even more surprised to know why—because I love you, Molly.

It seems strange to say those words for the first time on paper, but I couldn't leave without letting you know how I feel. It's not just the first time I've expressed those words to you, but the first time ever. I've never felt about another woman the way I feel about you. Before you came into my life I was lost, drifting. You changed everything for me.

I hope you know that I would do anything for you, give you anything you wanted if it was within my power to do so. And if all you want is your freedom, I will let you go.

As I write this note, I'm hoping with everything in my heart that you will be on the plane with me when it goes back to Tesoro del Mar tonight. But I want you to know that whatever you decide, I will love you always.

Eric

Molly raced down the stairs, Eric's letter clenched in her fist. She found her grandmother in the kitchen, humming to herself as she dropped spoonfuls of batter onto a tray. Her grandfather was at the table, drinking a cup of coffee and munching on warm oatmeal-raisin cookies.

The scene was homey and normal—a snapshot of the life she'd claimed she wanted, and a picture that was completely wrong without Eric in it.

Her grandmother looked up, smiled at her. "Want some cookies, honey?"

"Fresh pot of coffee, too," her grandfather said. "Decaf."

She shook her head. "No, thanks. Did you know Eric was gone?"

"Of course." Theresa slid the tray into the oven.

"He came into the garage to say goodbye, and to thank us for our hospitality." Lawrence chuckled. "And he said it with a straight face, even after four nights on that awful sofa bed."

Molly sank into a chair across from her grandfather. "And then he just left?"

Theresa's brow furrowed. "You didn't know he was going back today?"

"I didn't know he was going back *without me*."

"I would think you'd be relieved," her grandmother said. "You were the one who told me how incompatible you are."

Molly sighed. "You told him the bird story, didn't you?"

Theresa sniffed. "It's a good story."

"What bird story?" Lawrence asked, reaching for another cookie.

Molly shook her head. "The same story that she told me after my fiancé came home from Vegas married to my sister."

"Actually, it wasn't quite the same," Theresa said. "Having the bird come back with a mate this time would have completely changed the message."

"I love you, Grandma, but you've got to let me live my life."

"That's just what I told Eric," her grandmother said. "And living your life means accepting responsibility for your own choices. You can choose to stay or you can choose to go, but now there will be no doubt that the choice is yours."

Molly looked at her grandfather. "Has she always been this sneaky?"

"One of the reasons I married her," he agreed. "I wanted to be sure she'd always be on my side."

"So what's it going to be?" Theresa asked her granddaughter.

Molly stood up. "I'm going to fly."

* * *

There were charter flights to Tesoro del Mar twice a week.

Eric knew that and tried to take comfort in the fact that if Molly wasn't at the airport by the time Anton was ready to go, it would be easy enough for her to take another plane to the island. Assuming, of course, that she wanted to come back. And right now, with no sign of Molly anywhere, he knew that was a big assumption.

"I'm going to do the final flight check," Anton said.

But it was more a question than a statement, and Eric knew he was seeking confirmation that Eric intended to stick with their schedule.

The pilot had been surprised when the prince arrived without Molly and asked if she'd been delayed. Eric had told him, honestly, that he wasn't certain if Molly would be flying with them. Anton had never been one to question his boss and he didn't do so now, but Eric knew he was puzzled by the response.

"Go ahead," he said now.

The pilot nodded and ducked outside.

He would walk around the outside, visually confirming that everything was as it should be, then double-check all the gauges and instruments that had already been double-checked. Anton was nothing if not meticulous about the care and operation of his plane.

While he was waiting, Eric opened his laptop and checked his e-mail. He'd had a brief meeting with Scott while he was in town, updating his friend on the progress of DELconnex International. He knew he wouldn't be able to focus on work, but if he was staring at the computer screen, he wouldn't be staring out the window watching for Molly.

He read a few e-mails—and read them again when he realized he hadn't comprehended a single word the first time through.

When he heard footsteps on the metal stairs, he closed the lid and pushed the computer aside.

But when he looked up, it wasn't Anton in the doorway— it was Molly.

Her smile was soft, her eyes warm and glowing with the familiar light he loved.

"Is this plane going to Tesoro del Mar?" she asked.

He stood up, wanting nothing so much as he wanted to haul her into his arms and hold on to her, to know for sure that she was there, that she was real. But the choice needed to be hers, so he stayed where he was standing and said, "It can go wherever you want to go."

"I want to go home," she said, and breached the distance between them.

Then she was in his arms and he was holding her as close as their baby would allow. And she was holding him, too.

"It's almost four o'clock," he murmured the words into her hair.

She tilted her head back. "Have you been waiting long?"

"I feel as if I've been waiting for you my whole life," he said, tightening his arms around her.

"I was going to make you wait longer," she admitted. "I was going to wait in the hangar until Anton started the engines, but I thought that might be cutting it too close."

"You wanted me to suffer," he guessed.

"I figured it was only fair considering that I've been suffering for months knowing that I was falling in love with you and believing you could never feel the same way."

"It turns out you were wrong," he said.

"I was wrong about something else," she admitted. "I thought I needed you—at least for the sake of our baby—and I resented you for that. But when we came back to Texas, I realized that I could make a life for her on my own if it was what I wanted.

Maybe I couldn't give her the kind of life you could, but it would be a good one.

"But the more I thought about that, the more I realized that while I *could* do it, it wasn't what I wanted to do. I want to raise our child together. I want to spend my life with you."

"Your wish—" he brushed his lips against hers "—is my command."

After the debacle at the airport, Molly wasn't surprised to return to Tesoro del Mar to find that the news of her pregnancy had made headlines in all the local papers. Another Royal Baby in the New Year? Prince Eric a Daddy? And, her least favorite, Heir Apparent, above a photo of her in profile with the baby bulge clearly visible.

In response to all the furor, Eric decided to hold a press conference with Molly by his side, confirming that they were expecting a child early in the new year. It was their first official public appearance together, and though Molly had worried about having so much attention focused on her, she was glad that she and Eric would no longer have to hide their relationship or her pregnancy.

It was on their way back home after the press conference that Molly said, "I want to get married on Christmas Eve."

Eric shifted so that he was facing her. "Do you mean in general, if you ever get married?" he asked. "Or do you mean that you want to marry me?"

"I want to marry you."

"*This* Christmas Eve?"

She nodded, grinning. "Think we can pull off a royal wedding in two months?"

"We can do anything if it means putting my ring on your finger," he said, and sealed the promise with a long, slow kiss.

Molly melted against him, her heart sighing with contentment even as her body started to stir again with longing.

"Why Christmas Eve?" he asked later.

"Because Christmas hasn't been a happy occasion for me in a very long time," she admitted, "and I want to change that."

"What happened?"

She swallowed around the tightness in her throat. "My dad died on Christmas Eve. It will be ten years ago this year."

He tucked her closer to him. "I can see how that would put a damper on the holidays."

She nodded.

"Christmas Eve mass is a huge celebration here," he told her. "And it would be a perfect opportunity to introduce you as my wife to the people of Tesoro del Mar."

"You do realize I'm going to be hugely pregnant by Christmas Eve, don't you?"

He rubbed his hand over the curve of her belly. "You mean, you're not hugely pregnant now?"

She swatted him playfully. "Just remember, that's your baby that has me so bent out of shape."

"Our baby," he said, and dipped his head to kiss her lips, then her belly, then her lips again. "Another good thing about getting married on Christmas Eve is it would be convenient for your family to stay and spend the holidays with us."

She was touched that he wanted to include them, but she shook her head. "As much as I'd love to have my family here, I don't think that's a likely scenario. My grandmother refuses to even go near an airport, never mind set foot on an airplane. Abbey and Jason are finally getting their marriage back on track and are busy with the restaurant, and Fiona and Scott are just settling into their lives as newlyweds."

"Would it be easier, then, if we got married in Texas?"

"I'm going to be thirty-eight weeks along by Christmas Eve," she reminded him. "I can't imagine any doctor giving approval for me to fly so close to the end of my pregnancy."

"We could go back now, stay there for the wedding and after, until the baby's born."

She stared at him, stunned that he would even make such a suggestion. "You'd be willing to do that?"

"I love you," he said simply.

And she knew then, without a doubt, that it was true.

She kissed him softly, appreciatively. "Thank you for even considering it," she said. "But I want to be married, have our baby and start our life together right here."

Now that the date had been set, Molly was busy overseeing preparations for the big day. They'd decided to have the ceremony in the main parlor, which—along with the rest of the house—was being transformed by the small army that Carla had hired expressly for that purpose. While the holiday decorating was a project she would usually have tackled herself, the housekeeper insisted that everything had to be on a much grander scale this year because they weren't just preparing for the celebrations of the season but for the next royal wedding.

When the work was finished, it seemed that there wasn't a doorway in the entire house that wasn't draped with evergreen boughs and velvet ribbons or a table that wasn't adorned with a pot of holiday flowers or a vase of pretty glass balls. As Eric and Molly walked through the house, she was both awed and amazed by the attention to detail and couldn't think of a single thing she would change—until they got to the front parlor and she saw the towering but sadly barren tree beside the fireplace.

"Decorating the Christmas tree was one of our family traditions," Eric explained. "Every year, it was something my father, my mother and my brothers and I did together. I'd like to continue that tradition for our family."

Molly had been feeling twinges in her lower back as they walked through the house, but she didn't tell Eric because she knew he would insist that she rest, and she really wanted to share in this tradition with him. So they decorated the tree together, stringing up what seemed like thousands of tiny lights, unwinding miles of thick gold ribbon, hanging hundreds of shiny red and gold balls.

When the last ornament had finally been hung, Molly stood back in the circle of Eric's arms to admire their efforts.

"It looks pretty good for our first Christmas tree, doesn't it?" he said.

Our first Christmas. The words were a promise of years to come, of their future together, and they brought tears to her eyes. "It looks great," she agreed. "But there's still something missing."

"The tree topper," he suddenly remembered, and gestured to a large box on the table—a box she knew hadn't been there a moment before.

She opened the lid to reveal an exquisite angel with a delicately sculpted porcelain face and arms, in a flowing gown of elegant ecru lace over cream-colored satin. The wings were iridescent and shot through with gold threads. There was a gold ribbon around her waist, and at the end of the ribbon—

Her breath caught in her throat.

Eric smiled. "I know we've taken a lot of steps out of order in our relationship," he said. "But I thought we should be formally engaged before we got married."

"It's…wow."

He smiled and steered her over to the sofa, gently nudging her to sit. She sank onto the soft edge, her knees trembling, her heart pounding so hard the discomfort in her back was momentarily forgotten.

She didn't know why she was so nervous—they'd already set the date for the wedding and plans were well underway. But the thoughtfulness and romance of the moment seemed to have knocked her off her feet—and that was before Eric got down on one knee beside her.

He untied the ribbon, freeing the circle of gold and diamonds to drop into his palm.

"It's not a traditional engagement ring," he admitted. "In fact, it wasn't originally an engagement ring at all, but an eternity band that my father gave to my mother for their twenty-fifth wedding anniversary. When my mother died, it came to me.

"The circle of diamonds is said to represent unending love," he explained, taking her left hand in his. "As I will love you, Molly. Forever and always."

Chapter Fifteen

Eric slid the ring onto Molly's finger and linked their hands together. She squeezed his. Hard. He noticed her other hand had gone to her stomach and her face had gone pale.

"What's wrong?" he asked.

"I'm not sure. I've been having these twinges in my lower back for a few hours that I didn't think were anything, but now…"

"Now what?"

"I think I've been having…contractions."

"But—" He didn't know what to say. It was as if everything inside of him, including his brain, had gone numb with shock. "But you're not due until the new year."

"I'm aware of that," she said, a little breathlessly.

"And first babies are more commonly late than early," he added.

"Yeah, well, tell that to your daughter."

"Lara went early with William," he noted. "But only a few

days, and he wasn't her first. Matthew didn't come until four days after the due date."

"Eric!"

He shook his head, and turned his attention back to the woman who was going to have his baby—maybe a lot sooner than either of them had anticipated.

"Do you think you could…call the…doctor?"

Eric raced to the phone.

Dr. Marotta asked about the frequency and duration of Molly's contractions, whether her water had broken, if she was having back pain, spotting or bleeding. Eric's answers were "every fifteen to twenty minutes," "about sixty seconds," "no," "yes" and "thank God, no." To which the doctor advised that there was probably nothing to get excited about just yet, but he would come over to check the mom-to-be, anyway.

"The baby's not due for another three weeks," Eric said when the doctor had finished his exam.

Dr. Marotta's eyes sparkled with humor. "Babies come when they're ready not when their fathers are, Your Highness."

"Should she go to the hospital?"

The doctor looked at Molly. "Have you changed your mind about wanting to have the baby at home?"

"No," Molly told him. "Not if there's no risk to the baby."

"At this point, there's nothing to suggest either you or the baby are in any danger," Dr. Marotta assured her.

Which wasn't the unconditional guarantee Eric had hoped for.

The doctor left them with his cell-phone number and instructions to call when her contractions were coming about five minutes apart, or sooner if they had any questions.

When the door had closed behind the departing doctor, Molly squeezed Eric's hand. "I'm sorry."

"Why are you sorry?"

"Because I know it was important to you for us to be married before she was born."

"What's important," he said, "is that she's born healthy."

"Dr. Marotta doesn't seem worried that she's coming early, does he?"

His only response was a quick shake of his head and a terse, "No."

"Then you shouldn't be, either," she told him, and he realized she hadn't been seeking reassurance, but to reassure.

"I know," he said, then admitted, "I'd just feel better if you were in the hospital where they have all the high-tech equipment and the fancy drugs."

She managed to smile because she knew he was genuinely concerned. She'd had a few moments herself in which she'd second-guessed the decision to have their baby in the house where she and Eric had been living for the past six months—the house where he and his brothers had been born. But as her due date grew nearer, she grew more settled in her conviction that it was the right thing to do. She didn't have a lot to give to her baby in the way of family history so she felt it was important to help carry on whatever traditions she could.

She squeezed Eric's hand again, but this time it was an involuntary response to the contraction that tightened her womb. The contractions weren't so painful—not yet, anyway—but they were irregular, and it was the unexpectedness that always jarred her.

"Are you sure you don't want drugs?" Eric asked.

"Right now I'm not sure of anything," she admitted. "Except that I'm really glad you're here with me."

"As if I'd be anywhere else."

They took a long walk around the grounds together while Carla bustled around nervously and Stefan prepared a light snack for the mother-to-be. Then they decided to follow the doctor's advice and get some rest, because he'd warned that rest wouldn't be an option when the contractions increased in frequency and intensity.

Molly did manage to nap briefly, and when she woke, she found her back snuggled tightly against Eric's front, his hand splayed over the curve of her belly and the rigid shaft of his arousal pressing against her buttocks.

"I'm guessing that you're not sleeping," she said dryly.

He chuckled softly. "I was resting—until you started squirming around."

"I apologize."

"Please don't."

She smiled, then sucked in a breath as a contraction hit.

Eric's hand moved in gentle, soothing circles over her belly. "You managed to sleep through a couple of mild ones," he said. "And they're still about fifteen minutes apart."

She put her hand over his, linking their fingers together. "I just want so much for her to be born."

"We've done everything we can to speed things along. Now we just have to be patient."

"We haven't quite done everything," she noted, deliberately wriggling against him.

"Molly," he warned.

She rolled over—not an easy task considering her current size and condition—so that she was facing him. "Don't you remember what that book said about sexual activity helping to bring on labor?"

"Yeah." He swallowed. "I remember."

"Lara told me it worked for her when she was pregnant with Matthew."

He winced. "Please. I love my sister-in-law, but I don't want to think about her and my brother...you know."

"Then you probably don't want to know that Jewel also advocated its success."

"No—in fact, I think now would be a good time for you to stop talking," he said.

She closed her mouth.

Then she reached down between their bodies and pressed her hand to the front of his pants, stroking him through the fabric.

He groaned. "You're killing me here."

"I promise you—" she nibbled on his lip, tasting, teasing "—that isn't my intention."

"What do you think Dr. Marotta would say if he walked in here right now?"

She scraped her teeth over his jaw. "He'd probably say that you should have locked the door."

"I'm not convinced he would approve of this."

"He was the one who made a point of saying that he'd be gone a couple of hours."

She kissed him again, slowly, deeply, using her tongue and teeth on his mouth while her hands got busy with his belt. Then she reached inside and—

He rolled off of the mattress.

She wasn't sure whether to be insulted or amused by how quickly he moved away from her. "Where are you going?"

His only response was to flip the lock on the door, and her heart rate kicked up a notch.

Molly smiled as he came back to the bed. His pace was a little more leisurely now, his movements deliberate, the heat in his eyes scorching.

She'd thought her sex drive would decrease as the size of the baby increased, but found that the opposite seemed to be true. Both of Eric's sisters-in-law had assured her that wasn't unusual, though Molly couldn't remember how the topic had come up in conversation or why it had been so easy for her to talk about such intimate topics with the women who were married to Eric's brothers.

The mattress dipped as Eric lowered himself onto it, and when he brushed his lips against hers, all other thoughts fled her mind.

"We've probably got about an hour left," he told her.

"An hour," she echoed on a sigh as his hands skimmed down her sides to the hem of her nightshirt, then below.

She sucked in a breath at the rush of air that cooled her heated flesh when he yanked the garment up and over her head, then giggled when he unceremoniously tossed it aside and pounced on her. "You don't seem so uncertain now."

"I realized this will probably be my last chance to get naked with you for the next couple of months, and I certainly wasn't going to let that opportunity go."

But despite the teasing words, it wasn't his own gratification he seemed concerned with, but hers. He kissed her, slowly and deeply, exploring her mouth with his lips and teeth and tongue. She'd never known a man who derived so much pleasure from just kissing—and still gave so much more.

And while he was kissing her, he was touching her. His hands skimmed over her body, from her shoulders to her elbows to her wrists. From her hips to her belly to her breasts. Gentle strokes, featherlight touches and tantalizing caresses.

He let her guide him, using her soft sighs and murmurs to direct every pass of his hands and touch of his lips. He was so incredibly focused, so selflessly giving, that she forgot this was supposed to be about hurrying her labor along as she lost herself in the pleasure he was giving her.

His palms grazed over the tight buds of her nipples, a light touch that nevertheless shot rockets of sensation through her body. She gasped, then moaned when his hands closed over her breasts, squeezing gently.

Then he dipped his head, and his mouth—that wonderfully talented mouth—closed around one peaked nipple and he suckled.

She felt her womb tighten and tense with pain, but there was pleasure, too, as he continued to use his lips and tongue on her.

She felt the rush of liquid between her thighs as the spasms continued to wrack her body and her fingers dug into his shoulders as she held on through the waves that lifted her up and up.

Molly's labor started in earnest after that. As Dr. Marotta had warned, there was no opportunity to rest or relax when her contractions stretched to two minutes and weren't coming much further apart than that.

Through it all, Molly never once cried out in pain or screamed at him. She remained quietly and intently focused, she kept her breathing regular and steady without needing to be coached to do so and she kept her gaze focused on the vase of fresh flowers on the other side of the room, which Carla had brought in as a focal point. In fact, Molly was doing such a good job managing her own labor that Eric was beginning to feel extraneous.

He knew she wasn't deliberately shutting him out. She was just trying to handle giving birth as she'd handled everything else in her life since her father had died and her former fiancé had abandoned her—on her own.

Her grandmother had said that Molly was too stubborn for her own good, but Eric understood that she didn't like to depend on anyone else because there had never really been anyone she could depend on. He was determined to prove to her that he was that someone.

So while she never asked for his help, he stayed by her side. He offered her ice chips, he wiped her face and throat with a cool cloth. And he noticed that she eventually shifted her focus from the flowers to him.

Then, when the doctor's examination confirmed that she was fully dilated and ready to start pushing, she reached for his hand and linked their fingers together. "Stay with me?"

"Always," he promised her, and meant it.

And he was right there to hear the first cries when their baby was born twenty-two minutes later.

It didn't take long for Molly and Eric and Princess Margaret Theresa Santiago to settle into a routine. The routine basically being that the princess cried and both of her parents jumped, which meant that the baby was always fed and dry and being cuddled in one pair of arms or another, and her mother and father were exhausted.

By day four, Molly was ready to suggest a postponement of their wedding, certain she would end up sleepwalking down the aisle. It was a testament to his own state of fatigue that Eric actually considered it.

It was Carla who put her foot down—she'd been working her tail off to make sure everything was ready for the royal wedding and, dammit, there was going to be a royal wedding. The day before Christmas Eve, she called in reinforcements—bringing in Lara and Jewel to take turns with the baby so her exhausted parents could sleep.

So it was that Molly awoke on Christmas Eve morning feeling rested—and with enough energy to be excited about finally becoming Eric's wife. When Maggie started to demand her breakfast, Molly tucked her against her breast as Eric wandered out of the bathroom, fully dressed.

"What are you doing up so early?"

"I've got to get to the airport to pick up your Christmas gift."

"My Christmas gift is at the airport?"

He glanced at his watch. "They will be in about an hour."

Her breath caught. "They?"

He lowered himself onto the edge of the mattress and leaned over to kiss her softly. "My family's going to be here for our wedding. I thought that yours should be, too."

"But we talked about this—"

"And you didn't think I could get your grandmother on an airplane," he remembered.

"She's coming?"

"Both your grandparents and Fiona and Scott." He shrugged. "One of the perks of having access to a private plane."

"You think my grandmother actually got on it?"

"I know she did. It's not one of those questionable commercial aircraft, you know," he said, no doubt an exact quote of Theresa's words. "And she figured if the Santiago jet was good enough for the royal family of Tesoro del Mar, it was good enough for her."

She smiled through her tears. "This is, without a doubt, the best Christmas present ever."

He shook his head. "It doesn't even compare to what you gave me."

She stroked a finger gently over the baby's cheek. "She is pretty incredible, isn't she?"

"She is," he agreed. "But I didn't just mean our daughter."

"Well, your other presents are wrapped and under the tree, and you're not getting them until tomorrow."

He put his arms around her, so their baby was snuggled between them. "I was referring to hope and happiness and dreams for our future together."

She tipped her head back. "I gave you all that?"

"You changed my life," he told her. "The day I saw that neon sign as I drove around the curve in the highway."

"Jason wants to get rid of the neon," she told him. "It doesn't fit with the image they want for the restaurant."

"We'll have the sign shipped over here and hang it above the bed," he said. And though she smiled again, he had to ask, "Are you okay with the changes they're making?"

"It's their restaurant now," she said simply.

"Do you miss it?"

She shook her head. "How could I when I have you and Maggie, and now a contract to write children's books?" The offer had come through less than a week earlier, and Molly had been so stunned when the editor had told her why he was calling that she'd dropped the phone, inadvertently hanging up on him. Thankfully, he'd called right back.

"Your grandmother is so tickled about that."

"She always said I was a writer."

"She was right." He snuggled her close. "You haven't asked why Abbey and Jason aren't here."

"This would be difficult for my sister," Molly said. "I understand."

He shook his head. "She wanted to be here—she was very excited about meeting her niece and, up until two days ago, she and Jason planned to make the trip, too."

"What happened?"

"Family Services called, asking if they could take in a seven-month-old boy. They know it might only be a temporary placement," he said, "but they couldn't turn him down."

Molly nodded, her throat tight. "I think it's going to be a really good Christmas for Abbey and Jason this year, too."

"Speaking of Christmas," Eric said, lifting the now-sleeping baby from her arms, "it's going to be just that in less than twenty-four hours, so if we want to be married before then, you'd better get up and start getting ready."

"I want to be married before then." Molly took the hand he offered and slid out of bed and into his arms. "I'm ready for my happily ever after to begin."

Epilogue

PRINCE CELEBRATES HOLIDAY WITH
WEDDING BELLS & BABY BOTTLES
by Alex Girard

The holiday season is a busy time, but this year it was even more so than usual for His Royal Highness Prince Eric Santiago. The former naval officer turned corporate exec celebrated Christmas Eve at Estado de las Morales, his family's ancestral estate on the northern coast, by exchanging vows with Molly Shea, a native of San Antonio whom he met while visiting a friend in Texas earlier this year.

The wedding was planned to precede the birth of the couple's first child, due early in the new year. The young princess, however, made her arrival three weeks early in order to be present at her parents' nuptials.

The intimate ceremony was witnessed by a small gathering of family and close friends. Afterward, the bride and groom attended Christmas Eve mass at the Cathedral to announce their marriage and present their daughter, Princess Margaret Theresa Santiago, to the people of Tesoro del Mar.

In response to the urging of the crowd, the prince pulled a sprig of mistletoe from his pocket and held it over his bride's head before giving her a kiss that was hot enough to warm even the coldest winter day, and sizzling enough to ensure that it was going to be a very happy Christmas for the newlyweds and their newly expanded family. Feliz Navidad!

* * * * *

CHRISTMAS WITH
THE PRINCE

MICHELLE CELMER

To my mom,
Who has been not only my teacher, my confidante,
and my most dedicated fan, but one of my best friends.
Love you!

One

Olivia Montgomery was attractive for a scientist.

Attractive in a brainy, geeky sort of way. From a distance, at least. And not at all what Prince Aaron had expected.

He watched her gaze up at the castle from his office window, a look of awe on her heart-shaped face, her bow mouth formed into a perfect *O* beneath eyes as large as dinner plates.

He supposed it wasn't every day that a woman was asked to uproot her entire life, stay at a royal castle for an indeterminable period and use her vast knowledge to save an entire country from potential absolute financial devastation.

Of course, from what he'd read of their new guest, her life to date had been anything but typical. Most kids didn't graduate from high school at fifteen, receive their Ph.D. at twenty-two and earn a reputation as a pioneer in the field of botanical genetics at twenty-four. He would swear she didn't look a day over eighteen, due in part to the long, blondish-brown hair she wore pulled back in a ponytail and the backpack she carried slung over one shoulder.

He watched as Derek, his personal assistant, led her into the castle, then he took a seat at his desk to wait for them, feeling uncharacteristically anxious. He had been assured that in the field of genetic botany, she was the best. Meaning she could very well be their last hope.

Specialist after specialist had been unable to diagnose or effectively treat the blight plaguing their crops. A disease that had begun in the east fields, and spread to affect not only a good portion of the royal family's land, but had recently been reported in surrounding farms, as well. Unchecked, the effects could be financially devastating to their agriculturally based economy.

His family—hell, the entire country—was counting on him to find a way to fix it.

Talk about pressure. He used to believe that his older brother, Christian, the crown prince, had it rough, carrying the burden of one day taking over as ruler, and the responsibility of marrying and producing a royal heir. But to Aaron's surprise, after a slightly rocky start, Chris seemed to be embracing his new title as husband.

For Aaron, the thought of tying himself down to one woman for the rest of his life gave him cold chills. Not that he didn't love women. He just loved lots of different women. And when the novelty of one wore thin, he liked having the option of moving on to something new. Although, now that Chris was blissfully married off, their mother, the queen, had taken an active and unsettling interest in Aaron's love life. He never knew there were so many eligible young women with royal blood, and his mother seemed hell-bent on setting him up with every single one of them.

She would figure out eventually that all the meddling in the world wouldn't bring him any closer to the altar. At least, he hoped she would. She could instead focus on marrying off his twin sisters, Anne and Louisa.

Several minutes passed before there was a rap at Aaron's office door. Undoubtedly Derek had been explaining policy for meeting members of the royal family to their guest. What she should and shouldn't do or say. It could be a bit overwhelming. Especially for someone who had never been in the presence of royalty before.

"Come in," he called.

The door opened and Derek appeared, followed

closely by Miss Montgomery. Aaron rose from his chair to greet her, noticing right away her height. He was just over six feet tall, and in flat-heeled, conservative loafers she stood nearly eye level. It was difficult to see her figure under the loose khaki pants and baggy, cable-knit sweater, although she gave the impression of being quite slim. *Too* slim, even. All sharp and angular.

Missing was the lab coat, pocket protector and cola-bottle glasses one might expect from a scientist. She wore no makeup or jewelry, and was for all accounts quite plain, yet she was undeniably female. Attractive in a simple way. Cute and girlish. Although at twenty-five, she was definitely a woman.

"Your Highness," Derek said, "May I introduce Miss Olivia Montgomery, of the United States." He turned to Miss Montgomery. "Miss Montgomery, may I present Prince Aaron Felix Gastel Alexander of Thomas Isle."

Miss Montgomery stuck her hand out to shake his, then, realizing her error, snatched it back and dipped into an awkward, slightly wobbly curtsy instead, her cheeks coloring an enchanting shade of pink. "It's an honor to be here, sir—I mean, Your Highness."

Her voice was softer than he'd expected. Low and breathy, and dare he say a little sexy. He'd always found an American accent undeniably appealing.

"The honor is mine," he said, reaching out for a shake. She hesitated a second, then accepted his hand. Her hands were slender and fine-boned, with long fingers that wrapped around his with a surprisingly firm grip. Her skin was warm and soft, her nails short but neatly filed.

She gazed at him with eyes an intriguing shade— not quite brown, and not quite green—and so large and inquisitive they seemed to take up half her face. Everything about her was a little overexaggerated and…unexpected.

But she couldn't be any less his type. He preferred his women small and soft in all the right places, and the more beautiful the better. Not particularly smart, either, because frankly, he wasn't in it for the conversation. The fewer brains, the less likely he was to become attached. As long as she could navigate a golf course or squash court, or rock a pair of cross-country skis. Sailing experience was a plus, as well, and if she could climb a rock wall, he would be in sheer heaven.

Somehow he didn't see Miss Montgomery as the athletic type.

"I'll be in my office if you need me, sir," Derek told him, then slipped out of the room, closing the door behind him. As it snapped shut, he could swear he saw Miss Montgomery flinch.

He gestured to the chair opposite his desk. "Miss Montgomery, make yourself comfortable."

She set her backpack on the floor beside her and sat awkwardly on the very edge of the cushion. She folded her hands in her lap, then unfolded them. Then she tucked them around the sides of her thighs and under her legs. She looked very *un*comfortable.

"I apologize for being so late," she said.

He perched on the corner of his desk. "I hear you hit some bad weather on the way over."

She nodded. "It was a bumpy flight. And I'm not real crazy about flying to begin with. In fact, I might look into taking a ship home."

"Can I offer you a drink, Miss Montgomery?"

"No, thank you. And please, call me Liv. Everyone does."

"All right, Liv. And because we'll be spending quite some time together, you should call me Aaron."

She hesitated, then asked, "Is that...allowed?"

He grinned. "I assure you, it's perfectly acceptable."

She nodded, her head a little wobbly on the end of a very long and slender neck. She had the kind of throat made for stroking and nibbling. But somehow he didn't see her as the nibbling type. She had shy and repressed written all over her. No doubt, he could teach her a thing or two. Not that he intended to. Or even possessed the desire.

Well, maybe just a little, but purely out of curiosity.

"My family apologizes that they couldn't be here to greet you," he told her. "They're in England to see my father's cardiologist. They'll be back Friday."

"I look forward to meeting them," she said, although she sounded more wary than enthusiastic.

She had no reason to be apprehensive. In the history of his father's reign as king, her visit might very well be the most anticipated and appreciated. Not that she was offering her services for free. They had agreed to make a handsome donation to fund her research. Personally she hadn't asked for anything more than room and board. No special amenities, or even a personal maid to tend to her care.

"I'm told that you looked at the disease samples we sent you," he said.

She nodded, not so wobbly this time. "I did. As well as the data from the other specialists."

"And what conclusion have you drawn?"

"You have yourself a very unusual, very resistant strain of disease that I've never seen before. And trust me when I say I've pretty much seen them all."

"Your references are quite impressive. I've been assured that if anyone can diagnose the problem, it's you."

"There is no *if.*" She looked him directly in the eye and said firmly, "It's simply a matter of *when.*"

Her confidence, and the forceful tone with which she spoke, nearly knocked him backward.

Well, he hadn't seen that coming. It was almost as though someone flipped a switch inside of her and a completely different woman emerged. She sat a little straighter and her voice sounded stronger. Just like that, he gained an entirely new level of respect for her.

"Have you thought about my suggestion to stop all agricultural exports?" she asked.

That was *all* he'd been thinking about. "Even the unaffected crops?"

"I'm afraid so."

"Is that really necessary?"

"For all we know, it could be lying dormant in the soil of areas that *appear* unaffected. And until we know what this thing is, we don't want it to get off the island."

He knew she was right, but the financial repercussions would sting. "That means we have only until the next season, less than five months, to identify the disease and find an environmentally friendly cure."

Environmentally friendly so that they could maintain their reputation as a totally organic, green island. Millions had been spent to radically alter the way every farmer grew his crops. It was what set them apart from other distributors and made them a valuable commodity.

"Can it be done in that time frame?" he asked.

"The truth is, I don't know. These things can take time."

It wasn't what he wanted to hear, but he appreciated her honesty. He'd wanted her to fly in, have the problem solved in a week or two, then be on her way, making him look like a hero in not only his family, but also his country's eyes.

So much for that delusion of grandeur.

"Once I get set up in the lab and have a few days to study the rest of the data, I may be able to give you some sort of time frame," she said.

"We have a student from the university on standby, should you need an assistant."

"I'll need someone to take samples, but in the lab I prefer to work alone. You have all the equipment I need?"

"Everything on your list." He rose to his feet. "I can show you to your room and give you time to settle in."

She stood, as well, smoothing the front of her slacks with her palms. He couldn't help wondering what she was hiding behind that bulky sweater. Were those breasts he saw? And hips? Maybe she wasn't as sharp and angular as he'd first thought.

"If you don't mind," she said, "I'd rather get right to work."

He gestured to the door. "Of course. I'll take you right to the lab."

She certainly didn't waste any time, did she? And he was relieved to know that she seemed determined to help.

The sooner they cured this blight, the sooner they could all breathe easy again.

Two

Liv followed her host through the castle, heart thumping like mad, praying she didn't do something stupid like trip over her own feet and fall flat on her face.

Prince Aaron was, by far, the most beautiful man she had ever laid eyes on. His hair so dark and soft-looking, his eyes a striking, mesmerizing shade of green, his full lips always turned up in a sexy smile.

He had the deep and smoky voice of a radio DJ and a body to die for. A muscular backside under dark tailored slacks. Wide shoulders and bulging pecs encased in midnight-blue cashmere. As she followed him through the castle she felt hypnotized by the fluid grace with which he moved.

He was...perfect. An eleven on a scale of one to

ten. And the antithesis of the scientists and geeks she was used to keeping company with. Like William, her fiancé—or at least he would be her fiancé if she decided to accept the proposal of marriage he had stunned her with just last night in the lab.

Fifteen years her senior and her mentor since college, Will wasn't especially handsome, and he was more studious than sexy, but he was kind and sweet and generous. The truth was, his proposal had come so far out of left field that it had nearly given her whiplash. They had never so much as kissed, other than a friendly peck on the cheek on holidays or special occasions. But she respected him immensely and loved him as a friend. So she had promised to give his proposal serious thought while she was away. Even though, when he'd kissed her goodbye at the airport—a real kiss with lips and tongue—she hadn't exactly seen fireworks. But sexual attraction was overrated and fleeting at best. They had respect and a deep sense of friendship.

Although she couldn't help wondering if she would be settling.

Yeah, right. Like she had a mob of other men pounding down her door. She couldn't even recall the last time she'd been on a date. And sex, well, it had been so long she wasn't sure she even remembered how. Not that it had been smoking hot anyhow. The one man she'd slept with in college had been a budding nuclear physicist, and more concerned with mathematical equations than figuring out sexual complexities. She bet Prince Aaron knew his way around a woman's body.

Right, Liv, and I suppose the prince is going to show you.

The thought was so ridiculous she nearly laughed out loud. What would a gorgeous, sexy prince see in a nerdy, totally *unsexy* woman like her?

"So, what do you think of our island?" Aaron asked as they descended the stairs together.

"What I've seen of it is beautiful. And the castle isn't at all what I expected."

"What did you expect?"

"Honestly, I thought it would be kind of dark and dank." In reality, it was light and airy and beautifully decorated. And so enormous! A person could get hopelessly lost wandering the long, carpeted halls. She could hardly believe she would be spending weeks, maybe even months, there. "I expected stone walls and suits of armor in the halls."

The prince chuckled, a deep, throaty sound. "We're a bit more modern than that. You'll find the guest rooms have all the amenities and distinction you would expect from a five-star hotel."

Not that she would know the difference, seeing as how she'd never been in anything more luxurious than a Days Inn.

"Although…" He paused and looked over at her. "The only feasible place for the lab, short of building a new facility on the grounds, was the basement."

She shrugged. It wouldn't be the first time she'd worked in a basement lab. "That's fine with me."

"It used to be a dungeon."

Her interest piqued. "Seriously?"

He nodded. "Very dark and dank at one time, complete with chains on the wall and torture devices."

She gazed at him skeptically. "You're joking, right?"

"Completely serious. It's been updated since then of course. We use it for food and dry storage, and the wine cellar. The laundry facilities are down there, as well. I think you'll be impressed with the lab. Not dark or dank at all."

Because the majority of her time would be spent staring in a microscope or at a computer screen, what the lab looked like didn't matter all that much to her. As long as it was functional.

He led her through an enormous kitchen bustling with activity and rich with the scents of fresh baked bread and scintillating spices. Her stomach rumbled and she tried to recall the last time she'd eaten. She'd been way too nervous to eat the meal offered on the plane.

There would be time for food later.

Aaron stopped in front of a large wood door that she assumed led to the basement. "There's a separate employee entrance that the laundry staff use. It leads outside, to the back of the castle. But as a guest, you'll use the family entrance."

"Okay."

He reached for the handle but didn't open the door. "There is one thing I should probably warn you about."

Warn her? That didn't sound good. "Yes?"

"As I said, the basement has been updated."

"But…?"

"It did used to be a dungeon."

She wasn't getting his point. "Okay."

"A lot of people died down there."

Was she going to trip over bodies on her way to the lab or something? "Recently?"

He laughed. "No, of course not."

Then she wasn't seeing the problem. "So…?"

"That bothers some people. And the staff is convinced it's haunted."

Liv looked at him as though he'd gone completely off his rocker.

"I take it you don't believe in ghosts," Aaron said.

"The existence of spirits, or an afterlife, have never been proven scientifically."

He should have expected as much from a scientist. "Well, then, I guess you have nothing to fear."

"Do you?" she asked.

"Believe in ghosts?" Truthfully, he'd never felt so much as a cold draft down there, but people had sworn to hearing disembodied voices and seeing ghostly emanations. There were some members of the staff who refused to even set foot on the stairs. Also there was an unusually high turnover rate among the laundry workers. But he was convinced that it was more likely overactive imaginations than anything otherworldly. "I guess you could say I try to keep an open mind."

He opened the door and gestured her down. The stairwell was narrow and steep, the wood steps creaky under their feet as they descended.

"It is a little spooky," she admitted.

At the bottom was a series of passageways that led to several different wings. The walls down here were still fashioned out of stone and mortar, although well lit, ventilated and clean.

"Storage and the wine cellar are that way," he said, pointing to the passages on the left. "Laundry is straight ahead down the center passage, and the lab is this way."

He led her to the right, around a corner to a shiny metal door with a thick glass window that to him looked completely out of place with its surroundings. He punched in his security code to unlock it, pulled it open and hit the light switch. The instant the lights flickered on he heard a soft gasp behind him, and turned to see Liv looking in wide-eyed awe at all the equipment they'd gotten on loan from various facilities on the island and mainland. The way one might view priceless art. Or a natural disaster.

She brushed past him into the room. "This is perfect," she said in that soft, breathy voice, running her hands along pieces of equipment whose purpose he couldn't begin to imagine. Slow and tender, as if she were stroking a lover's flesh.

Damn. He could get turned on watching her do that, imagining those hands roaming over him.

If she were his type at all, which she wasn't. Besides, he wasn't lacking for female companionship.

"It's small," he said.

"No, it's perfect." She turned to him and smiled, a dreamy look on her face. "I wish my lab back home were this complete."

He was surprised that it wasn't. "I was under the impression that you were doing some groundbreaking research."

"Yes, but funding is an issue no matter what kind of work you're doing. Especially when you're an independent, like me."

"There must be someone willing to fund your research."

"Many, but there's *way* too much bureaucracy in the private sector. I prefer to do things my way."

"Then our donation should go far."

She nodded eagerly. "The truth is, a few more weeks and I might have been homeless. You called in the nick of time."

She crossed the room to the metal shipping containers that had preceded her arrival by several days. "I see my things made it safely."

"Do you need help unpacking?"

She vigorously shook her head. "There are sen-sitive materials and equipment in here. I'd rather do it myself."

That seemed like an awful lot of work for one person. "The offer for the assistant is still good. I can have someone here Friday morning."

She looked at her watch, her face scrunching with confusion. "And what's today? The time change from the U.S. has me totally screwed up."

"It's Tuesday. Five o'clock."

"P.M.?"

"Yes. In fact, dinner is at seven."

She nodded, but still looked slightly confused.

"Out of curiosity, when was the last time you slept?"

She scrunched her face again, studied her watch for a second, then shrugged and said, "I'm not sure. Twenty hours at least. Probably more."

"You must be exhausted."

"I'm used to it. I keep long hours in the lab."

Twenty hours was an awfully long time, even for a workaholic, and he'd traveled often enough to know what jet lag could do to a person. Especially someone unaccustomed to long plane trips. "Maybe before you tackle unpacking the lab you should at least take a nap."

"I'm fine, really. Although, I guess I wouldn't mind a quick change of clothes."

"Why don't I show you to your room."

She looked longingly at all of the shiny new equipment, then nodded and said, "All right."

He switched off the lights and shut the door, hearing it lock automatically behind him.

"Will I get my own code?" she asked.

"Of course. You'll have full access to whatever and wherever you need."

He led Liv back through the kitchen and up the stairs to the third floor, to the guest rooms. She looked a bit lost when they finally reached her door.

"The castle is so big and confusing," she said.

"It's not so bad once you learn your way around."

"I don't exactly have a great sense of direction. Don't be surprised if you find me aimlessly wandering the halls."

"I'll have Derek print you up a map." He opened her door and gestured her in.

"It's beautiful," she said in that soft, breathy voice. "So pretty."

Far too feminine and fluffy for his taste, with its flowered walls and frilly drapes, but their female guests seemed to appreciate it. Although he never would have pegged Liv as the girly-girl type. She was just too…analytical. Too practical. On the surface anyhow.

"The bathroom and closet are that way," he said, gesturing to the door across the room. But Liv's attention was on the bed.

"It looks so comfortable." She crossed the room to it and ran one hand over the flowered duvet. "So soft."

She was a tactile sort of woman. Always stroking

and touching things. And he couldn't help but wonder how those hands would feel touching him.

"Why don't you take it for a spin," he said. "The lab can wait."

"Oh, I shouldn't," she protested, but she was already kicking off her shoes and crawling on top of the covers. She settled back against the pillows and sighed blissfully. Her eyes slipped closed. "Oh, this is heavenly."

He hadn't actually meant right that second. The average guest would have waited until he'd left the room, not flop down into bed right in front of him. But he could see that there was nothing average about Olivia Montgomery.

At least she hadn't undressed first. Not that he wasn't curious to see what she was hiding under those clothes. He was beginning to think there was much more to Liv than she let show.

"You'll find your bags in the closet. Are you sure you wouldn't like a maid to unpack for you?"

"I can do it," she said, her voice soft and sleepy.

"If you change your mind, let me know. Other than that, you should have everything you need. There are fresh towels and linens in the bathroom. As well as toiletries. If you need anything else, day or night, just pick up the phone. The kitchen is always open. You're also welcome to use the exercise room or game room, day or night. We want you to feel completely comfortable here."

He walked to the window and pushed the curtain aside, letting in a shaft of late-afternoon sunshine. "You have quite a lovely view of the ocean and the gardens from here. Although there isn't much to see in the gardens this time of year. We could take a walk out there tomorrow."

Or not, he thought, when she didn't answer him. Then he heard a soft rumbling sound from the vicinity of the bed.

She had turned on her side and lay all curled up in a ball, hugging the pillow. He walked over to the bed and realized that she was sound asleep.

"Liv," he called softly, but she didn't budge. Apparently she was more tired than she'd realized.

He found a spare blanket in the closet, noticing her luggage while he was in there, and the conspicuously small amount of it. Just two average-size bags that had seen better days. The typical female guest, especially one there for an extended stay, brought a whole slew of bags.

He reminded himself once again that Liv was not the typical royal guest. And, he was a little surprised to realize, he liked that about her. It might very well be a refreshing change.

He walked back to the bed and covered her with the blanket, then, for reasons he couldn't begin to understand, felt compelled to just look at her for a moment. The angles of her face softened when she slept, making her appear young and vulnerable.

She's not your type, he reminded himself.

If he was going to be honest with himself, his "type" had plenty to offer physically, but intellectually, he was usually left feeling bored and unfulfilled. Maybe it was time for a change of pace.

Seducing a woman like Liv might be just what he needed to spice things up.

Three

It was official. Liv was lost.

She stood in an unfamiliar hallway on what she was pretty sure was the second floor, looking for the staircase that would lead her down to the kitchen. She'd been up and down two separate sets of stairs already this morning, and had wandered through a dozen different hallways. Either there were two identical paintings of the same stodgy-looking old man in a military uniform, or she'd been in this particular hallway more than once.

She looked up one end to the other, hopelessly turned around, wondering which direction she should take. She felt limp with hunger, and the backpack full of books and papers hung like a dead weight off one shoulder. If she didn't eat soon, her blood sugar was going to dip into the critical zone.

She did a very scientific, eenie-meenie-minie-moe, then went left around the corner and plowed face-first into a petite, red-haired maid carrying a pile of clean linens. The force of the collision knocked her off balance and the linens fell to the carpet.

"Oh my gosh! I'm so sorry!" Liv crouched down to pick them up. "I wasn't watching where I was going."

"It's no problem, miss," the maid said in a charming Irish brogue, kneeling down to help. "You must be our scientist from the States. Miss Montgomery?"

Liv piled the last slightly disheveled sheet in her arms and they both stood. "Yes, I am."

The maid looked her up and down. "Well, you don't much look like a scientist."

"Yeah, I hear that a lot." And she was always tempted to ask what she did look like, but she was a little afraid of the answer she might get.

"I'm Elise," the maid said. "If you need anything at all, I'm the one to be asking."

"Could you tell me where to find the kitchen? I'm starving."

"Of course, miss. Follow this hallway down and make a left. The stairs will be on your right, about halfway down the hall. Take them down one flight, then turn right. The kitchen is just down the way."

"A left and two rights. Got it."

Elise smiled. "Enjoy your stay, miss."

She disappeared in the direction Liv had just come from. Liv followed her directions and actually found the kitchen, running into—although not literally this time—Prince Aaron's assistant just outside the door.

"Off to work already?" he asked.

"Looking for food actually. I missed dinner last night."

"Why don't you join the prince in the family dining room."

"Okay." She could spend another twenty minutes or so looking for the dining room, and possibly collapse from hunger, or ask for directions. "Could you show me where it is?"

He smiled and gestured in the opposite direction from the kitchen. "Right this way."

It was just around the corner. A surprisingly small but luxurious space with French doors overlooking the grounds. A thick blanket of leaves in brilliant red, orange and yellow carpeted the expansive lawn and the sky was a striking shade of pink as the sun rose above the horizon.

At one end of a long, rectangular cherry table, leaning casually in a chair with a newspaper propped beside him, sat Prince Aaron. He looked up when they entered the room, then rose to his feet.

"Well, good morning," he said with a smile, and her stomach suddenly bound up into a nervous knot.

"Shall I take your bag?" Derek asked her.

Liv shook her head. That backpack had all of her research. She never trusted it to anyone else. "I've got it, thanks."

"Well, then, enjoy your breakfast," Derek said, leaving her alone with the prince. Just the two of them.

Only then did it occur to her that she might have been better off eating alone. What would they say to each other? What could they possibly have in common? A prince and an orphan?

The prince, on the other hand, looked completely at ease. In jeans and a flannel shirt he was dressed much more casually than the day before. He looked so...*normal*. Almost out of place in the elegant room.

He pulled out the chair beside his own. "Have a seat."

As she sat, she found herself enveloped in the subtle, spicy scent of his aftershave. She tried to recall if William, her possibly-soon-to-be fiancé, wore aftershave or cologne. If he had, she'd never noticed.

The prince's fingers brushed the backs of her shoulders as he eased her chair in and she nearly jolted against the sudden and intense zing of awareness.

He was *touching* her.

Get a grip, Liv. It wasn't like he was coming on to her. He was being *polite* and she was acting like a schoolgirl with a crush. Even when she *was* a schoolgirl she had never acted this way. She'd been above the temptation that had gotten so many other girls from high school in trouble. Or as her last foster mom, Marsha, used to put it, *in the family way.*

Then the prince placed both hands on her shoulders and her breath caught in her lungs.

His hands felt big and solid and warm. You are not going to blush, she told herself, but already she could feel a rush of color searing her cheeks, which only multiplied her embarrassment.

It was nothing more than a friendly gesture, and here she was having a hot flash. Could this be any more humiliating?

"Do you prefer coffee or tea?" he asked.

"Coffee, please," she said, but it came out high and squeaky.

He leaned past her to reach for the carafe on the table, and as he did, the back of her head bumped the wall of his chest. She was sure it was just her imagination, but she swore she felt his body heat, heard the steady thump of his heart beating. Her own heart was hammering so hard that it felt as though it would beat its way out of her chest.

Shouldn't a servant be doing that? she wondered as he poured her a cup and slid it in front of her. Then he *finally* backed away and returned to his chair, resuming the same casual, relaxed stance—and she took her first full breath since she'd sat down.

"Would you care for breakfast?" he asked.

"Please," she said, though her throat was so tight,

she could barely get air to pass through, much less food. But if she didn't eat something soon, she would go into hypoglycemic shock. She just hoped she didn't humiliate herself further. She was so used to eating at her desk in the lab, or in a rush over the kitchen sink, she was a little rusty when it came to the rules of etiquette. What if she used the wrong fork, or chewed with her mouth open?

He rang a bell, and within seconds a man dressed in characteristic butler apparel seemed to materialize from thin air.

"Breakfast for our guest, Geoffrey," he said.

Geoffrey nodded and slipped away as stealthily as he'd emerged.

Liv folded her hands in her lap and, because most of her time was spent huddled over her laptop or a microscope, reminded herself to sit up straight.

"I trust you slept well," the prince said.

She nodded. "I woke at seven thinking it was last night, then I looked outside and noticed that the sun was on the wrong side of the horizon."

"I guess you were more tired than you thought."

"I guess so. But I'm anxious to get down to the lab. You said I'll get a password for the door?"

"Yes, in fact…" He pulled a slip of paper from his shirt pocket and handed it to her. As she took it, she felt lingering traces of heat from his body and her cheeks flushed deeper red.

She unfolded the paper and looked at the code—

a simple seven-digit number—then handed it back to him.

"Don't you want to memorize it?" he asked.

"I just did."

His eyes widened with surprise, and he folded the paper and put it back in his pocket. "Your ID badge will be ready this morning. You'll want to wear it all the time, so you're not stopped by security. It will grant you full access to the castle, with the exception of the royal family's quarters of course, and any of our agricultural facilities or fields."

"You mentioned something about a map of the castle," she said, too embarrassed to admit that she'd actually gotten lost on her way to breakfast.

"Of course. I'll have Derek print one up for you."

"Thank you."

"So," Prince Aaron said, lounging back in his chair and folding his hands in his lap. "Tell me about yourself. About your family."

"Oh, I don't have any family."

Confusion wrinkled his brow. "Everyone has family."

"I'm an orphan. I was raised in the New York foster care system."

His expression sobered. "I'm sorry, I didn't know."

She shrugged. "No reason to be sorry. It's not your fault."

"Do you mind my asking what happened to your parents?"

It's not like her past was some big secret. She had always embraced who she was, and where she came from. "No, I don't mind. My mom died a long time ago. She was a drug addict. Social services took me away from her when I was three."

"What about your father?"

"I don't have one."

At the subtle lift of his brow, she realized how odd that sounded, like she was the product of a virgin birth or something. When the more likely scenario was that her mother had been turning tricks for drug money, and whoever the man was, he probably had no idea he'd fathered a child. And probably wouldn't care if he did know.

She told the prince, "Of course *someone* was my father. He just wasn't listed on my birth certificate."

"No grandparents? Aunts or uncles?"

She shrugged again. "Maybe. Somewhere. No one ever came forward to claim me."

"Have you ever tried to find them?"

"I figure if they didn't want me back then, they wouldn't want me now, either."

He frowned, as though he found the idea disturbing.

"It's really not a big deal," she assured him. "I mean, it's just the way it's always been. I learned to fend for myself."

"But you did have a foster family."

"Families," she corrected. "I had twelve of them."

His eyes widened. "Twelve? Why so many?"

"I was…difficult."

A grin ticked at the corner of his mouth. *"Difficult?"*

"I was very independent." And maybe a little arrogant. None of her foster parents seemed to appreciate a child who was smarter than them and not afraid to say so, and one who had little interest in following their *rules.* "I was emancipated when I was fifteen."

"You were on your own at *fifteen?*"

She nodded. "Right after I graduated from high school."

He frowned and shook his head, as if it was a difficult concept for him to grasp. "Forgive me for asking, but how does an orphan become a botanical geneticist?"

"A *lot* of hard work. I had some awesome teachers who really encouraged me in high school. Then I got college scholarships and grants. And I had a mentor." One she might actually be marrying, but she left that part out. And that was a big *might.* William had never given her this breathless, squishy-kneed feeling when he touched her. She never felt much of anything beyond comfortable companionship.

But wasn't that more important than sexual attraction? Although if she really wanted to marry William, would she be spending so much time talking herself into it?

The butler reappeared with a plate that was all but

overflowing with food. Plump sausages and eggs over easy, waffles topped with cream and fresh fruit and flaky croissants with a dish of fresh jam. The scents had her stomach rumbling and her mouth watering. "It looks delicious. Thank you."

He nodded and left. Not a very talkative fellow.

"Aren't you eating?" she asked Prince Aaron.

"I already ate, but please, go ahead. You must be famished."

Starving. And oddly enough, the prince had managed to put her totally at ease, just as he'd done the night before. He was just so laid-back and casual. So…*nice*. Unlike most men, he didn't seem to be put off or intimidated by her intelligence. And when he asked a question, he wasn't just asking to be polite. He really listened, his eyes never straying from hers while she spoke. She wasn't used to talking about herself, but he seemed genuinely interested in learning more about her. Unlike the scientists and scholars who were usually too wrapped up in their research to show any interest in learning about who she was as a person.

It was a nice change of pace.

The prince's cell phone rang and he unclipped it from his belt to look at the display. Concern flashed across his face. "I'm sorry. I have to take this," he said, rising to his feet. "Please excuse me."

She watched him walk briskly from the room and realized she was actually sorry to see him go. She couldn't recall the last time she'd had a conversation with a man who hadn't revolved in some way around her research, or funding. Not even William engaged in social dialogue very often. It was nice to just talk to someone for a change. Someone who really listened.

Or maybe spending time with the prince was a bad idea. She'd been here less than a day and already she was nursing a pretty serious crush.

Four

"Any news?" Aaron asked when he answered his brother's call.

"We have results back from Father's heart function test," Christian told him.

Aaron's own heart seemed to seize in his chest. Their father, the king, had been hooked to a portable heart pump four months ago after the last of a series of damaging attacks. The procedure was still in the experimental stages and carried risks, but the doctors were hopeful that it would give his heart a chance to heal from years of heart disease damage.

It was their last hope.

Aaron had wanted to accompany his family to

England, but his father had insisted he stay behind to greet Miss Montgomery. *For the good of the country,* he'd said. Knowing he'd been right, Aaron hadn't argued.

Duty first, that was their motto.

"Has there been any improvement?" Aaron asked his brother, not sure if he was ready to hear the answer.

"He's gone from twenty percent heart capacity to thirty-five percent."

"So it's working?"

"Even better than they expected. The doctors are cautiously optimistic."

"That's fantastic!" Aaron felt as though every muscle in his body simultaneously sighed with relief. As a child he had been labeled the easygoing one. Nothing ever bothered Aaron, his parents liked to brag. He was like Teflon. Trouble hit the surface, then slid off without sticking. But he wasn't nearly as impervious to stress as everyone liked to believe. He internalized everything, let it eat away at him. Especially lately, with not only their father's health, but also the diseased crops, and the mysterious, threatening e-mails that had been sporadically showing up in his and his siblings' in-boxes from a fellow who referred to himself, of all things, as the Gingerbread Man. He had not only harassed them through e-mail, but also managed to breach security and trespass on the castle grounds, slipping in and out like a ghost despite added security.

There had been times lately when Aaron felt he was days away from a mandatory trip to the rubber room.

But his father's health was now one concern he could safely, if only temporarily, put aside.

"How much longer do they think he'll be on the pump?" he asked his brother.

"At least another four months. Although probably longer. They'll retest him in the spring."

Aaron had been hoping sooner. On the pump he was susceptible to blood clots and strokes and in rare cases, life-threatening infections. "How is he doing?"

"They had to remove the pump to test his heart and there were minor complications when they reinserted it. Something about scar tissue. He's fine now, but he's still in recovery. They want to keep him here an extra few days. Probably middle of next week. Just to be safe."

As much as Aaron wanted to see his father home, the hospital was the best place for him now. "Is Mother staying with him?"

"Of course. She hasn't left his side. Melissa, the girls and I will be returning Friday as planned."

The girls being Louisa and Anne, their twin sisters, and Melissa, Chris's wife of only four months. In fact, it was on their wedding night that the king had the attack that necessitated the immediate intervention of the heart pump. Though it was in no way Chris and Melissa's fault, they still felt responsible for his sudden downturn.

"Now that Father is improving, maybe it's time you and Melissa rescheduled your honeymoon," Aaron told him.

"Not until he's off the pump altogether," Chris insisted, which didn't surprise Aaron. Chris had always been the responsible sibling. Of course, as crown prince, slacking off had never been an option. But while some people may have resented having their entire life dictated for them, Chris embraced his position. If he felt restricted by his duties, he never said so.

Aaron wished he could say the same.

"Did Miss Montgomery arrive safely?" Chris asked.

"She did. Although her flight was delayed by weather."

"What was your first impression of her?"

He almost told his brother that she was very cute. And despite what she'd told him, he couldn't imagine her as ever being difficult. She was so quiet and unassuming. But he didn't think that was the sort of *impression* Chris was asking for. "She seems very capable."

"Her references all checked out? Her background investigation was clean?"

Did he honestly think Aaron would have hired her otherwise? But he bit back the snarky comment on the tip of his tongue. Until their father was well, Chris was in charge, and that position deserved the same respect Aaron would have shown the king.

"Squeaky-clean," Aaron assured his brother. "And after meeting her, I feel confident she'll find a cure."

"Everyone will be relieved to hear that. I think we should—" There was commotion in the background, then Aaron heard his sister-in-law's voice, followed by a short, muted conversation, as though his brother had put a hand over the phone.

"Is everything okay, Chris?"

"Yes, sorry," Chris said, coming back on the line. "I have to go. They're wheeling Father back to his room. I'll call you later."

"Send everyone my love," Aaron told him, then disconnected, wishing he could be there with his family. But someone needed to stay behind and hold the fort.

He hooked his phone on his belt and walked back to the dining room. Liv was still there eating her breakfast. She had wiped out everything but half of a croissant, which she was slathering with jam. He didn't think he'd ever seen a woman polish off such a hearty meal. Especially a woman so slim and fit.

For a minute he just stood there watching her. She had dressed in jeans and a sweater and wore her hair pulled back into a ponytail again. He couldn't help grinning when he recalled the way she seized up as he put his hands on her shoulders, and the deep blush in her cheeks. He knew he wasn't exactly playing fair, and it was wrong to toy with her, but he'd never met a woman who wore her emotions so blatantly on her sleeve. There was little doubt that she was attracted to him.

She looked up, saw him standing there and smiled. A sweet, genuine smile that encompassed her entire face. She wasn't what he would consider beautiful or stunning, but she had a wholesome, natural prettiness about her that he found undeniably appealing.

"Sorry about that," he told her, walking to the table.

"S'okay," she said with a shrug, polishing off the last of her croissant and chasing it down with a swallow of coffee. "I think that was the most delicious breakfast I've ever eaten."

"I'll pass your compliments on to the chef." Instead of sitting down, he rested his arms on the back of his chair. "I'm sorry to say you won't be meeting my parents until next week."

Her smile vanished. "Oh. Is everything all right?"

"My father's doctors want to keep him a few days longer. Just in case."

"It's his heart?" she asked, and at his questioning look, added, "When I was offered the position, I looked up your family on the Internet. A ton of stuff came back about your father's health."

He should have figured as much. The king's health had been big news after he collapsed at Chris's wedding reception. But other than to say he had a heart "problem," no specific information had been disclosed about his condition.

"He has advanced heart disease," Aaron told her.

Concern creased her brow. "If you don't mind my asking, what's the prognosis?"

"Actually, he's in an experimental program and we're hopeful that he'll make a full recovery."

"He's getting a transplant?"

"He has a rare blood type. The odds of finding a donor are astronomical." He explained the portable heart pump and how it would take over all heart function so the tissue would have time to heal. "He's very fortunate. Less than a dozen people worldwide are part of the study."

"Heart disease is genetic. I'll bet you and your siblings are very health-conscious."

"Probably not as much as we should be, but the queen sees to it that we eat a proper diet. You know how mothers are." Only after the words were out did he realize that no, she probably didn't know, because she'd never had a real mother. He felt a slash of guilt for the thoughtless comment. But if it bothered her, she didn't let it show.

She dabbed her lips with her napkin, then set it on the table beside her plate. Glancing at the watch on her slender wrist, she said, "I should get down to the lab. I have a lot of unpacking to do."

He stepped behind her to pull her chair out, and could swear he saw her tense the slightest bit when his fingers brushed her shoulders. She rose to her feet and edged swiftly out of his reach.

He suppressed a smile. "You're sure you don't need help unpacking?"

She shook her head. "No, thank you."

"Well, then, lunch is at one."

"Oh, I don't eat lunch. I'm usually too busy."

"All right, then, dinner is at seven sharp. You do eat dinner?"

She smiled. "On occasion, yes."

He returned the smile. "Then I'll see you at seven."

She walked to the door, then stopped for a second, looking one way, then the other, as though she wasn't sure which direction to take.

"Left," he reminded her.

She turned to him and smiled. "Thanks."

"I'll remind Derek to get you that map."

"Thank you." She stood there another second, and he thought she might say something else, then she shook her head and disappeared from view.

The woman was a puzzle. Thoughtful and confident one minute, then shy and awkward the next. And he realized, not for the first time, that she was one puzzle he'd like to solve.

After a long morning in the fields and an afternoon in the largest of their greenhouse facilities, Aaron looked forward to a quiet dinner and an evening spent with their guest. Even though normally he would arrange some sort of physical, recreational activity like squash or tennis or even just a walk in the gardens, he was more interested in just talking to Liv. Learning more about her life, her past. She was the first woman in a long time whom he'd found both attractive and intellectually stimulating. And after a few drinks to loosen her up a bit, who knew where the conversation might lead.

He changed from his work clothes and stopped by her room on his way downstairs to escort her to the dining room, but she wasn't there. Expecting her to already be at the table waiting for him, he headed down, but found all of the chairs empty.

Geoffrey stepped in from the pantry.

"Have you seen Miss Montgomery?" Aaron asked.

"As far as I know she's still in the lab, Your Highness."

Aaron looked at his watch. It was already two minutes past seven. Maybe she'd lost track of the time. "Will you wait to serve the first course?"

Geoffrey gave him a stiff nod. "Of course, Your Highness."

A servant of the royal family as long as Aaron could remember, Geoffrey prided himself on keeping them on a strict and efficient schedule. Tardiness was not appreciated or tolerated.

"I'll go get her," Aaron said. He headed through the kitchen, savoring the tantalizing scent of spicy grilled chicken and peppers, and down the stairs to the lab. Through the door window he could see Liv, sitting in front of a laptop computer, typing furiously, papers scattered around her.

He punched in his code and the door swung open,

but as he stepped into the room, Liv didn't so much as glance his way.

Her sweater was draped over the back of her chair and she wore a simple, white, long-sleeved T-shirt with the sleeves pushed up to her elbows. Her ponytail had drooped over the course of the day and hung slightly askew down her back.

"It's past seven," he said softly, so as not to startle her, but got no response. "Liv?" he said, a little louder his time, and still she didn't acknowledge that he was there.

"Olivia," he said, louder this time, and she jolted in her chair, head whipping around. For a second she looked completely lost, as though she had no clue where she was, or who *he* was.

She blinked several times, then awareness slid slowly across her face. "Sorry, did you say something?"

"It's past seven."

She stared at him blankly.

"Dinner," he reminded her.

"Oh…right." She looked down at her watch, then up to her computer screen. "I guess I lost track of time."

"Are you ready?"

She glanced up at him distractedly. "Ready?"

"For *dinner.*"

"Oh, right. Sorry."

He gestured to the door. "After you."

"Oh…I think I'll pass."

"Pass?"

"Yeah. I'm right in the middle of something."

"Aren't you hungry?"

She shrugged. "I'll pop into the kitchen later and grab something."

"I can have a plate sent down for you," he said, even though he knew Geoffrey wouldn't be happy about it.

"That would be great, thanks," she said. "By the way, were you down here earlier?"

He shook his head. "I've been in the field all day."

"Does anyone else know the code for the door?"

"No, why?"

"A while ago I looked over and the door was ajar."

"Maybe you didn't close it all the way."

"I'm pretty sure I did."

"I'll have maintenance take a look at it."

"Thanks," she said, her eyes already straying back to the computer screen, fingers poised over the keys.

Geoffrey wouldn't consider it proper etiquette for a guest of the royal family to refuse a dinner invitation and then dine alone at a desk, but even he couldn't argue that Liv was not the typical royal guest.

She could eat in the bathtub for all Aaron cared, as long as she found a cure for the diseased crops.

"I'll have Geoffrey bring something right down."

She nodded vaguely, her attention back on her computer. He opened his mouth to say something else, but realized it would be a waste of breath. Liv was a million miles away, completely engrossed in whatever she was doing.

Doing her job, he reminded himself. They hadn't flown her in and paid good money so that she could spend her time amusing him.

He wondered if this was a foreshadow of what her time here would amount to. And if it was, it was going to be a challenge to seduce a woman who was never around.

Five

Liv studied the data that had been compiled so far regarding the diseased crops and compared the characteristics with other documented cases from all over the world. There were similarities, but no definitive matches yet. She wouldn't know for sure until she compared live samples from other parts of the world, which she would have to order and have shipped with expedited delivery.

She yawned and stretched, thinking maybe it was time for a short break, and heard the door click open.

She dropped her arms and turned to see Prince Aaron walking toward her. At least this time there was actually someone there. Despite a thorough check from a maintenance man, she'd found the door open several times, and once she could swear she'd seen someone peering at her through the window.

"Dinner not to your liking?" he asked.

Dinner? She vaguely remembered Geoffery coming by a while ago.

She followed the direction of his gaze to the table beside her desk and realized a plate had been left for her. Come to think of it, she was a little hungry. "Oh, I'm sure it's delicious. I was just wrapped up in what I was working on."

"I guess you were. You haven't slept, have you?"

"Slept?" She looked at her watch. "It's only ten."

"Ten *a.m.*," he said. "You've been down here all night."

"Have I?" It wouldn't be the first time she'd been so engrossed in her work that she forgot to sleep. Being in a lab with no windows probably didn't help. Unless she looked at her computer clock, which she rarely did, it was difficult to keep track of the time, to know if it was day or night. She'd been known to work for days on end, taking catnaps on her desk, and emerge from the lab with no idea what day it was, or the last time she'd eaten.

And now that she'd stopped working long enough to think about it, she realized that her neck ached and her eyes burned with exhaustion. A good sign that it was time for a break.

"When we hired you, we didn't expect you to

work 24/7," he said, but the playful smile said he was just teasing her.

"It's just the way I work." She reached back to knead the ache that was now spreading from her neck into the slope of her shoulders.

"Neck ache?" he asked, and she nodded. "I'm not surprised. Although gripping the muscles like that is only going to make it hurt more."

"It's stiff," she said.

He expelled an exasperated sigh and shook his head. "Why don't you let me do that."

Him?

She didn't think he was serious…until he stepped behind her chair. He was actually going to do it. He was going to rub her neck. He pushed her hands out of the way, then draped her ponytail over her left shoulder.

"Really," she said. "You don't have to—"

The words died in her throat as his hands settled on her shoulders.

The warmth of his skin began to seep through the cotton of her shirt and her cheeks exploded with heat. And as if that wasn't mortifyingly embarrassing and awkward enough, he slipped his fingers underneath the collar of her shirt. She sucked in a surprised breath as his hands touched her bare skin.

"The trick to relax the muscle," he told her, "is not to pinch the tension out, but to instead apply even pressure."

Yeah, right. Like there was any way she was going

to be able to relax now, with his hands touching her. His skin against her skin.

He pressed his thumbs into the muscle at the base of her neck and, against her will, a sigh of pleasure slipped from her lips. He slid his thumbs slowly upward, applying steady pressure. When he reached the base of her skull, he repeated the motion, until she felt the muscles going limp and soft.

"Feel good?" he asked.

"Mmm." Good didn't even begin to describe the way he was making her feel. Her head lolled forward and her eyes drifted shut.

"It would be better with oil," he said. "Unfortunately I don't have any handy."

The sudden image of Prince Aaron rubbing massage oil onto her naked body flashed through her brain.

Oh, no. Don't even go there, Liv. This was not a sexual come-on. He was just being polite. Although at that moment she would give anything to know what it would feel like. His oily hands sliding across her bare skin...

As if that would ever happen.

He sank his thumbs into the crevice beside her shoulder blades and a gust of breath hissed through her teeth.

"You have a knot here," he said, gently working it loose with his thumbs.

"You're really good at this," she said. "Did you take a class or something?"

"Human anatomy."

"Why would a prince in an agriculturally based field need a human anatomy class?"

"It might surprise you to learn that there was a time when I was seriously considering medical school."

Actually that didn't surprise her at all. She had the feeling there was a lot more to Prince Aaron than he let people see. "What changed your mind?" she asked.

"My family changed it for me. They needed me in the family business, so I majored in agriculture instead. End of story."

Somehow she doubted it was that simple. There was a tense quality to his voice that belied his true feelings.

"I guess that's the benefit of not having parents," she said. "No one to tell you what to do."

"I guess" was all he said, and she had the distinct impression she'd broached a subject he preferred not to explore. He gave her shoulders one last squeeze, then backed away and asked, "Feel better?"

"Much," she said, turning toward him. "Thank you."

"Sure," he said, but the usual, cheery smile was absent from his face. In fact, he looked almost…sad. Then she realized the inference in what she'd just said. His father was *dying,* his only hope a risky experimental procedure, and here she was suggesting that not having parents was a good thing.

Here he was being nice to her, and she was probably making him feel terrible.

Way to go, Liv. Open mouth, insert foot.

"Aaron, what I said just then, about not having parents—"

"Forget it," he said with a shrug.

In other words, *drop it.*

The lack of sleep, especially after that relaxing massage, was obviously taking its toll on her. She was saying stupid and inappropriate things to a man she knew practically nothing about. A virtual stranger.

A stranger who had the authority to fire her on a whim if it suited him.

"You should get some rest," he said.

He was right. She was long overdue for a power nap. "Now, if I can just find my way back to my room," she joked.

"Didn't Derek bring you a map?"

She looked down at her desk, papers strewn everywhere. "It's here. Somewhere."

He smiled and gestured to the door. "Come on, I'll walk you up."

"Thank you." She slipped her laptop in her backpack and slung it over her shoulder, grabbing the plate of uneaten food on her way out.

Even though he was silent, the tension between them seemed to ease as she followed the prince out of the lab and up the stairs. She left the plate in the kitchen and received a distinct look of disapproval from the butler.

"Sorry," she said lamely, and he answered with a stiff nod. That on top of what she'd said to the prince filled her with a nagging sense of guilt as they walked up to her room. She was obviously way out of her league here. This was going to take a lot of getting used to.

When they reached her door, she turned to him and said, "Thanks for walking me up."

He smiled. "My pleasure. Get some rest."

He started to turn away.

"Aaron, wait!"

He stopped and turned back to her.

"Before you go, I wanted to apologize."

His brow furrowed. "For what?"

"What I said in the lab."

"It's okay."

"No, it isn't. It was really…thoughtless. And I'm sorry if I made you feel bad."

"Liv, don't worry about it."

"I mean, I basically suggested you would be better off without parents, which, considering your father's health, was totally insensitive of me. My verbal filter must be on the fritz."

He leaned casually against the doorjamb, a look of amused curiosity on his face. "Verbal filter?"

"Yeah. People's thoughts go through, and the really dumb and inappropriate stuff gets tossed out before they can become words. Lack of sleep must have mine working at minimum capacity. I know it's a pretty lame excuse. But I'm really, *really* sorry. I'm just an employee. I have no right asking you personal questions or talking about your family, anyway."

For several long, excruciating seconds he just looked at her, and she began to worry that maybe he really was thinking about firing her. Then he asked, "Will you have dinner with me tonight?"

Huh?

She insulted him, and he invited her to share dinner with him? She might have thought he was extending a formal invitation just to be polite, but he looked sincere. Like he really *wanted* to have dinner with her.

"Um, sure," she said, more than a touch puzzled.

"Seven sharp."

"Okay."

"I'll warn you that Geoffrey loathes tardiness."

"I'll be on time," she assured him.

He flashed her one last smile, then walked away.

She stepped into her room and shut the door, still not exactly sure what just happened, but way too tired to try to sort it out. She would think about it later, after she'd had some sleep.

As inviting as the bed looked, the draw of a steaming shower was too appealing to resist. The sensation of the hot water jetting against her skin was almost as enjoyable as Aaron's neck massage had been. After her shower she curled up under the covers, planning to sleep an hour or two before heading back down to the lab.

She let her tired, burning eyes drift shut, and when she opened them again to check the clock on the bedside table, it was six forty-five.

* * *

Liv had been so wracked with guilt when Aaron walked her to her room this morning, she hadn't been paying attention to how they got there. And of course her handy map was in the lab, buried under her research. Which was why, four minutes before she was supposed to be in the dinning room, she was frantically wandering the halls, looking for a familiar landmark. The castle was just so big and quiet. If only she would run into someone who could help. She was going to be late, and she had the feeling she was already in hot water with Geoffrey the butler.

She rounded a corner and ran—literally—into someone.

Plowed into was more like it. But this time it wasn't a petite maid. This time it was a hulk of man, built like a tank, who stood at least a foot taller than her own five-foot-ten-inch frame. If he hadn't caught her by the arms, the force of the collision probably would have knocked her on her butt.

He righted and swiftly released her.

"Sorry," she apologized, wondering how many more royal employees she would collide with while she was here. "It was my fault. I wasn't looking where I was going."

"Miss Montgomery, I presume?" he said in a slightly annoyed tone, looking, of all places, at her chest. Then she looked down and realized she'd forgotten to pin on her ID badge. She pulled it from the outer pocket of her backpack and handed it to him. "Yeah, sorry."

His badge identified him as Flynn, and she couldn't help thinking that he looked more like a *Bruno* or a *Bruiser.*

He looked at the photo on her badge, then back at her, one brow raised slightly higher than the other. He didn't say, *You don't look like a scientist,* but she could tell he was thinking it.

He handed it back to her. "You should wear this at all times."

"I know. I forgot." She hooked it on her sweater, managing not to skewer her skin as she had yesterday. "Maybe you can help me. I'm trying to get to the dining room," she told him. "I've lost my way."

"Would you like me to show you the way?"

She sighed with relief. "That would be wonderful. I'm about three minutes from being late for dinner, and I'm already in the doghouse with Geoffrey."

"We can't have that," he said, gesturing in the direction she'd just come from. "This way, miss."

This time she paid attention as he led her downstairs to the dining room and she was pretty sure that she would be able to find her way back to her room. But she would keep the map with her at all times, just in case.

Prince Aaron was sitting in the dining room waiting for her, nursing a drink, when they walked in.

"I found her, Your Highness," Flynn told him.

"Thank you, Flynn," the prince said.

He nodded and left, and Liv realized it was no accident that she'd encountered him in the hallway.

"How did you know I would get lost?" she asked him.

He grinned. "Call it a hunch."

He rose from his chair and pulled out the adjacent chair for her, and as she sat, his fingers brushed the backs of her shoulders. Was he doing it on purpose? And if so, why did he feel the need to touch her all the time? Did he get some morbid kick out of making her nervous?

The only other time she'd had an experience with a touchy-feely person was back in graduate school. Professor Green had had a serious case of inappropriately wandering hands that, on a scale of one to ten, had an ick factor of fifteen. All of his female students fell victim to his occasional groping.

But unlike her professor, when Aaron touched her, she *liked* the way it felt. The shiver of awareness and swift zing of sexual attraction. She just wished she knew what it meant.

He eased her chair in and sat back down, lounging casually, drink in hand. "Would you like a drink? A glass of wine?"

"No, thank you. I have to stay sharp."

"What for?"

"Work."

He frowned. "You're working tonight?"

"Of course."

"But by the time we finish dinner, it will be after eight o'clock."

She shrugged. "So?"

"So, I have an idea. Why don't you take a night off?"

"Take a night off?"

"Instead of locking yourself in the lab, why don't you spend the evening with me?"

Six

The confused look on Liv's face was as amusing as it was endearing. She was as far from his type as a woman could be, yet Aaron wanted inside her head, wanted to know what made her tick.

Geoffrey appeared with the first course of their dinner, a mouthwatering lobster bisque. He knew this because he'd managed to sneak a taste before the chef had chased him out of the kitchen.

"How about that drink?" he asked Liv.

"Just water, please. Bottled, if you have it."

Geoffrey nodded and left to fetch it.

"You never answered my question," he said.

She fidgeted with her napkin. "I'm here to work, Your Highness."

"Aaron," he reminded her. "And you just worked a twenty-four-hour shift. Everyone needs a break every now and then."

"I had a break. I slept all day."

He could see he was getting nowhere, so he tried a different angle: the guilt card. He frowned and said, "Is the idea of spending time with me really so repulsive?"

Her eyes widened and she vigorously shook her head. "No! Of course not! I didn't mean to imply…" She frowned and bit her lip.

He could see that she was this close to giving in, so he made the decision for her. "It's settled, then. You'll spend the evening with me."

She looked hesitant, but seemed to realize that she had little choice in the matter. "I guess one night off wouldn't kill me."

"Excellent. What do you do for fun?"

She stared blankly.

"You do have fun occasionally, right?"

"When I'm not working I read a lot to catch up on the latest scientific discoveries and theories."

He shot her a skeptical look.

"That's fun."

"I'm talking social interaction. Being with other human beings."

He got a blank look from Liv.

"What about sports?" he asked.

She shrugged. "I'm not exactly athletic."

A person would never know it by her figure. She

looked very fit. He knew women who spent hours in the gym to look like Liv, and would kill to have a figure like that naturally.

"Do you go to movies?" he asked. "Watch television?"

"I don't get to the movies very often, and I don't own a television."

This time his eyes widened. "How can you not own a television?"

"What's the point? I'm never home to watch it."

"Music? Theater?"

She shook her head.

"There must be *something* you like to do besides work and read about work."

She thought about it for a moment, chewing her lip in concentration, then she finally said, "There is *one* thing I've always wanted to try."

"What's that?"

"Billiards."

Her answer surprised him. "Seriously?"

She nodded. "It's actually very scientific."

He grinned. "Well, then, you're in luck. We have a billiards table in the game room, and I happen to be an excellent teacher."

Ten minutes into her first billiards lesson, Liv began to suspect that choosing this particular game had been a bad idea. Right about the time that Aaron handed her a cue and then proceeded to stand behind her, leaning her over the edge of the table, his body pressed to hers, and demonstrating the appropriate way to hold it.

Hard as she tried to concentrate on his instructions, as he took her through several practice shots, she kept getting distracted by the feel of his wide, muscular chest against her back. His big, bulky arms guiding her. His body heat penetrating her clothes and warming her skin. And oh, did he smell good. Whatever aftershave or cologne he'd used that morning had long since faded and his natural, unique scent enveloped her.

It's just chemical, she reminded herself. And wholly one-sided. He wasn't holding her like this for pleasure, or as some sort of come-on. He was giving her a billiards lesson. Granted, she'd never had one before, but it stood to reason this was the way one would do it. Although the feel of him guiding the cue, sliding it back and forth between her thumb and forefinger, was ridiculously erotic.

If he did have some other sort of lesson on his mind, one that had nothing to do with billiards, she was so far out of her league that she couldn't even see her own league from here. Although, she had to admit, the view here was awfully nice.

"Have you got that?" Aaron asked.

She realized all this time he'd been explaining the game to her and she had completely zoned out. Which is absolutely unlike her. She turned her head toward him and he was so close her cheek collided with his chin. She could feel his breath shifting the wisps of hair that had escaped her ponytail.

She jerked her head back to look at the table, swallowing back a nervous giggle. Then she did something that she hardly ever did, at least, not since she was a rebellious teen. She *lied* and said, "I think I've got it."

He stepped back, racked up the balls, then said, "Okay, give it a try."

She lined the cue up to the white ball, just the way he'd shown her, but she was so nervous that when she took the shot she hit the green instead, leaving a chalky line on the surface. She cringed and said, "Sorry."

"It's okay," he assured her. "Try it again, but this time get a little closer to the ball. Like this." He demonstrated the motion with his own cue, then backed away.

She leaned back over, following his actions, and this time she managed to hit the ball, but the force only moved it about six inches to the left, completely missing the other balls, before it rolled to a stop. "Ugh."

"No, that was good," he assured her. "You just need to work on your aim and put a little weight behind it. Don't be afraid to give it a good whack."

"I'll try."

He set the cue ball back in place and she leaned over, lining it up, and this time she really whacked it. A little too hard, because the ball went airborne, banking to the left, right off the table. She cringed as it landed with a sharp crack on the tile floor. "Sorry!"

"It's okay," he said with a good-natured chuckle, rounding the table to fetch the ball. "Maybe not quite so hard next time."

She frowned. "I'm terrible at this."

"You just started. It takes practice."

That was part of the problem. She didn't have *time* to practice. Which was exactly why she was hesitant to try new things. Her motto had always been, If you can't be the best at something, why bother?

"Watch me," he said.

She stepped aside to give him room. He bent over and lined up the shot, but instead of keeping her eyes on his cue, where they were supposed to be, she found herself drawn to the perfect curve of his backside. His slacks hugged him just right.

She heard a loud crack, and lifted her gaze to see the balls scattering all over the table.

"Just like that," he said, and she nodded, despite the fact that, like before, she hadn't been paying attention. He backed up and gestured to the table. "Why don't you knock a few around. Work on your aim."

Despite her awkwardness, somehow Aaron always managed to make her feel less…inept. And after some practice and a couple of false starts, she was actually getting the hang of it. She even managed to keep all the balls on the table where they belonged and sink a few in the pockets. When they played a few actual games, she didn't do too badly, although she had the sneaking suspicion he was deliberately going easy on her.

After a while, despite having slept most of the day, she started yawning.

"Maybe we should call it a night," he said.

"What time is it?"

"Half past twelve."

"Already!" She had no idea they'd been playing that long.

"Past your bedtime?" he teased.

"Hardly." As if on cue, she yawned again, so deeply moisture filled her eyes. "I don't know why I'm so sleepy."

"Probably jet lag. It'll just take a few days for your system to adjust. Why don't you go to bed and get a good night's sleep, then start fresh in the morning."

As eager as she was to get back down to the lab, he was probably right. Besides, she really needed samples and her assistant wouldn't be here until the next morning. Maybe she could take some time to catch up on a bit of reading.

"I think maybe I will," she told him.

He took her cue and hung it, and his own, on a wall rack. "Maybe we can try this again, tomorrow night."

"Maybe," she said, and the weird thing was that she really wanted to. She was having fun. Maybe *too* much fun. She had a job to do here. That disease wasn't going to cure itself. It had been hours since she'd even thought about her research, and that wasn't at all like her.

"I'll walk you to your room," Aaron said.

"I think I can find my way." They were somewhere on the third floor, and if she took the nearest steps down one floor she was pretty sure she would be near the hallway her room was on.

"A gentleman always walks his date to the door," he said with a grin. "And if nothing else, I am *always* a gentleman."

Date? Surely he was using that word in the loosest of terms, because she and Aaron were definitely not *dating*. Not in the literal sense. He meant it casually, like when people said they had a *lunch date* with a friend. Or a *dinner date* with a work associate.

She picked up her backpack from where she'd left it by the door, slung it over her shoulder and followed him out into the hall and down the stairs. She wanted to remember how to get there, should she ever decide to come back and practice alone every now and then.

"By the way, do you play poker?" he asked as they walked side by side down the hall toward her room.

"Not in a long time."

"My brother, sister and I play every Friday night. You should join us."

"I don't know…"

"Come on, it'll be fun. I promise, it's much easier than billiards."

She wondered if that would be considered proper. The hired help playing cards with the family. Of course, since she'd arrived, he'd treated her more like a guest than an employee.

"If you claim you have to work," he said sternly, "I'll change the door code and lock you out of the lab."

She couldn't tell if he was just teasing her, or if he would really do it. And who knows, it might be fun. "They won't mind?"

"My brother and sister? Of course not. We always invite palace guests to join in."

"But I'm not technically a guest," she said as they stopped in front of her door. "I work for you."

He was silent for a moment as he seemed to digest her words, looking puzzled. Finally he said, "You don't have the slightest clue how valuable you are, do you?"

His words stunned her. Her? Valuable?

"What you've been through. What you've *overcome...*" He shook his head. "It makes me feel very insignificant."

"I make you feel that way?" she asked, flattening a hand to her chest. *"Me?"*

"Why is that so hard to believe?"

"You're royalty. Compared to you, I'm nobody."

"Why would you think you're nobody?"

"Because...I am. What have I ever done?"

"You've done a hell of a lot more than I ever have. And think of all that you still have the chance to do."

She could hardly believe that Aaron, a *prince,* could possibly hold someone like her in such high esteem. What was he seeing that no one else did?

"I'm sure you've done things, too," she said.

He shook his head. "All of my life I've had things

handed to me. I've never had to work for *anything*. And look at the adversity you've overcome to get where you are."

She shrugged. "I just did what I had to do."

"And that's my point exactly. Most people would have given up. Your determination, your *ambition,* is astounding. And the thing I like most is that you don't put on airs. You don't try to be something that you're not." He took a step closer and his expression was so earnest, so honest, her breath caught. "I've never met a woman so confident. So comfortable in her own skin."

Confident? Was he serious? She was constantly second-guessing herself, questioning her own significance. Her worth.

"You're intelligent and interesting and kind," he said. "And fun. And I'm betting that you don't have a clue how beautiful you are."

Did the guy need glasses? She was so…plain. So unremarkable. "You think I'm beautiful?"

"I don't think you are. I *know* you are. And you wouldn't believe how much I've wanted to…" He sighed and shook his head. "Never mind."

She was dying to know what he was thinking, and at the same time scared to death of what it might be. But her insatiable curiosity got the best of her.

Before she could stop herself she asked, "You wanted to do what?"

For a long, excruciating moment he just looked at

her and her heart hammered relentlessly in anticipation. Finally he grinned that sexy simmering smile and told her, "I wanted do this." Then he wrapped a hand around the back of her neck, pulled her to him and kissed her.

This was not the wishy-washy version of a kiss that Liv had gotten from William the day she left. Not even close. This kiss had heart. And soul. It had soft lips and caressing hands and breathless whimpers—mostly from her.

It was the kind of kiss that a girl remembered her entire life, the one she looked back on as her first *real* kiss. And she was kissing him back just as enthusiastically. Her arms went around Aaron's neck, fingers tunneled through his hair. She was practically *attacking* him, but he didn't seem to mind. She felt as though she needed this, needed to feed off his energy, like a plant absorbing the sunlight.

She kept waiting for him to break the kiss, to laugh at her and say, *Just kidding* or *I can't believe you fell for that!* As if it was some sort of joke. What other reason would he have for kissing someone like her? But he didn't pull away. He pulled *her* closer. Her breasts crushed against the solid wall of his chest, tingling almost painfully, and just like that, she was hotter and more turned on than she'd ever been in her life.

But what about William?

William who?

Aaron's hands were caressing her face, tangling through her hair, pulling the band free so it spilled out around her shoulders. He pulled her closer and she nearly gasped when she felt the length of his erection, long and stiff against her belly. Suddenly the reality of what she was doing, where this was leading and the eventual conclusion, penetrated the lusty haze that was clouding her otherwise-rational brain. In the back of her mind a guilty little voice asked, *Is this how you treat the man who asked you to marry him?*

She didn't want to think about that. She wanted to shut him out of her mind, pretend William didn't exist. But he *did* exist, and he was back in the States patiently awaiting an answer from her. Trusting that she was giving his proposal serious thought.

She broke the kiss and burrowed her head against Aaron's shoulder, feeling the deep rise and fall of his chest as he breathed, the rapid beat of his heart. Her own breath was coming in shallow bursts and her heart rate had climbed to what must have been a dangerously high level. Had anyone under the age of seventy ever actually died of heart failure brought on by extreme sexual arousal?

"What's wrong?" he asked, genuine concern in his voice.

She struggled to catch her breath, to slow her pounding heart. "We're moving too fast."

He chuckled. "Um, technically, we haven't actually done anything yet."

"And we shouldn't. We *can't*."

He was quiet for several seconds, then he asked, "Are you saying you don't want to? Because, love, that kiss was hot as hell."

He called her *love*. No one had ever used a term of endearment like that with her. Certainly not her foster parents. Not even William. It made her feel special. Which made what she had to do next that much harder.

"I want to," she said. "A lot."

He rubbed his hands softly up and down her back. "Are you…afraid?"

She shook her head against his shoulder. She was anything but frightened, although maybe she should have been, because nothing about this made any sense. It wasn't logical, and her entire life revolved around logic and science.

Maybe that was what made it so appealing.

"There's something I haven't told you," she said.

"What is it?"

She swallowed the lump in her throat and looked up at him. "I'm kind of…engaged."

Seven

"You're *engaged?*" Aaron backed away from Liv, wondering why this was the first time he'd heard this. Especially when he considered all of the blatant flirting that had been going both ways between them the past couple of days. Well, some of it went both ways, but in all fairness he was always the one to initiate it.

"Um…sort of," she said, looking uneasy.

Sort of? "Wait, how can a person be *sort of* engaged? And if you are engaged, why aren't you wearing a ring?"

"We kinda didn't get to that part yet."

He narrowed his eyes at her. "What part did you get to exactly?"

"He asked me, and I told him I would think about it."

There was this feeling, low in his gut. A surge of sensation that he didn't recognize. The he realized he was jealous. He envied a complete stranger. "Who is *he?*"

"His name is William. We work together."

"Another scientist?"

She nodded. "He's my mentor."

"Are you in love with him?" he asked.

She hesitated a moment, then said, "He's a good friend. I have an immense amount of respect for him."

Was that relief he'd just felt? "That isn't what I asked you."

She chewed her lip, as though she was giving it deep consideration, then she said, "Love is highly overrated."

Normally he would have agreed, but this was different. *She* was different. He couldn't imagine Liv being happy with a man she only *respected.* She deserved better. She'd fought all of her life to get exactly what she wanted. Why quit now?

And how did he know *what* she wanted when he barely knew her?

Somehow, he just did. And she was special. He couldn't even vocalize exactly why. It was just something he knew deep down.

"He must be a damned good shag, then," Aaron said, aware of how peevish he sounded.

He expected a snappy response, a firm, *Butt out, buster,* or *Mind your own business.* Instead Liv bit her lip and lowered her eyes. It didn't take him long to figure out what that meant.

He folded his arms across his chest and said, "You haven't slept with him, have you?"

"I didn't say that."

But she didn't deny it, either. "Out of curiosity, how long have you been dating this William fellow?"

Her gaze dropped to her feet again and in went the lip between her teeth. She didn't say a word. But her silence said it all.

"Are you telling me that you two have never even dated? Let me guess, you've never kissed him, either?"

She leveled her eyes on him. "I have so!"

He took a step toward her. "I'll bet he doesn't make you half as hot as I do."

He could tell by her expression, from the sudden rush of color to her cheeks, that he was right.

"I wasn't *that* hot," she said, but he knew it was a lie.

"You won't be happy," he said. "You're too passionate."

She looked at him like he was nuts. "I've been accused of a lot of things, but being passionate is not one of them."

He sighed. "There you go, selling yourself short again."

She shook her head in frustration. "I can't believe we're having this conversation. I hardly even know you."

"I know. And that's the bizarre part, because for some reason I feel as though I've known you forever." He could see by her expression that she didn't know how to respond to that, and she wasn't sure what to make of him. And oddly enough, neither did he. This wasn't at all like him.

She grabbed the knob and opened her door. "I should get to sleep."

He nodded. "Promise me you'll think about what I said."

"Good night, Aaron." She slipped inside her room and closed the door behind her.

He turned and walked in the direction of his own room. What he'd told her wasn't a lie. He'd never met anyone quite like her. She sincerely had no idea how unique, how gifted she was.

At first he'd planned only to seduce Liv and show her a good time while she was here, but something had happened since then. Something he hadn't expected. He really *liked* her. And the idea of her marrying this William person—a man she obviously didn't love—disturbed him far more than it should have.

Liv closed the door and leaned against it, expelling a long, deep breath.

What the heck had just happened out there? What did he want from her? Was he just trying to seduce her? To soften her up with his sweet words? Or did he really mean what he said? Did he really think she was interesting and fun? And *beautiful*. And if she really was, why had no one told her until now?

Just because no man had said the words, it didn't mean it wasn't true. And although she would never admit it to his face, he was right about one thing, no man had ever made her even close to as hot as he just had. With barely more than a kiss. Had it gone any further, she may have become the first scientifically genuine victim of spontaneous human combustion.

And oh how she had wanted it to go further. But to what end? A brief, torrid affair? Yeah, so what if it was? What was so wrong with that? They were consenting adults.

Yeah, but what about William?

So what if William wasn't an above-average kisser, and who cared that he didn't get her all hot and bothered the way Aaron did. William was stable and secure, and he respected her, and she was sure that he thought she was beautiful, too. He just wasn't the type of man to express his feelings. She was sure that once they were married he would open up.

But what if he didn't? Was that enough for her?

She heard a muffled jingle coming from her backpack and realized her phone was ringing. She pulled it out and saw that it was, *speak of the devil,* William. She hadn't spoken to him since she left the States. No doubt he was anxious for an answer.

She let it go to voice mail. She would call him

back tomorrow once she'd had a night to think things through. When she'd had time to forget how Aaron's lips felt against hers, and the taste of his mouth, and what it had been like to have his arms around her, his fingers tangling in her hair.

What if she never forgot? Could she go through life always wondering *what if?* Would it really be so awful, for once in her life, to do something just because she wanted to. Because it felt good. It wasn't as if he would want a relationship, and frankly, neither would she. Just one quick roll in the hay. Or maybe two. Then she could go home to William, who would never be the wiser…and live the rest of her life in guilt for betraying him.

Ugh.

But if they weren't technically engaged yet, could it really be counted as cheating?

As she was changing into her pajamas, her cell phone rang again. It was William. She considered letting it go to voice mail again, then decided she at least owed him a few words.

When she answered, his voice was filled with relief.

"I thought maybe you were avoiding me." He sounded so apprehensive and vulnerable. So unlike the confident, steadfast man she was used to, and the truth was, hearing him that way was just the slightest bit…off-putting. It knocked the pedestal she'd always kept him up on down a notch or two.

"Of course not," she said. "I've just been very busy."

"Is this a bad time? I could call back later."

"No, this is fine. I was just getting ready for bed. How have you been?"

"Swamped." He gave her a rundown on everything that had been going on in the lab since she left.

When he'd finished his dissertation, she asked him again. "How are *you,* William?"

"Me?" He sounded confused, probably because they never really talked about their personal lives.

"Yes, *you.*"

Finally he said, "Good. I'm good."

She waited for him to elaborate, but he didn't. Instead he asked, "How are *you?*"

Exhausted, but excited, and having more fun than I've ever had in my life, not to mention nursing a pretty serious crush, and considering an affair with, of all people, a prince.

But she couldn't tell him that. "I'm…good."

"The reason for my call," he said, getting right to the point—because William *always* had a point. "I was just wondering if you'd given any thought to my proposal."

He said it so drily, as though he were referring to a work proposal and not a lifetime commitment.

"I have," she said. "It's just…well, I've been so busy. I'd like a little more time to think it over. It's a huge decision."

"Of course. I don't mean to rush you. I realize that it probably came as something of a surprise."

"A little, yes. I never realized you had those kinds of feelings for me."

"You know that I deeply respect you. Both personally and professionally. We make a good team."

Yes, but a good professional relationship and a good marriage were two entirely different animals. Again she had to wonder, did she want to marry a man who respected her, or one who loved her? A man whom she worked well with, or one who found her so sexually appealing he couldn't keep his eyes, or hands, off her? One who made her feel all warm and breathless and squishy inside, the way Aaron did.

Don't even go there, she warned herself. Aaron had no place in this particular equation. Besides, for all she knew William would be fantastic in bed. She'd always considered good sex more of a perk than a necessity.

If that was true, why wasn't she jumping at his offer?

"Can I ask you a question, William?"

"Of course."

"Why now? What's changed from, say, two months ago?"

"Well, I've been doing a lot of thinking lately. I've always imagined that one day I would get married and have a family. And as you know, I'm not getting any younger. It seemed like a good time."

It sounded so logical, but that hadn't exactly been what she was hoping for.

"I guess what I want to know is, why me?"

"Why you?" he said, sounding puzzled. "Why not you?"

"What I mean is, was there a particular reason you asked *me*?"

"Who else would I ask?"

She was seriously fishing here, and he just didn't seem to get it. She wasn't desperate enough to beg for a kind word or two. Like, *You're beautiful* or *I love you.* That would come with time.

Then why, deep down, was a little voice telling her that this was all wrong?

"Things are just so crazy right now," she told him. "Can you give me a few weeks to think about it?"

"Of course," he said, his tone so patient and reasonable that it filled her with shame. "Take your time."

They made random and slightly awkward small talk for several minutes, and William seemed almost relieved when she said she had to go.

She hung up wondering what kind of marriage would they have if the only thing they ever talked about was work? And even worse, he didn't seem all that interested in getting to know her on a personal level. Would that just take time? Or should the years she had already known him have been time enough?

She thought of Aaron, who asked her questions and seemed genuinely interested in getting to know her. Why couldn't William be more like that?

Thoughts like that wouldn't get her anywhere.

William would never be like Aaron—a rich, charming prince. Which was a good thing, because as she'd reminded herself so many times now, Aaron, and men like him, were out of her league. Granted, she had never actually had a relationship with a man like Aaron, but she wasn't so naive that she didn't know the way these things worked. Even if Aaron did find her interesting at first, see her as a novelty, it wouldn't take him long to grow bored with her, for him to realize that she wasn't as special as he thought. Then he would be back to pursuing a proper mate. A woman with the right family and the proper breeding.

Yet she couldn't help but think of all the fun they could have in the meantime.

Eight

Liv was on her way to breakfast the following morning when she was greeted—more like accosted—by one of Aaron's sisters at the foot of the stairs on the main floor. Was it Friday already?

She was nowhere near as tall as her brother and had a slim, frail-looking build, and while they didn't exactly look alike, there was a strong family resemblance. She was dressed in a pale pink argyle sweater and cream-colored slacks and wore her hair pulled back in a low bun. In the crook of one arm she cradled a quivering ball of fur with bulging eyes. A dog, Liv realized. Probably a shih tzu.

The first impression that popped into Liv's head

was sweet and demure. Until the princess opened her mouth.

She squealed excitedly when she saw Liv and said, "You must be Olivia! I'm Aaron's sister Louisa."

Liv was so stunned by her enthusiasm—weren't princesses supposed to be poised and reserved?—she nearly neglected protocol and offered a hand to shake.

"It's nice to meet you, Your Highness," she said, dipping into a slightly wobbly curtsy instead. She had barely recovered when Louisa grabbed her hand and pumped it enthusiastically.

"Call me Louisa." She scratched the canine behind its silky ears. "And this is Muffin. Say hello, Muffin."

Muffin just stared, his little pink tongue lolling out of his mouth.

"I can't tell you how excited we are to have you here," she said, smiling brightly. "Aaron has told us *wonderful* things about you."

Liv couldn't help but wonder exactly what he'd told them. She would be mortified if he'd said something about their kiss last night. Having had the entire night to think it over, she decided that it would definitely never happen again. At least, not until she'd decided what to do about William. Although, probably not then, either. What she needed to concentrate on was the job she had come here to do.

"Has my brother been a good host?" Louisa asked.

Good didn't even begin to describe the sort of

host he'd been. "He has," Liv assured her. "He's made me feel very welcome."

"I'm so glad. I can't *wait* for you to meet the rest of the family! Everyone is so excited that you're here."

"I'm anxious to meet them, too."

"Well, then, let's go. Everyone should be having breakfast."

Everyone? As in, the *entire* family? Louisa expected her to meet them all at once?

Her heart slammed the wall of her chest. She never had been much good in groups of people. She preferred one-on-one interaction. She opened her mouth to object, but Louisa had already looped an arm through hers and was all but dragging her in the direction of the dining room. Liv felt like a giant beside her. Too tall, awkward and totally unrefined.

This was a nightmare.

"Look who I found!" Louisa announced as they entered the dining room. She probably didn't mean to, but she gave the impression that Liv had been aimlessly wandering the halls when this was the first morning she *hadn't* gotten lost.

She did a quick survey of the room and realized that other than Geoffrey, who was serving breakfast, there were no familiar faces. Where was Aaron?

Aaron's brother and his wife sat at one side of the table, while his other sister sat across from them.

"Everyone, this is Olivia Montgomery," Louisa

gushed. "The scientist who has come to save our country!"

Wow, no pressure there. She stood frozen beside Louisa, unsure of what to say or do. Then she felt it. The gentle and soothing pressure of a warm hand on her back. Aaron was standing there to rescue her.

She turned to him, never so happy in her life to see a familiar, friendly face. He was dressed to work in the field, in jeans and a soft-looking flannel shirt over a mock turtleneck.

He must have sensed how tense she was because he said under his breath, so even Louisa wouldn't hear, "Relax, they won't bite."

Miraculously, his deep, patient tone did just that. Her tension and fear seemed to melt away. Most of it at least. As long as Aaron was there, she was confident the introductions would go well. He would never feed her to the wolves.

His hand still on her back, he led her to the table where his brother sat.

"Liv," Aaron said, "meet my brother, Prince Christian, and his wife, Princess Melissa."

"Your Highnesses," she said, dipping into a near-perfect curtsy.

Prince Christian rose to his feet and reached out to shake her hand. She shifted her backpack to the opposite shoulder and accepted it.

His grip was firm and confident, his smile genuine. "I know I speak for everyone when I say it's an honor and a relief to have you here with us."

She pasted on her face what she hoped was a confident and capable smile. "I'm honored to be here."

"If there's anything you need, anything at all, you need only ask."

How about a valium, she was tempted to say, but had the feeling he might not appreciate her brand of humor. Instead she said, "I will, thank you."

"My parents send their regards and apologies that they weren't here to welcome you. They'll return in several days."

Liv wasn't sure if she was supposed to know the facts surrounding their father's situation, so she only nodded.

"You've already met Princess Louisa," Aaron said. "And this is my other sister, Princess Anne."

Louisa and Anne may have been twins, but they didn't look a thing alike. Anne was darker. In color, and considering her guarded expression, in personality, as well.

"Your Highness," Liv said, curtsying in her direction. She was getting pretty good at this.

"I understand you think you can find a cure for the diseased crops," Anne said, sounding slightly antagonistic, as though she questioned Liv's credentials. Was Anne trying to intimidate her? Put her in her place?

It was one thing to question Liv personally, but as a scientist, they wouldn't find anyone more capable.

She lifted her chin a notch. "I don't *think* I can, Your Highness. I *will* find a cure. As I told Prince Aaron, it's simply a matter of time."

A vague smile pulled at the corners of Anne's mouth. If it had been some sort of test, it appeared Liv had passed.

"Shall we sit?" Aaron said, gesturing to the table.

She turned to him. "Actually, I was planning to get right to work."

He frowned. "You're not hungry?"

Not anymore. The idea of sitting and eating breakfast surrounded by his entire family was only slightly less intimidating than facing a firing squad. "If I could get a carafe of coffee sent down to the lab that would be great."

"Of course." He addressed the butler. "Geoffrey, would you take care of that, please?"

Geoffrey nodded, and although Liv couldn't say for sure, he might have looked a bit peeved.

"It was nice to meet everyone," Liv said.

"You'll join us for dinner?" Princess Melissa asked, although it came across as more of a statement than a question.

Before she could form a valid excuse to decline, Aaron answered for her, "Of course she will."

She wanted to turn to him and say, *I will?,* but she held her tongue. Besides, much as she'd like to, she couldn't avoid them forever.

She would feel so much more comfortable if they

treated her like the hired help rather than a guest and left her to her own devices.

"I'll walk you down to the lab," Aaron said, and though her first instinct was to refuse his offer, she didn't want everyone to think there was a reason she shouldn't be alone with him. Like the fact that she was scared to death he would kiss her again. And even more terrified that if he did, she wouldn't be able to make herself stop him this time.

He led her from the room, and when they were in the hall and out of earshot he said, "I know they can be intimidating, especially Anne, but you can't avoid them forever. They're curious about you."

"I just want to get an early start," she lied, "before my assistant arrives."

He shot her a we-both-know-that's-bull look.

"You don't have to walk me to the lab."

"I know I don't." His slightly mischievous grin said he was going to regardless, and the warmth of it began melting her from the inside out. When he rested a hand on her back to lead her there, her skin tingled under his touch.

If this was the way things would be from now on, she was in *big* trouble.

"I think we need to talk," Aaron told Liv as they walked through the kitchen to the basement door.

"About what?" she asked and he shot her a what-do-you-think look. She frowned and said, "Oh, *that*."

"In the lab," he said, "where we can have some privacy." She nodded and followed him silently through the kitchen and down the stairs. She wasn't wound nearly so tight as she'd been facing his family. She'd been so tense when he stepped into the dining room that he was hesitant to touch her for fear that she might shatter.

She trailed him down the stairs and waited while he punched in the door code. When they were in the lab with the door closed, she turned to him and said, "I've decided that what happened last night can't ever happen again."

So, she thought she would use the direct approach. That shouldn't have surprised him. And he was sure she had what she considered a very logical reason for her decision.

He folded his arms across his chest. "Is that so?"

"I'm serious, Aaron." She did look serious. "I talked to William last night."

An unexpected slam of disappointment and envy pegged him right in the gut.

"You've made your decision, then?" he asked, knowing that if she'd said yes to the engagement, he would do everything in his power to talk her out of it. Not for himself of course, but for her sake.

All right, maybe a *little* for himself.

"I haven't made a decision yet, but I told William that I'm still considering it. And until I accept or refuse his proposal, I don't feel it's right to…*see* anyone else."

He grinned. "See."

"You know what I mean."

"Why?"

His question seemed to confuse her. "Why?"

"You're not engaged. Admittedly you're not even *dating* him. So, logically, *seeing* me or anyone else wouldn't technically be considered infidelity."

She frowned. "You're splitting hairs."

"Not to mention that, if you really *wanted* to marry him, why would you need time to think about it? Wouldn't you have said *yes* as soon as he asked?"

She looked troubled, as though she realized he was right, but didn't want to admit it. "It's…complicated."

"And you think it will be less complicated after you're married? You think he'll miraculously change?"

"That's not what I meant."

"It doesn't work that way, Liv. Problems don't go away with the vows. The way I hear it, they usually get worse."

She expelled a frustrated breath. "Why do you even care? Or is this just your way of trying to get me in bed?"

He grinned. "Love, if I wanted in your knickers, I'd have been there last night."

Her cheeks blushed bright pink.

He took a few steps toward her. "I'm not going to insult your highly superior intelligence and say I don't want to get you into bed. But more than that, I like you, Liv, and I don't want to see you make a mistake."

"Ugh! Would you please stop saying that I'm making a mistake?"

"Are you afraid you're going to start believing me?"

"You think that my sleeping with you *wouldn't* be a mistake?"

He knew now that she'd at least been thinking about it. Probably as much as he had. "No, I don't. In fact, I think it would be beneficial to us both."

"Well, you're not exactly biased, are you?" She collapsed in her chair and dropped her head in her hands. "I want to do the right thing, and you're confusing me."

"How could anything *I* say confuse you? Either you want to marry him, or you don't."

"I don't know if I want to marry *anyone* right now!" she nearly shouted, looking shocked at her own words.

Then why fret over it? "If you're not ready to get married, tell him no."

She looked hopelessly confused and completely adorable. He could see that she wasn't used to not having all the answers. For some reason it made him like her that much more.

She gazed up at him, eyes clouded by confusion. "What if I don't get another chance?"

"To marry William?"

"To marry *anyone!* I do want to get married someday and have a family."

"What's stopping you?"

"What if no one else ever asks?"

That was the most ridiculous thing he'd ever heard. She was an attractive, desirable woman that any man would be lucky to have. If she spent some time outside of her lab and living her life, she might already know that. Men would probably be fighting each other to win her hand.

He knelt down in front of her chair, resting his hands on her knees. "Liv, trust me, someone will ask. Someone you want to marry. Someone you *love*."

She gazed into his eyes, looking so young and vulnerable and confused. What was it about her that made him want take her in his arms and just hold her? Soothe her fears and assure her that everything would be okay. But even if he'd wanted to, she didn't give him the chance. Instead, she leaned forward, wrapped her arms around his neck and kissed him.

Nine

That guilty little voice inside Liv was shouting, *Don't do it, Liv!* But by then it was already too late. Her arms were around Aaron's neck and her lips were on his. She was kissing him again, and he was kissing her back. The feel of his mouth, the taste of him, was already as familiar as it was exciting and new. Maybe because she'd spent most of the night before reliving the first kiss and fantasizing what it would feel like to do it again. Now she knew. And it was even better than she remembered. Better than she could ever have imagined.

Aaron cupped her face in his hands, stroking her cheeks, her throat, threading his fingers through her hair. She hooked her legs around his back, drawing him closer, clinging to him. She might have been embarrassed by her brazen behavior, but she felt too hot and needy with desire to care. She needed to feel him. She just plain *needed* him. Nothing in her life had ever felt this good, this…right. She hadn't even known it was possible to feel this way. And she wanted more—wanted it all. Even though she wasn't completely sure what *it* was yet. Was this just physical, or was there more to it?

Of course not. What did she think, they were going to have some sort of relationship? She didn't want that any more than he did. Her work was too important to her.

That didn't mean they couldn't have a little fun.

She tugged the tail of his flannel from the waist of his jeans, but he grabbed her hands and broke the kiss, saying in a husky voice, "We can't."

Shame burned her cheeks. Of course they couldn't. Hadn't she just told him that very same thing? What the hell had she been thinking? Why, the instant she was near him, did she seem to lose all concept of right and wrong?

She jerked her hands free and rolled the chair backward, away from him. "You're right. I'm sorry. I don't know what I was thinking. This isn't like me at all."

He looked puzzled for a moment, then he grinned and said, "I don't mean *ever.* I just meant that we can't *here*. Any minute now Geoffrey is going to walk through that door with your coffee, not to mention the lab assistant who's due here this morning."

"Oh, right," she said, feeling, of all things, relieved. When what she should have felt was ashamed of herself, and regretful for once again betraying William. Although, as Aaron had pointed out, she and William weren't technically a couple.

You're rationalizing, Liv. When there was absolutely nothing rational about this scenario. This was not the way the world was supposed to work. Brainy, orphaned scientists did not have flings with rich, handsome princes. No matter what the storybooks said.

Nothing that felt this wonderful could possibly be good for her.

"We can't do this again," she told him. "Ever."

Aaron sighed. "We're back to that again?"

"It's wrong."

Aaron rose from his knees and tucked his shirt back in. "It felt pretty good to me."

"I'm serious, Aaron."

"Oh, I know you are."

So why didn't he look as though he was taking her seriously? Why did she get the feeling he was just humoring her?

"I have to get to work," he said. "I'll see you at dinner?"

Was that a statement or a request? She could say no, but she suspected he wouldn't take no for an answer, and that if she tried to skip it, he would come down to the lab and fetch her. At least with his family around he wouldn't try anything physical with her. At least, she hoped he wouldn't. She seriously doubted his family would approve of Aaron messing around with the hired help. Especially one who ranked so abysmally low in the social ladder.

"Seven sharp," she said.

He leaned over and before she could stop him, he gave her a quick kiss—just a soft brush of his lips against hers, but it left her aching for more—then he walked to the door. As he opened it, he turned back to her and said, "Don't forget about the poker game tonight." Then he left, the door closing with a metallic click behind him.

Ugh. She had forgotten all about that. But she already said she would play, so she doubted he would let her back out now.

As much as she didn't want to spend the evening with his family, she dreaded even more spending it alone with him.

She turned to her desk, reaching for the pen she'd left beside her keyboard, but it wasn't there. She searched all over the desk, under every paper and text. She even checked the floor, in case it had somehow rolled off the desk, but it wasn't there. It was as if it had vanished into thin air.

She got a new one from her backpack, and as she was leaning over she heard a noise behind her, from the vicinity of the door. She thought maybe it was Geoffrey with her coffee, or her lab assistant, but when she turned, there was no one there.

And the damn door was open again.

After breakfast Aaron pulled Chris aside and asked, "So, what did you think of Liv?"

"Liv?"

"Miss Montgomery."

Chris raised one brow. "We're on a first-name basis, are we?"

Aaron scowled a him. "I'm being serious."

Chris chuckled. "I'll admit she's not at all what I expected. She doesn't look like a scientist and she's much younger than I imagined. She does seem quite confident, though, if not a bit...*unusual*."

"Unusual?"

"Not the typical royal guest."

Despite having thought that very same thing, Aaron felt protective of Liv. "What does that matter, so long as she gets the job done?"

Chris grinned. "No need to get testy. I'm just making an observation."

"An observation of someone you know nothing about." Knowing his siblings had the tendency to be more judgmental, Aaron wouldn't tell them about Liv's past. Not that he believed she had anything to be ashamed of—quite the contrary in fact—but the things she'd told him had been in confidence. If they wanted to know more about her, they would have to ask themselves—which he didn't doubt they would.

"If I didn't know better, I might think you fancy her," Chris said. "But we all know that you prefer your women with IQs in the double digits."

Even though he couldn't exactly deny the accusation, Aaron glared at him. "By the way, I invited her to our poker game tonight."

Chris looked intrigued. "Really? She doesn't strike me as the card-playing type."

Aaron wanted to ask, *What type does she strike you as?*, but he was afraid he might not like the answer he got. "Are you saying you don't want her to play?"

Chris shrugged. "It's fine with me. The more the merrier." He looked at his watch. "Is there anything else? I have a conference call in fifteen minutes."

"No, nothing else."

Chris started to turn away, then stopped and said, "I almost forgot to ask, have there been any new developments since I left?"

Aaron didn't have to ask Chris what he meant. It had been in the back of everyone's minds for months now. The person who referred to himself as the Gingerbread Man. "No e-mails, no security breaches. Nothing. It's as if he disappeared into thin air."

Chris looked relieved. "I hope that means it was a harmless prank, and we've heard the last of him."

"Or it could mean that he's building up to something big."

His relief instantly turned to irritation. "Always the optimist."

Aaron grinned. "I like to think that I'm realistic. Whoever he was, he went through an awful lot of trouble breaching our security systems. All I'm saying is that we should keep on our toes."

"I'll keep security on high alert, but at some point we'll have to assume he's given up."

"Call it a hunch," Aaron said, "but I seriously doubt we've seen or heard the last of him."

In her life Liv had never met such an inquisitive group of people. It must run in the family because during dinner she was overwhelmed by endless questions from every side of the table. And like their brother, they seemed genuinely interested in her answers. They asked about her work and education mostly, and they were nothing if not thorough. By the end of the evening she felt picked over and prodded, much like one of the soil samples she'd studied that afternoon. It could have been worse. They could have completely ignored her and made her feel like an outsider.

"See?" Aaron whispered as they walked to the game room to play cards. "That wasn't so bad."

"Not too bad," she admitted.

As they took seats around the table, Geoffrey took

drink orders while Prince Christian—Chris, as he'd asked her to address him—divvied out the chips.

"We start with one hundred each," Aaron told her. "I can front you the money."

She hadn't realized they would play for real money. In college and grad school the stakes had been nickels and dimes, but one hundred euros wasn't exactly out of her budget range. She'd checked the exchange rate before leaving the U.S. and one hundred euros would be equivalent to roughly one hundred thirty-one dollars, give or take.

"I can cover it," she told him.

He regarded her curiously. "You're sure?"

Did he think she was that destitute? "Of course I'm sure."

He shrugged and said, "Okay."

She was rusty the first few hands, but then it all started to come back to her and she won the next few rounds. A bit unfairly, she would admit, even though it wasn't exactly her fault. Besides, she was actually having fun.

Louisa apparently didn't play cards. She sat at the table with her dog, to her siblings' obvious irritation, chatting.

"Where are you from originally?" she asked Liv. She was definitely the friendlier of the twins. A glass-is-half-full kind of girl. And Liv used the term *girl* because Louisa had so sweet a disposition.

"I'm from New York," Liv told her.

"Your family still lives there?" she asked.

"Five card draw, nothing wild," Chris announced, shooting Louisa a look as he shuffled the cards.

"I don't have family," Liv said.

"Everyone has some family," Melissa said with the subtle twang of a Southern accent. Aaron had mentioned that she was born on Morgan Isle, the sister country of Thomas Isle, but had been raised in the U.S. in Louisiana.

"None that I know of," Liv told her. "I was abandoned as a small child and raised in foster homes."

"Abandoned?" Melissa repeated, her lower lip beginning to quiver and tears pooling in her eyes. "That's *so* sad."

"Easy, emotio-girl," Chris said, rubbing his wife's shoulder. When the tears spilled over onto her cheeks, he put down the cards he'd been dealing, reached into his pants pocket and pulled out a handkerchief. Neither he nor anyone else at the table appeared to find her sudden emotional meltdown unusual.

Melissa sniffed and dabbed at her eyes.

"You all right?" he asked, giving her shoulder a reassuring squeeze.

She gave him a wobbly nod and a halfhearted smile.

"You'll have to excuse my wife," Chris told Liv. "She's a little emotional these days."

"Just a little," Melissa said with a wry smile. "It's these damn fertility drugs. I feel like I'm on an emotional roller coaster."

"They're trying to get pregnant," Aaron told Liv.

"She's a scientist, genius," Anne said. "I'm sure she knows what fertility drugs are for."

Aaron ignored her.

"I don't know much about it myself, although I have a colleague who specializes in fertility on a genetic level," Liv said. "I never realized how common it is for couples to have some fertility issues."

"We're trying in vitro," Melissa said, tucking the handkerchief in her lap while Chris finished dealing. "Our doctor wanted us to wait and try it naturally for six months, but I'm already in my midthirties and we want at least three children, so we opted for the intervention now."

"We do run the risk of multiples," Chris said. "Even more so because obviously twins run in the family. But it's a chance we're willing to take."

It surprised Liv that they spoke so openly to a stranger about their personal medical issues, although she had found that, because she was a scientist, people assumed she possessed medical knowledge, which couldn't be further from the truth. Unless the patient happened to be a plant.

"I'll open for ten," Aaron said, tossing a chip in the pot, and everyone but Anne followed suit.

She threw down her cards and said, "I fold."

"I can hardly wait to have a little niece or nephew to spoil. Or both!" Louisa gushed. "Do you want children, Olivia?"

"Someday," Liv said. After she'd had more time to develop her career, and of course she would prefer to be married first. Would William be that man? Would she settle out of fear that she would never get another chance? Or would she take a chance and maybe meet a man she loved, and who loved her back? One who looked at her with love and affection and pride, the way Chris looked at Melissa. Didn't she deserve that, too?

If she never married and had kids, would it be that big of a tragedy? She always had her work.

"I love kids," Louisa said. "I'd like at least six, maybe eight."

"Which is why when you meet men, they run screaming in the opposite direction," Anne quipped, but her jab didn't seem to bother her sister.

"The right man is out there," Louisa said, with a tranquil smile and a confidence that suggested she had no doubt. She was probably right. What man wouldn't want to marry a sweet, beautiful princess? Even if it meant having an entire brood of children.

"We all know that Aaron doesn't want kids," Anne said, shooting Liv a meaningful look.

Did she suspect that something was going on between Liv and her brother? And if so, did she honestly believe that Liv would consider him as a potential father to her children? Nothing could be further from the truth. If they did have a fling, which was a moot point because she had already decided they wouldn't, she would never expect more than a brief affair.

Unsure of how to react, Liv decided it was best to give her no reaction at all and instead studied her cards.

"I'm just not cut out to be a family man," Aaron said to no one in particular. If he caught the meaning of his sister's statement, he didn't let on. Or maybe he was saying it for Liv's benefit, just in case she was having any delusions of grandeur and thought they had some sort of future together.

"You would have to drop out of the girl-of-the-month club," Anne said with a rueful smile and a subtle glance in Liv's direction.

"And miss out on that fantastic yearly rate they give me?" Aaron said with a grin. "I think not."

"Are we going to talk or play?" Chris complained, which, to Liv's profound relief, abruptly ended the conversation.

Louisa tried occasionally to engage them in conversation, earning a stern look from her oldest brother each time. She finally gave up and said good-night around ten. Half an hour later Melissa followed. At eleven-thirty, when Liv was up by almost two hundred euros, they packed it in for the night.

"Good game," Chris said, shaking her hand, and added with a grin, "I hope you'll give us a chance to win our money back next week."

"Of course," she said, although she would have to throw the game to make it happen.

"I'll walk you to your room," Aaron said, gesturing to the door, and he had a curious, almost sly look on his face. Something was definitely up.

"Why are you looking at me like that?" she asked.

"Because we finally get some time alone."

Ten

The idea of being alone with Aaron again both terrified and thrilled Liv, then he went and added another level of tension by saying, "You do realize that counting cards is considered cheating."

Oh damn.

She really hadn't thought anyone was paying that close attention. They were playing for only a couple hundred euros, so what was the harm?

She plastered on a look of pure innocence that said, *Me? Cheat?* But she could see he wasn't buying it.

She sighed and said, "It's not my fault."

He raised one disbelieving brow at her.

"I don't even do it consciously. The numbers just kind of stick in my head."

"You have a photographic memory?"

She nodded.

"I wondered how you managed to memorize the code for the lab door so quickly. Although for the life of me I don't understand how you kept getting lost in the castle."

"It only works with numbers."

For a second she though he might be angry, but he shot her a wry smile instead. "At least you made a bit of money for your research."

He apparently had no idea of the going rate for genetic research. "A couple hundred euros won't get me very far."

"You mean thousand," he said.

"Excuse me?"

"A couple hundred thousand."

She nearly tripped on her feet and went tumbling down the stairs. "That's not even funny."

He shrugged. "I'm not trying to be funny."

"You're serious?"

"*Totally* serious."

"You said we were starting with one hundred."

"We did. One hundred thousand."

She suddenly felt weak in the knees. All this time she thought she'd been betting a dollar or ten, it had actually been thousands? What if she'd lost? How would she have ever paid her debt?

"I'll give the money back," she said.

"That would look suspicious. Besides," he reminded her, "you already told Chris you would play again next Friday."

Damn it, she had, hadn't she? If the rest of the family figured it out, they might think her some sort of con artist. Next week she would just have to lose on purpose, claim that her first time must have been beginner's luck, then pretend to be discouraged and vow never to play again. Only she and Aaron would know the truth.

When they reached her room she opened the door and stepped inside. A single lamp burned beside the bed and the covers had been turned down. Standing in the doorway, she turned to him and said, "I had fun tonight."

He leaned against the doorjamb, wearing that devilish, adorable grin. "Aren't you going to invite me in?"

"No."

"Why not?"

"I told you earlier, we can't be…intimate." Just saying the word made her cheeks flush.

"You said it, but we both know you didn't mean it." He leaned in closer. "You want me, Liv."

She did. So much that she ached. He smelled so good and looked so damn sexy wearing that wicked, playful smile, and he was emitting enough phero-mones to make any woman bend to his will.

"That doesn't make it right," she told him, but

with a pathetic degree of conviction. She didn't even believe herself.

Which was probably why, instead of saying good-night and closing the door in his face, Liv grabbed the front of his shirt, pulled him into her room and kissed him.

He reacted with a surprised, "Oomf," which she had to admit gave her a decadent feeling of power. But it took him only seconds to recover, then he was kissing her back, pulling her into his arms. He shut the door and walked her backward to the bed, tugging the hem of her shirt free from the waist of her pants. She did the same to him, their arms getting tangled. They broke the kiss so that they could pull the shirts over their heads, and the sight of his bare chest took her breath away. He didn't even seem put off by her very plain and utilitarian cotton bra. His eyes raked over her, heavy with lust, and when his hands settled on her bare skin, she shuddered. He was so beautiful, so perfect, she could hardly believe it was real. That he wanted someone like her.

It's just sex, she reminded herself, although deep down, it felt like more.

He tugged the band from her hair and it spilled down around her bare shoulders.

"You're beautiful," he said, looking as though he sincerely meant it. She wished she could see what he saw, see herself through his eyes for one night.

He lowered his head, brushing his lips against the

crest of one breast, just above the cup of her bra. She shuddered again and curled her fingers through his hair.

"You smell fantastic," he said, then he ran his tongue where his lips had just been, up one side and down the other, and a moan slipped from between her lips. "Taste good, too," he added with a devilish grin.

"What are we doing?" she asked.

He regarded her curiously. "As a scientist, I'd have thought someone would have explained it to you by now."

She couldn't help but smile. "I know *what* we're doing. I just don't understand *why*."

"I don't know what you mean."

"Why me?"

She expected him to tease her, to tell her that she was underestimating herself again; instead his expression was serious.

"Honestly, I'm not sure." He caressed her cheek with the backs of his fingers. "All I know is, I've never wanted a woman the way I want you."

She might have suspected it was a line, but his eyes told her that he was telling the truth. That he was just as stunned and confused by this unlikely connection as she was.

Then he kissed her and started touching her, and she didn't care why they were doing it, her only thought was how wonderful his hands felt on her skin, how warm and delicious his mouth felt as he tasted and nipped her. With a quick flick of his fingers he unhooked her bra, and as he bared her breasts, he didn't seem to notice or care how voluptuous she wasn't, and as he drew one nipple into his mouth, flicking lightly with his tongue, she didn't care, either. He made her feel beautiful and desirable.

There was this burning need inside her like she'd never felt before, a sweet ache between her thighs that made her want to beg him to touch her, but he was still concentrating all of his efforts above her waist—and it was driving her mad.

Thinking it might move things along, she ran her hand down his chest to his slacks, sliding her fingers along his waistline, just below the fabric, then she moved her hand over his zipper, sucking in a surprised breath when she realized how long and thick he felt. She should have expected that he would be perfect everywhere.

She gave his erection a gentle squeeze and he groaned against her cleavage.

He reached behind him and she wasn't sure what he was doing, until he tossed his wallet down on the mattress. Intelligent as she was, it took her several seconds to understand why, and when she did—when she realized that he kept his condoms in there—the reality of what they were doing and exactly where this was leading hit her full force.

The fading flower who in college wouldn't even let a man kiss her until the third date was about to have sex with a man she'd known only four days. A playboy prince who without a doubt was far more experienced than she could ever hope to be.

So why wasn't she afraid, or at least a little wary? Why did it just make her want him that much more?

"Take them off," he told her, his voice husky.

She gazed up at him, confused. Only when she saw the look on his face did she realize how aroused he was, and that she was rhythmically stroking him without even realizing it. Reacting solely on instinct.

"My pants," he said. "Take them off now."

With trembling fingers she fumbled with the clasp, then pulled down the zipper. She tugged the slacks down, leaving his boxers in place.

"All of it," he demanded, so she pulled the boxers down, too. "Now, do that again."

She knew what he wanted. He wanted her to touch him again. She took him in her hand and the skin was so hot, she nearly jerked her arm back. Instead she squeezed.

The point of touching him, or at least, part of the point, had been so that he would touch her, too, but so far he was the one getting all of the action. With that thought came a sudden jab of concern that he was one of *those* men. The kind who took pleasure and gave nothing in return. She'd never been with a man who had taken the time to even try to please her, so what made her think Aaron would be any different?

Before she could even complete the thought, Aaron clasped her wrist to stop her. "That feels too good."

Wasn't that the point?

But she didn't argue because he *finally* reached down to unfasten her chinos—much more deftly than she'd managed with his. He eased her pants and panties down together and she kicked them away.

"Lie down," he said, nodding toward the bed. She did as he asked, trembling with anticipation. But instead of lying down beside her, he knelt between her thighs. If she had been more experienced with men, or more to the point, with men like *him,* she probably would have known what was coming next. Instead it was a total surprise when he eased her thighs open, leaned forward and kissed her there. She was so surprised, she wasn't sure what to do, how to react. Then he pressed her legs even farther apart and flicked her with his tongue. The sensation was so shockingly intimate and intense she cried out and arched off the bed. He teased her with his tongue, licking just hard enough to drive her mad, to make her squirm and moan. When she didn't think she could stand much more he took her into his mouth and every muscle from head to toe locked and shuddered in ecstasy, sending her higher and higher, and when it became too much, too intense, she pushed his head away.

She lay there with her eyes closed, too limp to do more than breathe. She felt the bed shift, and the warmth of Aaron's body beside hers. She pried her eyes open to find him grinning down at her. "Everything all right?"

It took all of her energy to nod. "Oh, yeah."

"Are you always that fast?"

"I have no idea."

"What do you mean."

"No man has actually ever done that."

He frowned. "Which part?"

"Either. Both. The few men I've been with weren't exactly…adventurous. And they were more interested in their own pleasure than mine."

"Are you saying no man has ever given you an orgasm?"

"Nope."

"That's just…*wrong*. There's nothing more satisfying for me than giving a woman pleasure."

"Really?" She didn't think it worked that way. Or maybe he was in a class all by himself.

"And you know the best part?" he said.

"Huh?"

He grinned that wolfish smile. "I get to spend the rest of the night proving it to you."

In his life Aaron had never been with a woman so responsive or easy to satisfy as Liv. She climaxed so quickly, and so often, just using his hands and mouth, that it sort of took the challenge out of it. But the way he looked at it, he was helping her make up for lost time. Those other men she'd been with must have been totally inept, completely self-absorbed or just plain stupid. That gave all men a bad rap. He'd never seen anything as fantastic as Liv shuddering in ecstasy, eyes blind with satisfaction.

"I want you inside me," she finally pleaded, gazing up at him with lust-filled eyes, and he couldn't resist giving her exactly what she wanted. He grabbed a condom and tore the package open with his teeth. He looked down at Liv and realized she was staring at his hard-on with a look on her face that hovered somewhere between curiosity and fascination.

"Can I do it?" she asked, holding out her hand.

He shrugged and gave her the condom. "Knock yourself out."

He expected her to roll it on; instead she leaned forward and took him in her mouth. Deep in her mouth. He groaned and wound his hands through her hair, on the verge of an explosion.

She took him from her mouth, looked up at him and grinned.

"I figured it would go on better this way. Besides, I've always wanted to try that."

She could experiment on him anytime. And he truly hoped she would.

He gritted his teeth as she carefully rolled the condom down the length of him.

"Like that?" she asked.

"Perfect," he said, and before he could make another move she lay back, pulling him down on top of her, between her thighs, arching to accept him.

She was so hot and wet and *tight* that he nearly lost

it on the first thrust. And though he was determined to make it last, she wasn't making it easy. Her hands were all over him, threading through his hair, her nails clawing at his back and shoulders, and she wrapped those gloriously long legs around his waist, whimpering in his ear. Then she tensed and moaned and her body clamped down around him like a fist, and it was all over. They rode it out together, then lay gasping for breath, a tangle of arms and legs.

"I had no idea it could be like this," she said.

Neither did he. "You say that as if we're done."

She rose up on one elbow and looked down at him, her expression serious. "I can't marry William."

"That's what I keep telling you," he said. He just hoped she hadn't decided to set her sights on him instead. They had fantastic sexual chemistry, but that didn't change the fact that he had every intention of remaining a free man. William wasn't the right man for her, but neither was he.

"If I wanted to marry him, I would feel guilty right now, wouldn't I?"

"I would think so."

"I don't. Not at all. In fact I almost feel...*relieved*. Like this huge weight has been lifted from my shoulders."

"That's good, right?"

She nodded. "I'm not ready to get married. And even if I was, I can't marry a man I don't love, that I'm not even sexually attracted to. I want more than that."

"You deserve more."

"I do," she agreed, looking as though, for the first time in her life, she finally believed it. "We have to keep this quiet."

"About William?"

"No. About us. Unless…" She frowned.

"Unless what?"

"Well, maybe we shouldn't do this again."

"Don't you think that's a bit unrealistic? Since you got here we haven't been able to keep our hands off each other."

"Then we'll have to be very discreet. Anne already suspects something."

He shrugged. "So what?"

"I'm going to go out on a limb here and assume that your family wouldn't approve of you slumming it with the hired help."

"You're a *guest*," he reminded her. "Besides, I don't give a damn what my family thinks."

"But I do. I spent most of my life trying not to be one of *those* girls. Having sex for the sake of sex."

"This is different."

"Is it really?"

He wanted to say yes, but they were by definition having an affair. And although he hated to admit it, if he were sleeping with a woman of his own social level, his siblings wouldn't bat an eyelash. Liv's humble beginnings and lack of pedigree put her in an entirely different category.

Even though *he* didn't think of her any differently than a duchess or debutante, she was probably right in believing other people would.

It wasn't fair, but it was just the way the world worked. No point in making this any more complicated than necessary.

"They won't hear a word about it from me," he told her.

"Thank you."

"Now," he said with a grin, "where were we?" He pulled her down for a kiss, but just as their lips met, his cell phone began to ring. "Ignore it."

"What if it's something about your father?"

She was right of course. He mumbled a curse and leaned over the edge of the bed to grab it from the floor. He looked at the display and saw that it was Chris. He answered with an irritated, "What?"

"Sorry to wake you, but we need you in the security office."

He didn't tell him that he hadn't been sleeping. And that he had no intention of sleeping for quite some time. He and Liv weren't even close to being finished. "It can't wait until morning?"

"Unfortunately, no. Besides, you wouldn't want to pass up the opportunity to say I told you so."

Eleven

The Gingerbread Man, as he liked to call himself, was back in business.

Posing as hospital housekeeping staff, he'd made it as far as the royal family's private waiting room. Hours after he was gone, security found the chilling calling card he'd left behind. An envelope full of photographs of Aaron and his siblings that the Gingerbread Man had taken in various places. The girls shopping in Paris, and one of Chris taken through the office window of a building where he'd recently had a meeting with local merchants. Every shot of Aaron showed him with a different woman.

It wasn't a direct threat, but the implication was

clear. He was watching them, and despite all of their security, they were vulnerable. And either he'd gotten bolder or he'd made a critical error, because he'd let himself be caught on the hospital surveillance. Aaron stood in the security office with Chris watching the grainy image from the surveillance tape.

"How in the hell did he get so close to the king?" Aaron asked.

"His ID checked out," Randal Jenkins, their head of security, told him. "He must have either stolen a badge from another employee or fabricated one. He never actually looks up at the camera, so he may be difficult to identify."

"We need to tighten down security at the hospital," Chris told him.

"Already done, sir."

"The king knows?" Aaron asked.

"He and the queen were informed immediately as a precaution," Jenkins said. "The London police are involved, as well. They're talking with the hospital staff to see if anyone remembers him, and they're suggesting we take the news public, run the security tape on television in hope that someone will recognize him."

"What do you think?" Aaron asked his brother. "Personally, I'd like to see this lunatic behind bars, but it's your call."

"Take it to the public," Chris told Jenkins. "And until we catch him, no one will leave the castle

without a full security detail, and we'll limit any un-
necessary travel or personal appearances."

"That will be difficult with the holidays approach-
ing," Aaron said. "Christmas is barely a month away."

"I'm confident that by then he'll be in custody,"
Chris said.

Aaron wished he shared that confidence, but he
had the feeling that it wouldn't be that easy.

Though Aaron assured her that the king was fine
and it was nothing more than a security issue that
needed his attention, Liv tossed and turned, sleeping
fitfully. She roused at 5:00 a.m. so completely awake
that she figured she might as well get to work.

The castle was still dark and quiet, but the kitchen
was bustling with activity.

"Getting an early start, miss?" Geoffrey asked,
sounding almost…friendly.

"I couldn't sleep," she told him.

"Shall I bring you coffee?"

Was he actually being *nice* to her? "Yes, please.
If it's no trouble."

He nodded. "I'll be down shortly."

Liv headed down the stairs, grinning like an idiot.
Though it shouldn't have mattered what Geoffrey
thought of her, she couldn't help but feel accepted
somehow, as if she'd gained access to the secret club.

As she rounded the corner to the lab door, she
stopped abruptly and the smile slipped from her face.

She distinctly remembered turning out the lights last night before going up for dinner. Now they were blazing. The assistant, a mousy young girl from the university, didn't have a code for the door. As far as Liv knew, no one but herself, Aaron, Geoffrey and the security office had access, and she couldn't imagine what business they might have down there.

She approached the door cautiously, peering through the window. As far as she could see, there was no one there. So why did she have the eerie sensation she was being watched?

"Problem, miss?"

Liv screeched with surprise and spun around, her backpack flying off her shoulder and landing with a thud on the ground. Geoffrey stood behind her carrying a tray with her coffee.

She slapped a hand over her frantically beating heart. "You scared me half to death!"

"Something wrong with the door?" he inquired, looking mildly amused, the first real emotion she had ever seen him show.

"Do you know if anyone was down here last night?" she asked.

"Not that I'm aware of." He stepped past her and punched in his code. The door clicked open and he stepped inside. Liv grabbed her backpack and cautiously followed him.

"I know I turned out the lights when I left last night, but they were on when I came down."

"Maybe you forgot." He set the coffee down on the table beside her desk.

When she saw the surface of her desk, she gasped.

He turned, regarding her curiously. "Something wrong, miss?"

"My desk," she said. The papers and files that had been strewn everywhere were now all stacked in neat piles. "Someone straightened it."

"They're just trying to get your attention," he said, pouring her a cup of coffee.

"Who?" Had someone been snooping down there?

"The spirits."

Spirits?

She had to resist rolling her eyes. It surprised her that a man as seemingly logical as the butler would buy in to that otherwordly garbage. "I don't believe in ghosts."

"All the more reason for them to ruffle your feathers. But you needn't worry, they're perfectly harmless."

It would explain how the door kept opening on its own, when security claimed the log had shown no record of the keypad being used, and maintenance had found nothing amiss with the controls. Yet she still believed it was far more likely that someone was messing with her head or trying to frighten her. Maybe even Geoffrey?

But why?

"Shall I call you for breakfast?" Geoffrey asked.

"I think I'll skip it," she said.

Geoffrey nodded politely, then let himself out of the lab.

Liv wasn't exactly looking forward to facing Aaron's family again. What if someone else had figured out how she'd done so well at poker? Or even worse, what if they knew Aaron had been in her room last night?

If it were possible, she would stay holed up in her lab until the day she was able to go home to the States.

She took her computer out of her backpack and booted it up. As she did every morning, she checked her e-mail first and among the usual spam the filter always missed, she was surprised to find a message from William. There was no subject, and the body of the e-mail said simply, *Just checking your progress.* That was it. Nothing personal like, *How are you?* Or, *Have you made a decision yet?*

She was going to have to tell him that she couldn't marry him. Let him down easy. She would be honest and explain that she just wasn't ready to marry anyone yet, and hope that it wouldn't affect their friendship or their working relationship.

But she couldn't do it through e-mail; that would be far too impersonal, and she hadn't yet worked up the nerve to call him. Maybe it would be better if she waited until she flew home and did it face-to-face.

But was it really fair to string him along? If he knew what she'd been up to last night…

A pleasant little shiver tingled through her body

when she recalled the way Aaron had touched her last night. The way he'd driven her mad with his hands and his mouth. Just thinking about it made her feel warm all over. Even though deep down something was telling her that she would end up regretting it, that she was way out of her league and headed for imminent disaster, she could hardly wait to be alone with him again.

Maybe last night was a total fluke and the next time they had sex it would only be so-so, even though she doubted it. If she kept thinking about it, about *him,* she wouldn't get a thing done today.

She answered William's mail with an equally impersonal rundown of her progress so far, and asked him to please go over the data she planned to send him later that afternoon—a fresh eye never hurt— then she got back to work analyzing the samples her assistant had taken yesterday.

Although she usually became engrossed in her work, she couldn't shake the feeling that she was being watched, and kept looking over to the door. The window wasn't more than ten-by-ten inches square, but a few times she could swear she saw the shadow of a figure just outside. Was it possible that Aaron or one of his siblings had someone keeping an eye on her? What did they think she might be doing down there, other than saving their country from agricultural devastation?

Or maybe it was just her mind playing tricks.

Some time later she heard the sound of the door clicking open, and thought, Here we go again. She was relieved when she heard footsteps moving in her direction. Assuming it was probably Geoffrey fetching the empty coffee carafe, she paid no attention, until she felt a rush of cool air brush past her and the unmistakable weight of a hand on her shoulder. She realized it had to be Aaron, there to say good morning. She pried herself away from her computer and spun in her chair to smile up at him, but there was no one there. She looked over at the door and saw that it was still firmly closed.

She shot to her feet and an eerie shiver coursed through her. It had to be her imagination. Could she have dozed off for a second? Maybe dreamed it?

If she had been sleeping, she wouldn't feel completely awake and alert. She glanced back up at the door and saw distinct movement outside the window, then it clicked and swung open. She sat there frozen, expecting some ghoulish apparition to float through, relieved when it was Aaron who stepped into the lab.

Her apprehension must have shown because when he saw her standing there, he stopped in his tracks and frowned. "You look as though you've just seen a ghost."

"Do you have someone spying on me?"

Taken aback by Liv's question, Aaron said, "Good morning to you, too."

"I'm serious, Aaron. Please tell me the truth."

Not only did she look serious, but deeply disturbed by the possibility. How could she even ask him that? "Of course not."

"You mean it?"

"Liv, if I felt you needed constant supervision, I never would have invited you here."

"Could your brother or one of your sisters have someone watching me?"

"I can't imagine why they would."

She shuddered and hugged herself. "This is too weird."

He walked over to her desk. "What's wrong?"

"I keep getting this feeling like someone is watching me, and when I look up at the window in the door, I see a shadow, like someone is standing just outside."

"Maybe someone on the laundry staff has a crush on you," he joked, but she didn't look amused. "I don't know who it could be."

"You know that the door kept popping open yesterday, and the technician said there wasn't anything wrong with it. Then this morning when I came down here, the lights were on and I know I turned them off last night."

He shrugged. "Maybe you thought you did, but didn't hit the switch all the way or something."

"Then explain how the papers that were strewn all over my desk were stacked neatly this morning."

He frowned. "Okay, that is kind of weird."

"There's something else."

"What?"

She looked hesitant to tell him, but finally said, "This is going to sound completely crazy, but a few minutes before you came in I heard the door open and footsteps in the room, then someone touched my shoulder, but when I turned around no one was there and the door was closed."

He might have thought it was crazy, but he'd heard similar stories from the staff. "Lots of people have reported having strange experiences down here."

"I don't believe in ghosts," she said, but without a whole lot of conviction. "Scientific labs aren't typically hot spots for paranormal activity."

"But how many labs have you been in that used to be dungeons?"

"None," she admitted.

"If it eases your mind, no one has ever been physically harmed down here. Just frightened."

"I don't feel as though I'm in physical danger. It's just creepy to think that someone is watching me. And—" she shuddered again "—*touching* me."

"Do you want to leave?"

"You mean, permanently?"

He nodded. God knows he didn't want her to; they needed her expertise and would be hard-pressed to find someone equally qualified, but he would understand if she had to.

"Of course not," she said, and he felt a little too relieved for comfort.

He tried to tell himself that he was only concerned

for his country's welfare, but he knew that was non-sense. He wanted more time with Liv. At least a few weeks to get her out of his system.

He grinned and told her, "I guess that means I'll just have to protect you."

He wrapped a hand around her hip and tugged her to him. She resisted for about half a second, then gave in and melted into his arms, resting her head on his shoulder. She felt so warm and soft and she smelled delicious. If they weren't in the lab, he would already be divesting her of her clothing.

"I had fun last night," he said and he could swear he felt her blush.

She wrapped her arms around him and hugged herself to his chest. "Me, too. Did you resolve your security problem?"

"In a manner of speaking." Because it wasn't a secret, and she would eventually be informed of the security lockdown, he figured he might as well tell her about the Gingerbread Man.

"That's really creepy," she said, gazing up at him. "Why would someone want to hurt your family?"

Aaron shrugged. "There are a lot of crazy people out there."

"I guess."

He kissed the tip of her nose. "I didn't think I'd find you in the lab. I figured, because it's the week-end, you might not be working today. I thought you might be up to a game of billiards."

"I work every day."

"Even Sunday?"

She gazed up at him and nodded. "Even Sunday."

"That reminds me. Chris wanted to know how long you'll need for the holidays."

She looked confused. "Need for what?"

"To go home."

"Oh, I won't be going home. I don't celebrate Christmas."

"Why not?" he asked, thinking that maybe it was some sort of religious issue.

She shrugged. "No one to celebrate with, I guess."

He frowned. "You must have friends."

"Yes, but they all have families and I would feel out of place. It really is not a big deal."

But it was. It was a very big deal. The thought of her spending the holidays alone disturbed him in a way he hadn't expected. It made him...*angry*. If her so-called friends really cared about her, they would insist she spend the holidays with them.

"If you're worried about me getting in the way, I'll keep to myself," she assured him. "You won't even know I'm here."

What kind of person did she think him to be? "That is the most ridiculous thing I've ever heard," he said, and she looked startled by his sharp tone. "I won't let you spend Christmas alone. You'll celebrate with us."

"Aaron, I don't think—"

"This is *not* negotiable. I'm *telling* you. You're spending the holidays with my family."

She opened her mouth to argue, so he did the only thing he could to shut her up. He leaned forward, covered her lips with his and kissed her.

Twelve

Aaron was making it really difficult for her to tell him no. Literally. Every time they came up for air, and she would open her mouth to speak, he would just start kissing her again. She was beginning to feel all soft and mushy-brained and turned on. Yet she couldn't shake the feeling they were being watched.

She opened one eye and peered at the door, nearly swallowing her own tongue when she saw a face staring back at her through the window. A woman she didn't recognize, with long, curly blond hair wearing some sort of lacy bonnet. Liv's first thought was that someone had discovered their secret, and they were both in big trouble. Then before her eyes the face went misty and translucent and seemed to dissipate and disappear into thin air.

She let out a muffled shriek against Aaron's lip, then ripped herself free so fast that she stumbled backward, tripped over her chair and landed on her rear end on the hard linoleum floor.

"Bloody hell, what's wrong?" Aaron asked, stunned by her sudden outburst.

She pointed to the door, even though whoever, or *whatever,* she'd seen in the window was no longer there. "A f-face."

He spun around to look. "There's no one there."

"It disappeared."

"Whoever it was probably saw you looking and ran off."

"No. I mean, it actually disappeared. One minute it was there, and the next minute it vanished. I don't even know how to explain it. It was as if it…dissolved."

"Dissolved?"

"Like mist." It was scary as hell, but the scientist in her couldn't help feeling intrigued. She had always clung to the belief that there was no such thing as heaven or an afterlife. When you were dead, you were dead. Could this mean there was some sort of life after death?

He looked at the window again, then back to her, still sprawled on the floor. "Are you saying that you saw a ghost?"

"A few days ago I never would have believed it,

but I can't think of any other logical explanation."
And for some reason, seeing it with her own eyes,
knowing it was real, made her more curious than
frightened. She wanted to see it again.

He held out a hand to help her up, and when she
was on her feet he tugged her back into his arms. "If
someone was watching us, alive or otherwise, they
nearly got one hell of a view, because I was about two
seconds from ravishing you."

So much for being discreet. "Suppose someone on
this plane of existence did happen to come down and
look in the window?"

"So we'll cover it," he said, nibbling on her neck.
"A sheet of paper and some tape should do the trick."

What he was doing felt deliciously wonderful, but
now wasn't the time for fooling around. Although she
had the feeling that when it came to women, he was
used to getting his way. If he was going to be with
her, he was going to have to learn to compromise.

"Aaron, I have to work," she said firmly, planting
her hands on his chest.

"No, you don't," he mumbled against her skin.

She gave a gentle but firm shove. "Yes. *I do.*"

He hesitated a moment, then grudgingly let her go.
"Do I get to see you at all today?"

Though she could easily work late into the evening, if he had to compromise, then so should she.
"How about a game of billiards tonight after dinner?"

He grinned. "And after billiards?"

She just smiled.

"I'm holding you to it," he said, backing toward the door.

"Oh, and about Christmas," she said.

"It's not up for discussion."

"But your family—"

"Won't mind at all. Besides, if Melissa were to get wind of you spending the holidays alone, she would probably have an emotional meltdown."

He was probably right. If Aaron didn't insist she join them, Melissa probably would. Or maybe she was rationalizing.

Compromise, Liv. Compromise.

"Okay," she said, and that seemed to make him very happy.

"See you at dinner," he said as he walked out.

She'd never had what anyone would consider a conventional Christmas holiday. Her foster families never had money for gifts and extravagant meals. If she got candy in her stocking—hell, if she even *had* a stocking—it was a pretty good year. It used to make her sad when the kids at school returned after the holiday break sporting new clothes and handheld video games and portable CD players, but she'd learned to harden her heart.

Even now Christmas was just another day to her. But she would be lying if she said it didn't get a *little* lonely, knowing everyone else was with their families.

But there were definite benefits, too. She didn't

have to fight the holiday crowds shopping for gifts, or have outrageous credit card bills come January. The simpler she kept her life, the better. Although it might be a nice change to spend Christmas somewhere other than alone in the lab. With a real family.

Or maybe, she thought as she sat down in front of her computer, it would make her realize all that she'd been missing.

Liv fidgeted beside Aaron as they neared the king's suite. His parents had returned from England yesterday, several days later than expected due to mild complications caused by the reinsertion of the pump. But he was feeling well, in good spirits and happy to be home with his family.

"Maybe we shouldn't bother them," Liv said, her brow furrowed. "I'm sure the king needs rest."

"He *wants* to meet you," he assured her. She'd grown much more comfortable in the castle this past week. She seemed to enjoy spending time with his siblings, and the feeling was remarkably mutual. Even Anne had lowered her defenses within the past few days and seemed to be making a genuine effort to get to know Liv, and of course Louisa loved everyone.

He took Liv's hand and gave it a reassuring squeeze, and even though no one was around, she pulled from his grasp. He was breaking her rule of no public displays of affection. Although he was quite sure that if his siblings hadn't already begun to suspect their affair, it was only a matter of time. Nearly every moment Liv wasn't in the lab, Aaron was with her and he'd spent every night for the past seven days in her room.

If they did suspect, no one had said a word to him.

"I'm so nervous. I'm afraid that when I curtsy I'm going to fall on my face."

"If you fall, I'll catch you," he assured her. He knocked on the suite door then pushed it open, feeling Liv go tense beside him.

His father had dressed for the occasion, though he was reclined on the sofa. His mother rose to greet them as they entered the room.

"Liv, meet my parents, the King and Queen of Thomas Isle. Mother, Father, this is Olivia Montgomery."

Liv curtsied, and even though it wasn't the smoothest he'd ever seen, she was nowhere close to falling over.

"It's an honor to meet you both," she said, a slight quiver in her voice.

"The honor is all ours, Miss Montgomery," his father said, shaking her hand, which she did gingerly, Aaron noticed, as though she worried she might break him. "Words cannot express how deeply we appreciate your visit."

His mother didn't even offer to shake Liv's hand. Maybe the king's health and all that time in the hospital was taking its toll on her. Although she'd seemed fine yesterday. Just a bit tired.

"My children speak quite highly of you," the king said, and added with a grin, "in fact, I hear you're something of a card shark."

Liv smiled nervously. "I'm sure it was beginner's luck, Your Highness."

"I'm assuming you've had time to work since you arrived," his mother said and her curt tone took him aback.

Liv looked a little stunned as well, so Aaron answered, "Of course she has. I practically have to drag her out of the lab just to eat dinner. She would work around the clock if I didn't insist she take a break every now and then."

She ignored him and asked Liv in an almost-demanding tone, "Have you made any progress?"

As was the case when she talked about her work or someone questioned her professionally, she suddenly became the confident and assertive scientist. The transformation never ceased to amaze him.

"I'm very close to discovering the strain of disease affecting the crops," she told his mother. Usually she explained things to him in layman's terms, so he had at least a little hope of understanding what she was talking about. She must have been trying to make a point because when she explained her latest developments to his mother, she used all scientific terms and jargon. Though the queen had spent the better part of her life farming, botanical genetics was *way* out of her league.

By the time Liv finished with her explanation, his mother looked at least a little humbled.

"Would you mind excusing us, Miss Montgomery," the queen said. "I need to have a word with my son."

"Of course," Liv said. "I need to get back down to the lab anyway. It was a pleasure to meet you both."

"I'll walk you out," Aaron said, leading her from the room.

When they were in the hallway with the door closed, Liv turned to him and said, "I'm so sorry."

Her apology confused him. He should be the one apologizing for his mother's behavior. "For what? I thought you were fantastic."

She frowned, looking troubled. "I was showing off. It was rude of me."

"Love, you've earned the right to show off every now and then."

"Your mother hates me."

"Why would she hate you?"

"Because she knows."

He frowned. "Knows what?"

She lowered her voice, even though they were alone. "That something is going on between us."

"How could she?"

"I don't know, but that was a mother lion protecting her cub. Her message clearly said back off."

"You're being paranoid. I think between my

father's health, the security breach at the hospital and the diseased crops, she's just stressed out."

Liv didn't look as though she believed him, but she didn't push the issue.

"I'll come see you in the lab later." He brushed a quick kiss across her lips, ignoring her look of protest, then let himself back into his parents' suite. He crossed the room to where they still sat, determined to get to the bottom of this.

"What the bloody hell was that about?" he asked his mother.

"Watch your tone," his father warned.

"*My* tone? Could she have been any more rude to Liv?"

"Don't think I don't know what's going on between you two," his mother said.

So Liv had been right. She did suspect something. He folded his arms over his chest. "And what *is* going on, Mother?"

"Nothing that your father and I approve of."

"You haven't even been here, so how could you possibly know what's been going on? Do you have the staff watching me?"

"There's someone I want you to meet," she said. "She's a duchess from a *good* family."

Unlike Liv who had *no* family, was that what she meant? That was hardly Liv's fault. "If you're concerned that I'm going to run off and marry Liv, you can stop worrying."

"It isn't proper. She's not of noble blood."

If his mother had the slightest clue about the behavior of those so-called *proper* women she set him up with, she would have kittens. The spoiled brats whose daddies gave them everything their hearts desired, while they dabbled in drugs and alcohol, and were more often than not sexually promiscuous. Liv was a saint in comparison.

"Maybe you should take the time to know her before you pass judgment."

"I know all I need to. She's not good enough for you," his mother said.

"Not *good* enough? I can safely say she's more intelligent than all three of us combined. She's sweet, and kind, and down-to-earth. And she could very well be saving our *asses* from total financial devastation," he said, earning a stern look from his father. "Can you say that of your princesses or duchesses?"

"The decision has already been made," his mother said. "You'll meet the duchess next Friday."

Since Chris married Melissa, their mother had been determined to find Aaron a wife, and even though he'd told her a million times he didn't want to settle down, the message seemed to go in one ear and out the other. But he'd gone along with the blind dates and the setups because it was always easier than arguing. Easier than standing up for himself.

He thought of Liv, who had fought like hell for everything she'd ever gotten, how strong she was, and wondered what had he ever done but settle? From the day he was born his family told him who he was supposed to be. Well, he was tired of compromising himself, tired of playing by their rules. It ended today.

"No," he said.

She frowned. "No, what?"

"I won't meet her."

"Of course you will."

"No, I won't. No more blind dates, no more setups. I'm finished."

She huffed out a frustrated breath. "How will you ever find a wife if you don't—"

"I don't *want* a wife. I don't want to settle down."

She rolled her eyes. "Every man says that. But when the right one comes along you'll change your mind."

"If that's true, I'll find her without your help."

She gave him her token you-would-be-lost-without-me-to-run-your-life look. "Aaron, sweetheart—"

"I mean it, Mother. I don't want to hear another word about it."

She looked stunned by his demand; his father, on the other hand, looked amused. "He's made his decision, dear," he said. And before she could argue, he sighed and said, "This conversation has worn me out."

"Why didn't you say something?" She patted his shoulder protectively and summoned the nurse, shooting Aaron a look that suggested his father's sudden fatigue was his fault. "Let's get you to bed. We'll talk about this later."

No, they wouldn't, he wanted to say, but for his father's sake he let it drop. She would come to realize that he wasn't playing by her rules any longer.

While the nurse helped his father into bed, his mother turned to him and said, "Please let Geoffrey know that your father and I will be taking dinner in our suite tonight."

"Of course."

She smiled and patted his cheek fondly. "That's a good boy."

A good boy? Ugh. What was he, twelve? He turned and left before he said something he regretted. She seemed to believe she'd won, but nothing could be further from the truth. Knowing Liv had made him take a good hard look at his own life and he didn't like what he was seeing. It was time he made a few changes.

Thirteen

The following Monday was December first and
overnight the castle was transformed to a holiday
wonderland. Fresh evergreen swags dotted with red
berries and accented with big red bows hung from the
stair railings, making everything smell piney and
festive, and mistletoe hung in every door and arch-
way. Life-size nutcrackers stood guard in the halls
and every room on the main floor had a Christmas
tree decorated in a different color and theme. From
one hung various styles and flavors of candy canes
and other sugar confections, while another was fes-
tooned with antique miniature toy ornaments. Some
were draped in all shades of purple, and others in

creamy whites. But the most amazing tree was in the ballroom. It stood at least twenty feet high, decorated in shimmering silver and gold balls.

The outside of the castle was the most incredible of all. What looked to be about a million tiny multicolored lights edged the windows and turrets and lit the shrubs.

Liv had never seen anything like it, and she couldn't help but get drawn into the holiday spirit. For the first time in her life Christmas wasn't something she dreaded or ignored. This time she let herself feel it, get caught up in the atmosphere. And she almost felt as if she had a family. Aaron's siblings made her feel so welcome, and Liv was particularly fond of the king. He was warm and friendly and had a surprisingly thorough understanding of genetic science and an insatiable curiosity. They had many evening conversations about her research, sitting by the fire in the study sipping hot cider.

"Science is a hobby of mine," he once told her. "As a child I used to dream of being a scientist. I even planned to go to university and study it. That was before I was crown prince."

Much the way Aaron had dreamed of being a doctor, she thought. "You weren't always crown prince?"

"I had an older brother, Edward. He would have been king, but he contracted meningitis when he was fifteen. It left him blind and physically impaired, so the crown was passed on to me. It's a bit ironic, really. We would spend hours in this very room, sitting by the fire. I would read to him, or play his favorite music. And now here I am, the incapacitated one."

"But only temporarily," she reminded him.

He just smiled and said, "Let's hope so."

The queen didn't share her husband's affection for Liv. She wasn't cruel or even rude. She was just…indifferent. Liv had overcome enough adversity in her life to understand that she couldn't let herself be bothered by the opinions of one person, but she would be lying if she said it didn't hurt her feelings just a little. Particularly because she was being judged not on the merits of her accomplishments, or even her morals, but on her lack of pedigree.

The Sunday before Christmas a blizzard dropped nearly a foot of snow and Liv let Aaron talk her into trying cross-country skiing. He wanted to take her to their ski lodge on the other side of the island, but with the Gingerbread Man still on the loose, the king insisted they stay on the castle property.

As Liv anticipated, she spent the better part of the first hour sitting in the snow.

"It just takes practice," Aaron told her as he hauled her back up on her feet again, and she actually managed to make it two or three yards before she fell on her face. But he assured her, "You're doing great!"

As inept as she felt, and embarrassed by her lack of coordination, Aaron's enthusiasm was contagious and she found that she was having fun. Since she arrived on Thomas Isle, he had introduced her to so many things that she otherwise would have never tried. If not for him, she would still be in her lab 24/7, working her life away instead of living it.

As much fun as they had been having, Liv knew it wouldn't last. She was in the process of testing compounds in hope of finding one that would kill the disease, and when she found the right combination, there would be no reason for her to stay. Leaving would be hard because she'd grown attached to Aaron. In fact, she felt she may even be in love with him, but that didn't change who they were. Besides, he had made it quite clear that he didn't want to be tied down. It was destined to end, and all she could do was enjoy the time they had left together.

An hour before sundown, exhausted to the center of her bones and aching in places she didn't even know she could ache, Liv tossed down her poles and said enough.

"You have to admit that was fun," he said as they stripped out of their gear.

"Oh, yeah," she said, hissing in pain as she bent over to unclip the ski boots. "Spending an entire day sitting in the snow has always been my idea of fun."

He shot her a skeptical look.

"Okay," she admitted with a shrug that sent spirals of pain down her back. "Maybe it was a *little* fun."

"You were getting pretty good near the end there."

It was her turn to look skeptical.

"I'm serious," he said. "By the end of winter I'll have you skiing like a pro."

The *end* of winter? How long did he expect her to stay? Did he *want* her to stay? And even more important, did *she* want to?

Of course he didn't. It was just an off-the-cuff remark that he probably hadn't thought through.

They walked up the stairs—well, he walked and she limped—to her room.

"I'm going to dress for dinner," he said. "Shall I pick you up on my way back down?"

"I don't think so."

"Are you sure?"

"Not only am I not hungry, but I'm exhausted and everything hurts. I'd like to lie down for a while."

"I'll come by and check on you later." He brushed a quick kiss across her lips, then headed to his room. She still wasn't comfortable with him showing her physical affection where someone might see. Although she didn't doubt that his family knew what was going on. They had just been kind enough not to say anything. She was sure they saw it for what it was. A fling. But she still didn't feel comfortable advertising it.

She went into her room and limped to the bathroom, downing three ibuprofen tablets before she stepped into the shower. She blasted the water as hot as she could stand, then she toweled off and crawled into bed naked. She must have fallen asleep the instant her head hit the pillow because the next thing she remembered was Aaron sitting on the edge of the mattress.

"What time is it?" she asked, her voice gravelly with sleep.

"Nine." He switched on the lamp beside the bed and she squinted against the sudden flood of light. "How do you feel?"

She tried to move and her muscles screamed in protest. "Awful," she groaned. "Even my eyelids hurt."

"Then you're going to like what I found," he said, holding up a small bottle.

"What is it?"

He flashed her one of his sexy, sizzling smiles. "Massage oil."

He eased back the covers, and when he saw that she was naked, he growled deep in his throat. "I swear, you get more beautiful every day."

He'd told her that so many times, so often that she was beginning to believe him, to see herself through his eyes. And in that instant in time everything was perfect.

He caressed her cheek with the backs of his fingers. "I love…"

Her heart jolted in her chest and she thought for sure that he was going to say he loved her. In that millisecond, she knew without a doubt that her honest reply would be, *I love you, too.*

"…just looking at you," he said instead.

The disappointment she felt was like a crushing weight on her chest, making it difficult to breathe. Tell him you love him, you idiot! But she couldn't do that. Love wasn't part of this arrangement. Instead she didn't say a word, she just wrapped her arms around him and pulled him down for a kiss. And when he made love to her, he was so sweet and gentle that it nearly brought her to tears.

She loved him so fiercely it made her chest ache, and she desperately wanted him to love her, too.

She wasn't sure how much longer she could take this.

It took some convincing on his part, but Aaron talked Liv into another afternoon of skiing on Christmas Eve. And despite her reservations she did exceptionally well. So well that he looked forward to introducing her to other recreational activities, like biking and kayaking and even low-level rock climbing. The problem was, she probably wouldn't be around long enough. He was sorry for that, but in a way relieved. He'd grown closer and more attached to Liv than he had any other woman in his life. Dangerously close. And even though he knew he was walking a very fine and precarious line, he wasn't ready to let go yet.

Christmas morning he woke Liv at 5:45 a.m., despite the fact that they had been up half the night making love.

"It's too early," she groaned, shoving a pillow over her head.

He pulled it back off. "Come on, wake up. We're gathering with everyone in the study at six."

She squinted up at him. "*Six?* What for?"

"To open presents. Then afterward we have a huge breakfast. It's been a tradition as long as I can remember."

She groaned again and closed her eyes. "I'd rather sleep."

"It's *Christmas*. And you promised you would spend it with me and my family, remember?"

"I was thinking that you meant Christmas dinner."

"I meant the entire day." He tugged on her arm. "Now come on, get up."

She grumbled about it, but let him pull her to an upright position. She yawned and rubbed her eyes and asked, "What should I wear?"

"Pajamas." At her questioning look, he added, "It's what everyone else will be wearing."

She made him wait while she brushed her hair and teeth, and when they got to the study his siblings and sister-in-law were already gathered around the tree, waiting to open the piles of gifts stacked there. Their father sat in his favorite armchair and their mother beside him at the hearth. Geoffrey stood at the bar pouring hot cider. Christmas music played softly and a fire blazed in the fireplace.

"Hurry up, you two!" Louisa said excitedly.

"I shouldn't be here," Liv mumbled under her breath, standing stiffly beside him, looking as though she were about to go to the guillotine.

"Of course you should." When she refused to move, he took her hand and pulled her over to the tree and sat her by Louisa. The second she was off her feet she pulled her hand from his.

"Merry Christmas!" Louisa gushed, giving Liv a warm hug, and after a slight hesitation, Liv hugged her back. If anyone could make Liv feel like part of the family, it was Louisa. Although right now she just looked overwhelmed. She looked downright stunned when Anne, who wore the santa hat and passed out the gifts, announced, "And here's one for Olivia from the king and queen."

Liv's jaw actually dropped. "F-for me?"

Anne handed it to her. "That's what the tag says."

She took it and just held it, as if she wasn't sure what to do.

"Aren't you going to open it?" Aaron asked.

"But I didn't get anything for anyone."

His mother surprised him by saying, "Your being here is the only gift we need."

Liv bit her lip, picking gingerly at the taped edge of the paper, while everyone else tore into theirs enthusiastically. It was almost as though she had never opened a gift before or had forgotten how. What disturbed him most was that it might be true. When was the last time anyone had given her anything?

She finally got it open and pulled from the layers of gold tissue paper a deep blue cashmere cardigan.

"Oh," she breathed. "It's beautiful."

"You keep the lab so dreadfully cold," his mother said. "I thought it might come in handy."

"Thank you so much."

Anne passed out another round of gifts and this time there was one for Liv from Chris and Melissa, a pair of thick wool socks.

"For skiing," Melissa told her.

Louisa got Liv a silver bracelet decorated with science-themed charms, and Anne gave her a matching cashmere mitten, scarf and hat set. Aaron had gotten her something, too, but she would have to wait until later to get it.

The last present under the tree was for the king and queen from Chris and Melissa. Their mother opened it and inside was what looked like an ultrasound photo. Did that mean…?

"What is this?" their mother asked, looking confused.

"Those are your grandchildren," Chris said with a grin. "All three of them."

"Three grandchildren!" his mother shrieked, while his father beamed proudly and said, "Congratulations!"

"They implanted five embryos," Melissa said. "Three took. It's still very early, but we couldn't wait to tell you. My doctor said everything looks great."

Aaron had never seen his mother look so proud or

excited. She knelt down to hug them both, then *everyone* was hugging Chris and Melissa and congratulating them.

"Isn't it great? I'm going to be an uncle," Aaron said, turning to Liv, but she wasn't smiling or laughing like the rest of them. In fact, she looked as though she might be sick. "Hey, are you okay?"

She shook her head and said, "Excuse me," then she bolted from the room, seven startled pairs of eyes following her.

"What happened?" his mother asked, and Louisa said, "Did we do something wrong?"

"I don't know," Aaron said, but he was going to find out.

Fourteen

Liv reached her room, heart beating frantically and hands shaking, and went straight to the closet for her suitcase. She dropped it on the bed and opened it just as Aaron appeared in the doorway.

"What happened down there?" he asked, looking concerned. "Are you okay?"

"I'm sorry. Please tell everyone that I'm *so* sorry. I just couldn't take it another minute."

He saw her suitcase and asked, "What are you doing?"

"Packing. I have to leave."

He looked stunned. "Was being with my family really that awful?"

"No, it was absolutely wonderful. I had no idea it could be like that. I just… I can't do this anymore."

"What do you mean? I thought we were having fun."

"I was. I *am*. The time we've spent together has been the best in my life."

She started toward the closet to get her clothes, but he stepped in her way, looking so hopelessly confused she wanted to hug him. "So what's the problem?"

Did he honestly have no idea what was going on? "I know it's illogical and totally irrational, but I've fallen in love with you, Aaron."

She gave him a few seconds to return the sentiment, but he only frowned, looking troubled, and it made her inexplicably sad. She hadn't really believed he would share her feelings, but she had hoped. But as she had reminded herself over and over, the world just didn't work that way. Not the world she lived in.

"We don't have any further to go with this," she said. "And I'm just not the kind of person who can tread water. I think it would be better for us both if I leave now. The work I have left to do, I can finish in my lab in the States."

"You can't leave," he said, looking genuinely upset.

"I have to."

"I *do* care about you."

"I know you do." Just not enough. Not enough for her, anyway. She wanted more. She wanted to be part of a family, to feel as if she belonged somewhere. And not just temporarily. She wanted forever.

She wanted it so badly that she ached, but she would never have that with him.

His brow furrowed. "I just… I can't…"

"I know," she assured him. "This is not your fault. This is *all* me. I never meant to fall in love with you."

"I…I don't know what to say."

Just tell me you love me, she wanted to tell him, but Aaron didn't do love. He didn't get serious and settle down. And even if he did, it wouldn't be with someone like her. She didn't fit in. She wasn't good enough for someone like him.

"I'll pack up the lab today," she told him. "Can you arrange for a flight off the island tomorrow?"

"Won't you at least have dinner with us? It's Christmas."

She shrugged. "It's just another day for me."

That was a lie. It used to be, but after this morning it would forever be a reminder of how wonderful it could be and everything she'd been missing out on, and so *desperately* wanted. In a way she wished she'd never met Aaron, that he'd never called for her help. She would still be living in blissful ignorance.

"You should get back to your family," she told him.

"You're sure I can't convince you to spend the day with us?"

"I'm sure."

He looked disappointed, but he didn't push the issue, and she was relieved because she was this close to caving, to throwing herself into his arms and saying she would stay as long as he wanted. Even if he couldn't love her.

"I'll have Geoffrey bring your gifts up and inform you of your travel arrangements," he said.

"Thank you."

"You're *sure* I can't change your mind?"

There was an almost pleading look in his eyes, and she wanted so badly to give in, but her heart just couldn't take it. "I can't."

"I'll leave you alone to pack."

He stepped out of the room, closing the door behind him, and though it felt so final, she knew she was doing the right thing.

She packed all of her clothes, leaving out one clean outfit for the following day, then she went down to the lab to start packing there, feeling utterly empty inside.

She never had seen the ghost again, but she'd made her presence known by occasionally stacking Liv's papers, hiding her pen or opening the lab door. Maybe she should have felt uncomfortable knowing she wasn't alone, but instead the presence was a comfort. She'd even caught herself talking to her, even though the conversation was always one-sided. She realized now that when she was gone she might even miss her elusive and unconventional companion.

She was going to miss everything about Thomas Isle.

Geoffrey came down around dinnertime with a

plate of food. She wasn't hungry, but she thanked him anyway. "I bet you're happy not to have to deal with me anymore," she joked, expecting him to emphatically agree.

Instead his expression was serious when he said, "Quite the contrary, miss."

She was too stunned to say a word as he turned and left. And here she thought he viewed her as a nuisance. The fact that he hadn't only made her feel worse.

She packed the last of her equipment by midnight, and when she went up to her room, waiting for her as promised were the gifts the family had given her and the itinerary for her trip. She sat down at the desk by the window writing them each a note of thanks, not only for the presents, but for accepting her into their home and treating her like family. She left them on the desk where Elise would find them when she cleaned the room.

She climbed under the covers around one-thirty, but tossed and turned and slept only an hour or two before her alarm buzzed at seven. She got out of bed feeling a grogginess that even a shower couldn't wash away. At seven-forty-five someone came to fetch her luggage, then a few minutes later Flynn from security came to fetch her.

"It's time to go to the airstrip, miss," he said.

"Let's do it," she said, feeling both relieved and heartsick. She wanted so badly to change her mind, to stay just a little bit longer and hope that he would see he loved her. But it was too late to turn back now. Even if it wasn't, she knew in her heart that it would be a bad idea.

She followed Flynn down the stairs to the foyer, and when she saw that the entire family lined up to say goodbye, the muscles in her throat contracted so tight that she could barely breathe. This was the last thing she'd expected. She had assumed her departure would be as uneventful as her arrival.

The king was first in line. If she had expected some cold and formal goodbye, a handshake and a "have a nice life," she couldn't have been more wrong. He hugged her warmly and said, "I've enjoyed our talks."

"Me, too," she said, realizing he was the closest thing she had ever had to a father figure. She hoped with all her being that the heart pump was successful and he lived a long, productive life. Long enough to see his daughters marry and his grandchildren grow. She wasn't a crier, but she could feel the burn of tears in her throat and behind her eyes. All she could manage to squeak out was, "Thanks for everything."

The queen was next. She took Liv's hands and air kissed her cheek. "It's been a pleasure having you with us," she said, and actually looked as though she meant it.

"Thank you for having me in your home," Liv said.

Chris and Melissa stood beside the queen. Chris kissed Liv's cheek and Melissa, with tears running in a steady river down her face—no doubt pregnancy hormones at work—hugged her hard. "Watch the mail for a baby shower invitation. I want you there."

If only. It was a lovely thought, yet totally unrealistic. She was sure by then they would have forgotten all about her.

Louisa scooped her up into a bone-crushing embrace. "We'll miss you," she said. "Keep in touch."

Anne hugged her, too, though not as enthusiastically. But she leaned close and Liv thought she was going to kiss her cheek, but instead she whispered, "My brother is a dolt."

Of all the things anyone could have said to her, that was probably the sweetest, and the tears were hovering so close to the surface now that she couldn't even reply.

Aaron was last, and the one she was least looking forward to saying goodbye to. He stood aside from his family by the door, hands in his pants pockets, eyes to the floor. As she approached he looked up at her.

The tears welled closer to the surface and she swallowed them back down. Please let this be quick and painless.

"You'll contact me when you have results," he said, all business.

She nodded. "Of course. And I'll send you updates on my progress. At the rate it's going, you should have it in plenty of time for the next growing season."

"Excellent." He was quiet for a second, then he said in a low voice, "I'm sorry. I just can't—"

"It's okay," she said, even though it wasn't. Even though it felt as though he was ripping her heart from her chest.

He nodded, looking remorseful. She had started to turn toward the door when he cursed under his breath, hooked a hand behind her neck, pulled her to him and kissed her—*really* kissed her—in front of his entire family. He finally pulled away, leaving her feeling breathless and dizzy, said, "Goodbye Liv," then turned and walked away, taking her heart with him.

The flights to the U.S. couldn't have been smoother or more uneventful, but when Liv got back to her apartment and let herself inside it almost didn't feel like home. She'd barely been gone a month, but it felt as if everything had changed, and there was this nagging ache in the center of her chest that refused to go away.

"You just need sleep," she rationalized.

She climbed into bed and, other than a few trips to the bathroom, didn't get back out for three days. That was when she reminded herself that she'd never been one to wallow in self-pity. She was stronger than that. Besides, she needed to see William. She hadn't spoken to or even e-mailed him in weeks. Maybe they could have a late lunch and talk about his proposal and she could let him down easy.

She tried calling him at the lab, but he wasn't there and he wasn't answering his house or cell phone. Concerned that something might be wrong, she drove to his house instead.

She knocked, then a minute later knocked harder. She was about to give up and leave when the door finally opened.

Being that it was the middle of the afternoon, she was surprised to find him in a T-shirt and pajama bottoms, looking as though he'd just rolled out of bed.

"Oh, you're back," he said, and maybe it was her imagination, but he didn't seem happy to see her. Maybe he was hurt that she hadn't readily accepted his proposal. Maybe he was angry that she'd taken so long and hadn't been in contact.

"I'm back," she said with a smile that she hoped didn't look as forced as it felt. She thought that maybe seeing him again after such a long time apart would stir up feelings that had been buried or repressed, but she didn't feel a thing. "I thought we could talk."

"Um, well…" He glanced back over his shoulder, into the front room. "Now's not the best time."

She frowned. "Are you sick?"

"No, no, nothing like that."

Liv heard a voice behind him say, "Billy, who is it?"

A *female* voice. Then the door opened wider and a young girl whom Liv didn't recognize stood there dressed in, of all things, one of William's T-shirts.

"Hi!" she said brightly. "Are you a friend of Billy's?"

Billy?

"We work in the lab together," William said, shooting Liv a look that said, *Go along with it.* He obviously didn't want this girl to know that she and William had had anything but a professional relationship. Which, if you wanted to get technical, they never really had.

"I'm Liv," Liv said, because William didn't introduce them. She had the feeling he wished she would just disappear. "And you are?"

The girl smiled brightly. "I'm Angela, Billy's fiancée."

Fiancée? William was *engaged?*

She waved in front of Liv's face a hand sporting an enormous diamond ring. "We're getting married in two weeks," she squealed.

"Congratulations," Liv said, waiting to feel the tiniest bit of remorse, but what she felt instead was relief. She was off the hook. She didn't have to feel bad for turning him down.

"Could you give us a second, Angie?" he said. "It's work."

"Sure," she said, smiling brightly. "Nice to meet you, Liv."

William stepped out onto the porch, closing the door behind him. "I'm so sorry. I wasn't expecting you."

If he'd answered his phone, he would have been, but she was pretty sure they had been otherwise occupied. "It's okay," she said. "I only came here to tell you that I can't marry you."

"Yes, well, when you stopped calling, I just assumed…"

"It just wasn't something I wanted to do over the phone. I guess it doesn't matter now."

"I'm sorry I didn't have a chance to prepare you. I mean, it was very sudden. Obviously."

"I'm very happy for you." And jealous as hell that even he had found someone. Not that he didn't deserve to be happy. It just didn't seem fair that it was so easy for some people. Of course, falling in love with Aaron had been incredibly easy. The hard part was getting him to love her back.

He smiled shyly, something she had never seen him do before, and said, "It was love at first sight."

She left William's house feeling more alone than she had in her entire life. She'd gone from having seven people who accepted her as part of the family—even if the queen had done it grudgingly—to having no one.

Fifteen

Aaron sat in his office, staring out the window at the grey sky through a flurry of snow, unable to concentrate on a single damn thing. He should be down in the greenhouse, meeting with the foreman about the spring crops, but he just couldn't work up the enthusiasm to get his butt out of the chair. The idea of another long season of constantly worrying about growth rates and rainfall and late frosts, not to mention pests and disease, gave him a headache. He was tired of being forced into doing something that deep down he really didn't want to do. He was tired of duty and compromise and putting everyone else's wishes ahead of his own. And even though it had taken a few days for him to admit it to himself, he was tired of shallow, meaningless relationships. He was sick of being alone.

He missed Liv.

Unfortunately she didn't seem to share the sentiment. It had been two weeks since she left and he hadn't heard a word from her. Not even an update on her progress. Yet he couldn't bring himself to pick up the phone and call her. Maybe she'd run back to William.

"Are you going to mope in here all day?"

Aaron looked up to see Anne standing in his office doorway. "I'm working," he lied.

"Of course you are."

He scowled. "Do you need something?"

"I just came by to let you know that I talked to Liv."

He bolted upright in his chair. "What? When?"

"About five minutes ago. She wanted to update us on her progress. And inquire about father's health."

"Why did she call you?"

Anne folded her arms across her chest. "Gosh, I don't know. Maybe because you *broke her heart.*"

"Did she say that?"

"Of course not."

"Well," he said, turning toward the window, "she always has William to console her."

"William?"

"He's another scientist. He asked her to marry him before she came here." Not that Aaron believed for a minute she would actually marry William. Not when she admitted she loved Aaron.

"Oh, so *that* was what she meant."

He swiveled back to her. "What?"

"She mentioned that, with the wedding coming up, it might be several weeks before we get another update. I just didn't realize it was *her* wedding."

She was actually going to do it? She was going to compromise and marry a man she didn't love? How could she marry William when she was in love with Aaron?

The thought of her marrying William, or anyone else for that matter, made him feel like punching a hole in the wall. And why? Because he was jealous? Because he didn't like to lose?

The truth hit him with a clarity that was almost painful in its intensity. He loved her. She couldn't marry William because the only man she should be marrying was him.

He rose from his chair and told Anne, "If you'll excuse me, I need to have a word with Mother and Father."

"Something wrong?" Anne said with a grin.

"Quite the opposite." After weeks, maybe even *years* of uncertainty, he finally knew what he had to do.

Aaron found his parents in their suite watching the midday news. "I need to have a word with you."

"Of course," his father said, gesturing him inside.

He picked up the remote and muted the television. "Is there a problem?"

"No. No problem."

"What is it?" his mother asked.

"I just wanted to let you both know that I'm flying to the States today."

"With the Gingerbread Man still on the loose, do you think that's wise?" his father asked.

"I have to see Liv."

"Why?" his mother demanded.

"So I can ask her to marry me."

Her face transformed into an amusing combination of shock and horror. "*Marry* you?"

"That's what I said."

"*Absolutely not.* I won't have it, Aaron."

"It's not up to you, Mother. This is my decision."

"Your father and I know what's best for this family. That girl is—"

"Enough!" his father thundered, causing both Aaron and his mother to jolt with surprise. It had been a long time since he'd been well enough to raise his voice to such a threatening level. "Choose your words carefully, my dear, lest you say something you'll later regret."

She turned to him, eyes wide with surprise. "You're all right with this?"

"Is there a reason I shouldn't be?"

"I know you're fond of her, but a *marriage?* She isn't of noble blood."

"Do you love her, Aaron?" his father asked.

"I do," he said, never feeling so certain of anything in his life.

He turned and asked Aaron's mother, "Do you love our son?"

"What kind of question is that? Of course I do."

"Do you want him to be happy?"

"You know I do. I just—"

"Since Liv has come into his life, have you ever seen him so happy?"

She frowned, as though she didn't like the answer she had to give. "No...but..."

He took her hand. "She's not of noble blood. Who cares? She's a good person. Thoughtful and sweet and kind. If you'd taken any time to get to know her, you would realize that. Royal or not, our son loves her, so she deserves our respect. And our *acceptance*. Life is too short. Shouldn't he spend it with someone who makes him happy? Someone he loves?"

She was silent for a moment as she considered his words, and finally she said, "I want to state for the record that I'm not happy about this."

Aaron nodded. "So noted."

"However, if you love her and she loves you, I suppose I'll just have to learn to accept it."

"You have our blessing," his father told him.

"There's one more thing. I'm going back to school."

His mother frowned. "What for?"

"Because I still need a few science credits before I can apply to med school."

"*Med* school? At your age? What in heaven's name for?"

"Because I've always wanted to."

His father mirrored her look of concern. "But who will oversee the fields?"

"I'm sure we can find someone capable to fill my position. You'll manage just fine without me."

The king didn't look convinced. "Why don't we discuss this when you get back? Maybe we can reach some sort of compromise."

He wanted to tell his father that he was through compromising, but this was a lot to spring on them in one day. It would be best if he gave it some time to sink in.

"All right," he agreed. "We'll talk about it when I get home."

"I want you to take a full security detail with you," his father said. "I know we haven't had any more threats, but I don't want to take any chances."

"Of course," he agreed, and as he left his parents' suite to make the arrangements, he felt an enormous weight had been lifted from his shoulders. That for the first time instead of just watching his life pass by before him, he was finally an active participant. And he knew with a certainty he felt deep in his bones that until he had Liv by his side, life would never be complete.

And he would do anything to get her back.

* * *

It was late in the evening when his limo pulled up in front of Liv's apartment. The building was very plain and unassuming, which didn't surprise him in the least. Hadn't she claimed to spend most of her time in the lab? He hoped she wasn't there now, or, God forbid, at William's place. Not that he wouldn't hunt her down and find her wherever she happened to be. And if William tried to interfere, Aaron might have to hurt him.

Flynn opened the door for him.

"I'm going in alone," Aaron told him.

"Sir—"

"I don't imagine there's an assassin staked out on the off chance that I drop by. You can wait outside."

He nodded grudgingly. "Yes, sir."

Aaron went inside and took the stairs up to the third floor. Her apartment was the first on the right. There was no bell, so he rapped on the door. Only a few seconds passed before it opened, and there stood Liv wearing flannel pajama bottoms and a faded sweatshirt, looking as sweet and sexy and as irresistible as the first time he'd met her.

She blinked several times, as if she thought she might be imagining him there. "Aaron?"

He grinned. "The one and only."

She didn't return his smile. She just looked…confused. In every scenario he had imagined, she had immediately thrown herself into his arms and thanked him for saving her from a life of marital disaster. Maybe this wouldn't be quite as easy as he'd anticipated.

"What are you doing here?" she asked.

"Can I come in?"

She glanced back inside the apartment, then to him, looking uneasy. Had it not occurred to him that William could be there, in her apartment?

"Is someone...*with* you?" he asked.

She shook her head. "No, it's just that my apartment is kind of a mess. I'm getting ready to do some redecorating."

"I won't hold it against you," he said.

She stepped back and gestured him inside. Her apartment was small and sparsely furnished. And what furniture she did have was covered in plastic drop cloths.

"I was getting ready to paint," she explained. She didn't offer to take his coat, or clear a seat for him. "What do you want?"

"I'm here to prevent you from making the worst mistake of your life."

She frowned and looked around the room. "Painting my apartment?"

She looked so hopelessly confused that he had to smile. "No. I'm here to stop you from marrying a man you don't love."

"Why would you think I'm getting married?"

It was his turn to look confused. "Anne said..."

Before he could finish the sentence, reality slapped him in the face. Hard. He'd been set up. Anne was trying to get him off his behind, so he would go after Liv. And he'd given her just the ammunition she needed when he told her about William.

The next time he saw his sister, he was going to give her a big hug.

"I take it you never said anything to my sister about a wedding?"

She shook her head.

"So, you're definitely not marrying William," he confirmed, just to be sure.

"I should hope not, considering he's engaged to someone else."

That was by far the best news Aaron had had all day.

"What difference does it make?" she asked. "Why do you care who I marry?"

"I care," he said, taking a step toward her, "because the only man you should be marrying is me."

Her eyes went wide with disbelief. "I beg your pardon?"

"You heard me." He got down on one knee and pulled the ring box from his coat pocket. He opened it, offering her the five-carat-diamond family ring that sat nestled in a bed of royal-blue velvet. "Will you, Liv?"

For several excruciating seconds that felt like hours, she just stared at him openmouthed, and he began to wonder if she'd changed her mind about him, if, now that they'd been apart for a while, her affection for him had faded. For an instant he genuinely worried that she would actually tell him no.

But when she finally spoke, she said, "You don't want to get married. You're not cut out to be a family man. Remember?"

"Liv, you told me that you love me. Is that still true?"

She bit her lip and nodded.

"And I love you. It took me a while to admit it to myself, but I do. And I couldn't imagine spending the rest of my life with anyone else."

A smile twitched at the corner of her mouth. "What about that excellent rate you get from the girl-of-the-month club?"

He grinned. "I already cancelled my subscription. The only girl I want in my life is you. Now, are you going to make me kneel here all night?"

"But what about your parents? They'll never let you marry a nonroyal."

"They've already given their blessing."

Her eyes went wide. "Your *mother* gave her blessing? Did you have to hold a gun to her head?"

"I'll admit she did it grudgingly, but don't worry, she'll come around. If we give her a grandchild or two, she'll be ecstatic."

"You want that?" she asked. "You really want children?"

"Only if I can have them with you, Liv."

That hint of a smile grew to encompass her entire face. "Ask me again."

He grinned. "Olivia, will you marry me?"

"Yes." She laughed as he slid the ring on her finger, then he pulled her into his arms. "Yes, Your Highness, I definitely will!"

* * * * *

THE PRINCE SHE
NEVER FORGOT

SCARLET WILSON

This book is dedicated to our newest family addition
Luca Cole Dickson, already gorgeous,
well-behaved and utterly charming.
The ladies in his later life won't stand a chance!

PROLOGUE

Ten years earlier

SHE COULD FEEL the electricity in the air, feel the excitement. It seemed as if everyone in the world had decided to celebrate New Year's Eve in Paris.

She was jostled along with the crowd, being practically carried off her feet on the route from the Champs-élysées towards the Eiffel Tower.

'Aren't you glad you came?' her friend Polly screamed in her ear, sloshing wine over her sleeve. 'This is the best place in the world right now.'

'Yes, it is,' murmured Ruby.

It certainly beat sitting at home in her flat, brooding over the job that wasn't to be or the boyfriend who never should have been.

Polly gave a squeal. 'The fireworks will be starting in an hour. Let's try and get near the front!'

Ruby nodded as she was shouldered from behind. There were ten in their group but it was getting harder and harder to stick together. 'I need to find a bathroom before we head to the fireworks,' she whispered to Polly. 'Give me five minutes.'

There were cafés and bars open all the way along the Champs-élysées, but unfortunately for her just about every female in the city seemed to have the same idea that she had.

She waved to Polly, 'Go on without me. I'll meet you at the sign we saw earlier.'

The group had already planned their night with precision. Dinner on a riverboat. Drinks in the hotel. A walk along the Champs-élysées and rendezvous at the Eiffel Tower for the fireworks. They'd already picked the spot they planned to stand at in case anyone got lost—which on a night like tonight was a certainty.

She stood in a queue for an eternity before finally heading back out to the thronging crowds. In the thirty minutes it had taken to get access to a bathroom it seemed the whole of Paris had started to congregate in the streets.

The crowds were sweeping along the Avenue George V, carrying along anyone who happened to be standing close enough. It was one part terrifying, one part exhilarating.

The crowd was even thicker at the Rue de l'Université. The street was packed, with everyone heading directly to the base of the Eiffel Tower. Ruby glanced at her watch. Visiting the bathroom hadn't been such a good idea. There was no way she was going to be able to find her friends in this crowd.

But she wasn't too worried. The mood of the crowd was jubilant. People were drinking wine and singing. The atmosphere and heavy police presence made her feel safe—even if she was alone.

Around her she heard dozens of different accents: snatches of English, Italian and Japanese all mixed in with French. The streets were lit with multi-coloured lights and a variety of decorations and garlands left over from Christmas. She unfastened the buttons on her red wool coat. She'd expected Paris to be cold in December, but the heat from the people around her meant the temperature was rising.

She clutched tightly onto the bag strung diagonally in front of her, keeping her hand clasped over the zipper. Pickpockets were rife in Paris at New Year's. They'd all been warned to keep a close hold of their belongings.

Her phone beeped just as she was in sight of the Eiffel Tower and she struggled to move out of the thronging crowd. It had practically ground to a halt, with people from behind still pressing ahead. The streets were packed. There was no way forward.

She moved sideways, unzipping her bag and pulling out her phone.

Where are you?

It was from Polly. Her friends were obviously waiting at their designated meeting point.

She typed quickly. Not sure if I can get to you, but I'll try. She pressed Send just as someone bumped her from behind and the phone skittered from her hand.

'Oh, no!'

It was kicked one way, then another, quickly going out of sight. She tried to push her way through the crowd sideways, but that proved impossible. It was a sea of people. And she was heading in the wrong direction.

'Hey, watch out. Ouch!'

Her feet were trampled, her ribs elbowed and the wind knocked from her. It was impossible. She looked up for a few seconds, to try and make her way through the crowd, then looked down again amongst the stampeding feet, trying to track down her phone.

A thud to her shoulder sent her flying into a group of rowdy Germans.

'Sorry...sorry.'

They were laughing and joking and smelling of beer. She tried to find her way through but it was virtually impossible. There seemed to be nowhere to go.

Her chest started to tighten. They weren't doing or saying anything untoward, but the sheer amount of people meant they'd started to crowd around her, closing in. She tried to take a deep breath and lifted her elbows up, edging her way to the side. But the only place she seemed to be moving was closer and closer.

There was a waft of beer-soaked breath on her cheek. Too close. Too invasive. A hand at her back, someone pressing against her hip.

'Let me out. Let me through. Move, please!'

A hand reached down between her shoulders, grabbing her coat and pulling her upwards. The air left her lungs momentarily and her feet were still stuck amongst the crowd. A strong arm wound around her waist and pulled her clear. Her feet stopped unsteadily on a wall at shoulder height to the throng.

'Are you okay?'

She was teetering on the wall. The hand and arm that had steadied her had pulled away the instant she was free. She reached and grabbed hold of the dark sleeve in front of her, trying to regain her balance.

The voice sounded again. 'Are you okay? Are you drunk?' There was a slight edge of disappointment to the voice.

She steadied herself on the wall, taking a deep breath of relief before turning around to speak to her rescuer. How dared he accuse her of being drunk?

But the words died in her throat. Bright blue eyes and a broad chest obstructed her view.

Even on a dark Paris night those blue eyes would have attracted her attention. He was tall, dark-haired, with a broad chest, wearing a simple white T-shirt and jeans with a dark wool coat on top. Trust her to find the best-looking guy in Paris and have no reliable witnesses. No one would believe her.

She automatically lifted her hands. 'No. No, I'm not drunk. I just got stuck in a crowd going in the opposite direction from me.'

His demeanour changed. The skin around his eyes

creased as he smiled. 'What? You're going home already? You don't want to see the fireworks?'

His accent sent tingles across her skin. He sounded French, with a little something else.

He was teasing her, and now she could actually breathe she could take a little teasing.

She sighed. 'No. I'm not going home. Not tonight anyway. Of course I want to see the fireworks.' She held out her hands to the bodies pressed below. 'Just not like this.' The crowd had ground to a halt. She stared across at the sea of people. 'I was supposed to be meeting my friends.'

'You are lost?' He sounded concerned.

'Not exactly.' She turned back to face him, getting a whiff of woody aftershave. 'We were meeting at a sign near the Eiffel Tower.' She shook her head. 'I have absolutely no chance of getting there now.'

She had no intention of leaving the safety of this wall any time soon. She only hoped his friends weren't all about to join them and there'd be no room for her to stay here.

He smiled as he looked down at all the people below. 'You could be right. I'm sorry if I startled you but you looked frightened. I thought you were beginning to panic in the crowd.'

Her heart had stopped fluttering in her chest and her breathing was settling down. It had been an odd feeling, and so not like her. Ruby Wetherspoon didn't tend to panic.

'I was. Thank you. I've never really been in a crowd like that before.

It had definitely been a bit claustrophobic.' She shook her coat free, letting some air circulate around her, and pulled her red hat from her hair.

'There—that's much better.'

'It certainly is.'

He was smiling appreciatively at her and for a second she was unnerved. But, no. There was nothing predatory about her rescuer. He had kind eyes, even if the man exuded sex appeal from twenty paces. If her up-close-and-personal alarm was going off it wasn't because she was scared—it was because it had been jolted back into life. About time too.

He nodded slowly. 'Crowds can be…difficult.'

It was an odd choice of words, but then again her hesitant French would sound much poorer than his English.

'And you'd know?' She was curious.

His face crinkled. It seemed her half-inquisitive, half-sarcastic question was lost on him.

She held out her hand towards him. 'Ruby. Ruby Wetherspoon from England.'

His warm hand closed around hers. 'Alex,' he said simply.

Her eyes glanced up and down his body. White T-shirt, blue jeans and black boots. But the dark wool coat seemed a little strange for a young guy—a little formal.

'Are you from here?'

The corners of his lips turned upwards. 'Close enough.'

Mystery. She liked it. Perfect for New Year's Eve.

Under normal circumstances she might have felt a little nervous, a little wary around a mysterious stranger. But Alex didn't give her those kind of vibes.

Trust your instincts. That was what her gran had always told her. And she should have. Because if she had she probably wouldn't have found her boyfriend in bed with her ex-best friend. Truth was, she couldn't wait to see the end of this stinker of a year.

She glanced around. For the moment they were the only two people perched on this precarious wall. 'Well, Alex from "close enough", where are your friends? Am I about to get trampled and thrown back to the crowd when they all want a place on this wall?'

She sent a silent prayer upwards. What was the betting they were all gorgeous and female?

He shrugged. 'I lost them too. I climbed up here to look for them. Then I decided I liked the view.'

She turned to face where he was looking. Of course. A perfect view of the Eiffel Tower. For now it had a row of white lights running up the outside of its edges. The sun had set a few hours ago and it stood out like a beacon in the dark sky.

She'd been so busy fighting her way through the crowd that she hadn't really had time to stop and take in the sight.

'Wow. I just remembered why I came here,' she breathed.

A few people shouldered past beneath them, knocking into her feet, and she wobbled again. His arm rested around her waist to steady her, and he didn't move it once she'd regained her balance.

'So, why is an English girl in Paris for New Year's Eve?'

Why, indeed? She was still asking herself that question. And Mr Gorgeous Mysterious Stranger didn't really need the whole truth. Maybe just a tiny part.

'Visiting a boyfriend?' he added.

It was a loaded question. Was he really testing to see if she was taken?

She sucked in a deep breath and tried not to let the idiot smile that was whooping and dancing around in her brain actually appear. 'My flatmate Polly persuaded me it was time to try something new. We usually spend every New Year's in London. We did try a Scottish lodge once, but that was a disaster. Snowed in with no power and no booze.'

He was laughing at her now.

She held out her hands. 'What girl would say no to Paris on New Year's? This place is just amazing...' Her voice tailed off. 'And, to be honest, I'm not sorry to see this year go.'

'You've had a bad year?'

'Somewhere between a wrecking ball and a demolition derby.'

She could almost see his brain trying to make sense of her words.

'Ahh. You sound sad. But surely not everything about this year can have been bad?'

Perfect. Her own Pollyanna.

He was right. Of course he was right. She'd just needed someone to remind her.

She gave a little nod. 'Of course not. There have been a few good things. I qualified this year.'

'As what?'

'A speech and language therapist.'

'Well, that sounds great. Congratulations.'

She nodded. 'Yeah. Yes, it is.'

Three years doing a course she'd absolutely loved. Her placements had been fabulous, letting her practice all her skills and making her realise exactly what she wanted to do.

'So why aren't you jumping for joy? You'll get to do the job that you want. Some people would give anything for that.'

His voice sounded a little wistful.

Wow. She must sound an ungrateful misery-guts. But there was something easy about talking to a perfect stranger. Someone who didn't know all the people or personalities involved. Someone completely independent.

'I should be. I know. It's just that I really, really wanted to work in one area. I did two training stints there, but by the time I'd qualified there was only one job and they gave it to someone with more experience.' She shrugged. It still stung. She'd had her heart set on working there.

'Where was it?'

'In London. A specialist speech and language unit attached to the biggest children's hospital. I loved it there. The staff were really special and the kids...they just made my heart melt.'

'What kind of things did you do there?'

He seemed genuinely interested.

'I worked with children with specific language impairment and language disorders. Those kids made progress every day.' She held up her finger and thumb. 'Even if it was just in the tiniest way.' She smiled again, caught up in the memories. 'I even worked with children with hearing problems. Seeing the look on their faces when they got a cochlear implant and heard for the first time…' She shook her head. 'It was magical. It was exactly what I wanted to do.' She lifted her eyes to meet his. 'These things stay with you for ever.'

He was looking at her with such intensity, such sincerity, that it took her breath away. Here, in a city with over two million people, he was looking only at her.

She couldn't imagine how she'd done it, but she seemed to have completely captured his attention—just as he'd captured hers.

His voice was low and deep. 'So you don't have a job now?'

Even the timbre of his voice sent butterflies along her skin. Those two glasses of wine earlier seemed to have finally hit her system. Any minute now she was going to have to find some food before her brain was truly addled. No guy could have this kind of effect on a girl? Not in real life anyway.

She shook her head in an attempt to find some clear thoughts. 'I do. And I don't mean to sound ungrateful. I've got a job at a stroke unit, working with patients who've suffered a stroke and are having trouble with speech.'

He kept smiling at her—one minute looking serious, the next as if she amused him. Those teeth were perfect. Too perfect. He must be a model. He probably advertised toothpaste.

He raised his eyebrows. 'But that sounds just as important as the other job.'

Clear, rational thought. Easy when you didn't dream about the place where you wanted to work every night.

She cringed. 'I know. I *know*. I don't mean to sound like that. I'm lucky to have a job. Not everyone on my course got one. And once I get there I know that'll love it.' She gave a sad smile. 'It's just not what I'd hoped for, that's all.'

She heard him suck in a deep breath. 'We don't always get what we hope for, Ruby.'

His voice was serious. It made her curious.

He couldn't possibly have any idea of the kind of thoughts that were circulating in her head right now. Her imagination was running riot. Handsome mysterious Frenchman. Gorgeous, smelling good enough to eat. Polly wouldn't believe a word of this. Any minute now someone would pinch her and she'd wake up.

Time to get back to reality. Time to get a little nosey.

'So, Alex. What do *you* do? Do you work around here?'

He shook his head. 'I'm like you—just visiting for New Year. I'm in business. Boring things. Investment banking.'

Smash. The first dream broken. Not a model. But what interested her most was how he'd described his job. This guy gave very little away.

'Why do you do it if it's boring?'

'Because I'm expected to. It's a job.'

Another tell-nothing answer. The less he said, the more she was curious.

His phone buzzed and he pulled it from his pocket and frowned.

'Is it your friends? Are they looking for you?' She looked through the crowd, expecting to see a bunch of Amazonian blondes charging in to steal their prize back.

He shook his head. 'Nothing like that.' He stuffed the phone back in his pocket.

Ruby bent forward and peered into the crowd below. 'I dropped my phone. It's probably smashed to smithereens.'

'Smithereens? What is that?

He wrinkled his nose. It made him even cuter, if that was humanly possible.

'You know—broken into lots and lots of tiny pieces. Irreparable.'

He nodded. 'Aha. Can't be fixed?'

She smiled. 'You got it.'

His hand tightened on her waist, edging her a little closer, and she didn't object. She liked his hand there. She was happy standing next to his shoulder with his arm anchored around her.

'So, your friends… The ones you're here with. Will they be looking for you?'

He gazed across the crowd. 'I'm quite sure they are.' He shrugged. 'But I don't always want to be found.'

Hmmm… More mystery. He was so good at deflecting questions. It was almost an art form.

He turned towards her, pulling her so they were face to face. 'Are you comfortable without *your* friends, Ruby Wetherspoon? Are you happy to watch the Paris fireworks with some strange man who pulled you from the crowd?'

It was the way he said it. The way he looked at her. The gentle smile on his face and the twinkle in his eyes. For a second she didn't want to breathe.

The wind caught her curls and blew them across his face. He laughed and took her hair in his hand, smoothing it down and tucking it behind her ear. She lifted her hand and put it on his chest. She could feel his warm skin on her palm through his thin T-shirt. She could feel the curling hairs on his chest.

The man just oozed sex appeal. If anyone had told her this time last year that she would be standing here, now, like this, she would have shaken her head in disbelief.

But right now there wasn't any place else she'd rather be. 'You're not a stranger,' she said simply. 'You're Alex.'

The countdown started around them.

Dix…neuf…huit…sept…

'Yes,' he murmured. 'Tonight I'm just Alex.'

The world around them exploded. Multi-coloured lights flickered up and down the outside of the Eiffel Tower. And Alex bent to kiss her.

The fireworks around her were nothing to the ones exploding in her brain. She didn't do this. She didn't do any of this. But everything about it felt right.

This was the kind of thing she could tell her grandkids about when she was an old woman. *I once kissed a gorgeous Frenchman in Paris on New Year's Eve.*

Because this *was* a fairytale. This wasn't real life.

Except Alex's kiss was more than a fairytale. It was right up there with an award-winning movie.

Tingles were going to places that tingles hadn't been in a long time. One of his hands was resting gently on her lower back—the other was holding the back of her head. Except it wasn't *holding* the back of her head…it was *caressing* the back of her head. His fingers tangled through her hair, gently moving with tantalising softness to the side of her face.

If she could capture this moment and stuff it in a jar she would keep it for ever.

His lips finally pulled free and she had to stop herself reaching out for more. When her eyes finally opened his blue gaze was on her, his fingers still on her cheek. She'd thought the moment would be gone. But it wasn't.

It was still exploding in the stars all around.

He smiled at her. People were still shouting in the street beneath their feet, jumping up and down, and a million mobile phones were being held aloft to capture the last few seconds of the firework display.

'Happy New Year,' he whispered.

'Happy New Year,' she murmured. She couldn't wipe the smile off her face. It would probably last for eternity.

They stood for a little while as the firework display

came to an end and the lights on the Eiffel Tower finally finished.

He grabbed her hand in his. 'What say we get away from all this? Do you want to find something to eat? To drink?'

Her eyes flickered towards the far-off sign where she was to meet her friends. People were still tightly packed around it. There was no way she would be able to find her friends, then fight her way back through the crowd to Alex. The choice was simple.

'Food sounds good.'

The crowd around their feet had dispersed a little. The excitement of the countdown and the end of the fireworks display had sent people dispersing into the surrounding streets.

He jumped down and reached his arms up to catch her around her waist as she sat on the top of the wall, and he placed her gently on the ground.

Getting through the crowd was much easier with Alex in charge. No one seemed to argue with a broad-shouldered, six-foot-four man. He swept her along easily, pulling her behind until most of the crowd was behind them.

For a few seconds she thought there was a strange group of men behind her—all in black, with earpieces. But seconds later they'd vanished and she forgot about them.

By the time they reached Avenue George V the street was still busy but the crowd was gradually beginning to thin out. There were a number of open restaurants and cafés still serving customers. Alex hesitated a second outside of the door of the Four Seasons, then pulled her over to one of the other nearby restaurants with tables on the street.

He pulled out a chair and gestured for her to sit down. She rubbed her hands together and smiled at his good manners. It had been a while since she'd met anyone who'd pull out a chair for her.

'Are you cold? We can sit inside.' He pointed at her fingers.

'No, it's fine.' The restaurant looked claustrophobic, packed with people. It was strange, but outside seemed more private.

A waiter appeared quickly and nodded to Alex.

'What would you like, Ruby? Wine? coffee?' He picked up a menu. 'Food?'

She smiled. 'I'll have a cocktail.' Her eyes scanned the menu. 'I'll have a Royal Pink Circus—and the biggest piece of cake they've got.'

Alex grinned and reached forward and grabbed the menu. 'What *is* that? Hmm…vodka, champagne, raspberries and violet syrup. Interesting choice.'

He turned and spoke in rapid French to the waiter.

Under the warm light from the restaurant she got a clear view of the man she'd just kissed. Under dim lights he'd been gorgeous. Under street lights…*wow*.

She couldn't help but smile. No phone. No camera to record the moment. Typical. Her friends would never believe this. His blue eyes stood out even from across the table, complemented by the lightly tanned skin she hadn't noticed before and the shadow along his chin.

'So, what plans do you have?'

She shrugged. 'I don't have my phone so I can't contact my friends.' She waved her arm. 'But it's fine. I know where I am from here. I can find my way back to my hotel.'

She gestured towards the Four Seasons.

'For a second I thought you were going to take me in there.' She glanced down at her red wool coat, jeans and boots. 'Somehow I don't think I would have got inside.'

He gave a little shake of his head. 'Oh, you would have got inside.' He reached over and took her hand. 'But I wasn't talking about right now. How long are you in Paris?'

Mysterious Alex was getting better by the second. He actually wanted to know if she was staying.

'Just another two days. We go home on Friday. What about you?'

'I don't really have a fixed timetable. I can go home any time. Do you want to do some sightseeing for the next two days? See a little more of Paris before you go home?'

Her heart gave a little leap. She was here with a group of friends, but Polly wouldn't mind if she spent some time with a sexy French guy—in fact after this last year she'd probably encourage her.

She nodded as the waiter appeared. 'That sounds fun.'

He set down the raspberry cocktail in a sugar-frosted glass. She took a tiny sip. The alcohol was stronger than she'd expected and the bubbles from the champagne flew up her nose. She choked and laughed.

'Wow|! This Royal Pink Circus is a doozy!'

'What does that mean?' asked Alex as he took a sip of his beer.

'You know—extraordinary, spectacular. A doozy.'

Next came the cake. If it could even be described as that. This was no delicate *petit-four*. This was honest-to-goodness the biggest piece of cake in the universe. Seven layers of sponge, cream, raspberries and sauce.

She picked up her fork and took a bite. 'Oh, wow…' She leaned back in the chair. It had been hours since she'd had dinner. Alex was smiling at her again, with a twinkle in his eye. 'Would you like a piece? This is to die for.'

He shook his head. 'Don't let me deprive you. I'm getting enough pleasure seeing the look on your face.'

'Didn't you order anything?' She waved at the empty space in front of him, poising her fork above the cake again.

'I did, but I asked the waiter to bring your cake first.'

She swallowed another heavenly spoonful, 'I could get used to this kind of consideration, you know.'

Something flickered across his face that made her wonder if she'd made some kind of dreadful *faux pas*.

But Alex just nodded in agreement. 'And I think I could get used to Ruby Wetherspoon, who knows how to eat a piece of cake.'

She licked her fork. 'What? Do the people around you not eat?'

He lifted his eyebrows as the waiter reappeared and put a plate down in front of him, with the biggest BLT and portion of French fries she'd seen in a long time. She reached over and grabbed a fry.

'Not like you,' came his amused reply.

She shrugged. 'They certainly don't skimp on portions here. I'll need to remember this place. What's it called?' She looked at the name and screwed up her face. 'Too difficult. I'll just need to remember it's next to the fairytale hotel.'

'The fairytale hotel?' He'd started to eat and was making short work of the fries.

She nodded her head sideways. 'Yeah, next door. Isn't that the hotel every little girl wants to stay in when she comes to Paris?'

'I thought that was Cinderella's Castle at Disneyland?'

'Yeah, well. I'm older now. Tastes change.' She eyed her cocktail again. 'You know, you're going to hate me. But this is going straight to my head. Do you think I could order a coffee instead?'

He gave a wave of his hand and ordered her a coffee.

The cocktail might be a little strong, but the cake was perfect. The restaurant was perfect. The ambience in the street was perfect. And Alex…? Even more perfect.

'Have you been up the Eiffel Tower yet?' he asked.

She nodded, then leaned across the table and whispered, 'Don't tell anyone, but I thought I was going to be sick. It was okay looking into the distance, but when I looked down…' She made a swaying motion in her seat and shook her head. 'Bad idea.'

He laughed. 'And have you been to Versailles and the Louvre?'

She nodded. 'I queued for ever to see the Mona Lisa.'

He raised his eyebrows. 'What did you think?'

She wrinkled her nose. 'Honestly? Smaller than I expected—and a bit dark. But do you know the strangest thing? I still wanted to reach out and touch it.'

'She mesmerised you. Just like she did Leonardo. What about Notre Dame? Have you been there yet?'

She nodded again.

He held up his knife and fork. 'How long have you been here?'

'Just a few days. We've tried to cram in as much as possible.'

'Is there anywhere you'd still like to see?'

'Of course! This is Paris.' She counted off on her fingers, 'I still want to visit the Sacré Coeur and Montmartre—oh, and the Père Lachaise cemetery.'

He took a drink of his beer. 'So, I offer to take you sightseeing and you want to visit dead people?'

He slid down in his chair a little—he seemed to be relaxing more and more as their conversation continued.

'Well, I guess I bring out the best in you.'

She laughed. 'It's supposed to be beautiful—enchanting. Haven't you ever walked around a cemetery before? In the summer it can be so peaceful. I actually quite like wandering around and looking at the inscriptions in the gravestones. There's a few in our local church that have a skull and crossbones on them, showing that people had the plague. It's fascinating.'

His smile spread from ear to ear. 'Ruby, every time I think I might know you a little you say something else that surprises me.'

'Is that bad?'

He shook his head. 'No, it's good. *Very* good.' He reached over and took her hand. 'I'm sure I can find some things in the next two days for us to visit.'

'But today's New Year's Day. Everywhere will be closed.'

'Don't worry about that. I'll work something out.'

She was so wrapped up in him—in the way he was smiling at her, the way he was flirting with her—that she almost didn't notice the men in long black coats until they were almost on top of them.

One of them put a black-gloved hand sternly on Alex's shoulder, bent down and spoke quietly in his ear. She couldn't make out a word.

'Alex? What's wrong? Who is this?'

The expression on his face changed instantly. First it was a flare of anger, then it was a pure panic. He stood up, sending his chair flying.

'Alex?'

The black-coated man barely even acknowledged her presence.

'Ruby, I'm sorry—I have to go.' He fumbled in his coat for his phone. 'Give me your number. I'll call you.'

Her hands went automatically to her bag. No phone. She'd lost it.

'I don't have my phone, and I can't remember what my number is.'

She felt like an idiot. Everyone should know their mobile number. And she did—she had it written down at home—but right now she couldn't tell him if her life depended on it.

'What's wrong, Alex?'

He shook his head. He wasn't focused on her any more. He looked shocked.

'It's my family. Tell me where you're staying. I'll send you a message.'

She rattled off the name of the low-budget hotel where they were staying. He mumbled something to the man behind him.

'I'm sorry. I need to go. I'll send you a message later.'

He walked around to her side of the table and bent to kiss her. It was the briefest moment, but his lips came into contact with hers in the lightest of kisses. A brush like a butterfly's wings.

And then he was gone.

Surrounded by black coats, disappearing down the street.

The fairytale was over.

January

Ruby crashed through the door with her shopping bags, work folders and uniform over her arm.

Polly was sitting cross-legged on the sofa, eating a plate of noodles. She nodded towards the kitchen. 'Come and sit down, Ms Misery. Noodles in the pot and wine in the fridge.'

She was knackered. Honestly and truly exhausted. Between the long hours and the killer commute every day, this job was proving tougher than she'd ever thought. But today had been a winner. Today she'd finally believed that her work had helped a patient regain a little part of his speech. 'No' had been the finest word she'd heard in a while.

She poured the wine and tipped the rest of the noodles into a bowl, kicking off her shoes and thudding down sofa next to Polly. 'What are you watching?'

'Just the news. How was your day?'

She put the first spoonful of noodles into her mouth. It was like a chilli explosion. Polly had a penchant for spicy foods, and as she was the cook in the house Ruby was getting used to it. She took a few quick gulps of wine to try and quell the burn.

Her eyes flickered to the screen and she inhaled quickly, coughing and spluttering as her noodles went down the wrong way.

Polly turned and laughed, leaning over and slapping her hand on Ruby's back. 'Was the chilli kick that strong?'

But Ruby couldn't answer. Her eyes were streaming.

She swallowed as best she could. 'Turn that up,' she said, pointing at the screen.

'What?' Polly mumbled, her mouth still full of food.

'Turn it up!'

She started throwing cushions and newspapers around, searching for the TV remote, which seemed to have an innate ability to hide whenever she left the house. Finally she spied it, hiding part-way under the sofa. She pointed it at the TV and pressed the volume button hard.

Polly just stared at her open-mouthed.

'There are unconfirmed reports that King Leopold of Euronia is seriously unwell.

'The normally quiet principality has seen a flurry of activity in the last few days as private jets have been seen landing at the state airport. Crown Prince Alexander has returned home after a recent sojourn in the US, where he was apparently working with MIT and Harvard University.

'Prince Alexander, the only child of widowed King Leopold, is rarely seen. He is an astute businessman who is passionate about his country. Rumours have circulated in the last few years about King Leopold's declining health and his lessening public engagements.

'Crown Prince Alexander was seen returning in a private jet in the early hours of New Year's morning, quickly followed by dignitaries from the surrounding area. We've been told to expect a statement in the next few minutes.'

'It's him,' Ruby croaked, pointing at the screen. 'It's Alex.'

It was almost as if an elephant had sat on her chest, stopping her breathing.

Polly dropped her fork and bowl on the table. 'What?' She glanced from Ruby to the TV and back again. 'Him? *He's* your Alex? Crown Prince…whatever?'

'Apparently.'

Her throat had dried like an arid desert. She picked up

the wine and gulped it down as if it were a glass of water, grimacing as it hit her tastebuds.

Her brain was in overdrive. Tiny words, tiny phrases, looks that had fleeted across his face and disappeared in an instant. Tiny pieces of a jigsaw puzzle she'd had no idea even existed.

A close-up picture of Alex emerging from a plane appeared on the screen and she gasped. He looked awful. He was still handsome, but his tanned skin was pale and there were lines around his eyes—even their blueness had dimmed.

He hadn't called. He hadn't left a message at all. At first she'd been irritated. Then, she'd been angry. Finally, she'd admitted to herself she was devastated.

But this was something else entirely. Her fairytale in Paris had never included a real live prince.

Polly started chattering in her ear. 'No wonder you were miserable. What a catch. Ruby—you kissed a *prince*!' She stared back at the screen. 'I wonder what's going on.'

The newsreader interrupted the next report mid-story. 'We're going to cross live now to Euronia for an announcement.'

A sombre-faced grey-haired, black-suited man stood on a podium. A sign appeared beneath him: 'Palace Principale'.

'What does that mean?' asked Polly.

'I have no idea.' Ruby shook her head.

The man started speaking. 'After consultation with the Crown Council, the principality of Euronia would like to announce that, with immediate effect, Crown Prince Alexander de Castellane will be taking over as Regent of Euronia as His Majesty King Leopold is no longer able to exercise his royal functions. The Crown Prince Alexander will now be known as Prince Regent.'

The picture cut back to the newsreader as he glanced up from reading the piece of paper in his hands. 'There are unconfirmed reports that King Leopold has suffered a catastrophic stroke, but no one at the palace is willing to comment on his medical condition. We'll bring you an update whenever we get one.'

Polly turned to face Ruby. 'Wow. Just…*wow*.'

Ruby felt sick. Her heart had squeezed when she'd seen the expression on Alex's face. How on earth must he be feeling?

She wanted to be angry with him—she really did. Why couldn't he have told her who he really was?

But deep down she knew the answer to that.

A real live prince wouldn't be looking for a girl like her. Not in this lifetime anyway.

CHAPTER ONE

Ten years later

'RUBY?' THE DEPARTMENT receptionist shouted at her again.

Too many things were circulating in her brain. She needed to refer one child to someone else, another to an oral surgeon, and speak to the dietician about another.

She turned round and was nearly knocked over by a giant flower display. Her stomach tied itself up in little knots.

Rena smiled as she tried to hold up the giant display. 'You've got flowers again. Even more gorgeous than the last time. And, oh, *so* expensive.' She looked thoughtful for a moment. 'It's been a little while since the last bunch. Do you realise that, on and off, it's been six years you've been getting these mysterious flowers? Right from when you started here. Surely you must have guessed by now who they're from?'

Ruby shook her head. 'I have no idea. The cards never say anything specific.' She pulled out the latest one. 'See? *"Thinking of you and wishing you well."*'

Rena frowned at the card in her hands. 'Have you tried phoning the florist to find out who sent them?' She was a regular amateur detective and could usually find a missing set of case notes in less than five minutes.

'Of course I have. But these places are used to things like this. They don't give anything away.'

'Well, whoever it is, money certainly isn't an object. These must have cost a fortune.' Rena reached up and touched one of the coloured petals. 'They smell gorgeous.' She frowned. 'Who have you seen lately that could have sent these?' She paused and bit her lip. 'Maybe it's Paul? Maybe he's trying for a reunion?'

Ruby shook her head. 'Paul would never send flowers like these.' Then she smiled. 'Paul would never send flowers full-stop. Which is why we're not together any more. That, and a whole lot of other things.'

Paul could never live up to the memory of Alex. Sometimes it felt like a figment of her imagination. Something so special that only she could remember. The only person she ever spoke to about it was Polly.

She'd tried to forget about him—she really had. She'd even lived with a lovely guy called Luke for a couple of years. But things just hadn't worked out between them, and in her heart she knew why. No matter how hard she tried, she just couldn't forget about her mysterious prince.

Rena smiled and touched Ruby's arm. 'Well, you've obviously got a devoted, secret admirer. It's romantic. It's mysterious. I could probably work it into a book somewhere.'

Ruby laughed. 'Rena, you write about murder and mayhem. I'm not sure I want to end up in one of your books!'

She cast her eyes over the flowers again. Stunning. Really stunning. Beautiful tropical colours. Red, pinks, yellows and oranges. Like a burst of sunshine on a rainy day.

She swallowed. The flowers had stopped for a few years. Right around the time when it had been all over the news that Prince Alex had married Princess Sophia of Leruna. A perfect fairytale princess. Dainty and blonde—nothing like Ruby. A baby had followed quickly afterwards. Followed by her tragic death due to breast cancer.

All that crammed into the space of two years. And not a single bunch of flowers over that time.

The coincidence played on her mind. The deliveries had started again around eighteen months ago. Could the flowers have been from Alex all along?

Something coiled deep inside her.

She walked over to the window and stared outside at the pouring rain of London. Another wasted five minutes thinking about her prince.

Her prince. What a joke. She'd never used those words out loud and never would. It was bad enough that they circulated around her brain.

Alex might have had tragedy, but he'd also had a life. Promotion for Ruby had come at a price. She'd been working so hard these last few years. Trying to change the lives of children who had been born with speech difficulties. It had left no time for her, no time for relationships, and no time to think about having a family.

The responsibilities of being in charge of a department in one of the best hospitals in London were relentless.

Sometimes she felt like a hamster, running in a wheel that she could never get off.

A porter brushed past, sending the scent of the beautiful flowers to meet her. It brought her back to reality quickly.

There was no point dreaming. She was nobody's princess.

And it was time to get back to work.

She was dashing around like a mad woman. Everyone in this hospital was the same. It had taken five different attempts for him to finally get some directions.

He stopped for a second to breathe. Ten years. Ten years since that night in Paris.

How different his life might have been. If his father hadn't been taken ill he would have met Ruby a few hours later in Paris and taken her sightseeing. That thought still made his stomach tighten.

She looked almost the same. Her dark curls were a little shorter. Her figure was just as curvy. But the expression on her face was more serious. Tired, even. And there were little lines around her eyes.

He didn't even want to look in the mirror lately. Although only ten years had passed since they'd last seen each other he was sure he'd aged about twenty.

The flowers he'd sent were sitting on the desk behind her. She wasn't even looking at them. Everyone else was oohing and aahing over them. But Ruby was too busy. Ruby was focused.

He watched her hurry around; she had a pile of cards in her hands.

'Seventeen new referrals,' she said to a nearby colleague, 'and Caroline is stuck in a traffic jam in the middle of London. How on earth are we going to get all these children assessed?'

He sucked in a breath. He'd never doubted for a second that Ruby would be dedicated to her work. But would it stand in the way of what he wanted her to do?

She tucked a curl behind her ear. It made his fingers tingle. *He'd* done that once.

'Can I help you?' someone asked him.

He shook his head. It was now or never.

He stepped forward. 'One of those referral cards will be from me.'

Ruby spun around to face him. The professional mask fell as quickly as the cards from her hand. His accent was unmistakable; she couldn't fail to recognise it.

'Alex,' she said. Nothing else. Her eyes locked on to his.

'Ruby.'

She tilted her head to the side, as if she were contemplating a million different questions, before sucking in a deep breath and giving a visible little shake of her head.

Ten years. Ten years since he'd run his fingers through those soft dark curls and looked into those chocolate-brown eyes. Ten years since he'd felt the silky softness of her skin, tasted the sweetness of her lips.

Every sensation, every touch, every taste flashed in front of him in an instant.

But Ruby wasn't caught in the same spell that he was.

She bent down to retrieve the cards and he knelt to help her. It was inevitable that their hands touched as they reached out towards the same card.

She pulled her hand away as if she'd been stung. 'Why, Alex? Why are you here?'

It was as if someone had reached into his chest and twisted his heart. There it was. In a few simple words a whole multitude of hurt. No one else would hear it. No one else would understand. But Ruby's deep brown eyes were fixed on his and he could see everything there. She looked wounded. Ten years on and her hurt was still easily visible.

But what did she see when she looked at him? He wasn't Alex the twenty-four-year-old any more—the bachelor Crown Prince with the world at his feet. He was a father. He was a widower. He was Prince Regent. The Prince continually in waiting.

And he was desperate.

In his head this had all been so easy. *Find someone you would trust with your daughter. Find Annabelle the expert help she needs.*

It had even seemed sensible to the palace advisors. If they'd questioned his choice of therapist at first, once they'd researched Ruby's qualifications and seen her recent publications all queries had vanished.

But now he was here in the flesh it was so much harder. Now he could see her. Now he could hear her. Now he could smell her. Her light floral scent was drifting around him.

He'd had no idea of the effect seeing Ruby again would have on him. Ten years... Ten years lost. Ten years of what might have been.

'Alex?'

The word jolted him and he smiled. No one called him Alex any more. No one had ever really called him just Alex.

He straightened up and handed her the final cards.

'I'm here because I need your help, Ruby.'

Any minute now a bunch of unicorns would come cantering along the hospital corridor, with exploding rainbows all around them.

She'd dreamt about Alex before. But never like this. Never in her workplace. All those dreams had been set back in Paris. Or in the Euronian palace that she'd looked at online.

But Alex standing in front of her at work, asking for her help…? She was obviously losing her mind.

He reached out and touched her bare arm. Short sleeves were essential in a hospital environment, to stop the spread of infection. This time she didn't pull away. This time she let the feel of the pads of his fingers spread warmth through her chilled arm.

He was really here.

This wasn't a strange hallucination due to overwork or lack of chocolate.

Ten years she'd waited to talk to this man again. Ten years waiting to ask him what the hell had happened back in Paris and why he'd never contacted her.

Alex—her Alex. *Her prince* was finally standing right in front of her.

He was every bit as handsome as she remembered. Better, even.

Tanned skin, dark hair and bright blue eyes. She'd sometimes wondered if she'd imagined how blue they were. But she hadn't. If anything she'd underestimated their effects. But, then again, she'd never seen Alex in daylight.

She wasn't imagining any of this. All six foot four of him was standing right in front of her.

Her eyes lowered to where his hand was touching her. Tiny electric pulses were shooting up her arm. She didn't know whether to cry or be sick.

Every part of her imagination had just turned into reality.

In a way, it was a relief. She *had* met Alex. He *did* remember her. So why was that making her so darn angry right now?

He pulled his hand back from her arm and she lifted her head, pulling her shoulders back. *He'd taken his hand away.* And it had left her feeling bereft. Now she was feeling angry with herself. She didn't have a sensible thought in her head right now.

She swallowed and looked him in the eye. 'How can I help you, Alex?' The words were automatic. It was all she could manage right now.

He looked around. 'Is there somewhere we can talk?'

She nodded and gestured with her arm for him to walk down the corridor, stopped at a door, pulled a key from her pocket and unlocked the door.

Her office. It even had her name on the door: 'Ruby Wetherspoon, Head of Speech and Language'. She'd done well. Most days she was proud. Today she had no idea how she felt.

The office was small, but neat and tidy. She pointed to a chair and invited him to sit. It was almost a relief to sit at the other side of the desk and have the heavy wooden structure between them.

'How exactly do you think I can be of assistance to you, Alex?'

Her words were formal, her professional façade slipping back into place. The juggling of the cards on the table-top was the only sign of her nerves. She hoped he wouldn't notice.

'It's not me. It's my daughter Annabelle. She's three years old now and she isn't speaking.'

Ruby nodded automatically. His daughter. Of course. Why else would be come to her?

She had this sort of conversation every day. This one wouldn't be much different.

'Three years old is still an acceptable age for speech development. All children develop at a different rate. Some children have a delay in their speech and language development. Have you had her hearing checked?'

He sighed. She was going back to basics—which was the correct thing for a health professional. But she could tell from his expression he'd heard it all before.

'I've had ten different professional opinions on Annabelle. The latest of which is selective mutism. Her hearing is fine. Her comprehension is fine. She doesn't seem to *want* to speak.'

She could feel herself bristle. Ten assessments on a child? Talk about overkill. Why not just let her develop at her own pace? She tried to be pragmatic.

'How does she communicate with those around her?'

'She signs.'

Ruby was surprised. 'Proper signing?'

He nodded. 'We have a member of staff who's deaf. She's been able to sign since she was young.'

It wasn't particularly unusual in children who were deaf, or in children who had deaf siblings. But it *was* unusual in a child who could apparently hear and speak.

She lifted her hands. 'Then maybe she thinks that's normal?'

He shook his head.

It was time to ask some more questions.

'Has Annabelle ever spoken? Ever said a few words?'

'Only on a few select occasions.'

Strange… Ruby couldn't help but be a little curious. Selective mutism was certainly unusual but she'd dealt with a few cases before. She'd even published some professional papers on it.

Ruby lowered her voice. 'Does she speak to you, Alex?'

The question was straight to the heart of the matter. It was a natural question for any health professional, but she saw him recoil. She'd seen this before. He felt this was his fault. She'd dealt with lots of parents who felt guilty about whatever issue their child had. Most of the time it was just hard luck. Genetics. A developmental delay. A head injury or similar accident.

She asked the most practical question. 'Does Annabelle have anything significant in her medical history?'

'No. Nothing.'

They sat in silence for a few seconds. She couldn't take it. She couldn't take it a second longer. Her professional façade was slipping. After all this time—just to turn up like this and expect her to help him—just because he asked? Did she have *mug* stamped across her forehead?

She couldn't even acknowledge the flutters in her stomach. She couldn't even explain her feeling when she'd heard his voice and turned to see him again after all this time. It had been like a sucker punch.

It was time to stop being so polite.

Ruby leaned back in her chair. 'I don't get it, Alex. After all this time, why come to me? Why come here? You must have plenty of people in Euronia willing to help with your daughter.'

His brow was lined with deep furrows that marred his handsome face. It made her feel self-conscious. She only had the lightest dusting of make-up on, to emphasise her brown eyes and pink lips. How much had she changed in the last ten years? Would he be disappointed by what she saw?

Why was he here? Why, after all this time, had he been convinced that this was the right thing to do?

'I want to feel as if I've tried everything possible for Annabelle. I haven't had faith in any of the people who have seen her and assessed her. And, whilst the latest diagnosis seems reasonable, I'm not happy at the treatment plan for Annabelle.'

Maybe that's because you should have left her alone to be a normal toddler. Ruby was still imagining what ten assessments had done to that poor child. But she couldn't say those words out loud.

It was difficult. This was Alex, her mysterious Frenchman—who wasn't a Frenchman after all. She'd never thought she'd come into contact with him for *work*. She never thought she'd come into contact with him again.

'What *is* the treatment plan for Annabelle?'

He pushed a folder he'd been carrying across the desk towards her. She opened it and scanned it quickly. Whilst the assessment might have been thorough, she didn't agree at all with what was in the plan, or with the conclusions it had already surmised.

Ever the professional, she raised her head and selected her words carefully. 'Every professional will have a different idea of the correct plan for your daughter. It's not really my place to disagree.'

He pointed to the file. 'What would *you* do?'

She opened her mouth automatically to speak, then closed it again. 'What does it matter?'

'Because I'd like you to come to Euronia and assess Annabelle for yourself. I'd like you to be the one to plan her care and treat her.'

He might as well have dumped a bucket of ice-cold water over her head. She was stunned. 'That's impossible.'

'No. It's not. I know you have a job here, and patients, but I've offered your Director of Services a generous annual bequest if you'll agree to come and work for me—for Annabelle,' he added quickly.

'What?' She stood up, the chair behind her flying backwards. 'You've done *what*?'

She couldn't believe her ears. The tiny glimmer of hope that he'd searched her out for any reason other than his daughter died in an instant. He might be a prince in another country, but he didn't seem much like a prince to her now.

'And you did that without speaking to me first?' She walked around the desk, reached down, and grabbed hold of his jacket, pulling him to his feet. 'How dare you, Alex? How *dare* you? Ten years later you think you can just walk into my life and *buy* me?'

Anger and the untold resentment that had festered for ten years came spilling out. This wasn't her. She never acted like this. But she just couldn't help it.

She shook her head fiercely, blazing with fury. 'You can't buy me, Alex. I'm not for sale.' She held out one hand. 'I have a job. Responsibilities. I have staff to take care of—patients to take care of.'

She stared at her other hand, still gripping tightly to the lapel of his jacket. What on earth was she doing? Her knuckles were white and she quickly loosened her grip and took a step backwards. Her heart was thudding in her chest. Her head was thumping.

'And you could do it better if you had two more permanent members of staff.' He cut her off before she had more time to think about it.

Her mouth fell open. 'What?'

'That's what I promised your director. Permanent funding for two more members of staff if they'll release you to work with Annabelle. Plus filling your post while you're gone.'

Her brain was whizzing. Two more members of staff could make a world of difference to this place. Time. It would give her staff time. The one thing she couldn't conjure up for them.

She hated rushing assessments. She hated not having enough time to allocate to the children who needed her. She hated having to turn children away because there just wasn't enough space for any more patients. Two more members of staff was a luxury she couldn't afford to ignore.

'Why on earth would you do this?'

He sat back down in his seat and put his head in his hands.

She'd read about everything that had happened to him in the last ten years. Now here he was, right in front of her, and she actually felt sorry for him.

She started shaking her head. 'It feels like blackmail, Alex. I haven't seen you in ten years. *Ten years!* Not a word from you—nothing. And now this.' She started pacing around the small office. 'I know what happened to your father. The whole world knows. But you never contacted me. You never said anything. I was left sitting in that hotel for two days, wondering if I'd imagined everything. Thank goodness Polly dragged me out and about.'

His head shot up. 'I did contact you. I sent a message.'

'I never got any message!' She was still angry.

'But I sent one. My head of security—he took it to the hotel. Gave it to the reception clerk. You *must* have got it.'

She shook her head and lowered her voice. 'There was no message, Alex. None. I waited and waited.'

She hated the way the words made her feel. She hated the way she wanted to reach out and grab them. Grab the fact that Alex *had* tried to reach her—no matter what else had happened in his life. But it was the expression on his face that was worse. He looked hurt. He looked injured.

But, most importantly, he looked tired.

She knelt down in front of him. His father had been sick for ten years. He had a country to run. His wife had died from cancer—she was assuming he'd nursed her through that—and he had a daughter whom he clearly loved but needed help with.

She reached up and touched his hand. Her skin coming into contact with his almost made her smile. Her pale skin against his tanned skin. A world of difference.

The sensation she felt touching his skin was still there.

Still electrifying. But she had to put a reality check on things.

She spoke quietly. 'Why now, Alex? Why me?'

It was only a few words but they meant so much more than she was actually saying. He knew that. He must.

He reached up and touched her cheek. *Zing.*

'Because there is no one else. No one else I could trust with the thing that is most precious to me.'

She blinked, trying to stop the tears forming in her eyes.

Nothing about wanting to see her again. Nothing about wanting to know how she was.

But he had just told her he trusted her with the thing most precious in the world to him. His daughter.

She didn't know whether to be happy or sad.

He pulled a picture from his wallet. A sad-looking blonde-haired toddler. She was beautiful. Just like her mother had been. But she wasn't laughing. She wasn't playing. She didn't look happy.

'Oh, Alex…' she breathed.

'Will you come?' His voice sounded as if it was breaking.

She stood up, her mind whirling. 'I'll need to think about it. You'll need to give me some time.'

How ironic. Ten years later she was asking him for time.

How on earth could she not do this? The picture of the little girl had broken her heart. She had no idea if she could help or not—but she could try.

Outside her office she could see figures rushing past. The hospital was always busy—never enough time to do everything. It was wearing her down. She loved her job, but the truth was she'd spent the last few months searching the vacancy bulletins.

One thing. If she did this one thing she could help this department and these kids for ever. Was it really such a hard task?

A chair scraped along the floor behind her. Alex had

stood up, a resigned look on his face. He nodded at the desk, 'I'll leave those things for you to look at. My contact details are there. Let me know when you make up your mind.'

He thought she was going to say no. And right now that was the way she was leaning. What would she do with her flat—her cat—if she left to go abroad?

The file and the photo of Annabelle sat on her desk. He had his hand on the door handle.

'Alex? How did you know where I was?'

It had bothered her since he'd first arrived.

His bright blue eyes fixed on hers. It was the first time she'd seen anything resembling the eyes she'd looked into ten years ago.

'I've always known where you were, Ruby,' he said quietly as he opened the door and walked down the corridor.

CHAPTER TWO

THE PLANE JOURNEY was smooth. The private jet immaculate. Any other person might have taken the opportunity to relax, but Ruby's stomach had been jittery ever since they'd left London.

She stared out of the window as the plane came into land. Her first sight of Euronia. A stunning, winding coastline overlooking the Mediterranean Sea. A population of two hundred thousand people over an area of only seventy kilometres. The rich and famous flocked here because of the tax benefits. The press loved Euronia because it seemed to host every celebrity wedding that had ever existed.

The plane landed quickly and glided to a halt on the Tarmac. She hadn't spoken to Alex since she'd seen him at the hospital. The number he'd given her had been for his secretary—a chirpy little man who'd been delighted when she'd said she would come to Euronia and had spoken with great fondness about Annabelle. He'd arranged everything. Even advising on what kind of clothing to bring and asking her for her dress and shoe size so he could provide some extra items if required.

The pilot and the stewardess had both been polite but formal. She wondered if they were used to fading into the background.

A black limousine was waiting for her.

'Welcome to Euronia, Ms Wetherspoon. It will only

take ten minutes to reach the palace. Please make yourself comfortable and help yourself to refreshments.'

Another man in black. She hid her smile. Any minute now she would hear the theme tune to that movie in her head. It was the same garb that the men in Paris had been wearing all those years ago. Those men had made her uncomfortable. This man was a little different. His eyes were scanning the horizon constantly. Was he a chauffeur or security?

She settled into the comfortable leather seats. The 'refreshments' in front of her were wine, champagne and beer. It was ten-thirty in the morning. What she'd actually like was a cup of tea.

She watched the scenery speed past.

Polly's words echoed in her ears. *'This isn't a movie. He's using you, Ruby. Don't get any ideas about this at all.'*

Her disdain had been apparent as soon as she'd heard what had happened. Polly had long since abandoned any romantic notions of her prince. She'd been the one to see exactly how devastated Ruby had been. But it was all right for Polly. She'd got her happy-ever-after—a doting husband and a baby in her arms.

'How long will you be gone?' she'd asked Ruby moodily.

'I have no idea.' And she really didn't. She couldn't plan anything until she'd assessed Annabelle.

The car swept through some regal gates, past armed guards and down a long pale yellow sweeping drive. The view over the Mediterranean was breathtaking.

No turning back. She was here now. She tugged at her pale green dress. It was a little more formal than what she normally wore, but at least it didn't crumple.

The palace came into view. Nicknamed the Pink Palace, the Palace Principale was built from pink and red sandstone. She'd seen pictures on the internet, but seeing it in reality was entirely different.

Ruby took a deep breath. There must be a million little

girls' birthday cakes all over the world based on this palace. Four square turrets and it seemed like hundreds of slim windows looked down on her. The palace doors were enormous, with wide sweeping steps leading up to them.

Intimidating. Definitely intimidating.

She would be lying if she claimed she'd never thought about this. Of course she had. Every girl had.

But every girl hadn't kissed a prince.

Oh, boy. She squeezed her eyes shut for a second. This was harder than she'd thought.

Actually being here in Euronia was much harder than she'd imagined it to be.

In her head this was a job. This was professional. So why was her heart fluttering so much? And why did she want to run back along that yellow driveway?

A man was standing at the top of the steps to greet her. It wasn't Alex. Of course it wasn't Alex. He hadn't even spoken to her on the phone.

She climbed the steps and looked out over the Mediterranean Sea. Lots of little white boats bobbed up and down on the beautiful blue water. *Little* boats? They probably cost more than she would earn in her lifetime. This was a whole other world.

But she was here to do a job, not to admire the scenery—no matter how beautiful it was.

The sooner she got started the better.

He watched her step from the car. She was picture-perfect. Her elegant legs were the first hint of what was to come as her slim figure emerged in a pale green dress that fluttered around her in the strong sea winds. It was an occupational hazard of having a palace on the sea.

His mother had always joked that one day a press photographer would get a picture of something they shouldn't. She'd been born before her time, and had been taken much too soon. She would have known exactly what to do with Annabelle.

He watched as Rufus, his private secretary, bustled around about Ruby. He would probably give her a headache in the first five minutes, but his heart was in the right place.

Rufus had organised everything once he'd known Ruby would be coming. From her favourite foods and TV shows to her clothes—everything would be taken care of. The only thing he'd asked for some input with was where to put her in the palace.

Alex hadn't been quite sure, but had finally decided she should be in the West Wing, overlooking the sea. The rooms there had always been his mother's favourites.

It only took a few moments before his phone rang.

'Your Majesty? I'm afraid there's a problem with our guest. Her accommodation is unsuitable. She's requesting rooms next to Princess Annabelle.' Rufus was so overwrought he was practically squeaking.

'Take her to the library. I'll be along directly.'

Five minutes. That was all it had taken for Ruby to cause turmoil in his life. He just hoped this wasn't a decision he'd live to regret.

He strode down the stairs and along the corridor towards the library. Rufus was flapping around the doorway. He wasn't used to people not going along with his plans.

'Where is she?' Alex looked around the empty room.

'She went upstairs to Princess Annabelle's quarters. She knows Annabelle isn't there but she said she wanted to make herself familiar with the place.'

Rufus cringed. The whole thing was probably giving him palpitations. It didn't take much these days.

Alex waved his hand. 'Leave this to me.'

He didn't need Rufus getting over-excited. What on earth was Ruby *doing*? She'd barely put her feet across the front door.

He bit his lip as he climbed the stairs at a rapid pace. She wasn't used to things like this. Maybe he should try and exercise a little patience. Ruby wasn't used to royal palaces and protocols. She was here because he'd asked her to be. She might have a job to do, but she was also his guest.

He reached Annabelle's rooms quickly. The door was open wide, giving a clear view of the palace gardens and the sea. Ruby was sitting on one of the window seats, but she wasn't admiring the view. One of Annabelle's stuffed toys was in her hands. It was a koala left by the Australian ambassador after his last visit. Ruby was looking around the room carefully.

He stood behind her, looking at her outline, seeing every curve of her body. It sent a rush of blood around his own body.

He hadn't quite imagined how this would feel. Ruby, sitting in his palace, with the backdrop he'd looked at every day for years behind her. It almost seemed unreal.

'Ruby, what are you doing in here?'

She sighed and turned to face him. The first thing that struck him was her big brown eyes. So dark, so deep, so inviting... He really needed to get hold of himself.

'There are rooms right next door to Annabelle's. It would be best if I stayed there.'

'Why?' The rooms he'd chosen for her in the West Wing were brighter, more spacious. The ones next to Annabelle were smaller, usually reserved for staff. 'The other rooms are nicer. They have more space.'

She waved her hand. She didn't look happy. Was she already regretting coming here?

'I need to be next to her, Alex. You forget—I live in London. These rooms will be a penthouse compared to my flat. I need to see her, Alex. I need to see her in her own environment. I need to see how she functions. I need to see how she communicates with those around her. She's three. I need to watch her in the place where she's most comfortable. I'm not just here to assess whether she can

actually speak or not. I need to assess her ability to understand—her cognitive abilities. I need to see how she inter-
acts with those around her.'

She held out her arm across the immaculately kept
room.

'Is this Annabelle's world?'

There was tinge of sadness to her words. As if to her
the beautiful rooms were clearly lacking.

'Where is she now?'

Professional Ruby. The one he'd never really experienced before. She wasn't having wishful thoughts about
him. She was concentrating on the job she was here to do.

He glanced at his watch. 'She's with her nanny. She
goes to the local nursery for a few hours twice a week. Her
nanny thought mixing with other children might be good
for her. She's due back any minute.'

Ruby nodded and smiled.

Alex continued. 'This isn't a big country. Annabelle will
go to the local school with the other children, just like I
did. My father always believed that to lead the people you
had to be part of the people.'

'He sounds like a very wise man.' She turned and looked
out over the sea. 'Where is your father? Is he here?'

He hesitated. They kept details about King Leopold
closely guarded. But this was Ruby. He trusted her with
the details of his daughter—why not his father?

'He's not here. He's in Switzerland.'

'Switzerland?'

'His stroke was severe. We have a hospital in Euronia,
but we don't have ICU facilities.'

She walked towards him, concern lacing her brow.
Clearly no one had told her about the protocol of remaining ten steps away from the Prince. He was glad. He could
see a tiny smattering of freckles across the bridge of her
nose. Had they been there before?

If asked, he would have said that every part of her face

had been etched on his brain. But these were new. It was disconcerting. A part of Ruby he hadn't kept in his head.

She put her hand on his chest. He could practically hear the alarms going off around the building.

'Ten years on your father still needs ICU facilities?'

He was trying not to concentrate on her warm skin penetrating through his shirt. 'Yes—and no. He did at first. His recovery was limited and slow. He was moved to a specialist rehab unit. But now he has frequent bouts of pneumonia and he needs assistance with breathing. He has to be kept near an ICU. Euronia doesn't have those facilities.'

'You could get them.'

Her voice was quiet. She knew exactly what she was saying. It was enough. The rest of the words didn't have to be said out loud. No one else around him would do this.

'I could,' he said gently. 'But my father wouldn't want people to see him the way he is now. It would break his heart.' His voice was strained. Even he could hear it.

It was so strange to have Ruby standing right here in front of him, in his daughter's room. He'd imagined her in many different scenarios over the years, but this had never been one of them.

In his darkest moments, when everything had seemed insurmountable, he'd always been able to close his eyes and go back to Paris, the fireworks and Ruby.

A perfect night. With a disastrous end.

She'd suited her red coat and hat that cold night. And for the last ten years that was the way he'd remembered her.

Ruby—with the sparkle in her eyes, the flirtatious laugh and the easy chatter. Every time he thought of her there were fireworks in the background. Fireworks that matched her personality and her vitality.

But today, in the sun, the pale green chiffon complemented her dark brown curls and brown eyes. The dress covered every part of her it should, but he hadn't expected her to look quite so elegant.

It was just the two of them. No palace staff. No interruptions.

'I've met so many different people, Ruby. I see masks, façades, the whole time. I've never seen any of that with you. Ten years ago I saw someone who was devastated at not getting her dream job—someone who wasn't afraid to say that to a stranger. All the people who have assessed Annabelle...'

He shook his head.

'None of them have felt genuine to me. Oh, they might be professionals in their field. They might have letters after their names. But most of them only tell me what they think I want to hear. Others try and blind me with science. I don't think any of them have ever wanted to find out who the real Annabelle is. They might be interested in the theory or psychology of why a three-year-old won't talk...'

He put his hand on his chest, directly over hers. One set of fingers intertwined with another.

'But none of them have cared in *here* about why she isn't speaking.'

He could lean forward right now. He could lean forward and capture her lips the way he did ten years ago.

Ruby's eyes were fixed on his. 'Well, no wonder.'

'No wonder what?'

'No wonder you came looking for me.'

CHAPTER THREE

IT TOOK ANNABELLE four long days to acknowledge Ruby's existence. At first she completely ignored her, preferring to communicate in her own way with her nanny.

The nanny, Brigette, was thankfully a dedicated and sensible woman. She'd spent all her life in Euronia and had been with the family since Annabelle's arrival. The little girl trusted her completely, but once Brigette realised Ruby was here to stay and help with Annabelle it was clear she was glad of the assistance. She loved the little girl but felt frustrated that she wasn't able to help more.

Ruby was patient. But Alex was hovering around her constantly, asking her questions, destroying her concentration and patience. Any time he appeared her senses went into overdrive. The timbre of his voice, the accent, could make her legs turn to mush.

She had to drive a little bit of her anger back into her head. Her anger that she was here for Annabelle—not for Alex. It didn't matter that it might be irrational. It was the only thing currently keeping her sane.

He appeared at her shoulder, his scent drifting around her. She didn't even turn around.

'Alex, you need to leave me to get on with the job. That's what I'm here to do.'

Annabelle was playing quietly in her room. Flitting between colouring at the table and drawing chalk pictures on her board. There was a television in her room, which she rarely watched, and a tablet on the chair next to her.

She was definitely an interesting study. She was a creative little girl. The drawers at her desk were filled with cardboard, paint, ribbon, glitter and glue. She was never happier than when she was covered in the stuff. But the life of a royal princess meant that she was continually being cleaned, tidied and paraded elsewhere.

The only time she showed interest in the tablet—which she could use easily—was when she watched clips of singing and dancing from films. *Annie*, *The Sound of Music* and *Seven Brides for Seven Brothers* seemed to be the favourites.

There was a mixture of melancholy and frustration that emanated from Alex when he watched Annabelle.

'But I'm her *parent*. Aren't you supposed to talk to me and give me a report?'

Ruby nodded and gave a little sigh. 'I suppose... But I haven't finished my full assessment of Annabelle yet. I can only give you my first impressions.'

She turned around to face him, conscious of the fact that she'd be subjected to his killer blue eyes.

'This will take longer than I thought. I have to wait until Annabelle is ready to communicate with me—to work with me. I'm not going to force myself on her. She's not that type of kid.'

The smile that spread across his face was one of complete relief. He put his warm hands on her shoulders. '*That's* why you're here, Ruby. You're the first person who's assessed Annabelle that has said that to me. You don't care about the time span. You care about the child.'

Because you're paying me to.

It was an uncomfortable thought racing around in her brain. She was used to working for the health service. She'd never seen private patients before. Every child she'd assessed had been given the best possible assessment. But the health services were pushed for time and it sometimes frustrated her. Here she didn't have those worries.

Everything about this was a whole new experience. Staying in a palace. Knowing that after ten years she might bump into Alex at any second. The *you're paying me to* thought had a tiny bit of self-preservation about it. It kept things in perspective. It kept her grounded. It reminded her why she was actually here.

Alex was still touching her shoulders. She was wearing a sundress and his fingers were in direct contact with her skin. The sensations that were currently running like little pulses down her arms were conflicting with all her previous thoughts.

'Why don't we do this somewhere else?

'What?'

Do what somewhere else? She felt panic rush through her. How exactly had she been looking at him?

He lifted his hand from her shoulder and waved it towards the window. 'I've not been a very good host. Let me show you a little of Euronia.' He looked down at her sandals. 'How do you feel about a walk?'

Her sandals were pretty, but flat and comfortable. Her curiosity had definitely flared. 'I feel fine about a walk.'

'Then let's go.'

'Don't you need to let your security team know first, Alex?'

He smiled again and shook his head. 'You know, you're the only person that actually calls me that.'

'What?'

'Alex. No one else calls me that.'

She shook her head in disbelief. 'What on earth *do* they call you?'

He shrugged. 'Prince Regent or Your Majesty. If it's someone I've known a long time they might call me Alexander.'

A different world.

She stepped right up to him, her nose only inches away from his. 'But I know you as Alex. Always have. Always will.'

He smiled and gestured for her to follow him, and led her down a huge array of corridors and out through one of the back doors of the castle.

The gardens were beautiful—colourful and perfectly groomed. She recognised the marble fountain from an old black and white picture she had seen of Alex and his future wife as children.

They walked across the immaculate expanse of green lawn towards the city. It was officially the smallest city in the world—not much bigger than an average town. But it had grown exponentially as the economy of Euronia had grown.

'Did you play in these gardens when you were a child?'

He nodded. 'Yes. There's a secret maze in the forest over there. And my father ordered a tree house to be built and it took the carpenter nearly a whole year.' He gave a little sigh. 'Annabelle is still a little young to play in it. I don't even think she'll like it.'

'Haven't you ever shown it to her?'

He shook his head. 'I've been too focused on other things when it comes to Annabelle. We haven't got around to anything like that.'

Ruby nodded and bit her tongue. It was important that she find out about the relationship between Alex and his daughter. It wouldn't do well for her to criticise, but she could already imagine the kind of recommendations she might make.

'Well, if you show it to me some time maybe I can give you some suggestions on how to make it more appealing to a little girl.'

He gave a little nod as they approached a gate in the high walls. Alex keyed in a code and the door swung open.

'Won't that set off alarms everywhere?'

'No. It's my code. They'll know it's me that's opened the door.'

The back entrance opened directly on to the sea cliffs. The breeze was startlingly stiff and she shivered. She should have brought a cardigan, but the light summer breezes on the castle balcony had been pleasing.

Her bright pink dress whipped around in the wind and Alex pulled off his jacket and put it over her shoulders. The first thing she noticed was the smell of his aftershave as she slid her arms into the jacket and pulled it around her.

'Do you do this often?'

'Of course.' He raised his eyebrows. 'Do you think I spend all my time holed up in the castle?'

'I have no idea, Alex. I have no idea what you do at all.'

She heard him suck in a breath. She wasn't trying to bring up the past, but if she wanted to help Annabelle she had to have a good idea about the environment in which she lived.

The walk into the centre of the city was pleasant. It was less than a mile and they browsed at the shop windows, with several of the shopkeepers coming out to speak to them. One gave Alex some cheese, another some ham wrapped in paper.

'Your favourite,' he said with a smile.

The clothing and jewellery shops were spectacular. No prices in any window. Ruby could only imagine how much things actually cost around here.

She was surprised at how relaxed everything was. The palace was much more formal. People nodded to Alex in the street, but no one seemed in awe of him.

They'd reached the casino in the middle of the city. 'Would you like to sample some of the best cake in Euronia?' he asked.

'Is it better than the cake in Paris?'

Their eyes met. It was a moment. A second for them both to remember that night ten years ago in Paris. Both of them were smiling, as if it were an automatic reaction to the memory.

He leaned forward a little, the heat from his body emanating towards her. 'The cake in Paris won't even come close to the cake in Euronia.'

She lifted her head. They were so close. 'Is that a promise?'

He slid his hand around her back and pulled out a chair for her. 'Absolutely.'

The café Alex had chosen was opposite the casino. She'd seen pictures of the place on the internet. Just about every visitor who came to Euronia visited this café and watched the coming and goings at the casino.

'Aren't you worried you'll get harassed here?'

He shook his head. 'It's Sunday. No cruise ships moor at Euronia on a Sunday and no bus tours run. Today's the best day for me to take a walk around.'

The owner of the café appeared and nodded at Alex. 'The usual coffee and cake, Your Highness?' Alex nodded. 'And for the beautiful lady?'

'You should go and look in the glass cabinet. The cakes are amazing.'

Ruby stood up and walked over to the cabinet, spending a few minutes talking to the café owner before finally settling on a strawberry and cream sponge.

It was surreal. Sitting in the warm sunshine of Euronia with Alex.

These were the kind of things that had drifted into her imagination in the early days. Fanciful thoughts of what might have been.

Alex seemed happy here—more relaxed than he was in the palace, which was strange, as that was his home.

He drank his steaming coffee and devoured a piece of chocolate cake as soon as it appeared. He held out his fork towards her. 'Try some.'

She hesitated, then leaned forward, opening her mouth.

'Mmm, it's delicious. You're right. The cakes here *are* nicer than in Paris.'

He licked some chocolate from his lips and nodded towards her strawberry and cream sponge. 'What? All of them?'

She raised her eyebrows at him and waved her fork. 'I'm warning you—Prince or no Prince. Touch my cake and I'll spear you with my fork.'

He threw back his head and laughed. 'I'm sure you offered me a piece of your cake in Paris.'

She winked at him as she took another bite. 'I might have. But I was trying to impress you then.' She smiled and shrugged. 'Those days are gone.'

'You're not trying to impress me now?'

'No,' she said solemnly. She reached one hand over to his. Her other one was poised carefully. 'I'm just trying to distract you so I can steal some more of your chocolate cake.'

Her fork swooped in and she grabbed another piece.

He held the hand resting over his. 'That's what I like about you, Ruby. What I remember. A girl who likes to eat cake.'

She licked her fork. 'It's my best talent. It's taken years and years of practice.'

She liked this. He was relaxed here. He was much more like the Alex she remembered. Around the palace he seemed so much more uptight.

'How long has the casino been open?' She watched the stream of people entering and leaving.

'Almost three hours.'

She glanced at her watch. 'But it's only one o'clock in the day. I thought gambling would be a night-time kind of thing.'

'Have you ever been to Las Vegas or Atlantic City?'

She shook her head. 'So people gamble here all day?'

He nodded.

'And is that good or bad?'

He fixed his blue eyes on hers. 'You mean for the people, or for the place?'

She shrugged, 'Both, I guess. I don't really know that much about gambling.'

'Neither do I. But tourism is one of the ways to bring money into Euronia. The new port means that cruise ships can easily moor here. We open up part of the castle for tours at different times of the year. We've spent money building five-star hotels that keep the rich and famous happy. And we have some of the most beautiful venues for weddings in the world. That, and the tax benefits, mean that Euronia thrives.'

She listened to his words carefully, hearing the underlying pride as he said them. Ten years ago there had been financial predictions that Euronia would have to be taken over by another country to remain viable. None of those predictions had come true.

'Is that why you went to Harvard and studied business—to find a way to help Euronia?'

He gave a rueful smile. 'If I'd had my way I would have gone to Harvard to study chemistry or physics.'

She sat back in her chair. 'Really? You like that kind of thing?'

He nodded. 'Of course I do. Doesn't every little boy want to be an astronaut? I still want to. Science, maths or engineering—that's what you need a degree in.'

She couldn't help but smile. This was the Alex she'd met back in Paris. This was the guy who'd kissed her until her toes tingled. This was the guy she'd lost a tiny little piece of her heart to.

'You really looked into this?'

'Of course I did.'

She finished the last piece of her cake and licked the fork. It had been delicious. Now she knew this place existed she would try to take a daily trip.

He glanced towards her and it sent a tingle right down to her toes. A cheeky look, a flirtatious look, a maybe-none-of-those-things look, but there was no denying its effect.

It made her feel exposed. It made her feel as if all those fleeting thoughts, all those ridiculous daydreams about being here in Euronia, were being instantly read in her mind.

'Now I'm sold on the cake here I want to come back.'

'I'll bring you any time you like.'

'Good. Because I want you to bring us tomorrow.'

'Us?'

'Yes. You, me and Annabelle. I've watched her in the palace. Later on I'm going to watch her at nursery. But I also need to see how the two of you interact together.'

'But you've seen her with me in the last few days.'

'That was in the palace. This is different.' She held out her hands. 'This is normal.'

He raised his eyebrows at her. 'My life isn't normal?'

She sighed. 'No, Alex. Your life isn't normal. But Annabelle's should be. She's just a little girl. I want to see her come and eat cake or ice cream with her dad.'

If it was possible his tanned face paled. He took a few moments, and she could almost see the thoughts flickering across his face.

Alex had been so relaxed around her for the last hour. She was just praying that the palace portcullis wasn't about to come down, slamming into place.

He gave a slow nod and lifted his bright blue eyes to meet hers. He didn't get it. When he looked at her like that it was magnetising. She couldn't pull herself away if she tried.

She hated it that after ten years he could still do that to her. Still make her feel as if she was the only person around. Make all the noise and people around them just fade into the background.

Her mouth was instantly dry. She wanted to lick her lips,

but was afraid of what that might suggest. It might let him know exactly what she was thinking. And none of her current thoughts could ever be acknowledged between them.

There was one way to break this spell.

'Tell me about your wife, Alex. Tell me about Annabelle's mother.'

There. He looked as if she'd just sucker-punched him. Truth be told, she really didn't want to talk to Alex about his wife. She didn't need to hear how beautiful or wonderful she'd been—the press had already let the world know that. She especially didn't want her stomach to clench so hard she might be sick.

But this was it. This was the way to stop her thinking about her prince. *Her prince*. She was still doing it. It was natural.

And this was a natural question to ask Alex. If she wanted to assess Annabelle properly she had to know the family circumstances.

'What do you want to know?' His voice was hoarse.

She signalled to the waiter. 'Can we have some water, please?' She needed to do something with her own scratchy throat.

The sun was shining down on them, warming her arms and legs. This should be perfect. She was sitting in the most gorgeous setting. From this café she could look across the square at the port and see million-dollar boats bobbing on the sea in front of her. Across from her was the guy she'd thought about for the last ten years.

But she'd just managed to ruin the mood completely. It was time to stop things being personal—it was time to be professional.

'What happened with Sophia? I've seen pictures of the two of you sitting on the fountain at the castle as children. You obviously knew her for a long time?'

He ran his fingers through his dark hair. She was conscious of the furrows in his brow, the lines around his eyes.

He took a deep breath. 'Sophia was my oldest friend. Even though she lived in a neighbouring country our fathers were constantly doing state business together. She was always here.'

Ruby sipped the water the waiter had brought. Nothing would get rid of the dryness in her throat. 'And...?'

He looked at her, then quickly looked away again—almost as if he was embarrassed to speak about Sophia in front of her.

She licked her lips. She wanted to tell him that she only needed to know about Annabelle. But her insides were churning. This was the moment when she'd hear the things she'd always known.

His voice had the slightest tremor. It was only because she was listening so intently that she noticed.

'Sophia came to me after everything had happened. After my father had had the stroke and I'd been made Prince Regent.' His hands went back to his hair. 'Things were a mess. I was totally consumed by finances, by looking for new opportunities for Euronia. But Sophia was sick. I knew it as soon as saw her.'

He sat back in his chair. His body was rigid. One hand clenched in a fist.

'I was furious. She hadn't told me anything.' He fixed his eyes on a point over her shoulder. 'The speculation was right. She had breast cancer. It was terminal. Sophia came and told me after she'd tried a number of treatments. She'd already made her mind up that she didn't want to do that any more.'

There was a sheen across his eyes and it made Ruby's heart ache for him. But down in the pit of her stomach there was something else. A tiny smattering of jealousy that he'd felt so much for this woman.

'So you got married?'

She tried to make it sound casual. But her voice was tight and she knew it. She just hoped he wouldn't notice.

Alex gave the slightest nod of his head.

'Sophia came to me. She told me her diagnosis. She told me the one thing she wanted in the world was to have a baby before it was too late. I couldn't say no to her. I just couldn't. I loved her. People had speculated for years that we would marry—but it never entered our heads. Sophia had plans—she had big plans. She was so creative...she loved art and design. But she also had a really inquisitive nature. She was torn between design and journalism. She loved to write. She had sketches and sketches of dress designs.'

He sighed,

'And then...' he lifted his hand '...the cancer.' He shook his head. 'It was as if all her dreams just evaporated. She'd already made up her mind before she came to see me. If we had a child together it would seal the fate of our two kingdoms. Sophia was an only child. When she died her whole dynasty would die with her. She didn't want that to happen.' His voice steadied. 'Neither of us wanted that to happen.'

He pressed his lips together.

'You probably already know this, but when Sophia's father dies Annabelle will be Queen of Leruna. If he dies before Annabelle comes of age I'll be Regent to the two principalities.'

His lifted his eyes and met her gaze full-on. The implications were huge. He was telling her he'd made a pact with his childhood friend. They'd married. They'd had a child together. They'd cemented their relationship and safeguarded the future of two countries. How noble.

She was trying hard not to be bitter. And there was still a tiny flicker of hope. He hadn't said Sophia was the love of his life. He'd said he loved her. That was different.

Ruby felt her voice wobble. 'She was really young to have breast cancer, Alex.'

'I know.' He paused. 'She had the gene.' It came out in a whisper.

Her breath caught in her throat. 'Sophia had the gene?' Everyone had heard about 'the gene' by now—the mutation linked with breast and ovarian cancer. 'What about Annabelle?'

He shook his head. 'I had her tested. She's not affected.'

Her breath left her in a whoosh. 'Oh, wow. You must be so relieved.' She toyed with the glass of water in her hands. 'I know it's a silly question, but was there nothing else they could do? It's just that…wouldn't the pregnancy have made a difference to her cancer? I thought they recommend that you don't get pregnant if you have that type of cancer?'

His face was serious. 'Sophia was very single-minded. She knew that she would die eventually. Having a child was the most important thing to her in the world. She could have had some type of chemotherapy while she was pregnant—but she refused. She did have some immediately following delivery. But she was so weak. So tired. She only took the treatment to prolong her time with Annabelle. Once she realised how sick it was making her, and how it really didn't make any difference to the outcome, she decided to stop everything. She wanted some time with Annabelle.'

'And did she have time with Annabelle?'

Ruby was trying to work out the impact on the child. Annabelle couldn't have been much more than a baby. Was there any chance that what had happened then might have had an impact on her future? It seemed unlikely. There was lots of debate as to when a child formed its first memories. Most researchers thought it happened around the age of three. But Ruby had seen a lot of things in her work that had made her question that.

'She had a few months. She spent every possible second with Annabelle. By the end she was just too tired, too sick. Annabelle was in her arms when she died. She was only eleven months old.'

'It must have been devastating for you.'

'She was my childhood friend—the person I grew up with. If my father hadn't had the stroke, if Sophia hadn't had breast cancer, lots of things might have been different.'

Something flickered across his eyes. A tiny moment of recognition. An awareness. A regret.

'I'm sorry, Ruby,' he whispered.

Tears filled her eyes. It was an acknowledgement, however brief, of what had happened between them. He was laying everything out on the table for her. It was just the two of them. No one else to interrupt. No one else to interfere.

He reached over and touched her cheek—just as he had all those years ago in Paris. He tucked a piece of hair behind her ear.

Silence. For the longest time. Lots of words unspoken.

His fingers stroked across her cheek. So many things wanted to spill out of her. But her frustration was dissipating. The years had passed. She couldn't be angry with him any more. She'd lived a whole ten years of her life without him. He'd always been in the background of her mind. No matter how hard she'd tried to push him away. But her memories of Alex were memories of one New Year's Eve and a moment in time.

The Alex she saw in front of her now was the one that really existed. A father. A prince with the responsibilities of a country—two countries. Someone who'd set aside his career ambitions to fulfil his duty to his country. Someone who'd just told her that he was sorry. That meant more than anything.

She'd been harbouring an illusion for the last ten years. Trouble was, the reality was better than the dream.

She felt a rush of blood to her cheeks, but Alex had reached across the table and taken her hand.

'Thank you, Ruby. Thank you for doing this for me. Thank you for doing this for my daughter.'

She stood up quickly. *His daughter.*

'It's time to go. I need to get back and plan for the nursery with Annabelle and her nanny.'

He was being kind. He was being sweet. He was thanking her for doing her job.

Her job. The one he was paying her to do.

If Alex was disturbed by her abruptness he didn't show it. He just signalled to the waiter and left some money on the table.

Her cheek was burning from where he'd touched her. It almost felt as if he'd left a mark on her skin.

She needed some distance. She needed some space.

Most of all she needed to remember why she was here—to assess a little girl. Nothing more. Nothing less.

CHAPTER FOUR

FOR A MOMENT earlier today Alex had been sure there was something in the air between him and Ruby.

He'd managed to persuade his security team to stay a comfortable distance away from them. He knew the palace must be suffocating for Ruby. But he'd never considered it might be suffocating to Annabelle.

Ruby was here to do a job. She'd already made an impact on his staff by insisting she stay in the staff quarters next to Annabelle. He'd tried not to smirk when he'd heard Rufus, his private secretary, scold her for calling him Alex.

'You must address him as Your Highness or Prince Regent,' he'd insisted.

But Ruby had laughed and waved her hand. 'Nonsense. He's Alex.'

There was a hum in the air around her. When she remembered, her manners could be impeccable. But most of the time she was just Ruby, and his staff were starting to warm to her.

Her focus on her task was obvious to all. She was unobtrusive, watching Annabelle and listening quietly. None of her assessment had put any demands on the child. After months of people trying to make Annabelle do things she clearly didn't want to, or examining her ears, tongue and throat, it was a refreshing change.

Ruby. She'd been fixed in his mind for the last ten years. Her brown curls, dark eyes, red coat and a carefree attitude had wrapped their way around him like cotton candy around a stick.

But it was other things he remembered too. The laughter in her eyes, the flirtation, the buzz between them. That moment when their lips had touched and the fireworks had started going off in his head as well as in the sky. Ruby had sent a rush of blood around his body. He'd never felt a connection like that. He'd never had a kiss like that again.

He remembered the feel of her warm curves filling the palms of his hand underneath that red coat. The skin on her cheek where he'd stroked it. Every sensation of just *being* around Ruby.

Part of what he remembered was reality, part fantasy. He hadn't wanted that night to end. To Ruby, he'd been just Alex. At that point in his life he'd been able to do that. But it had been the last night of his life to have that opportunity, and spending it with Ruby couldn't have been more perfect. If only it had ended differently.

He looked down and shuffled the ever-growing mound of papers on his desk. All things that needed his signature. Emails were all very well, but some things still required a signature.

He picked up the phone and dialled the number of the clinic in Switzerland. It didn't matter that he knew the doctors would phone him if they had any concerns. Or that he had a multitude of staff members to do it for him. After ten years, he still liked to keep a check of things on his own.

He moved the papers on the desk again, looking to find a letter for a foreign dignitary. Something fluttered to the floor. A photo. He picked it up and smiled. It was ten years old. Ruby, just the way he remembered her, taken by one of his security team on New Year's Eve. He'd only found out about it a few months later, when he'd wanted to track her down. His Head of Security had admitted they had some photographs and had looked into her past—all to check her authenticity.

It was of the two of them, sitting at the table in that café next to the Four Seasons. They were laughing. Ruby had her head thrown back, her dark hair was glossy, and she was smiling from ear to ear. But the thing that had always struck him about that picture was the way they were looking at each other. Even though Ruby was laughing she was still looking at him, and he at her.

A little moment captured in time.

A million different possibilities. A million different futures.

If he'd turned a different corner that night he'd never have met Ruby Wetherspoon, and that thought made his stomach twist almost as much as the thought of what might have been.

Deep down he knew his father would never have accepted his fascination with an English healthcare worker. He'd never fully understood it himself.

But no one could deny the connection between them. This picture was everlasting proof of that.

When he had his darkest moments—when the nights just seemed to last for ever—it was thoughts of Ruby that gave him comfort. Thoughts of being twenty-four again and having the world at his feet.

He sighed and opened a drawer to put the photo inside. Ruby had never been a threat and his security staff had filed their paperwork away.

He just couldn't do the same.

There it was again. That strange noise.

Ruby moved from the window seat, where she'd been watching the sun start to lower in the sky. Evenings could be long in the palace. Annabelle went to bed early and most of the time Ruby spent her time walking in the gardens, reading a book or talking to Polly on the phone.

Polly was still unimpressed.

The noise again. Was it a whimper?

She stood up quickly. Brigette, the nanny, had gone to bed earlier with a migraine. Could it be Annabelle?

Annabelle's door had been left open earlier, so Ruby walked out into the corridor and hesitated, her hand above the door handle. Part of her was worried. Annabelle wasn't that familiar with her yet. Maybe she would be scared if Ruby went into her room.

She took a deep breath as the whimper continued and pushed the door open. There was no way she could leave any child upset—whether they knew her or not.

The room was dark. Even though the sun hadn't set yet there were blackout blinds at the window. It only took her a few seconds to realise the bed was empty.

She sucked in a breath and suppressed her impulse to shout. Instead she flicked on the light switch and had a quick look around. Annabelle might still be in the room.

But she wasn't. Not under the bed. Not in the wardrobe—even though Ruby hadn't really expected her to be. Not in any corner of the room.

Her heart started thudding as she walked back to the door and quickly along the corridor. The missing child would cause mayhem. The implications were tremendous—and terrifying. She had to take a few seconds to be sure before she called the alarm.

There. In front of her. At the top of the stairs.

A tiny staggering figure in pink pyjamas.

Her legs broke into a run.

'Annabelle!'

She reached her seconds.

But Annabelle hadn't responded to her voice. And it was clear why. She was sleepwalking.

Ruby didn't have any experience with sleepwalking kids. She could vaguely remember something about not waking them up. But Annabelle was perilously close to the top of the staircase. She didn't hesitate. She just swept her up into her arms.

Annabelle's eyes were open, and the movement and embrace by Ruby seemed to give her a little start. Her whimpering stopped and she tucked her head into Ruby's neck.

There was no one else about. Not a single person in the corridor.

She hesitated. What next? She walked back along the corridor and paused at Annabelle's door. Her heart was still thudding after that horrible few seconds of thinking something might be wrong.

She couldn't put Annabelle back into her bed and risk it happening again. She'd need to talk to Brigette and Alex in the morning to see if this was normal for Annabelle. No one had mentioned it, and she knew in some kids it was common, but she couldn't risk Annabelle walking near the stairs again.

She walked back into her own room. There was plenty of space in her bed for both of them. At least then she'd know that Annabelle was safe.

Her eyes were still open. Ruby had no idea if it was just an automatic response in sleepwalking, or if on some level Annabelle was actually awake.

The little arms wound around her neck. Thank goodness for automatic reactions. Ruby just started to rock her.

Familiarity. That was what she needed for this little girl.

She kept her in her arms and walked next door, picking up Annabelle's favourite movie and taking it with her.

Background noise. That was all it needed to be. Something familiar so that if Annabelle woke up she'd be comfortable.

Ruby reached her hand out, juggling the weight of Annabelle on the other arm as she opened the case and slid the DVD inside the player.

They settled back on the bed. Annabelle adjusted her position. She seemed comfortable in Ruby's lap and made no attempt to move. Ruby piled the pillows around them.

If they were here for the long haul they might as well be comfortable.

The screen lit up bright blue as the titles for *Finding Nemo* appeared. Her own 'go to' film as well as Annabelle's favourite. She loved it just as much as any child, and had yet to meet a kid who wasn't enthralled by it.

Annabelle seemed to settle back against her and that was when Ruby *really* started to listen. She'd already heard Annabelle whimper. She had no doubt that on a physical basis the little girl could form sounds. The diagnosis of selective mutism seemed the most appropriate. She wondered if Annabelle spoke in *any* situation.

She seemed a little more awake now, but she hadn't made any sign to Ruby. Her head was definitely turned towards the TV screen, and she didn't seem to have any objection to being in Ruby's bed.

A new thought crossed her mind, completely unrelated to the sleepwalking. Company. This little girl wanted company.

And then it started. Little noises. Little sounds. Gasps when Nemo's mother disappeared. Small, slow body movements along with the music, and then—eventually—a little hum. Ruby did nothing. She didn't react at all. Just listened as Annabelle hummed along. A smile danced across the little girl's face. She was enthralled—lost in the story. Perfect. Just perfect.

She was only three. Her speech wasn't really too delayed. Maybe Annabelle needed a little encouragement and coaching instead of assessing and prodding. She would have to choose her words carefully when she explained all this to Alex. There was no magic wand that she could wave here. Annabelle had to be allowed to develop at her own pace.

Ruby settled back against the pillows. Annabelle's eyes were getting heavy. She would fall asleep soon—and then Ruby could think about this a little more…

* * *

'Ruby!'

Her eyes shot open. The first thing that struck her was the crick in her neck. The second thing that struck her was the three people standing in the doorway—all of them staring at her.

She tried to push herself up, but Annabelle was still curled in her lap, sleeping. Ruby couldn't even begin to imagine what she looked like—rumpled clothes, hair sticking up in every direction but the right one, and more than likely pillow creases on her face.

Brigette, Rufus and Alexander were standing in the doorway, three sets of eyes fixed on her. She tried to edge herself out from under Annabelle without disturbing her. The curtains were still drawn and the TV was flickering on the wall.

Alex rushed across the room. 'What on earth is going on? Why is Annabelle in here?' He seemed furious. 'Have you *any* idea what I thought when I saw her bed was empty?'

He was shouting now, unable to contain his anger.

Of course. The same horrible thought *she'd* had for a few seconds last night, when she'd saw Annabelle's empty bed. The horror. The worry.

She couldn't get the words out quickly enough. 'I'm sorry. I found her sleepwalking last night. She was close to the top of the stairs. I just grabbed her. Then I didn't know whether to try and wake her or not, so I brought her in here. I was worried she might do it again.'

Alex reached over and lifted his still sleeping little girl out of the bed. 'Sleepwalking? Why didn't you call me? Why didn't you call Brigette?'

He was angry with her.

'I'm her father. You should have come and got me if there was something wrong with Annabelle.'

Ruby shook her head. She understood his anger. She understood those seconds of panic.

'There was no one around, Alex. I had no idea if sleep-walking was normal for Annabelle or not. And she seemed to settle with me really quickly. She just wanted some comfort. I did plan to talk to you about it today.'

Alex shot her a look that left her in no doubt about his feelings. He didn't even say another word. Just turned and walked out of the room with Annabelle in his arms, still asleep.

She turned to Brigette. The last thing she wanted to do was get Annabelle's nanny in trouble. 'I'm sorry, Brigette. I knew you had a migraine. I didn't want to wake you when I felt as if I could deal with Annabelle on my own.'

Brigette brushed past her too, leaving Rufus the last person to lock his beady eyes on hers.

She sighed. 'I'm going to take a shower and get dressed.'

Rufus tutted at her and then spun on his heels and left. *Great. Just great.*

Now she was awake a little more she wanted to shout at them all to come back and tell them to calm down.

Annabelle was fine. They should talk about her sleep-walking and put steps in place to keep her safe.

But common sense told her this wasn't the time.

He hadn't spoken to Ruby in four days.

It was ridiculous. He'd snapped at her when there had been no reason to. But when Rufus had bustled along the corridor to tell him Annabelle was missing he'd panicked. He could have broken speed records with his bolt along the corridor.

The thought of something happening to his daughter... He couldn't even allow his brain to contemplate it.

But seeing Ruby asleep on the bed with Annabelle in her arms had knocked the wind from his heels.

After the instant relief he'd felt a wave of anger.

Their heads resting next to each other, the mish-mash of blonde curls and long brown hair, the way Ruby had been sheltering Annabelle in her arms had consumed him with an unexpected rage he hadn't felt in a long time.

She couldn't know that, against advice, on lots of occasions Sophia had taken Annabelle in to sleep next to her. She could never imagine that the impact of seeing his little girl in someone else's arms would flood him with unspeakable guilt.

He hadn't loved Sophia the way people thought he had. He had loved her like a best friend. A best friend who'd been cheated out of sleeping next to their little girl and seeing her grow up.

If Sophia was here now he was almost sure Annabelle wouldn't have any problems with her speech.

As for the sleepwalking…? Was that his fault too? It was yet another worry. Another failing. Something else to consult a whole array of doctors on.

He couldn't even begin to understand why it annoyed him all the more that it was Ruby who'd found the problem. She was under his skin in more ways than was imaginable.

Guilt was chipping away at him. Guilt for how he was feeling about Ruby. And guilt because he continually felt as if he were failing his daughter.

What would Sophia have thought? His friend would have dealt with things so much better than he could.

But if Sophia were here now he would never have seen Ruby again. And that was what burned away at his insides. That was what filled him with even more hideous guilt.

The last few days of being around Ruby had lit a fire inside him that had long since died. He could feel her presence everywhere. The staff in the palace seemed happier—less formal. It was almost as if her scent drifted in the air into every room. Light, flowery, lifting the mood.

She'd connected with most members of staff in her polite but informal manner. She wasn't afraid to ask questions, and more importantly she wasn't afraid to laugh. In the space of a few days the atmosphere around him seemed to have lightened. The palace had started to feel happy again.

Years of worry about his father's health, the economy of Euronia, and then the terminal diagnosis of Sophia, followed by the concerns about Annabelle, had made being here oppressive. Every tiny part of this place seemed to weigh on his shoulders relentlessly.

Seeing Ruby's connection today with Annabelle had been unexpected. He'd never realistically thought about someone else stepping into Sophia's shoes.

But he should have. It was inevitable.

At some point he would marry again—this time for love—and that woman would become a mother to Annabelle. He'd been so busy these last few years, and so stressed, he hadn't taken time to think of the impact of that.

The impact on the country. The impact on Annabelle. The impact on him.

And then, there she was, with her mussed-up curls parallel with his child's. Making him see something that everyone had probably already surmised.

It was time to move on.

But was he ready?

CHAPTER FIVE

THE CLOTHES WERE lying across her bed. Seventeen dresses of varying styles and colours—all with matching shoes.

'I don't understand. Did something happen to my clothes?'

Rufus shook his head. 'I told you I would arrange for some other clothing to be sent to the palace for you.'

She reached down and touched the nearest designer dress. It was red…beautiful. Like something you would wear to the Queen's garden party back in London. It certainly wasn't like anything she owned.

'But I'm not sure I really need these. I don't know how much longer I'll be here. And I've got clothes of my own.' She opened the wardrobe, revealing her few dresses, jeans, T-shirts and a couple of pairs of sandals and heels.

Rufus gave an almost imperceptible shake of his head. He turned to leave. 'They're here now—enjoy!' he said, and with a wave of his hand he disappeared, leaving her to perch on the edge of the bed, too nervous to touch some of the dresses.

'How very *Pretty Woman*.' She sighed. Her head was swimming. Was this another way for Alex to buy her? Did he want to dress her up like some doll?

Every dress was beautifully styled and there was a rainbow of colour. It was strange, but whilst they were all different none was in a style that she wouldn't wear. It was almost as if they'd given her friend Polly a free budget and the run of all the designer houses.

A silk one slid through her fingers. It was almost the same blue as Alex's eyes. She gave a little shudder.

Alex. He hadn't spoken to her for four days. Falling asleep with his daughter was obviously a no-no. But while it might have been a little unconventional she really thought everyone had overreacted.

The imaginary walls between herself and Annabelle had definitely started to crumble. The little girl wasn't completely ignoring her any more. Yesterday she'd sat next to Ruby as she'd thumbed through a book. After a while Ruby had asked her if she wanted her to read the story and Annabelle had given a little nod and slid closer.

It was a small step, but gaining Annabelle's trust was the most important thing of all.

She picked up another of the dresses. It was yellow— a colour she never usually wore—and it matched the sun outside and the flowers in the garden directly beneath her window.

She slipped off her T-shirt and Capri pants. The dress dropped over her head and fitted her curves as if it had been specially made for her. Everything was covered, from the round neckline to the flouncy skirt that fell to her knees. She reached behind to fasten the zip. It was a little tricky. She managed to pull it up to her bra strap. Then she reached her hands above her shoulders and over her back, trying to pull the material of the dress a little higher and grasp the zipper.

Someone cleared his throat loudly. She spun around.

She hadn't thought to close the door after Rufus had left. No one ever seemed to come down this corridor.

'Alex!' Colour flooded into her cheeks.

He was leaning in the doorway, his hands folded across his chest, with a cheeky smile on his face. She hadn't even heard his footsteps.

'What are you doing here?'

His smile just seemed to get broader. 'Looks like I'm helping a damsel in distress.' He stepped into the room and twirled his finger. 'Go on—spin around and I'll fasten it for you.'

It was amazing how quickly his presence could cause a buzz in the air around her. She sucked in a breath as she turned around.

Fastening a zip should take the briefest of seconds. But Alex waited. She could feel the material of her dress shifting slightly. The zipper must be in his hand. Then he stepped forward, closing the gap between them.

His head was at her shoulder. She could smell his aftershave—it was coiling its way around her. Who was the snake in that childhood film? Kaa, in *The Jungle Book*—with the hypnotic eyes that could make you do anything that he wanted. She was pretty sure Alex's eyes would have the same effect on her.

'I'm sorry I snapped at you,' he said quietly. 'I thought something was wrong with Annabelle.'

'Okay...' That was all she replied. Her breath was still caught somewhere between her chest and her throat. It was all she was capable of saying right now.

There was a drumming noise in her ears. Her heart was thudding against her chest as she waited to see what would happen next.

'I thought today we could go back to the café with Annabelle—like you asked me to.'

She smiled. Did that mean her mistake was being forgotten, or was this part of his apology? He still hadn't moved. He still hadn't fastened her zipper.

She nodded. Not breathing was getting difficult. 'Okay.'

'Do you like the dresses?'

She could feel his breath warm the skin on her shoulder.

'I love them—but I don't need them. Rufus didn't need to do that.'

'He didn't do it.'

She froze. One of his hands moved and rested on her hip.

This was all becoming remarkably familiar. Richard Gere was going to appear any second now. Didn't he buy Vivian a new wardrobe in *Pretty Woman*?

Her profession might not compare with Vivian's, but the thought of Alex purchasing a whole wardrobe for her was both mildly disturbing and somehow exciting. She didn't know whether to be insulted or overjoyed.

'I don't think I like this, Alex. You can't buy me. You can't dress me up as if I'm your little doll.' She could feel her stomach tighten.

But Alex just shook his head. 'I'm not buying you, Ruby. I don't care whether you wear the clothes or not.' He waved his hand. 'If you don't like them give them away—give them to charity. It makes no difference to me.'

He stepped a little closer.

'I guess I'm just not good at this. I'm trying to say sorry. Sorry about how I reacted over Annabelle. For a second I thought she was gone. I thought someone had kidnapped my daughter—I overreacted. And...' He waved his hands again. 'This is how I say sorry. Doesn't every woman like clothes?'

The tightness in her chest dissipated. It was clear he meant every word.

'What are you going to do if it happens again?'

He smiled. 'Silent alarms. Everywhere. If Annabelle opens her door in the middle of the night alarms will go off in my room, Brigette's room and in Security.' He looked over his shoulder and whispered. 'And, don't tell her, but we've actually had tracking devices sewn into all her pyjamas.'

She laughed. He was sorry, and he'd put steps in place to ensure Annabelle's safety. Of course he had. She hadn't doubted that for a second, but it made her mood lighten.

He nudged her, and pointed to the dresses as he slid a hand around her waist.

'Which is your favourite?'

He was so close. His lips were almost touching her ear. If she just moved her head a little...

'The blue one.'

'Why?'

'I like the colour.' The rush of blood was heating her cheeks. Her answer had been automatic.

She was conscious of the lightness of his fingers on her hip. Would he make the connection between the colour of the dress and the colour of his eyes? No. Guys didn't do that kind of thing.

This time his lips did brush against her ear. 'I like the red one. It reminds me of you in Paris. The same colour as your coat.'

A whole host of tiny centipedes were marching along her arms with their hundreds of legs, making every single hair stand on end.

His finger touched the skin of her back. She gasped. It wasn't cold—it was just unexpected. A thousand butterfly wings had just exploded on her back, and all the little nerve-endings were waiting for the next sensation.

He bent a little lower and whispered in her ear again. This time it felt as if his breath was caressing her skin.

'Ten years is a long time, Ruby.'

He pulled the zipper up with his finger inside, then ran it along the upper end of her spine, resting his fingers at the base of her neck.

Her legs were turning to jelly. It was ridiculous. It was nothing. But she felt as if she'd waited ten years for that.

Ten years of dreaming. Ten years of imagining. Ten years of hoping.

She stepped backwards. Against him. Into him. Feeling the full length of his body next to hers. Her eyes were fixed outside, on the gardens. If she turned around and looked at those blue eyes she might do something much more inappropriate than fall asleep next to his daughter.

She rested her head back against his chest. 'Yes, it is.'

Her voice was tinged with sadness.

They both stood there—neither moving. It was almost as if they were happy for this to be the first tiny step. The first real acknowledgment that their time ten years ago hadn't just been a figment of her imagination that she'd played over and over in her head.

She could feel the rise and fall of his chest against her back. The heat from his body through the thin fabric of her dress. It felt natural. It felt as if this was exactly the place she was supposed to stand. As if this was exactly the place she was meant to be.

His hand moved slightly from her hip around to her stomach. His other hand met hers and he threaded their fingers together in front of her.

This might be wrong.

It might be inappropriate.

But why did it feel so good?

'Your Highness?'

The voice came echoing down the hall and they sprang apart. Alex disappeared out of her door in flash to meet Rufus, who was muttering again.

Ruby's feet were stuck to the floor.

Had that really just happened?

Her body was telling her yes. Every sense seemed to be on fire.

But her brain was turning to mush. Sensible, rational thoughts seemed to have flown from the building.

Ruby was logical. Ruby was always sensible.

The one time in her life she hadn't been entirely sensible had been ten years ago in Paris. Ten years ago she'd acted on impulse. And look where that had got her.

But ten years ago she'd felt the same tiny flicker of

warmth and excitement that was burning inside her right now.

   This was the first time she hadn't felt like the hired help.

   This was the first time she'd felt as if she wasn't here just for Annabelle.

   Question was: what was she getting herself into?

CHAPTER SIX

ALEX'S HANDS WERE still shaking. That had been it. The situation that—in his head—he'd dreamed about being in.

Him and Ruby alone.

Getting private time in the palace was harder than it seemed.

Ruby's questions a few days ago had started to play on his mind. How much time *did* he actually get to spend with Annabelle?

He tried to be there most mornings when she had breakfast. He always tried to see her before bedtime. But in a world where visits to other countries were inevitable and midnight conference calls were normal it wasn't always possible.

Annabelle was the spitting image of her mother. He'd already been friends with Sophia at her age. And, although he loved his daughter with all his heart, sometimes she was a painful reminder of the friend he had lost.

Perhaps he'd overreacted when the nanny had mentioned Annabelle's speech seemed a little behind?

Alex had no experience with children. And the internet seemed like a dangerous tool sometimes. He'd paid for expert upon expert to assess her—all the while terrified that there was something wrong with his child.

When Ruby had said that as part of the assessment she wanted to see how Annabelle and Alex interacted with each other he'd felt a wave of panic. Was it a criticism? She hadn't made it sound like that. Maybe he was just feeling under pressure.

He'd planned carefully. He'd had someone pack a picnic to take to the palace grounds, then they would walk into the centre and have some ice cream—just as Ruby had suggested.

Then he gone to find Ruby and she'd been surrounded by the dresses he'd ordered and been half dressed.

Maybe not strictly true. But that glimpse of the skin on her back had been enough to send his blood pressure rising. When he'd offered to zip her up it had taken all his strength not to pull the zip down.

Alex was always in control. That night in Paris years ago had been the first time he'd shaken off his security team in years. Bumping into Ruby had made the whole night perfect. Having her in the palace again was bringing a whole host of sensations he hadn't acknowledged in years.

Rufus had mumbled in his ear all the way along the corridor. The look of surprise on his face to see Alex exiting Ruby's bedroom had spoken volumes without a single word being said.

Neither of them had acknowledged it. Alex had immediately started talking business and given Rufus a list of instructions for the rest of the afternoon.

Annabelle and her nanny were waiting at the main entrance for him. After a few minutes Ruby came down the main staircase carrying a bright pink ball in her arms. Her face was slightly flushed. A sure sign they'd been doing something they shouldn't.

Brigette gave a nod and left while Alex offered his hand to Annabelle and put the picnic basket over his arm.

'A picnic? You never said we were having a picnic,' said Ruby.

'Didn't I?'

He glanced at the ball, then at her feet. She was wearing a pair of white trainers with a yellow dress. It brought a smile to his face. Ruby didn't really worry about who might take her picture and claim she'd made a fashion *faux pas*.

'I didn't take you as a footballer.'

Ruby pulled at the skirt of her dress and smiled. 'I have lots of hidden talents. But maybe I should have worn something different—trousers, perhaps?'

He shook his head. 'I think your dress will be perfect. Now, let's go.'

There was a further little flush of colour in her cheeks. Both of them were remembering exactly why he liked the fact she was wearing a dress.

But Ruby wasn't giving anything away. She bent down in front of Annabelle. 'A picnic—wow. It's been years since I've been on a picnic. Why don't you take us to your favourite place in the palace grounds and we'll eat there?'

She gave Alex a little smile and walked out through the door, waiting for them to join her.

He could sense the general unease in the air. There were a few members of staff staring at them. Was it really so unusual that he spent time with his child—or had word spread even more quickly than he'd thought that he'd been seen leaving Ruby's bedroom?

He gave Annabelle's hand a squeeze and they walked out into the beautiful sunshine. Ruby's idea was good. He'd been trying to decide between going near where the horses were stabled, to the ornamental gardens, the duck pond or the palace maze. But Annabelle had other ideas. She was leading them around the side of the palace, her little footsteps assured.

It only took a few minutes, then she plunked herself down on the grass directly behind the ornamental fountain.

Alex blinked. This was the place where he'd had that picture taken with Sophia. They'd both been about Annabelle's page and the photo had been zoomed around the world with the press headline *'Future King and Queen?'*

Had Annabelle ever seen that picture? He wasn't sure,

but he could tell from a fleeting glance at Ruby's face that *she* certainly had.

Whatever her thoughts on the matter, she sat down next to Annabelle on the grass, not even waiting for him to lay out the picnic blanket he'd brought along.

The little girl started to fumble with her shoes. Ruby gave her a smile and knelt down next to her, taking off her white leather sandals and frilly socks.

She held out her hand to Annabelle and the two of them walked over to the fountain. Annabelle hadn't said a word and he was confused. How did Ruby know what she wanted?

He moved closer as Annabelle stood up on the wall surrounding the fountain and dipped her toes in the water. She let out a little laugh and he took a deep breath.

His little girl's laughter. How beautiful it was—and how rarely he'd heard it.

Annabelle was walking around the fountain now, holding Ruby's hand to keep her balance. She had the biggest smile on her face.

He walked in pace with Ruby. 'How did you know that's what she wanted to do?'

He couldn't take his eyes off his little girl. Couldn't believe how much she looked like her mother. It alarmed him how much he noticed.

Ruby shrugged. 'It's exactly what I would do if I were Annabelle's age.'

They reached the point where they'd started and Ruby put her arms around Annabelle's waist and swung her in the air.

'Whee!'

Annabelle laughed again as Ruby swooped her through the air and landed her on the blanket that he'd spread out. She picked up a corner of the blanket and started drying Annabelle's toes.

Alex opened the basket and started unpacking the food.

The palace chef had outdone himself, as usual, but the most curious thing was a small tub full of steamed-up food.

Annabelle gave a little shriek of excitement and grabbed it, pulling open the lid and searching for a spoon.

Ruby wrinkled her nose and leaned closer. 'Macaroni cheese? Is this one of Annabelle's favourites?'

Alex nodded. 'Apparently.' He peered in the basket. 'I'm not quite sure how it managed to find its way into the picnic basket, though.'

Ruby grabbed an apple, bit into it, then leaned back on her hands, staring up at the palace. 'I can't say I've ever had a picnic in front of a palace before.'

He stared up at the hundreds of windows. There might be a whole host of palace staff looking down on them at any moment. It might look like a private picnic, with no one visibly around them, but the truth was it was anything but.

He pulled a bottle of water out of the basket and popped the tab for Annabelle. 'Would you like to go and see the horses? Or the maze?'

She shook her head and continued to eat the macaroni. He reached into the basket for some more food, and squinted when his hand came into contact with something strange. A leg. A plastic doll's leg. And another doll. And another.

He pulled them out. One was in a princess dress, one in a swimsuit and one in a semi-naked state with her arms partway into a spacesuit.

He winked at Ruby. 'Ruby, I see you brought your dolls to play with.'

She laughed and grabbed the blonde astronaut, pushing her arms and legs into the silver and white suit and fastening it appropriately. 'Of course I did, Alex. I like playing with dolls.'

Annabelle's head shot up and she gave a little smile, abandoning the macaroni and walking over to the dolls.

Her comprehension was perfect. She understood everything that was going on around her. So why didn't she talk?

Ruby held up the princess doll and the swimsuit doll. 'Which one do you like best? The pink one or the purple one?'

He wondered what she was doing. Annabelle screwed up her face and shook her head. There were no pink or purple clothes.

Ruby just smiled, as if this was something she did every day—which she did. She held each doll higher. 'Oh, I *see*. Silly me. Blue or red, then?'

Annabelle came over and picked the doll wearing the pale blue dress and pointed towards her own.

Ruby nodded. 'You like blue, then?'

She gave Alex a secret smile. Every little thing she did was part of Annabelle's assessment. Every other person who had come to see her had been much more rigid in their processes, wanting Annabelle to do certain things at certain times. Being three was difficult enough. But Alex had been made to feel as if Annabelle was being difficult or uncooperative. She didn't seem that way with Ruby.

Annabelle took her dolls and walked over to the ornamental fountain with all three.

'I think they're all about to go for a swim—costumes or not,' murmured Ruby.

She seemed perfectly relaxed out here. She picked up a ham sandwich and started to eat. He reached in and pulled out his favourite. Tuna. Hardly royal. Probably not the thing that most Prince Regents would eat. But this had been Alex's favourite since he was a child.

The tension between them wasn't as high as it had been in the room when they were alone. But then again, they hadn't been on display there. He kept wondering if there *were* any unseen eyes watching what should be a private affair.

'She knows her colours. For a three-year-old that's good.' Ruby was watching Annabelle again.

'You can tell just from that?'

She shook her head. 'Oh, no. I've done a few other exercises as well.' She leaned forward and pulled her knees up, wrapping her dress around them. 'Listen…' she whispered.

Alex sat a little straighter, straining to hear what Ruby had heard above the constant trickle of water from the fountain.

There it was—floating across the air.

Ruby touched his arm. 'She's humming. She did that the other night with me.' She gave a tiny shake of her head. 'I know that one of the reports about Annabelle questioned whether she could even make sounds. But she can. You've heard her laugh. You've heard her squeal. And she can communicate with sign language. She's *choosing* not to speak.' A frown marred her complexion. 'I've just got to figure out why.'

Her eyes were fixed on Annabelle playing with her dolls. This was all so easy for Ruby. Annabelle was just a patient. She didn't have the same investment, the same emotional connection that he did. She didn't have the same frustrated feeling that there must be something else he could do. She was a professional with a puzzle to solve.

'You make it sound so easy.' He couldn't help the way the words sounded. He'd forced them out through gritted teeth.

But Ruby didn't react. She just kept looking at Annabelle. 'I don't think it's easy, Alex. I just think that you—and I—are going to have to be patient. That's the only way this can work.'

Her eyes met his. For a second he wasn't quite sure what she was talking about. They were talking about Annabelle, right? Because those words might sound as if she were talking about them instead.

'What's your first memory, Alex?'

'What?' He was surprised by her question.

She smiled at him. 'I can honestly say the first thing I remember is from around age seven. I was on holiday with my mum and dad in Boulogne in France. I can remember walking about with cases because we couldn't find our hotel. Then my father thought it would be interesting to go and watch the fishermen.' She gave a shudder. 'Watching fishermen gut their fish was not something I wanted to see as a seven-year-old.' She turned and smiled at him. 'That's my first real memory.'

He sat back a little, unsure where this was going. 'I can remember having to sit very still for a long, *long* time. It was at some awards ceremony and my father glared at me every time I moved. I hated the shirt and tie I was wearing because it felt too tight.'

She nodded. 'What age do you think you were?'

He shrugged. 'Around five, I think.'

She lifted her hand towards Annabelle. 'Here's the thing. Science tells us that the first three years are the most important for a child's brain development. It's the first time we're supposed to form memories—but I can't remember anything from back then. The experts tell us that young children's memories change over time, replacing old memories with new ones. So I'm looking at Annabelle and wondering what she remembers.'

'What do you mean?' This was starting to make him uncomfortable.

She interlinked her fingers. 'The brain has connections—hard wiring. Children's brains are like a sponge—they take in everything all around them. Children are born to learn. By their first year seventy-five per cent of the hard wiring is in place.' She pointed at Annabelle again. 'By age three ninety per cent of the hard wiring is there.'

She ran her fingers through her hair.

'Under the age of two, lots of their development depends

on attachment. I wonder if Annabelle's speech issues could actually be down to the loss of her mother.'

'What?' Alex shook his head. It was something he hadn't even considered. 'But she was only eleven months old when Sophia died.'

Ruby nodded slowly, 'Exactly. A baby recognises its mother's voice in the womb. Once it's born it puts the face and voice together. It responds to those. You said that Sophia was a good mother and spent most of her time with Annabelle?'

He nodded. 'Yes, she did.'

'Then for eleven months Annabelle's hard wiring was formed all around her mother.'

Ruby sat back, letting what she'd said sink around him. She seemed to know when she'd said enough.

She wasn't apportioning any blame. She wasn't being confrontational. She was being logical. She was giving him information and letting him think for himself what it might mean.

He sat quietly. Ruby was relaxed and Annabelle seemed happy. She was busy trying to drown all her plastic dolls in the ornamental fountain and probably block the pumps from here to eternity.

No matter what Ruby had just told him it was comfortable. It was relaxed.

The sandwiches disappeared quickly, followed by some little cakes at the bottom of the picnic basket. Ruby didn't feel the need to chatter and fill the silence. She was entirely happy to lie back on the blanket and watch Annabelle.

This was something he never got time to do any more.

There was always something to be signed, someone who needed to talk to him urgently. An email or a letter to write. A dignitary to entertain. A celebrity to pander to in order to bring extra publicity and business to Euronia.

Where was the time for Annabelle in all that?

Where was the time for him?

He never got time to be just a father. He never got time to be just Alex. Did anyone in the palace even think of him as just Alex?

He watched as Ruby moved, crawling on all fours, ignoring her dress and bare knees, creeping across the red stones to meet Annabelle and start splashing her with water from the fountain.

Annabelle shrieked in delight and ran around the fountain. It was the finest sound he'd ever heard.

Two minutes later Ruby had the pink plastic ball and was throwing it over the top of the fountain to Annabelle at the other side. But that was soon too safe—too ordinary. Within a few seconds they'd both climbed on the wall at each side of the fountain and were throwing the ball to each other while balancing precariously on the low wall.

He should intervene. He should tell them to stop being so silly. Last time they'd had to replace the blue tiles in the wall of the fountain it had taken for ever. He couldn't even remember the cost.

But both of them were laughing out loud. He couldn't remember the last time he'd seen Annabelle so happy. And it was Ruby who was responsible for that.

Something twisted inside him. Part of it was pride, part of it a little inkling of jealousy. Deep down he knew that *he* should be the one making his little girl laugh like that. But if it couldn't be him he was so glad that it was Ruby.

Ruby was genuine. Ruby related to his daughter in a way that none of the other professionals had.

He had been so right to bring her here.

Even when the palace officials had voiced their obvious concerns about his latest plans to get Annabelle assessed he'd known that this was the right thing to do.

He'd been right to remember the passion in her eyes when she'd spoken about missing out on the job she would have loved. He'd followed her for years…sent her unsigned flowers. He remembered his surge of pride when he'd found out she'd got her dream job, when she'd been promoted, when she'd published professional papers. All those things had made him happy for her.

Now, in a few short days, she'd started to connect with his daughter.

With him.

There was a scream, followed by a huge splash. A flash of moving yellow rushed before his eyes. He was on his feet instantly.

Annabelle's eyes were wide. She jumped down from her side of the fountain and ran around it towards the splash, meeting her father as they both peered down into the few feet of clear water.

Ruby was completely under the water, tiny bubbles snaking out from her mouth, her yellow dress billowing around her. Alex leaned over to put his hand in and pull her up—then gasped as she opened her eyes.

The expression on her face was priceless. Annabelle dissolved into fits of laughter as Ruby burst up through the surface of the water, shrieking with laughter.

Alex's eyes shot up towards the hundreds of windows of the palace. He could only imagine what anyone on his staff might say if they'd witnessed this.

But the laughter was infectious. And Ruby wasn't at all worried about the fact that her hair was sodden and she was soaked to the skin.

She reached towards his outstretched arm, smiled, and tugged sharply—pulling him straight in next to her.

Even though the sun was shining the water in the fountain was freezing.

His landing was partly cushioned by the soft body of Ruby. Water was dripping from the end of her nose, her hair was flattened to her head and her clothes hugged every part of her body.

'Who are you laughing at?' She winked.

He couldn't do anything other than laugh. Annabelle was still jumping up and down at the side of the fountain.

Ruby reached down and picked up a submerged princess doll. 'I came in to rescue the doll—what's your excuse?'

He smiled, their faces only inches apart. He lifted his eyebrows, 'Oh, I definitely came in to rescue Ruby.'

His arms were on either side of her, his chin just above her head. Every part of him was soaked.

'Who says I needed rescuing?' she quipped.

She didn't care. She didn't care about her wet clothes or how she looked. She wasn't constantly looking over her shoulder for a camera. Ruby was just Ruby.

And it was at that moment that he realised. Realised this was bigger than he ever could have imagined.

Every thought, every memory of this fountain had been imprinted on his brain for thirty-four years. That famous photo had been shared firstly in the newspapers, and later around the world on the internet.

Every single time he'd looked at this fountain it had brought back memories of Sophia and their childhood. He could clearly remember sitting on the edge of the fountain with her, banging his heels on the stonework.

But now, and for ever, every time he looked at this fountain this was what he'd remember. *This.* A water-soaked, laughing Ruby with a twinkle in her eyes and a bright-eyed little girl watching at the side.

Some memories were worth changing.

CHAPTER SEVEN

THERE WAS DEFINITELY something wrong with her. She was getting used to these clothes. She was getting used to opening the closet and seeing the rainbow colours of the beautiful garments hanging up and just waiting to be worn.

Her blue jeans had been stuffed in the back of the cupboard, along with her baseball boots. It had only been two weeks and she didn't even want to pull them out any more.

Even the pale green dress that she'd worn when she'd arrived—the best thing she had—looked like a poor cousin hanging beside all the designer clothes.

It made her skin prickle. She'd never been like this before. Every girl liked nice things. But she hadn't expected to get used to it so suddenly.

What would happen in a few weeks, when she was back in London, in her flat, wearing her healthcare uniform again? She'd always worn that uniform with pride. What on earth was happening to her?

Alex had been keeping to his side of the bargain and spending a certain amount of time with Annabelle. She'd been trying not to interfere—no matter how much she wanted to.

It was important that there was time for just father and daughter. But the rest of the palace staff didn't seem to understand that. She'd had no idea how busy Alex really was. It seemed that a country/principality didn't run itself.

After watching the constant interruptions of their father/daughter time she'd appointed herself guardian of that little part of the day. She'd started to stand guard outside the door.

By the time Annabelle was settled into her bed and he'd read a few stories to her there was usually a queue of people standing outside the bedroom, waiting to see Alex. Not one of them ever got past her.

The hard wiring talk seemed to have done the trick. It had given him the gentle kick up the backside he needed to say no to people who weren't his daughter. It was sad, but clear, that Alex hadn't been able to spend as much time with Annabelle as he would have liked.

Now he made it his priority. And Ruby's role was to make sure that father and daughter got that protected time together.

'Knock-knock.'

The voice made her jump. She was sitting in the palace library, looking out over the gardens.

This had quickly become her favourite room. The beautiful wood and paper smell crept along the corridor towards her and drew her in like a magnet. The dark wooden bookcases filled with beautiful hardback books seemed to suck her in every time she walked past. The set of steps that moved on a rail to reach the books at the top almost made her jump up and down with excitement. Every time she entered the room she climbed a few steps and moved them on just a little.

She'd even taken to bringing her computer down here and answering any emails she received from work in her favourite environment. She needed to stay in touch with her colleagues to make sure things were running smoothly back home. There were only a few emails each day—mainly about patients, asking for a second opinion or a referral route for a patient with unusual conditions. Nothing she couldn't handle from thousands of miles away.

She spun around in her chair. 'Alex? Is something wrong?'

He smiled. 'Do I only come and look for you if something is wrong?'

She leaned her elbow on the desk and rested her head on the heel of her hand. 'Let's see—maybe?'

She was teasing him. Sometimes he made it so easy. But most things were easy around Alex—except for the times when he was surrounded by palace staff. She could almost swear that Rufus stalked him from one end of the palace to the other.

'Well, let's change that. You've been here for a few weeks now, and apart from the palace grounds and a few walks into the city centre you've hardly seen anything of Euronia. How about we remedy that?'

He held his hand out towards her. She hesitated. Since the dress incident and the day at the fountain something had changed between them. It was happening slowly. Almost without her even noticing. But the way Alex looked at her was different.

Sometimes she caught him staring with the blue eyes of a man ten years younger, without the responsibilities of today on his shoulders. Those were her favourite moments.

Ten years of thinking about 'what ifs'… It was easy to pretend that she hadn't. That she'd been busy with work and life and relationships. But underneath all that there had always been something simmering beneath the surface.

Her first sight of him in her hospital department had knocked the breath from her lungs—not that she'd ever admit that. She had a hard time even admitting it to herself.

In her mind, Ruby Wetherspoon had never been that kind of girl. Dreaming of princes and happy-ever-afters. But her brain kept trying to interfere with her rational thoughts. It kept giving her secret flashes of holding hands, or more kisses. It kept making her imagine what might have happened on the rest of that night on New Year's Eve.

But there was no point dreaming of the past. Today was about looking to the future.

She was beginning to feel a glimmer of hope that there could *be* a future. Her confidence around Alex was starting to grow.

She stood up. The only 'what ifs' were for the here and now.

She reached out and took his hand, his warm skin enveloping hers. 'Where do you plan on taking me?' She looked down, 'And am I suitably dressed?'

He grinned. 'You might need alternative clothes.'

'Really? Why?'

He winked. 'You'll see.'

If the crew were surprised to see him accompanied by a lady they did their best to hide it. It had been a few months since he'd been out on the yacht, and in the past he'd always gone alone.

He hadn't even mentioned the yacht to Ruby, and her face had been a picture as they'd walked onto the dock.

She'd blinked at the gleaming white yacht. It was made of steel and over three hundred feet long.

He waved his arm, 'Ruby, I'd like you to meet the other woman in my life—the *Augusta*.'

'She's huge.' She could see all the staff on board. This wasn't a one-man sailing boat.

He nodded and headed over to the gangway. 'Five bedrooms and an owner's stateroom with living room, bedroom, bathroom and veranda. She's pretty much a guy's dream come true.'

Her foot hesitated at the gangway. His heart gave a little twist. He hadn't even asked her if she was afraid of water. *Please don't let this be a disaster.* He'd already arranged for some swimming and snorkelling gear to be dropped off at the yacht.

But her hesitation was momentary and she steadied

her balance on the swaying gangway by holding on to the rail.

'Shouldn't a boat have sails?' she whispered as they walked over the gangway.

'It's a yacht. And it doesn't need sails—it's got four diesel engines. It can probably go faster than some cars.'

She grinned and stopped mid-step, 'Well, aren't *we* a bit snippy about our boat?' She was clearly amused by his automatic response.

He wrinkled his nose. 'Snippy? What does that mean?'

She stepped a little closer. She'd changed into a pale blue dress and flat sandals. He could see the tiny freckles across the bridge of her nose and feel her scent invade his senses. It didn't matter that the smell of the Mediterranean Sea was all around them. The only thing he could concentrate on right now was the smell of some kind of flowers, winding its way around him.

'It means you don't like anyone calling your yacht a boat.' She waved her hand. 'Boat, ship, yacht—it's all the same to me.'

He laughed and shook his head. 'What's that word you use in the UK? Landlubber?'

She nodded as he guided her up on to the deck. 'I'll wear that badge with pride. I know absolutely nothing about sailing. The only boats I've ever sailed were the ones in my bath tub.'

There it was—that little twinkle in her eye. It happened whenever they joked together, whenever Ruby was relaxed and there was no one else around but them. He didn't see it often enough.

She settled into one of the white chairs as the yacht moved smoothly out from the port. The sea could be choppy around Euronia, but today it was calm.

His steward appeared. 'What would you like for lunch, Ms. Wetherspoon? The chef will make whatever you desire.'

He saw her visibly blanch. There were so many things he took for granted. At any time in the palace he could ask for whatever he wanted to eat. There was always staff available to cater to his tastes. Ruby looked almost embarrassed by the question.

'I guess since I'm on the sea it should be some kind of fish.' She shot the steward a beaming smile. 'What would you suggest?'

If the steward was surprised by her question he didn't show it. 'We have crayfish, mussels, clams and oysters. Or, if you prefer we have sardines—or bouillabaisse. It's a fish stew, practically our national dish.'

'That sounds lovely. I'll have that, thank you.'

The yacht was working its way along the coastline. Within a few minutes the pink palace came into view.

Ruby stood up. 'Wow! It looks so different, seeing it from the sea. It really does look like something from a little girl's toybox. It's gorgeous.'

Alex rolled his eyes. 'You can imagine how I felt as a teenager, living in a pink palace.'

She smiled. Her eyes were still sparkling. 'I *can* imagine. But look at it. It's impressive enough when you see it on land—but from here…? It's like something from a fairytale.'

'What's your favourite room?'

'In the palace?'

He nodded.

The steward had brought some champagne and an ice bucket and Alex popped the cork and started pouring the champagne into glasses.

She took a sip from the glass he handed her. 'It has to be the library. It's the smell. I love it. I could sit in there all day.'

'That was my mother's favourite room too. She was always in the library.'

Ruby turned to face him. 'You don't really talk about

your mother. What was she like? I've seen some photographs. She was beautiful.'

He nodded. 'Yes, she was. Most people talk about the clothes she wore and her sense of style. Marguerite de Castellane was known the world over for her beautiful wardrobe. But I remember my mother as having a really wicked sense of humour. And she was clever. She spoke four languages and brought me up speaking both English and French. She died from a clot in her lung—a pulmonary embolism. She'd had the flu and been off her feet for a few weeks. Her legs were swollen and sore—but she didn't tell anyone until it was too late.'

He couldn't help but feel a wave of sadness as he spoke about his mother. To everyone else she had been the Queen. But to an only child with an almost absent father his mother had been his whole world.

She'd kept him grounded. She'd made sure he attended the local school and the local nursery. She'd sent him shopping for bread at the bakers and meat at the delicatessen. Everything he'd learned about being a 'normal' person he'd learned from his mother.

His father had aged twenty years after she'd died. Still working, still ruling his country, but his heart hadn't been in it.

The relationship between father and son had always been strained. And it hadn't improved with age or with his father's ill health.

Ruby had little lines across her forehead now. Even when she frowned she still looked good. He felt a surge of emotion towards her.

He didn't talk to *anyone* about his mother. In years gone by he had spoken to Sophia, but that had been like talking to a friend. Ruby hadn't known his mother. She would only have whatever had been posted on the internet to refer to.

It felt good to share. She made it so easy to talk.

With her legs stretched out in front of her, sipping champagne from the glass, she looked right at home. But he knew she wasn't.

She might be comfortable around him, but she wasn't comfortable around the palace. The formalities of palace life were difficult for her.

She didn't ask or expect anyone to do things for her. Rufus had already mentioned how she'd ruffled some feathers by trying to do her own laundry or make her own toast.

'What about your family?'

She smiled. 'My mum and dad are both just about to retire. They've already told me they plan to move to the South of France. They bought a house there last month. They've holidayed there for the last ten years and have really got into the way of life.'

'Have they ever been to Euronia?'

She rolled her eyes and took another sip of champagne, holding the glass up towards him. 'Only billionaires come to Euronia, Alex.'

He was instantly defensive. 'That's not true. There are cruise ships moored every day in port, and we have bus tours that come across the border from France—'

'Alex.'

She leaned over and touched his arm. The palm of her hand was cool from holding the champagne glass.

'I was teasing.'

The smile reached right up into her eyes and he wrapped his hand over hers.

'Sometimes I'm just not sure.' He stayed exactly where he was. His eyes fixed on hers.

She wasn't shy. She didn't tear her gaze away. Her lips were turned upwards, but as he looked at her more closely her smile seemed a little sad.

'What do you think would have happened between us, Ruby?'

He didn't need to fill in the blanks. She knew exactly what he was talking about. He saw her take a careful breath in.

'I have no idea, Alex,' she whispered. 'Sometimes I've thought about it—thought about what might have happened if things had been different. But neither of us know. Neither of us can really imagine. Ten years changes a person. I'm not the girl I was in Paris, and you're not the boy.'

He nodded his head and grinned at her. 'You thought I was a *boy*?'

Now he was teasing. But she was right. They could spend hours talking about what might have been but it wouldn't do either of them any good. He'd spent too long thinking that Ruby had slipped through his fingers.

But she was right here. Right now.

He ran his palm along her arm. 'I thought about you, Ruby. I thought about you a lot. When you didn't reply to the message I left you I just assumed you'd changed your mind.' He met her gaze again, 'Or that you'd seen the news and didn't want any part of it.'

'Oh, Alex…' She lifted her hand and stroked her fingers through her hair. Her head shook slowly. 'I never got your message, Alex. And once I realised who you were I assumed you didn't want to know me—plain old Ruby Wetherspoon. You were a *prince*, for goodness' sake— with a whole country to look after. I didn't think you'd even remember me.'

He reached up and touched her cheek. 'You have no idea at all. And you've never been plain old Ruby to me.'

'The flowers… They were from you—weren't they?'

He nodded. 'I didn't want to interfere in your life. But then there came a time when it wasn't appropriate to send them any more.' His chest tightened as he said the words.

He didn't need to go into detail.

He'd always harboured hopes about Ruby. But once he'd known he had to make a commitment to Sophia it had become inappropriate to keep sending flowers to another woman. Alex would never have done something like that.

'I guess now I'm free to send you flowers again,' he said quietly.

'I guess you are.'

She gave him a little smile and set down her glass. The yacht was moving around the coastline, dancing along in the waves—just as they were dancing around each other.

'Why did you ask me to come, Alex? Why did you want me here?'

There it was again. That tiny tremble in her voice. He loved the fact that she was fearless. That she was courageous enough to ask the question out loud.

Ruby wasn't bound by a country. Ruby wasn't bound by two whole nations hoping she'd be able to keep them financially stable. Ruby didn't have to bite her tongue to prevent international incidents with foreign diplomats. Ruby had her own life—her own responsibilities. Could he really be honest? Was he willing to expose her to the world he lived in?

It was time to take a risk.

'I didn't just ask you here for Annabelle, Ruby. I need your help with my daughter. That much is clear.' He reached over and took her hand. 'But I asked you here for me too.'

She bit her lip. He could tell she was trying not to interrupt, but she just couldn't help it.

'But what does that *mean*, Alex? I need you to say it out loud.'

She was drawing a line in the sand. And she was right. He knew she was right.

He met her gaze and touched her cheek. 'I want us to have a chance, Ruby Wetherspoon. I'm not your everyday guy, and what I have isn't your everyday job. I'd like to see where this can take us, but I understand the pressure of being here and being with me. I don't want to expose you to anything before you're ready.'

She shook her head. 'Not enough. Who *am* I, Alex? Am I Ruby Wetherspoon, speech and language therapist for your daughter? Am I Ruby Wetherspoon the hired help who might catch your eye? Or am I Ruby Wetherspoon the girl you might decide to date?'

She stood up and walked across the deck, held on to the railing, looking out over the sea.

'You touch me, Alex. You kiss me. You bring me out on day trips that make my brain spin. What are you doing, Alex? What are *we* doing?'

He stood up to join her, and then slowed his movements as he neared. He didn't want to stand next to her. So he did what was the most natural thing in the world. He stood behind her, his full body against hers, with his arms wrapped around her waist, sheltering her from the sea winds.

He lifted his hand and caught her hair that was blowing in the breeze. 'Ruby, you can be whatever you want to be. But be warned: being around Alex de Castellane isn't easy. If you want to be the woman I date, that's fine. If you want to do that in public or private, that's fine with me too.'

He moved closer to her, whispering in her ear, nuzzling her.

'I lost you once, Ruby. I don't intend to lose you again. But I'll take your lead on this.'

He held his hands out towards the cliffs and the view of Euronia.

'The world out there can be hard. I want to give this a chance. I want to see where this will take us. I'd love to be able to walk down the street with you without everyone whispering—but that will never happen. I'm public property, Ruby. The world owns me. I don't want it to own you too. At least not until we're both sure about what we want.'

She turned herself towards him, tears glistening in her eyes.

He lowered his hands and wrapped them around her waist. 'What do you say, Ruby? Are you willing to give us a try?'

She wrapped her arms around his neck and stood on her tiptoes, whispering in his ear. 'I think I might need a little extra persuasion.'

'What kind of persuasion?' He liked the thought of where this might go.

'I might have questions. Conditions.'

He was surprised. 'Okay…' he said slowly. 'Like what?'

This time the expression on her face was a little bit cheeky, a little bit naughty. 'If we start dating do I get to look in all the palace rooms that are currently out of bounds to me?'

'*That's* what you want to know?' He couldn't help but smile.

'I also want to check for secret passages and dungeons.'

He nodded solemnly. 'That might be difficult. I'll have to see what I can do.'

'Can I slide down the banister?'

'That might be taking things a bit far.'

She shrugged. 'It'll save the staff from polishing.'

He nodded. 'True.' And then he sighed. 'I wish I'd thought of that explanation twenty years ago. You could have got me out of a whole heap of trouble.'

She stood up and whispered in his ear again. 'How about painting the palace a brighter shade of pink? Doesn't every girl want to live in a pink palace?'

He laughed. 'You don't think it's pink enough already? It might be every girl's dream but guess what? It's not every teenage boy's. I told you—I hated living in a pink palace.'

She shook her head. 'Silly boy. You just don't know what you had.'

He stopped smiling and touched her cheek. 'But I do now.'

She bit her lower lip again. He couldn't help but fixate

on it. They weren't entirely alone on this boat. But right now he didn't care. It seemed as if he'd been waiting for this moment for ever.

He bent forward and captured her lips against his. She met him hungrily, pushing herself against him and letting her fingers gently stroke the back of his neck. The sensation shot directly down his spine and into his groin.

He pulled back. There was a whole host of things running through his mind right now. But none was as important as being here with Ruby.

He grabbed her hand and pulled her inside.

'There are seven staff on this boat. They would never disturb us, but things aren't exactly private here. If we're going to see where this takes us we have to agree what you're comfortable with.'

She looked a little unsure. But her face was flushed and her hands were touching his waist—almost as if she didn't want to let go.

He glanced down at them and gave a laugh. 'Careful, Ruby. You've no idea where my *brain's* currently taking us.'

He opened the door and pulled her along a narrow corridor,

'I've made plans for us today. Let's cool off. There are some swimsuits inside this room along here. We'll anchor the boat, do a little swimming, and then have some dinner.' He stopped outside the door of one of the rooms and hesitated. 'It'll give you time to think.'

He was aware that she hadn't said anything—was terrified that he might have frightened her off. Ruby probably hadn't considered the real consequences of being involved with a prince and he'd just laid them all bare to her.

He'd lived with press intrusion all his life. But in his world it was slightly easier for men than women. When the heir to the throne in the United Kingdom had got married his new wife had been constantly under the glare of the spotlight. Even now every outfit she wore, every friend she spoke to, even the appointments in her diary were scrutinised continuously.

Euronia might not be the UK, but it was a hotspot for the rich and famous. The press were always lurking somewhere in the background. He was surprised no one had commented on Ruby's presence before now. She must have slipped under the radar as a member of staff. But that wouldn't last much longer.

Her smile faltered. 'Alex, what if we're making a mistake? What if we're both caught in the memory of ten years ago and what we've imagined and reality is totally different?' She looked up through heavy eyelids. 'We might not even *like* each other.'

His stomach twisted. It was true. It was a fair comment. But it went against his gut. It went against how he truly felt.

He didn't know Ruby that well. Someone, somewhere in the palace would have a report on her—they had one on every staff member. And his security staff would have the report from ten years ago on the woman he'd been with when they'd found him at the café in Paris. Someone would know which schools she'd attended in England, what the occupations of her mum and dad were, if she had any political affiliations.

But he didn't want to find out from a bit of paper. He wanted to find out in real time—with Ruby.

So he did what his gut told him to do. He leaned forward and brushed a kiss against her cheek. 'Then let's find out.'

She stepped inside and closed the door behind her, instantly feeling the coolness of the air-conditioned room. Her cheek burned from where he'd kissed her.

Kissed her—and left her. Walking down the corridor, leaving her to fixate on his backside and broad shoulders. She felt like someone from a bad movie.

Her stomach was turning over and over. *'Let's find out.'*

She'd waited ten years to find out. Ten years of secret thoughts and wild imagination. Did this mean anything between them was destined to fail?

She picked up her mobile and pressed the quick call button. She'd never needed to talk to someone so badly.

'Polly? Are you free? Can you talk?'

'Ruby? Where on earth have you been? I tried to call you three times yesterday. Are you coming home?'

'No. Not yet. And maybe…'

'Maybe what?' Polly got straight to the point. 'What's happening with you and Prince Perfect?'

Ruby sighed and leaned against the wall. 'He just kissed me, Polly. He kissed me and I didn't want him to stop.'

'Oh, no. Don't start all this dreamy kissing stuff again. Does this guy have stars and rainbows in his lips? One kiss and you go all squishy.'

She smiled. It was true. Trust Polly just to come out with it. 'I'm worried, Pol. He's told me he wants to give us a chance. He's asked me if I'm willing.'

'Willing to what? Flounce off into the sunset on matching unicorns? What exactly does he need you to be willing *for*?'

'To give us a go. To see where this takes us.' She started to slide down the wall. 'But I can't think straight, Pol. I'm just Ruby. I'm not a princess. I'm not a supermodel. How can I possibly live up to the expectations he has? I don't even know what fork to pick up at dinner.'

'Ruby Wetherspoon, you listen to me. This isn't about his expectations. This is about yours. You don't *need* to be a princess or a supermodel. You're better than both. He is lucky to have met you. He's lucky you agreed to go and help with his daughter. This isn't about you being good enough for him. The question is: is Prince Perfect good enough for *you*?'

Trust Polly. She could always boost her confidence and make her feel better. It was like having her own professional cheerleader and piranha all in one. But whilst she loved what Polly was saying, she just wasn't sure she believed it.

Polly hadn't finished talking. 'And as for the forks—just start on the outside and work your way in. Never fails.'

Ruby was shaking her head. 'I like him, Polly. I really like him. But this is a whole other country. There's so many people watching me. So many people watching *him*.'

'He's a prince, Ruby. What do you want?'

She sighed. 'I want to do normal things. I want to get to know him better. I want the chance to go out and have a glass of wine with him. I want to go to the cinema and fight about who is the best action hero or the best *Star Trek* captain—'

'Picard.' Polly cut her off quickly. 'It's always Picard.'

Ruby heard the squeak of furniture as Polly obviously sat down.

'I hate to break it to you, honey, but going for a glass of wine and heading to the multiplex is probably a no-no. Anyway—doesn't Alex have a whole cinema in the palace?'

'Probably. I don't know. I just can't think straight around him, Pol. He walks in a room and my whole body—it just *tingles*.' She gave a little shake as she said the words.

'Oh, no. No tingling. Definitely no tingling.'

'People here—they're different. The way they treat Alex. The way they treat me when I'm with Alex…'

Her voice drifted off as her train of thought started to take her down the railway line to mild panic.

'His mother spoke four languages. I can't do that. I know nothing about politics. Or history. Or modern studies. I only got a passing grade in geography because I memorised stuff about eroding coastlines.'

'What exactly do you think you're auditioning for here, Rubes? You're a speech and language therapist—an expert in your field. You've published professional papers. You work at one of the finest hospitals in London. Why do you think you're not good enough for him?'

She started shaking her head. 'It's not that I think I'm not good enough. I'm just worried. Alex wants to give us a chance—*I* want to give us a chance—but what about the rest of the world?'

'Hang the rest of the world, Ruby. This is *your* life. Not theirs.' Polly groaned. 'You know I want you back here with me. But *ten years*, Ruby. Ten years you waited for this guy to come back into your life. You can't let what anyone else thinks matter.'

Ruby straightened up. Polly was right. Alex was right. He was just trying to prepare her. Trying to let her understand that things might be difficult.

But Alex de Castellane wanted *her*—Ruby Wetherspoon. It had to mean something.

She walked over to the other side of the cabin. 'Oh, Pol. He's bought me clothes.'

'Again? What is he—a personal shopper or a prince?'

She lifted up a scrap of material from the bed and squinted at it—trying to imagine what it covered. 'Well, they're not clothes, exactly. More like tiny bits of cloth. I think they're supposed to be for swimming.' She started to laugh and shake her head as she moved her phone to snap a picture and send it to Polly. 'What on earth is *that* supposed to cover?'

There were five different styles of swimming costume on the bed, along with a whole host of scraps doing their best impression of itsy-bitsy teeny-weeny bikinis. She picked up the first and checked the label. At least they were her size—but there was no way she was wearing one in front of Alex. Not right now anyway.

There was a screech at the other end of the phone as Polly got the photo. She started howling with laughter. 'Gotta go, honey—the baby's crying. But, please—if you wear that you've got to send me a photo!'

Ruby smiled as the call was disconnected. She always felt better after talking to Polly. But Polly's life had moved on. They were still best friends. But Polly had a husband and a baby. She'd found her happy-ever-after. What about Ruby's?

She picked up a red swimsuit, slightly padded with a ruched front. Perfect. Something that actually covered the parts it should. It only took two minutes to put it on, and she grabbed a sheer black sarong to knot around her waist.

It was time to get out there.

Let's find out.

Alex was doing his best impression of a male model in white trunks. She gulped. She was going to have to avert her eyes. Either that or put a sign on her head saying that if she looked at that area it would make her knees go weak.

He was waiting for her out on deck and he led her around to the back of the yacht this time. Again there were some seats, but Alex had also laid down towels on a flat area overhanging the edge. There was no ladder down the side. This flat part seemed to have been designed purely for getting in and out of the sea.

She sat down on a white towel and blushed as she noticed his appreciative gaze. 'What do you normally use this for?'

'Diving. I used to do a lot of diving with friends. Nothing too spectacular. Just for fun. So when I commissioned the yacht I knew I wanted a diving platform attached.'

'You *commissioned* the yacht? You didn't just buy it from a catalogue? Just how rich are you, Alex?'

She was laughing as she said the words and turned to dip her toes in the water. Even though the sun was blistering hot the sea was cold.

'Youch!'

She pulled her feet back in as Alex laughed. 'Here.' He

tossed her some sunscreen. 'Put some of this on or you'll burn your nose.'

It was easy to forget how hot the sun was with the sea breezes around them. She smeared some sunscreen on her face, arms and legs, then stood behind him, poised to put some cream on his back.

But he grabbed her arm and pulled her into his lap. 'I've already got some. You, however, need some on *your* back. Give me that.'

He squirted some cream on his hands and started to rub it over her back. She was almost scared to move. Her position was precarious. They were right at the edge of the moored boat and she was balancing on his knees. Right now there were only two very thin pieces of fabric separating them. Her right arm was pressing against his bare chest, the dark curling hairs tickling her skin.

His hand movements slowed, going from initially brisk and efficient to sensual, circling her back, slipping under the straps on her shoulders and smearing cream across every part of her skin. She breathed in sharply and his hand circled lower, fingertips sweeping below her swimsuit.

His voice was husky, his accent thicker. 'You didn't like the bikinis?'

'I didn't like *me* in the bikinis.'

'Why ever not?' His fingers slowed and stopped, staying just underneath the back of her costume. 'You're a beautiful woman, Ruby.'

She felt her cheeks flush, instantly embarrassed by his words—which was ironic, really, since she was sitting half clothed in his lap. Could anyone see them, sitting here on the back of his yacht? In front of her all she could see was the Mediterranean Sea. There wasn't even another boat in sight.

His hand moved gently around her waist, touching the fabric of her costume and resting next to the knot of her sarong. 'This is definitely your colour. You suit red, Ruby. It seems as though your mother named you well.'

'My mother named me after the ruby slippers in *The Wizard of Oz*. But I'll tell her you appreciate her choice,' she teased.

This was too much. She was sitting here, feeling the rise and fall of his chest next to her arm, the warmth between his skin and hers. Their faces were inches apart. Not touching him properly was torture.

She moved that little inch, putting her hand at the back of his head and tugging him closer until their lips touched. His fingers started tugging at the knot on her sarong. It fell apart easily.

The kiss quickly intensified. She could easily tell the effect their close contact was having on his body—just as it was having an effect on hers. Kissing him was too easy.

They weren't in Paris any more. It wasn't New Year's Eve. But she could almost hear the fireworks going off in her head.

The sun wasn't heating her skin any more—Alex was. Every nibble, every tiny touch of his tongue electrified her. She let out a little moan as their kiss deepened, his hands running up and down the bare skin on her back.

'Ruby…' he muttered.

'What?' She didn't want him to stop. She didn't want this moment to end.

'We're out in the open. I know it doesn't feel like it, but…' His voice tailed off.

She was still kissing him, never wanting it to end.

A few minutes ago the sea had seemed deserted. But other boats had passed them on their journey around the coastline. And the crew might not come down here, but if she didn't stop this now…she might live to regret it.

She broke the kiss. 'Alex?'

'What?' He looked up, those gorgeous blue eyes connecting with hers.

She smiled. 'You're right. It's time to cool off.'

Her arms were still wrapped around him and she just leaned backwards, pulling them both into the cold blue sea.

The plunge was a little further than she'd expected, and the shock of the cold water on her skin pushed the air from her lungs as it closed around her. It only took a few seconds to push to the surface and break out into the warm sun. She was laughing and coughing and spluttering all at once.

She slicked her wet hair back from her face as Alex surfaced next to her, shaking his head and showering her with droplets of water.

'This is getting to be a habit,' he said as he swam next to her and put his hands around her waist underwater.

The cold water was doing nothing to dampen their desire and she wound her hands around his neck again as they trod water.

'It is, isn't it? Maybe you and I shouldn't be around water.' She laughed.

'What should we be around?' he asked as the waves buoyed them up.

'I don't know. Pink palaces, Eiffel Towers, fireworks and yellow dresses.' She could see the twinkle in his eye as she said those last words.

'Come on,' he gestured towards her. 'Let's swim around the boat. It might be best if we have some water between us.'

Her hand touched his arm as they separated in the water.

They laughed and swam around the boat, occasionally stopping next to each other as Alex told her a little more about his country.

'The caves down there were traditionally used by pirates.'

There were two dark caves carved into the bottom of the cliffs on the rocky shoreline. Her body had grown accustomed to the temperature of the water but she still gave a shudder.

'No way. Fairytales. Made-up stories.'

He lifted his hand out of the water. 'You forget—this is a land with a pink palace. You think we didn't have pirates?'

'When you put it like that it doesn't seem quite so crazy.'

'I'll show you some of the things in the castle vaults. I think my ancestors might have been in league with the pirates. Either that or they just kept everything once they'd captured the pirates.'

'Are you allowed to do that?'

He shrugged his shoulders as they continued to swim around the boat. 'We have some old doubloons, some jewellery and some weapons. The assumption is that they are Spanish, but the Spaniards didn't want them back when they were offered a few hundred years ago. There isn't enough to be of any real value—we've kept them safe because of the historical importance.'

She kept swimming. 'I'm going to add that to my list of conditions from earlier—a visit to the pirate caves.' She winked, 'I might even ask you to dress up.'

As they rounded the hull of the yacht another boat came into view. It was not quite as big as Alex's, but equally sleek in white and silver.

Alex sighed. 'Let's get back on board.'

'Do you know who owns that boat?'

He stroked out towards the diving platform. 'It's Randall Merr and his wife. They can be unbearable. I'll tell the crew to head back to port.'

Randall Merr. A billionaire with houses all over the world—including in Euronia.

Part of her stomach twisted. Maybe Alex didn't want to introduce her to his friends? Maybe he was embarrassed by her?

She put her head in the water and struck out towards the platform. Alex reached it first and turned round to help her out of the water, offering her a towel and her sarong.

The electricity between them seemed to have dissipated.

All of a sudden she felt very exposed—and it wasn't because she was wearing only swimwear. The magic bubble that she'd felt earlier around her and Alex had vanished in the blink of an eye.

'Ruby, what's wrong?'

He was picking up the other towels and the sunscreen from around them.

She started up the steps. 'Nothing's wrong. I'm going to put some clothes on.' She hated that tiny waver in her voice.

He caught her arm. 'Ruby, tell me what's wrong. Are you angry with me?'

The words that were spinning around in her brain tumbled out of her mouth unchecked. Nothing she would ever really want him to hear.

'Why would I be angry with you, Alex? You tell me it's up to *me* to decide how this goes—then as soon as we see someone you know you try and bundle me away. As if I'm some kind of employee you can't be seen with. Which, when you think about it, I really am—aren't I?'

His brow crumpled and confusion swept over his face. He shook his head and tightened his grip on her arm, pulling her hard against him. She was above him, on the first step of the stairs. Their faces were perfectly level.

'You think I want to hide you? After everything I've said?'

His nose was almost touching hers and his eyes were blazing. She'd angered him.

But instead of being intimidated she just felt another fire spark within her. 'Well, that's what it looks like.'

His lips connected with hers. His hands jerked her hipbones against his. This was no delicate kiss. This was no teasing, no playing with her. This was pure and utter passion.

His hands moved from her hips and his fingers tangled in her hair, tugging her head one way then another. His teeth clashed with hers and his tongue drove its way into her mouth. She could hardly breathe. He was devouring her.

He finally released her just as the white boat passed directly behind the yacht. It was so close the yacht bobbed wildly in its wake.

'There,' he growled, without even turning around. 'Randall Merr and his wife got a prime-time view. If you didn't want anyone to know about us it's too late. That woman practically has a satellite connection to the world's press.'

She gulped. Was that really what she wanted?

Truth was, she hadn't answered Alex because she was unsure.

She wasn't unsure about him. Not for a second. But she was definitely unsure about his world.

How could she possibly ever fit in to his lifestyle? She was already sure that some of the staff didn't like her and suspected something might be in the air between them.

She wanted the Alex she'd met ten years ago in Paris. The gorgeous, slightly mysterious man with a bit of an accent.

But that wasn't Alex at all. *This* was Alex. The acting ruler of one country and potentially the temporary head of another. The father of a young daughter. The son of a sick man. A businessman with the financial responsibility for all the inhabitants of his country.

Her Alex had only really ever existed in her head.

And whilst the living, breathing Alex in front of her was sexier than she could ever have dreamed of, she was still wondering if this was all a figment of her imagination.

After ten years he'd come looking for her.

After ten years he'd told her he'd let her decide the pace.

She was finding it hard to believe it. These were the kind of dreams she'd had ten years ago and never told anyone about.

Alex de Castellane had spent his life surrounded by supermodels and movie stars. They all flocked to his country—a tax haven. They all wanted to be seen with him, to be photographed with him.

And Alex, Prince Regent, was charming. He knew how to show interest and talk to people as if they were the only ones in the room. There was something enigmatic about him. And for most people it would be easy to get lost in his world.

But Ruby was different. Ruby wasn't looking for a fairytale.

Maybe the Alex she'd always imagined was just a figment of her imagination. Maybe he'd never really existed.

The man she'd spent a few hours with that night had been excited about life. Had had plans for the future. He'd offered to show her around Paris and she had gladly accepted.

Accepted the chance to spend a few more hours in his company. Accepted the chance to be the focus of his attention for a few more hours.

Would she have accepted any of it if she'd known his real identity?

Most of the world would have screamed *yes*. Most of the world would have claimed it was every girl's dream to be a princess. But most of the world wasn't Ruby Wetherspoon.

Her hand was still on his arm. Droplets of sea water were running down his skin, running from his hair down his chest. Physically, she wanted Alex. Emotionally, she wanted Alex. Mentally, she wanted Alex. But all wrapped up together?

It was terrifying. And she couldn't put it into words. She didn't know how to explain the feeling of wanting to reach out and grab him, yet feeling totally overwhelmed.

Right now she wanted to be back in her room at the palace. The room next to Annabelle's. She wanted to be curled up with Annabelle, watching a movie and observing her. In an environment of peace and calm. In a place where she felt safe.

A place where she didn't feel so exposed.

'Get changed. Ruby. Put some clothes on. I'll meet you back on deck and we'll have some food, then go back to the palace.'

The Alex of earlier was lost. The man who'd looked at her almost adoringly and whispered in her ear had vanished from her grasp.

The warm sea breeze had turned distinctly chilly. It swept around her, making every little hair on her arms stand to attention. She wrapped the towel around her shoulders.

Her feet slipped and squelched along the wooden-floored corridor until she finally reached the room with her clothes and she sagged down, wet and cold, onto the bed.

All of a sudden the designer bathing suits didn't seem quite so attractive any more.

She lay down on the bed—just for a second—and closed her eyes.

CHAPTER EIGHT

ALEX WAS HAVING trouble keeping his emotions in check.

Today, all he'd been able to think about was Ruby. He hadn't worried about share prices. About price indexes. About gas, electricity and oil prices.

Today he'd just thought about the beautiful, bright-eyed woman in front of him. For a time it had seemed perfect.

Their familiarity and warmth had developed over the last few weeks and he'd finally managed to put into words the things that had been circulating in his brain.

Then—*bam!* It felt as if everything was ruined.

He was pacing up and down the deck. The crew all seemed to have vanished into the mists—as if they knew he was brooding. Cold diet colas had appeared magically in a silver cooler. His steward had obviously realised that this wasn't the time for more champagne.

He couldn't even face eating right now. So much was circulating in his head that his stomach was churning over and over.

How had he managed to mess this up? He'd planned it in his head. *Give her time to think about this. Don't rush her.* He was sure he'd seen a flicker of doubt in her eyes and that had almost killed him. He was treading so carefully around her.

Then the Merrs and their darn boat. Mrs Merr had probably buzzed them deliberately. Anything to see what the Prince Regent was up to.

He'd thought he was giving Ruby time. He'd thought he was giving her space. Wasn't that what she wanted?

But a few moments ago she'd seemed angry—annoyed that he'd tried to hide her from prying eyes. He'd only been trying to protect her. But her words had practically sent a flare up.

He wanted to be seen with Ruby. He wanted to tell the world that he was willing to take a chance on where this might go.

But he was also terrified that harsh treatment by the world's press would send her running for the hills.

How on earth was he supposed to know what was right and what was wrong?

Would he ever be able to fathom the way Ruby's brain worked?

Right now it seemed unlikely.

He glanced at his watch. She hadn't appeared. He went into his cabin, pulled out his laptop and sat at the table.

Time. That was what he needed to give her.

In the meantime, he still had work to do.

Ruby hovered at the glass doors. He was concentrating fiercely on the laptop screen in front of him.

She'd sat down on the bed for just a minute and ended up sleeping for an hour. When she'd woken she'd been embarrassed. But it had been too late for that, so she'd showered and changed before coming out.

She'd half expected to find the boat moored back in the harbour, and was pleasantly surprised to find they were still out at sea.

Here, there was nowhere to run and hide. Here, she would need to talk to Alex.

She'd changed into a turquoise-blue maxi-dress and flat jewelled sandals and pulled her hair up into a ponytail. She wasn't trying to seduce Alex. She wasn't trying to entice him away from anything else.

She was here to have one of the hardest conversations of her life.

This had all crept up on her. She'd known it was always there—hovering in the background. But things had become crystal-clear to her.

It was so easy to think that this was about her. About whether she could stand the press attention or not. But it wasn't really. It was about him. She just had to be brave enough to say the words.

Her stomach growled loudly and he turned sharply in his chair.

'Ruby.'

It was more like a grunt than a greeting—not a good start. But it gave her the kick she needed. She took the few steps across the cabin and pulled out the chair opposite him.

'Sorry. I sat down for five minutes and fell asleep.'

'You obviously don't find my company riveting enough.'

It was a barb. And she could take it or she could react.

She leaned over and snapped the laptop shut on his fingers. 'Got your attention now?'

He snatched his fingers back and glared at her. 'I was working.'

'You're always working.'

It was as if all the barriers around them had come crashing down. Right now she wasn't afraid to say anything—and from the looks of it neither was he.

'Make up your mind what you want, Ruby.'

'I can't. There's too many variables.'

No nice words. No beating about the bush. Two people with everything at stake.

'Well, let's start with the things that can't change. The non-variables.'

She leaned over and grabbed a can from the silver bucket, popping the tab and taking a sip. This could take a while.

'Is this like a quiz show, Alex? Do I win something if I get the questions right?'

Their eyes locked. They both knew exactly what was at stake here. They both knew what the prize was.

He sucked in a deep breath and held his hand out for the can of cola. It was the first sign that this really was going to be a discussion.

His voice was low. 'I'm always going to be the King of Euronia. I'm always going to be father to Annabelle.'

She nodded. 'I've never questioned those things.'

He held her gaze. 'But I've never really told you that those are things that I *wanted*. Not just things that were forced upon me or inherited by birth. When I was young I thought being King would be a whole lot of pressure on my shoulders—with no say in it for me. As I've grown older I've accepted that not only is this my destiny, it's something I actually want.'

She ran her tongue along her lips. Deep down she'd always known this. Even though Alex hadn't told her who he was when they'd met. This wasn't just his inherited future. This was a future he was willing to embrace.

It was a first step. It was the first time he'd actually admitted to her what he wanted in life.

He leaned back in his chair a little. 'I went to the US to study and learn business. It was my idea, not my father's, but he fully supported it. The world is changing constantly—it's getting smaller—and Euronia needed to move into the twenty-first century.'

'And now?'

'Now I need to use everything that I've learned to help my country prosper.'

'So where does that leave us?'

So many things were sparking in her brain. Did Alex suspect what she was about to say to him?

'How do you feel about me, Ruby?'

The question blind-sided her. She knew they were having a frank discussion, but she hadn't expected him just to ask her outright.

'I…' Her voice tailed off as her brain tried frantically to find the right words.

He shook his head.

She hadn't even answered yet and she'd disappointed him. But how could she tell him how she really felt when they still hadn't dealt with the heart of the problem? She had to say the words.

'What if Sophia had lived?'

'What?' He looked confused. Blind-siding worked both ways.

'What if her cancer had been cured and she'd lived—what then?'

He shook his head. 'That would never have happened. Sophia's cancer was already terminal. Nothing was going to change that.'

'But what if it had? Would you still have married her? Still have had Annabelle? Would you have come looking for me at all?'

Her voice started to shake a little and she took a deep breath. She needed to be calm. She needed to be rational and not blinded by her emotions.

'I need you to be honest with me, Alex. I need you to be honest with yourself.' This was hurting more than she could ever have imagined. 'If Sophia was alive today, where would she feature in your life?'

'Don't paint her as the villain in this piece. You're angry with me because I married another woman. Just say it.' He blurted it out straight away.

'You're right. I *was* angry. More than that, I was bitterly disappointed—even though I'd no right to be. But I don't understand. If you'd really wanted to find me you could have. In fact, you did. You sent me those flowers. Why didn't you just come and see me? Why didn't you ever jump in your million-pound jet and come and find me?'

She was sounding desperate and she hated herself for

being like that. But if it was going to be all out there—then so be it.

'You didn't answer my message, Ruby. I left you a message—I got no reply. What was I supposed to do? Search for a woman who didn't want me to find her? Embarrass myself and put you in vulnerable position?'

She bit her lip. It was a reasonable reply. But it didn't make her like it any better.

He kept going.

'I thought my father was about to die. The things I'd been working towards were being thrust on me from a great height. I didn't have time to think about it any more—I had to just do it. No wonder my father had agreed for me to study business. The country's finances were in a mess. We were teetering on the brink of disaster. For the best part of three years I juggled finances, moved money, invested money, watched stock markets and persuaded people to come to Euronia—persuaded people to invest in Euronia. Most nights I got around four hours' sleep. I was a mess, Ruby. I didn't have time to sleep, let alone think. How would you have felt if you'd been around a man who was too busy to spend time with you? Too busy to talk? Too busy to sleep? What kind of a relationship would that have been?'

'But you found time for Sophia.'

She said it so quietly the words were barely a whisper above the hum of the yacht's engines.

Alex's eyes widened and his response was immediate. 'Sophia appeared just as things were starting to look up. She was desperate, Ruby. She was dying and she was my friend. Sophia's illness brought me back to reality. What's the point of taking care of a country if you can't take care of those around you?'

She could hear the emotion in his voice. It was starting to break. This was it. This was the whole crux of the mat-

SCARLET WILSON

127

ter. This was the enormous big grey elephant in the room and it was time to smash it to smithereens.

'So what happened with Annabelle, then?'

The words echoed around them. She hadn't really meant to say them out loud. They'd come into her brain and out of her mouth almost instantly. It was cruel. It was uncalled for.

It was unintentional.

He sat back sharply—almost as if she'd thrust a knife into his chest.

'You think it's my fault, don't you?'

She looked him straight in the eye. Everyone had danced around Alex. Everyone had chosen their words carefully. But this was it. This was the only way to give them a fighting chance.

'I think that when Sophia died Annabelle didn't just lose her mother, she lost her father too.'

She took a deep breath and continued.

'You keep claiming Sophia was only your friend. And you can tell me that as often as you like. But your little girl is the spitting image of her mother. Do you think I've not noticed that there's no photograph of her mother in her room? Do you think I don't see that little fleeting gaze of something when you look at her? Don't ask me what it is, Alex, but it's there. I've seen it. Children pick up on these things. And I think Annabelle has picked up on it. You don't want to be around her. She reminds you too much of what you've lost.'

She could almost see the shock registering on his face, but she couldn't stop.

She pointed her finger at him. 'I know you've been busy, but I don't think you've been as busy as you claim to be. When I laid it out for you that you *had* to spend time with her you managed to do it.'

She was hurting him. She could tell. And she really didn't want to. But it had to be said. She had to try and move them both forward.

'She's improving, Alex. She is. I know that when she's around you, and around me, she exists in her own little bubble. But it's our job to expand your daughter's world in a way that makes her feel safe.'

'This isn't about Annabelle. Today isn't about Annabelle. This is supposed to be about you and me.'

He looked stunned. Stunned that someone had challenged him on his feelings about Sophia. Stunned that someone was suggesting the reason his daughter might not be speaking was his fault.

It was only natural for him to try and deflect the conversation.

'But it can't be, Alex. It can't be until you deal with this first.' She kept her voice steady. 'Tomorrow I'm going to find the nicest photo I can of Sophia and put it in a frame next to Annabelle's bed. She needs to be able to look at her mother every day. She needs to know that there was someone in this world who loved and adored her.'

'You mean I don't?'

He was furious. His eyes were blazing. But no matter how much it made her stomach ache this was exactly what she had to do.

'Don't you get it, Alex? There can't be an "us". There can't be the start of anything between us until you face up to your past. Annabelle wasn't created in a dish. She wasn't a test tube baby. You slept with your wife. You created a child together. Part of you loved her.'

She waved her hand.

'Stop trying to tell me otherwise. I've accepted it, Alex, and so must you. If you want us to be seen together—if you want to kiss me like that again—then it has to be on the condition that you've grieved for your wife. It has to be on the condition that you can look at your daughter and love her the way you should.'

Tears started to roll down her cheeks.

'This isn't about me trying to decide if I want to be seen

in public with you or not. I can't even answer that yet—because we're not there yet. It's easy for you to put all the responsibility for this relationship on my shoulders. Because then you don't need to think about Sophia or Annabelle at all.'

The tears wouldn't stop. Her heart was breaking.

Alex's face had crumpled. She didn't have a single doubt that she loved this man sitting across from her. This proud, passionate, potential king.

It would be so easy to get swept along with the wonder of the pink palace, Euronia, and a prince who'd come looking for her after ten years.

She wanted him for herself. She really did.

She almost wished she could take back everything she'd just said and walk through that door again and wrap her arms around his neck and kiss him.

But this would always have been there.

This would eventually have festered between them.

She wanted to be free to love Alex. And she wanted him to be free to love her. Things just didn't feel like that right now.

'This is killing me, Alex,' she whispered.

He stood up sharply, his chair screeching along the floor. He ran his fingers through his hair. 'I need to think. I need to think about all this.'

His eyes were vacant. As if he couldn't look at her, couldn't focus.

The tables had turned completely.

He'd been telling *her* to take her time.

But the reality was after ten years it was Alex who needed to take his time.

She stood up and walked back towards the glass doors.

This time it was her turn to say the words. 'Take all the time you need.'

CHAPTER NINE

FOR TWO DAYS he avoided Ruby.

There was too much to think about—too much to absorb.

Any time he was around Ruby he was drawn to her and wanted to touch her.

But horrible little parts of what she'd said were keeping him awake at night.

The photograph part was easy. He knew exactly which picture to frame for Annabelle. It was embarrassing to think he hadn't even considered it before.

He—and the advisors around him—had just assumed that Annabelle wouldn't remember anything about her mother.

He hadn't deliberately kept her pictures away from Annabelle—he just hadn't thought to talk to Annabelle about her mother.

She was playing in her room now. One blonde doll seemed to be driving a racing car around the furniture and over most of the other toys. She was making noises again—a *brrrrmm* for the racing car and a gasp as the doll plummeted over the bedcovers.

His heart twisted in his chest. If Sophia had lived would their little girl have been like this? It was a horrible thing to consider. It meant facing up to facts—facing up to a responsibility that he'd thought he had fulfilled.

Ruby thought differently.

He couldn't hesitate any longer. He walked into the room, keeping his voice bright. 'Hi, Annabelle. I've brought a picture for you.'

He put the silver frame on Annabelle's bedside table.

There was an audible gasp. It almost ripped him in two.

The picture was almost exactly at Annabelle's head height. She tilted her head to one side, her eyes wide.

He could have picked from a million pictures of Sophia. Once Annabelle was old enough to use the internet she would find another million pictures of her mother online.

But this was his favourite. This had always been his favourite. It was the picture he still had of Sophia in his mind—not the frail, emaciated pale woman she'd become.

This picture had Sophia on a swing, her blonde hair streaming behind her, her face wide with laughter and her pink dress billowing around her. She was around eighteen in this picture and it captured her perfectly. It captured the fun-loving human being she'd been before illness had struck her down.

He had other pictures. Pictures of her holding Annabelle not long after the birth and in the following months. There were lots of those.

But all of those pictures were touched with inherent sadness. The inevitability of a life lost. He'd put some into a little album for Annabelle. Those were for another day.

She reached out and touched the photo, obviously captivated by the joy in the picture. That was the word it conjured in his brain. *Joy.*

He knelt beside her. 'That's your mama, Annabelle. She was a very beautiful woman and you look just like her. I thought it was time for you to have a photograph of your own.'

Her little brow furrowed for a moment. He could almost see her brain trying to assimilate the information. Her lips moved, making the M movement—but no sound came out.

He rested her hand at her back. 'Look—your dress is the same colour as hers.'

He could see the recognition on his little girl's face. His whole body ached. Why hadn't he done this sooner?

A wave of shame washed over him. He should have known to do this. He should have known that his daughter needed this. But Alex had no experience around children. He had no relatives with youngsters, and as an only child he didn't have much experience to draw on.

He'd had friends—peers—during his life. Sophia had been among them, as had his schoolmates and university friends. But he hadn't been exposed to a life of looking after other people's children.

His sole experience of children before the birth of Annabelle had been on royal tours, where he was expected to talk to kids and hold babies. That was all fine, but it only lasted minutes. It didn't give him a taste of real life.

He looked down at the little girl in front of him. She'd gone back to her dolls and was racing them around the room again. Just like any three-year-old should.

His eyes glanced between his daughter and the photo. The wave of grief was overwhelming. Ruby was right. Sophia *hadn't* just been his friend.

Would he have married her if she hadn't been sick? Probably not. Their relationship hadn't been destined to go that way. Sophia had had wanderlust. She would likely have travelled and married someone from a distant country.

But the genetics of life had changed all that.

He took a deep breath. He hadn't felt the surge of emotion around Sophia that he felt around Ruby. There hadn't been that instant connection. More like a slow-growing respect. But other than Ruby she was the only woman on this planet he'd actually felt anything for.

In his head it had all been about duty and loyalty. He hadn't wanted to let his heart get involved. But if he wanted to move on with Ruby he had to acknowledge that she'd been more than just a friend.

He held his hand out to Annabelle. 'Annabelle, honey. Come with Daddy. We're going to go and put some flowers on your mama's grave.'

Another tiny step. Another massive milestone.

When was the last time he'd visited Sophia's grave?

He knew for sure he'd never taken his daughter there.

That was all about to change.

The changes were subtle at first.

The first thing she noticed was the picture in the silver frame next to Annabelle's bed. It made her heart squeeze in her chest. One, because he'd done it himself, and two, because Annabelle's mother had indeed been beautiful.

She wasn't jealous. She couldn't bring herself to be jealous of a dead woman. Those initial little pangs of frustration had disappeared. On dark nights—for some horrible moments—she'd wanted this woman never to have existed. Irrational and unreasonable thoughts had filled her head momentarily: Sophia had stolen those ten years she could have had with Alex.

All nonsense.

Life was life.

There was a gorgeous little girl running about around her legs and that was what she should focus on.

Her brain could be logical. It could tell her that she was there to do a job. It could tell her that she was the best person possible for Annabelle.

And there were discernible changes in Annabelle. Small ones—as if the little girl's walls were being finally worn down.

She wasn't quite so reserved. Her play and interaction at the nursery had changed. Humming was rapidly becoming normal now. Little noises, little sounds would be made with excitement—or sometimes fright if they were watching *Finding Nemo* again.

A small flick-through book of photographs of Annabelle and her mother had appeared. The picture on the front was amazing. One half in black and white, one half in colour. Annabelle and her mother, both sitting on the fountain, at around the same age. Two captured moments in time.

Anyone who didn't know Annabelle would think it was the same little girl.

Ruby could already predict that in her teenage years Annabelle would blow up that picture for her bedroom wall.

The first time she'd flicked through the book with Annabelle talking her through the pictures had been hard. A weight had pressed down on her chest and it had been all she could do to stop the tears rolling down her cheeks. But it became easier, and soon part of their routine every day involved five minutes of flicking through the photos.

It had also become part of Alex's bedtime routine with Annabelle. The staff had finally got the message and stopped queuing outside the door at night. Alex was adamant that this time was Annabelle's.

And it had done them both good. Alex was more relaxed around his child. He knew what her favourite foods were. He knew who her best friends were at nursery. He could sing along to all the songs in *Finding Nemo*. And gradually the sad tone in his voice was replaced as he told stories of happy memories while they flicked through the photo album.

Ruby stayed in the background although she was working tirelessly with Annabelle. There were no more romantic interludes with Alex, no matter how much she hoped for them. No other heated moments when the air was so thick a wrecking ball couldn't pound its way through.

He still watched her. Sometimes when she lifted her head she would meet his bright blue gaze. The sparks were still there. They were both just treading more warily.

If they brushed hands as they played with Annabelle, or if he moved closer for any reason, the buzz thrummed through her body. Every part of her still wanted to be with him. But she was more confident around him.

She didn't feel the need to look like a supermodel. She didn't feel outclassed by visiting royalty. Alex wanted her. She knew it. He knew it.

Getting there was a slow process. But she could live with that.

Every day she learned something new about Euronia. About its history—the subterfuge, the pirates and the Kings. The history was chequered with colourful characters. Alex's father was probably the quietest ruler of them all.

He was still in Switzerland. Once Alex had flown there, when his father had suffered another bout of pneumonia and had to be ventilated. She'd offered to go but he'd asked her to stay with Annabelle. They both knew the little girl needed stability and she'd been happy to oblige.

The long summer came to a close around the end of September, when Ruby finally had to pull her cardigans out of her cupboard to cover her arms.

And before the leaves on the trees started to change colour Alex started to appear around her again.

At first it was simple. Coffee. Cake. Days sitting in the late summer sunshine in the café in the square. Their visits became so frequent that the café owner stopped asking her what she wanted. After she fawned over a new apricot sponge the café owner started to bake it for her every other day.

Then there was the lunches, and their time spent together that included Annabelle. Sometimes it was in the palace grounds. Sometimes it was in and around Euronia. Once he even took them to Monaco for the day.

This time it felt as if she was the one with the barriers in place and it was Alex who was chipping away at her walls. But it felt right. The momentum was building at a pace that felt comfortable for both of them, for Annabelle, and for the people around them.

Clothes kept mysteriously appearing in her wardrobe—all of them beautiful, all of them fitting perfectly. The palace staff had stopped being prickly around her. Her devotion to Annabelle was clear, but Alex's respect for her was even clearer. Even Rufus had started to come round, and had given her a key to the palace library so she could work undisturbed.

'Ruby?'

Her head shot up. It was late at night and she was sitting on one of the ancient chaise longues, with her feet tucked up underneath her, reading on her electronic tablet.

There were no fancy clothes tonight. Tonight she was wearing a sloppy white top, grey jogging trousers, and her hair was tied in a knot on top of her head.

'Is something wrong with Annabelle?'

It was the first thought that came into her head.

Alex crossed into the room, holding up his hand as he walked. 'No. She's fine. I was looking for you. I should have known I'd find you in here.'

There was a warmth in his eyes as he said the words, a flicker of a memory, and she remembered he'd told her this had been his mother's favourite room.

He pointed at the tablet. 'Isn't it sacrilege to read that in here?'

She shrugged. 'I couldn't work the ancient light switches. Every time I pressed one it seemed to light up the wrong part of the library. Plus, I like being in the dark.'

She pointed to the gardens outside, where some light from the fountain and its walls was spilling up to meet them.

'There's something nice about looking out over the world.'

She turned to face him.

'What have you got?'

He was holding something wrapped in brown paper in his hand, along with two large cups. The smell of something wonderful was winding its way through the air towards her.

'Midnight snacks.' He grinned as he sat down next to her. 'I was starving and went for a rummage around the kitchen to see what I could find.'

She lifted her eyebrows. 'I'm surprised Rufus's inbuilt internal alarm didn't go off at you stepping into the palace kitchens unattended.'

He shrugged. 'I was too. Here,' he handed one of the cups to her and she lifted it to her nose, inhaling.

'Soup?' She glanced at her watch. 'At one in the morning?'

He smiled. That goofy smile he sometimes gave when it was just the two of them. 'I'm hungry. Leena's soup is the best there is.' He held up the brown paper package. 'I even managed to find some freshly baked rolls.'

She opened it up and looked in. Fresh crusty bread in the middle of the night did have a certain appeal.

'Come on,' he said. 'It's no fun eating on your own.'

There was a twinkle in his eye. It was the most relaxed she'd seen him for a while. Spending time with his daughter was doing him the world of good. This wasn't the uptight guy who'd visited her months ago in her hospital department. This wasn't the guy who'd looked as if a permanent grey cloud was resting on his shoulders.

She moved over to the table and he joined her, breaking open his bread roll and dipping it into the soup.

'I've got something else to show you.'

He pushed a file across the table towards her. It was pale beige and looked official.

She flipped it open and gasped. A picture of her and Alex from ten years ago in Paris.

He shrugged. 'It always bothered me that you never

got my message. I trust my Head of Security. If he said he sent it I know he did. I had to work out what went wrong.'

'After all this time?'

It had always bothered her too. She'd assumed an absent-minded clerk just hadn't bothered passing the message on.

She looked at the file again. Read the notes. All of them were about her. It was more than a little unnerving. Then she let out a gasp. 'Oh, no!'

His hands closed over hers. 'What is it?'

She smiled at him. 'Hotel du Chat. That's not where I was staying. It says in the notes that your Head of Security left a message at Reception there.'

Alex's brow furrowed. 'He did. But that's what you told me.'

She squeezed his hand. 'Hotel du Champ, Alex. Not Hotel du Chat.' She shook her head. 'After all these years I don't know if that makes me feel better or worse.'

Alex put his head in his hands. 'I was so sure. So sure you said Hotel du Chat.'

'It was noisy, Alex. It was New Year's. You'd just had an urgent message about your father.' She took a deep breath. 'Mistakes happen.'

His finger reached up and touched her cheek. 'I hate mistakes,' he whispered.

'So do I.'

They sat in silence for a few seconds. Both of them letting the revelation wash over them. For Ruby, it felt like a relief. It didn't matter that Alex had assured her he'd tried to contact her. There had always been a tiny sliver of doubt.

But he had. And, strangely, it made her feel good. Maybe life would have been different. Who could possibly know? What she did know was that they couldn't change the past.

'What did the message say?' She couldn't help but ask. It had always played on her mind.

He gave a little nod and held her gaze. 'It was simple.'

He shrugged. 'We'd just met and barely had a chance to get to know each other. It said that I was sorry I couldn't meet you, that I really wanted to see you again but had been called away to a family emergency—something I really wanted to explain to you. I left my number and asked you to call as soon as you got my note.'

She gave a sad kind of smile. 'And that—as they say— was that.'

They sat in silence again for a few seconds, thinking of what-might-have-been.

There was no point second-guessing now. Time had passed. They'd found each other again. What happened next was up to them.

Alex pointed back to her soup. 'Better eat that before it gets cold.'

She nodded and picked up her spoon. 'This makes me feel as if I'm in one of those boarding schools that Enid Blyton wrote about and we're having a midnight feast.'

His brow wrinkled. 'She was a kids' author, wasn't she? I must have missed those books.' He gave her a wink. 'Boarding school wasn't so bad.'

'You went to boarding school?' She was fascinated.

'Not until I was twelve. I went to primary school here in Euronia. The same one that I'm planning on sending Annabelle to.'

Her bread was poised over the cup. 'Do you plan on sending her to boarding school when she's older?'

It was almost as if a little breeze had chilled her skin. It was all right joking about these things, but the thought of Annabelle going to boarding school in a few years made her blood run cold.

'I don't know that much about girls' boarding schools. Maybe... I'd need to see how she was doing first.'

It was a touch of relief, but not enough. She had no business saying anything. But she didn't care.

'I don't think you should.' The words were out before she'd thought about them.

'You don't?'

He seemed surprised. But the atmosphere between them was still relaxed. She felt able to continue.

'I just wonder if that will be the right environment for Annabelle.' She leaned across the table and touched his arm. 'I've something to tell you about today.'

'What is it?'

She gave him a smile. 'Today, when I was at the nursery watching Annabelle, I'm almost sure she spoke to another child.'

'What?'

She nodded. 'She was with a little boy. They were playing together. I was at the other side of the nursery but I saw her look up and her lips moved. The little boy's head snapped up, so she must have said something. But at that point she resorted to signing again. It was almost as if his reaction reminded her that she didn't talk.'

Alex looked as if he could hardly believe her. His face was a mixture of surprise and relief. 'But you didn't actually hear her?'

'No. I was too far away—and, believe me, it's bedlam in the nursery. The noise levels are incredible.'

'So, this is good. Isn't it?'

'I hope so. It's one of the concepts of selective mutism that in some situations children will talk and in others they won't.'

'What do you think?'

'I think that I can see changes all the time, Alex. They're slow, but steady. In my head, Annabelle is a little flower with all its petals tightly closed. It's only now that she's starting to bloom. We need to nurture her. We need to keep letting her develop at her own pace, her own speed.'

He nodded. 'I think so too. I didn't want to say anything, but when we were flicking through the pictures the other day it was almost as if the "mmm" sound was hovering around her lips. It wasn't quite there, it wasn't quite formed, but I could almost hear it in the air around us.'

'You think she was going to say Mum?'

He gave a rueful smile. His fingers moved. She was still touching his hand and this time he interlinked his fingers with hers.

'You think I'm just being silly? Is it just a father's wishful thinking?'

She shook her head. He was so sincere.

'I think you're being the same as any parent, Alex. You're putting the welfare of your child first.'

'And so are you.'

He said the words so quietly they took a few seconds to sink into her brain.

His bright blue eyes were fixed on her. The implication was clear. Alex was acknowledging something that she hadn't yet acknowledged herself.

Her other hand was still poised over the soup, with the already sodden piece of bread threatening to fall into the cup. Her hand was trembling. She couldn't pull her eyes away from his.

She dropped the bread in the soup and pushed it away. The library was mainly dark, the gardens outside giving only a glimmer of deep gold light. But it didn't matter how dim the light was—the only thing she could fixate on right now was him.

His other hand stretched over and tangled in her hair. She sucked in a breath as he stroked the back of her neck. Every part of her skin was tingling.

He moved. It was only one step but he was kissing her, pulling her up into his arms. She wrapped her hands around his neck. Last time he'd kissed her they'd been on the yacht. Tension had been in the air all around them. This time it was different.

This felt like the most natural thing in the world. Every

touch of his fingers sent shivers down her spine, building expectation.

This didn't feel as if a man with a kingdom was kissing her. This felt as though *Alex* was kissing her. Alex whom she'd met in Paris all those years ago.

The man she'd watched change over the last few weeks and months. The man who'd taken on board what she'd told him about his child and tried to make changes. He respected her opinion. He'd taken her seriously.

She didn't feel as if she were there as a paid employee any more. It felt like so much more. This felt natural. This felt right. This felt as if it were the place she was supposed to be.

He pulled away and looked down at her. He was smiling. The twinkle in his eyes was back.

'Ruby Wetherspoon…?'

She blinked, not quite sure where this was going. His voice was serious, but the smile hadn't moved from his face. It was almost as if he knew the answer before he asked the question.

'Yes?'

All she could concentrate on right now was the heat of his body against hers. She didn't care that she was wearing ratty clothes. She didn't care that her hair was a mess. All she cared about was the fact she was in Alex's arms.

'Would you do me the honour of coming to Euronia's Annual Charity Ball with me?'

Her throat instantly dried and she wanted to lick her lips. But she couldn't because Alex was kissing her again.

It was almost as if he knew that for a fraction of a second she'd be filled with doubts and he was determined to kiss them away.

This was the first official function he'd invited her to. They'd spent lots of time together—lots of time alone and with Annabelle—but this would be the first time Alex sent a message to the world.

He'd told her he would give her time. And she'd known that he needed time too.

But that time had passed. It felt as if they were both on an even footing. Both in a place where things could develop in the way they wanted.

So she said the thing that felt the most natural to her in the world.

'Yes, Alex. I'd love to.'

CHAPTER TEN

THE DRESS WAS BEAUTIFUL. More stunning than anything she could have imagined.

Red satin, with a ruched sweetheart bodice encrusted with silver crystals. It hung from the wardrobe door, the crystals glittering and sending sparkles around the room. There were matching silver sandals.

Her stomach was fluttering over and over. Her food tray lay on the table untouched. She couldn't even think about eating.

One of the palace staff had come and set her hair in rollers—a silent girl who'd been ruthlessly efficient: tugging the rollers into place within a few minutes, with strict instructions not to remove them until five minutes before she was ready to leave.

It felt so unreal. Even her face in the mirror looked unreal. The black kohl she occasionally put around her eyes had been smudged uselessly across one cheek. It had taken her two attempts before it looked anything like it should. And the red lipstick seemed too severe. It was a perfect match for her dress—together they would look magnificent—but next to her white skin and dark hair in the bathroom mirror she felt she looked more like the Wicked Queen in *Snow White*.

Doubts were creeping into every corner of her mind. Alex had asked her to come. His reasons seemed valid. But she was just an ordinary girl who knew nothing of visiting dignitaries or the traditions of other countries. At first this had seemed exciting, flattering and little fairytale-ish. Now it seemed terrifying. Every handshake, every nod of her head, every word she said could be wrong.

The last thing she wanted to do was embarrass him.

Maybe things would be better if she stayed in her room?

The door handle creaked and the door edged open. Ruby gasped, her hands automatically going to her bra-covered breasts and her bare abdomen.

But it was Annabelle, dressed in pink pyjamas and with sleepy eyes. She didn't seem the slightest bit concerned to see Ruby half dressed.

'Is something wrong Annabelle?' She knelt on the floor next to the little girl.

But Annabelle's eyes were wide as she looked at the sparkles on the red dress. She let out a little squeak of excitement and pulled her thumb from her mouth, reaching over to touch the dress.

It swung on its hanger, making the sparkles move like little stars in the sky.

The thumb had left a smudge on the delicate fabric, but Ruby didn't care. 'Do you like it, Annabelle?'

The little girl nodded. So Ruby let it swing some more, sending the sparkles further. She lifted Annabelle into her arms and swung her around, then picked up an abandoned book from the floor.

'Let me take you back to bed,' she said, slipping her arms into her satin dressing gown and padding next door.

She read the caterpillar book until Annabelle fell asleep. She almost wanted to stay there. It would be so much easier falling asleep next to Annabelle than putting on that dress and going out to meet the world.

Alex had asked her to accompany him. What exactly did that mean?

She was Ruby Wetherspoon from Lewisham. She couldn't speak any other languages. She didn't know how to address dignitaries. There was every chance she would seriously offend someone by not shaking their hand the correct way. Her stomach was turning over and over.

Annabelle looked so peaceful. Her attachment to Ruby was growing. It was Ruby she'd seek out now when she was looking for company. It was Ruby she wanted to draw pictures and play games with.

And these last few weeks had brought changes in her demeanour. She wasn't quite so shy. She was gaining confidence. She was interacting better with the children at nursery. She might not be talking, but every day Ruby heard more sounds and expressions. It was almost as if a tiny little valve had been released and she was becoming more comfortable.

Last night Ruby had been convinced that the humming along to *Finding Nemo* was becoming a murmur. She'd been careful not to react. She'd stayed exactly where she was, letting Annabelle lie in her arms until she'd fallen asleep and then gently sliding her arms out from underneath her.

The thought of going away and leaving this little girl was starting to play on her mind. The hospital in the UK had started to ask her for the date of her return. It seemed reasonable. She hadn't expected to be here this long. But the days had quickly turned into weeks, and the weeks into months. Euronia was starting to feel like home—no matter how many times Polly phoned her and told her it was time to return to London.

She wasn't sure she wanted to leave Annabelle.

She wasn't sure she wanted to leave Alex.

Where had *that* come from?

Her face flushed and she walked back into her own room, shedding her dressing gown and pulling the red dress from the hanger and stepping into it.

She sucked in her breath and slid the zip up at the back. It fitted perfectly—just like everything the palace had provided. The silver sandals were elegant, but comfortable. The only thing missing was jewellery.

Nothing really suited. Her plain gold earrings and chain looked paltry next to the designer gown. Maybe it would be better with nothing at all?

She smiled at her reflection in the mirror. With the rollers removed her dark hair was hanging in curls, covering her shoulders. The boning and the crystals on the dress gave her a more curvaceous shape than normal. And now, with the dress in place, her skin didn't look quite so pale or her lips so red.

Her hands trembled as she took off her gold earrings.

Tonight she was going to a ball in the palace.

Tonight she was going to a ball with her own prince.

Just for tonight she might actually be a princess.

Just for tonight she might actually look as if she was worthy of Alex.

And tonight, for the first time, she might actually feel as if she was part of a couple—even if it was only in her head.

Alex had been pacing for the last thirty minutes, wondering when Ruby would appear.

The palace was buzzing. It had been over a year since there had been a ball at the palace. When his mother and father had ruled there had been several balls every year, all raising money for various charities.

Alex had given some instructions on which charities he wanted to support, and the various people he wanted to invite. But all the details had been dealt with by his staff.

In less than a few minutes over a thousand people would be in the palace. He had guards in all corridors, letting the guests know which areas were open to the public and which were not. The corridor that held Ruby and Annabelle certainly wasn't.

He walked along its length, cursing himself for not saying goodnight to Annabelle earlier. He opened her door just a crack—she was already sleeping, her book and a stuffed caterpillar beside her on the bed.

He walked across the room and dropped a kiss on her forehead before quietly closing the door behind him. His fingers tightened around the black velvet box in his hands. He was still unsure. This felt right—he just didn't know how Ruby would react.

He knocked on her door before he could change his mind.

She opened the door and met him with a smile. 'Hi, Alex. What do you think?'

There was a tremor in her voice. An uncertainty.

He couldn't speak. He must have the dopiest smile on his face right now. What did he *think*? She'd just blown him away!

Ruby was always gorgeous—usually understated, but gorgeous nonetheless. But he'd never seen Ruby the grown-up.

The scarlet dress was stunning. Elegant without giving anything way. Hugging her curves but sweeping the floor and keeping everything covered. The beads along her bodice sparkled in the dim evening light snaking through the windows. Her hair had been styled into large curls, covering her bare shoulders. She was wearing more make-up than usual, but it was perfect. Highlighting her flawless skin, dark brown eyes and red lips.

He held out the black box towards her. 'You look *almost* perfect, Ruby.'

'Almost?'

It was obvious she knew he was teasing her. She stepped forward, reaching out for the box.

He could tell she was nervous—her hands were trembling slightly. Would she know he was nervous too?

She lifted the lid and let out a little gasp. The diamonds were dazzling. The jewels on her dress paled in comparison to these. He knew instantly he'd done the right thing.

'Alex…' Her eyes were wide. 'Where did these come from?' She held up one of the earrings, its thirty hanging diamonds bright and clear.

'They were my mother's. I knew you were nervous about tonight. I thought it might be nice if you had something of hers to wear.'

'You want me to wear *these*?' She looked almost terrified. 'But they must be worth a fortune.' Her fingers went automatically to her earlobe. 'What if I lose one?'

He shook his head and smiled. 'You won't. Don't worry.'

'But—'

'But nothing.' He spun her around to face the full-length mirror in the room and held up one of the earrings next to her ear. 'Can't you see how perfect it looks?'

She could hardly argue. Her face said exactly how she was feeling.

She put her hand up over her heart. 'They're beautiful. They set off the dress perfectly.' She turned around towards him. 'How did you know?'

'Because my mother had impeccable taste, Ruby. It wouldn't have mattered what you wore tonight—these earrings were always going to be a perfect match.' He bent a little lower and whispered in her ear. 'You have a lot in common with her.'

'What does that mean?'

'It means that you look beautiful.' He pressed the earrings into her hand. 'Here—put them on and let's go.'

She stood in front of the mirror, putting the earrings in place, then stopped for a second to study her reflection. She was trying to calm herself. Trying to steady herself for the night ahead.

He put his arms on her shoulders. 'You're going to be the most beautiful woman in the room, Ruby Wetherspoon.'

He was standing by her shoulder, looking at their reflection in the glass. He knew she was nervous. He was nervous himself. Although this was meant to be a private function, nothing could ever really be private when a thousand people were involved.

This would be the first time since Sophia had died that he'd officially invited someone to be his partner. He was well aware of how some of his guests might react. But the charity ball had always been an informal occasion. In a way, it might give Ruby a taste of what could lie ahead.

He hadn't even broached that question with her on the yacht. There had been too much more to deal with. But now the time was right.

He slid his hand into hers. 'Are you ready? Because you look beautiful.'

She nodded slowly and touched the glittering diamonds in her ears. 'I'm ready now.' She sounded more confident. More sure.

He didn't have a shadow of a doubt. His mother would have loved Ruby Wetherspoon.

The first disaster was tripping over her dress. Even though it was gorgeous, and made-to-measure, she wasn't standing quite as straight as she should be. As a result the bottom seam of the dress kept catching on her toes.

A strong hand at her elbow stopped her face-planting on the floor. At first she thought it was Alex, but he was on her other side. A quick glance proved it to be one of the waiters, with a whole silver tray of canapés in his other hand.

He gave her a little conspiratorial nod. 'Mind your step, m'lady.'

She gathered up part of the dress in her hand. Her stomach was turning over and over. Another waiter proffered a tray with champagne flutes but she shook her head—champagne was the last thing she needed right now.

Alex turned and smiled at her. It was the first time she'd really seen him in formal dress. He'd been pressed up behind her next to the mirror, and she'd been so dazzled by the diamonds that she hadn't noticed how handsome he looked. The black dress uniform suited him perfectly, with its sweeping red sash across his chest and adorned with several gold medals.

It hadn't even occurred to her that the sash was the exact same red as her dress. Had Alex done that deliberately?

They walked through the ballroom doors side by side. It wasn't so bad. There was no audible hush when they appeared, just a few quiet gestures and murmurs.

Alex immediately went into charm mode—working the room and talking to lots of the guests, his arm behind her, gently guiding her from person to person. Sometimes he spoke in French, sometimes in German. After the first few words she was mainly lost, and just nodded and smiled along, shaking a proffered hand when appropriate.

The diamonds had felt dazzling in her ears upstairs—if a little ostentatious—but in this room it was clear that Ruby was the least adorned woman there. Everywhere she turned there were rings the size of rocks and twinkling tiaras.

She'd recognised a few faces from royal families across Europe, all in dazzling jewels. And even the movie stars and supermodels were adorned with diamond necklaces and bracelets.

A blonde actress—one of her favourites—was right in front of her. She was immaculate, as usual, in a figure-hugging black dress high at the neck but with virtually no back. How she kept the dress in place was a mystery to Ruby.

She spun on her heels and tilted her head, unashamedly studying Ruby. Waves of discomfort washed over her, along with a distinct flow of blood to the cheeks. She was determined not to be intimidated.

She held out her hand. 'Maria Cochette? It's a pleasure to meet you. I'm Ruby Wetherspoon.'

Her hand stayed in the air for the longest time.

'I know who you are.'

The Italian accent that sounded so cute on screen was harsh in real life. Maria's eyes swept up and down Ruby with obvious distaste. The dress that had felt so perfect up-stairs suddenly felt old-fashioned and overdone.

This was a woman who had charmed in every inter-view Ruby had ever watched. She exuded elegance and grace. But the look she was giving Ruby now held none of those things.

She moved closer, still ignoring Ruby's outstretched hand. Her voice lowered. 'So how did you do it? How did little Plain Jane manage to catch the Prince's eye?' She sneered. 'Or was it just too easy for him to do the hired help?' The vulgar words were spat out. 'Lydia Merr told me about you. She said you weren't even eye candy—and she was right.'

Ruby had never been a girl for conflict. But if she'd been any other place, at any other time, she would have punched the perfect Maria clean in the face. Alex had warned her that Mrs Merr was a renowned gossip, and it seemed their kiss hadn't gone unnoticed.

For the first time that night she drew herself up to her full height. She almost felt her dress lift from the floor. Up close, Maria wasn't so perfect. Botox had made her eye-brows arch unevenly. Her suntanned skin couldn't hide the wrinkles around her eyes.

Ruby lifted her hand up to her ears and smiled sweetly, though she knew her eyes would be shooting daggers. She'd dealt with too many difficult patients and members of staff over the years to simper around a woman like this.

'I guess some of us have hidden talents, Maria. Or maybe our core values and ethics are just apparent.' She let her fingers run over the sparkling drop diamonds. 'Do you like the earrings Alex gave me to wear? They were his mother's.'

The diamonds were elegant, in contrast; the bling from Maria was almost blinding her.

She met the cold grey eyes with another smile. 'I always think that less is more, don't you?'

She didn't wait for an answer—just turned and walked away, ignoring the stifled noise of indignation behind her.

Ruby never behaved like that. But something had burned inside her. Was it the way Maria had looked at Alex? Or her total disrespect for Ruby?

Her stomach flipped over. Would this be something she would need to get used to?

She almost stumbled over her feet. Where had *that* thought come from? This was their first official outing together. It might lead to nothing.

But all of a sudden, even after all their talks and all this time, Ruby felt woefully unprepared. Alex had said nothing to her, but this almost felt like a test to see how she would do. A test she was about to fail spectacularly if her exchange with Maria was anything to go on.

She looked around the room. She didn't have a single friend here.

It was a sobering thought.

And all of a sudden she felt very alone. When was the last time she'd spoken to Polly?

She was planning on spending Christmas with her parents in France—that was only a few weeks away—but for the first time since she'd got here she missed her colleagues, she missed her friends, she missed her flat.

It was this. It was here—standing in this room with hundreds of people and the only person who had her back was Alex.

It was as if he felt the vibe across the room. He looked up and his gaze met hers, and he gave her a quizzical are-you-all-right? look. It was impossible, but she felt as if she could see the bright blue of his eyes even from this distance.

He started to walk towards her and her feet automatically moved in response. All she could do was smile. It didn't matter who else was in the room. The only person who mattered was Alex. And he was looking at her as if he felt exactly the same way.

The voices, the jewels, the chatter all around her just faded to background noise. Her smile was getting broader by the second. It was the strongest urge, the greatest pull she'd ever felt. Like metal being drawn towards a magnet from a million miles away.

Several people tried to talk to him as he made his way towards her, but Alex didn't even blink—he just kept his eyes focused entirely on her.

Seconds later he filled her entire view. For another second both of them hesitated. Then his arms were around her waist, her hands were resting on his shoulders.

'Are you okay?'

'I am now.'

She'd never felt more sure of anything. This time there *was* a hush in the room. Their actions had attracted everyone's attention.

But Alex's bright blue eyes were still fixed on hers. 'You're the most beautiful woman in the room, Ruby.'

His voice was low, for her ears only.

'That's the way I always feel around you,' she murmured.

'Good.'

His lips met hers. She could hear the audible gasps around her but she didn't care. Alex was kissing in her in front of everyone. Alex was making his intentions clear.

It was as if she could soar. Soar above the shocked faces in the ballroom and soar above the pink palace. The kiss in Paris had been special—had been electric—but this kiss was everything. He spun her around as he kissed her and they both started to laugh. Knowing entirely how it looked.

He pulled his lips back, their noses still touching. 'You're mine, Ruby Wetherspoon. And the whole world knows it.'

'And you're mine right back.'

She'd never thought she'd say those words. She'd never thought she'd believe them. But this moment was hers. Hers and Alex's.

'I don't really want to look around,' she said. 'I don't want anyone to spoil what's happening between us.'

His eyes were still fixed on her face. He was smiling. 'Who could do that?'

It was almost as if a gong had sounded. Some ancient clanging noise reverberating around the room. But it was actually the opposite.

Silence. Pure and utter silence.

No one was talking. No one was murmuring. All she could hear was her and Alex breathing. Every tiny hair on her arms stood on end. It was as if someone were walking over her grave.

'Alex?'

He looked up and his hands dropped from her waist. There was an elderly couple standing in the doorway. Immaculately regal. Both were staring at Alex.

It took her a few seconds. She'd never met or seen pictures of Sophia's parents. But for a reaction like this it had to be them.

She glanced nervously at Alex. How much had they seen? Had they seen him kiss her, or just hold her?

Those few seconds whilst he gathered himself seemed to stretch into hours. She saw everything. The fleeting moment of panic followed by the worry of what to do next.

Her heart plummeted. He'd been carried away. He hadn't thought of the consequences of kissing her in front of everyone. This was a disaster.

Every eye in the room flicked between them and Sophia's parents.

She heard Alex suck in a deep breath, then his hand moved over and took hers.

The feeling of skin against skin was unexpected. Her gaze fixed on their hands as he intertwined their fingers. He moved forward in long strides and she struggled to keep up, having to gather her dress in her hand to stop it from tangling around her feet again.

He gave a courteous bow to the King and Queen. 'Ruby Wetherspoon, I'd like you to meet Annabelle's grandparents—King Henry and Queen Isabelle of Leruna.'

Her brain was racing. What on earth would they think of her?

There were a few expanding seconds of silence. Then their immaculate breeding kicked into place.

The King gave a nod of his head, 'Ms Wetherspoon.'

The Queen took a little longer. But her wide-eyed look had disappeared. Ruby could almost tell that to this woman composure was everything.

She held out a hand towards her. Ruby felt a second of panic—was she supposed to shake it or kiss it?

Alex made the tiniest movement and she reached out and shook the Queen's hand. Something from fairytales long ago made her curtsy. 'It's a pleasure to meet you, Queen Isabelle.'

As she stood up it was clear the Queen was regarding her carefully. Her heart was fluttering madly in her chest. If she didn't calm down soon she'd end up in a crumpled heap on the floor. She felt as if the whole room was watching her. Anything she did right now would be crucial. Her actions and demeanour would temper what everyone in the room thought of her.

It was as if a lightbulb had gone off in her head. All of a sudden she realised just how much of a chance Alex had taken on her.

She sucked in a breath. She was worthy. She was worthy of his faith in her. She just had to show it.

She was still holding the Queen's hand, and Isabelle's eyes were starting to smart with disapproval.

Despite her glittering tiara and her sumptuous silver gown, Ruby knew a clear way to connect with this woman. In her job she'd managed to charm the most difficult family members over the last ten years, and she could do it again now.

'It's been a pleasure to work with Annabelle these last few months. She's such a wonderful little girl and she's making real progress.'

Isabelle looked a little startled at the familiarity. People probably didn't speak to her like this. But as soon as Annabelle's name was mentioned it was clear she was interested.

'You're the speech therapist.' There was just the slightest hint of distaste—as if she were trying to put Ruby in her place.

'She's my friend.' Alex's words were quiet, but firm. Shooting a crystal-clear message across the tension-laden air. It was like a subtle counter-attack.

But this woman with decades of experience didn't even blink. Her eyebrows rose a little. 'Progress? Is she starting to talk?'

She was clearly surprised.

Ruby nodded and moved closer to her, away from the prying ears that were straining all around the room to hear their conversation.

Alex shot her a look that was a cross between pure relief and pleading, and with an almost imperceptible nod engaged the King in conversation, leading him over towards a drinks tray.

Ruby held out her hand to let the Queen lead the direction of their steps, and was unsurprised to find her leading them towards the entrance to another room filled with antique mahogany chairs. The door was closed quickly behind them by one of the palace attendants.

The Queen settled herself in one of the chairs and arranged her skirts around her before gesturing to Ruby to sit down too.

'Tell me about Annabelle.'

Ruby smiled. 'I've seen definite progress in the last few months. It's slow. But steady. I don't dispute the diagnosis of selective mutism. But do you know that in some cases children will speak in some circumstances but not others?'

The Queen gave the smallest of nods, so Ruby continued. 'Annabelle was silent when I got here. Over the last weeks and month we've noticed noises.'

'Noises?'

'Yes. Gasps of excitement. Whoops of pleasure. Whimpers when we're watching scary movies.'

'My granddaughter *whoops*?' There was an amused edge to her voice.

'Yes, she does. But that's not all—she often hums along to some of the songs in her favourite films. She seems to do it quite unconsciously—usually when she's most relaxed or when she's tired.'

'And she's that way around *you*?' The timbre of the Queen's voice had changed slightly.

'It's taken her a while to get to know me,' said Ruby quickly. 'But she's been spending more time with her father.'

Part of her wondered if she should be saying this. She didn't want to make it sound as if Alex had neglected Annabelle in any way at all.

'We've made sure that all the palace staff knows that his time with Annabelle is to be uninterrupted. It's time they spend alone—together.'

She was starting to get nervous and her mouth was running away from her. She wanted to be clear that she wasn't trying to push herself between Alex and his daughter. The last thing she wanted was for the Queen to think she was trying to take Sophia's place.

'And is this working?' There was a tone of slight disbelief. As if she didn't quite understand the significance.

'It's definitely working. Annabelle is changing. Her confidence has increased in leaps and bounds. She's a different little girl than the one I met when I arrived.'

For the smallest of seconds—almost instinctively—the Queen's eyes narrowed. She straightened herself in her chair, pulling herself up to her full height. 'Why do you think my granddaughter doesn't talk, Ms Wetherspoon?'

There was a whole host of things she could say here. But experience had taught her to go with her instinct.

'I think she misses her mother,' she said simply.

There was the tiniest sound. A little gasp from the Queen. Then the woman's eyes clouded, as if they were fogged by impending tears.

It was the clearest and most confident Ruby had felt all evening. Isabelle might be a distinguished queen—something that was way out of Ruby's realm of expertise—but she was also a concerned grandmother—something Ruby *could* understand.

Ruby leaned over and squeezed her hand, and then changed position, gathering her dress and kneeling in front of the Queen.

'Science tells us that even babies can form memories. Annabelle heard and recognised her mother's voice for nine months in the womb, and then for another eleven months after she was born.' She let go of the skirts in her hand and pressed her other hand over her heart. 'She remembers her mother in *here*.'

Her voice was becoming huskier. She wasn't trying to upset the Queen, but she felt it was important to be honest with her.

'Alex has put a picture of Sophia next to Annabelle's bed. He has made a picture album with photos of the two of them—as children they almost look like twins. It has pictures of Sophia alone, and pictures of her with Annabelle.' She squeezed the Queen's hand again. 'He talks about her every night with Annabelle.'

If the Queen disapproved of Ruby using the familiar form of Alex's name she didn't show it. A slow tear trickled down her cheek. 'He does?'

Ruby nodded. 'It's not sad. It's not morbid. He just tells her a little story—something about her mother—and they move on to something else. They play a game. Watch some TV together.'

The older woman's lips were trembling. 'And who has helped him to do that?'

Isabelle's pale grey eyes were fixed on hers. Ruby took a deep breath. 'I have. Everything about their relationship has changed. I think Alex had a lot of grief locked up inside. Talking and spending time with his daughter has helped them both.'

The Queen's gaze was fixed on Ruby. 'You did this? You did this for them?'

A flash of recognition crossed her eyes, along with a whole host of fleeting emotions.

Ruby could step back at this point. She could fall into professional mode. It would keep her safe. It would keep her guarded. But the Queen had already seen Alex's arms around her. Maybe she had seen more. It was time for honesty.

'I care about them. I care about them both very much.'

The Queen licked her lips. 'Do you think my granddaughter will ever talk?'

'I can't say for sure—but I do think so. I think she spoke the other day at nursery. I think she might have said something to one of the other children. But I didn't want to make a scene. I didn't want to draw her attention to the fact. We all have to be patient.'

'And are *you* patient, Ruby Wetherspoon?'

The question shocked her. It might sound simple, but the Queen clearly wasn't talking about Annabelle's speech any more. She meant something else entirely.

Was she brave enough to be honest?

I've waited ten years were the words on her lips.

'I am.'

There were another few moments' silence. It was almost as if the Queen were taking time to digest all she'd told her. She shifted a little closer to the edge of the chair—a little closer to Ruby.

'Alexander was Sophia's safe place.'

Her voice was shaky, but controlled. Her silver-grey eyes were fixed on Ruby's.

'He was the one person she trusted to give her the ultimate gift.'

Ruby's stomach squeezed. It would always hurt. It would always reach little parts of her that she couldn't share.

Her voice was shaking too. 'Annabelle is a beautiful gift. Of that there is no doubt.'

Their eyes met again and she felt the common understanding between them. This woman had lost her precious daughter. Her life would never be the same again.

If she wanted to she could hate Ruby. She could make life difficult for Alex. She could make their relationship impossible.

But it seemed she had no wish to do that.

'I'm glad my granddaughter has someone who has her best interests at heart. I'm glad that Alexander is looking to build a life for himself and his daughter again.'

She pushed herself up from the chair and gave a little nod to Ruby with the hint of a smile.

'And I would very much like to hear my granddaughter speak.'

Ruby straightened up and her knees gave an unexpected crack. She let out a nervous laugh—it certainly displaced any anxiety in the room.

Queen Isabelle gave her a serene smile. 'I'm tired. But if I retired for the evening now people would talk. We should return to the ballroom together. I'll be able to leave after a while.'

Ruby nodded. Of course. People had seen them leave the ballroom together and their tongues would wag if they didn't return together.

Then the Queen did something she didn't expect. She held out her elbow towards Ruby. An invitation to take it. Before it had been polite and because they were in company. In the confines of this room, when it was just the two of them, it was something she didn't have to do.

Ruby didn't hesitate. She slid her arm next to the Queen's and joined her in walking towards the door.

Isabelle's smile had stayed on her face. 'Beautiful earrings, Ms Wetherspoon. They seem familiar. Queen Marguerite had exquisite taste, didn't she?'

Ruby's heart squeezed inside her chest. *She knew.* She knew Alex had given them to her to wear this evening.

They walked through the door arm in arm.

The glass doors from the ballroom leading out to the gardens were open, letting the cool fresh air sweep in. Ten years ago New Year's Eve in Paris had been cold, but winter in Euronia was much warmer. People drifted in and out of the ballroom and the gardens as the music played.

People were curious about her now. Alex appeared by her side every ten minutes or so, introducing her to diplomats and other royals. They shook her hand and gave her guarded smiles. The celebrity guests were much more up-front. Apart from her earlier encounter with Maria Cochette, everyone else seemed to want to be her new best friend. It was odd. Perhaps it was the fact that Alex had kissed her in front of everyone. His message had been clear.

The scene that everyone had expected in front of Sophia's parents hadn't materialised. When she'd re-entered the ballroom on the arm of Queen Isabelle some mouths had dropped open. Even Alex had looked a bit shocked, but he'd covered it well.

His hands had appeared at her waist a little later and his mouth at her ear. 'What did you do?' he whispered.

'I told the truth,' she said simply, and he'd twirled her around in the next dance.

The evening passed by in a flash. She didn't even notice when the King and Queen of Leruna slipped away—she was too busy focusing on Alex.

He was more attentive than ever, leaving her in no doubt

of his attentions. Every tiny brush of his fingertips on her skin ignited the fire within her. Every time he caught her eye, or gave her a smile from across the room, she felt as if she were the only person there.

When finally the last person left her feet were throbbing and her jaw was aching from smiling so much.

Alex appeared at her side and took the champagne glass from her hand. 'Are you tired?'

She shook her head. 'No. I don't want this night to end.'

He took her hand in his and led her up the huge curved staircase and along the corridor towards his rooms. Their footsteps quickened as they walked, their anticipation building.

He swung the door of his apartment wide. She'd never been in here before. Alex had always been around her and Annabelle in their rooms, or in the main parts of the palace. She'd had no reason to visit his rooms.

The room was stark. Different from the other very ornate rooms in the palace.

No antique furniture. No sumptuous furnishings. It was white and black—like a modern apartment in the middle of New York—certainly not what she expected to find in a pink palace.

'Alex?'

She turned to face him and her heart squeezed at the expression on his face. These were the rooms he'd shared with his wife. He didn't need to say anything. Everything in this room had been stripped bare—just like his heart. She understood in a heartbeat.

She closed the door quietly behind her and stepped over to him. 'Oh, Alex…'

She ran her fingers through his hair as he closed his eyes.

Everything—all their conversations—had been about *her* being ready. But the truth was it was about *him* being ready too.

Part of this was painful. Because after tonight she'd

never been more sure about what she wanted. It was Alex. It had always been Alex. It would always be Alex.

But did he really want her? Or was she just someone to plug the gap his wife had left?

It should unsettle her that these were the rooms he'd shared with his wife. It should make her feel uncomfortable. But she had a feeling that there wasn't a single part of Sophia left in here.

Her fingers were still running through his hair—his hands were planted firmly on her hips. She stepped closer to him and placed a gentle kiss on the soft skin at the side of his neck.

'Are you ready for this, Alex? Are you ready for us?'

Every knot inside him was beginning to unravel. He'd held himself in check all night. From the first second he'd seen Ruby in her red dress he'd wanted to have her in this position. She was everything to him. And now he was finally free to say it—finally free to let the world know.

The arrival of Sophia's parents had been more than unexpected. They were always invited to formal occasions at the palace. But since Sophia's death they'd never attended.

They saw Annabelle on regular occasions, but they were always private times.

He'd been horrified when they'd arrived—horrified that their first view of Ruby was in his arms with his mouth on hers.

With a few hours' hindsight he realised that Queen Isabelle must have heard through the grapevine about Ruby. They'd attended with the sole reason of meeting the woman who might replace their daughter in his affections.

Isabelle had always known the truth of their relationship and their marriage. But she'd supported them both every step of the way. She'd once told Alex that there were lots of forms of love. Some with fireworks, some with steady steps, and some with bonds of loyalty that would forsake all others.

The King had mentioned nothing of Ruby at all. He'd spoken to Alex at length about business worries and difficult negotiations.

When Alex had watched Ruby and Queen Isabelle leave the room together he'd felt sick. *Should he intervene?* But he'd been almost sure that Ruby wouldn't want that.

And when they'd returned some time later Queen Isabelle had been serenely graceful, as always, when she'd told Alex that Ruby seemed like 'a nice girl'.

His sense of relief had been enormous.

And now here they were. In the one place he'd wanted to bring her all night.

'I've been ready for ten years, Ruby,' he whispered in her ear. 'I've waited a long time for this.'

'Me too.'

Her brown eyes were fixed on his. Just like that night in Paris. The only thing missing was the reflection of the fireworks.

Ruby... Every bit as beautiful as she'd been ten years ago. Those brown eyes seemed to pull him right in, touching his heart and his soul. For the first time in ten years he was free to love exactly who he wanted to love. He had the strength and the power of his convictions and he knew what was right for him and what was right for his child. *Who* was right for him and who was right for Annabelle.

Ruby might not be Annabelle's mother, but her patience and affection for his little girl was clear. Their relationship had changed exponentially. Ruby spent hours playing with her, not just assessing the little girl. Trust had built between them. When Annabelle smiled at Ruby and looked at her in that way she had, it made his heart melt.

His little girl was every bit as much in love with Ruby as he was.

He ran his fingers along her velvet skin, from her fingertips to her shoulders. She gave a little shudder of pleasure as she smiled at him. When his fingers reached her shoulders he swept one hand along the back of her neck and traced the other gently across her décolletage. His fingers stopped mid-point as she closed her eyes and swayed a little. The curve of her breasts was highlighted in the figure-hugging dress. If Ruby knew who'd actually designed it for her, and how much it had cost, she would probably be horrified.

His hands joined at the back of the dress, where he caught the zipper in his fingers and started to release it slowly. She was holding her breath as he inched it lower. The shimmering red fabric slid from her frame and puddled on the floor at her feet as he tangled his fingers in her hair and pulled her against him.

Kissing Ruby before had been tantalising. Magical. Full of expectations and promise.

Kissing Ruby in his room as he shucked off his jacket and trousers was more than he could ever have imagined. He walked backwards, pulling her with him as they sank down on to the white bed.

The eiderdown enveloped them both. He'd dreamed about this for the last ten years. But the reality was far more incredible than his imagination could ever have envisaged. And he could envisage quite a bit.

He pulled his lips back for a second as his fingers brushed against her underwear. 'Are you sure about this, Ruby? Because there's no going back. This has to be right for both of us.'

She was holding her breath again, fixing him with her chocolate eyes. His fingers danced along her silky-smooth skin.

Her perfect red lips broke into a smile as she pressed against him. 'This is right, Alex. This has *always* been right.'

And then she kissed him again and he forgot about everything else.

CHAPTER ELEVEN

PEOPLE WERE LOOKING at her. People were fixing their eyes on her and muttering under their breath. She'd been in the shops in the city centre on lots of occasions recently but she'd never noticed this.

Even Pierre in the baker's shop wasn't his usual friendly self. He hardly even made eye contact before he handed her a brown paper bag of baked goods and waved his hand at her attempt at payment.

It made her feel uneasy. She might not speak fluent French, but she'd always muddled through and felt welcome in Euronia before.

This morning had been so strange.

The thing that she'd secretly dreamed about for such a long time had finally come true. Waking up in Alex's arms had been fantastic.

Stealing along the corridor with her dress clutched around her hadn't been quite so fantastic. But she hadn't been sure if any of the staff—in particular Rufus—might routinely go into Alex's room to wake him.

There was still so much about the palace protocols she had to learn. And last night she hadn't thought to ask Alex about any of these things—there had been far too many other sensations occupying her mind.

It had seemed so much easier to duck out and get back to her room to shower and dress. But once she'd got ready her stomach had begun churning again.

On one hand she'd wanted to go back to Alex's room. On the other she'd wanted to give him a little space. And yet they had to talk about what would happen next. About Annabelle. About Sophia's parents. All the things they hadn't really focused on last night when they'd been in each other's arms.

She loved him. She was sure of it. She just hadn't told him yet.

Maybe tonight they would be able to re-enact the whole thing. Maybe she could tell him then. But the truth was as soon as Alex had started kissing her everything else had gone out of the window except the feel of his body pressed against hers. The touch of his fingers on her skin. The sensation of his lips on her neck…

The newspapers outside one of the nearby shops fluttered in the wind. Something caught her attention. It was the colour on the front page. The exact colour of one of the dresses in her wardrobe back at the palace.

Her feet were drawn automatically. Her hand was pushing back the fluttering pages.

Princess Ruby?

The words leapt out at her and she jumped backwards on the pavement. *No. It couldn't say that.* Her heart was pounding in her chest. What on earth…?

She stepped forward again. Pushing the front page back and scanning the page. It was totally in French. She couldn't understand what was written at all.

But she really didn't need to understand. The picture said it all.

It must have been taken a few months before—just after she'd arrived. She and Alex were sitting at the café and her bright pink dress was fluttering around her—just as the newspaper pages were doing today.

But it was the moment that the picture had captured.

That second when Alex had leaned forward and cradled her cheek. He was looking at her as though she was the only person in the world and she was looking at him exactly the same way.

That moment had literally been the blink of an eye. A tiny, private fragment of two lives captured for eternity for the world.

And it had changed everything.

It was printed alongside a picture from the ball. Ruby in her long red dress with diamonds glittering in her ears.

Some eagle-eyed journalist had found and printed a picture of Alex's mother wearing the same earrings years earlier.

She couldn't understand any of the words that were written. But she could understand the panic clamouring in her chest.

No. Just when things between her and Alex seemed to be heading in a perfect direction.

What was happening between them was private. It wasn't for the world's consumption. She felt indignant. She felt angry. She felt stupid.

Alex was a prince—at some point would be King.

This would always be the life of whoever he showed interest in. She was a fool to think otherwise. And this was exactly what he'd tried to warn her about.

She leaned back against the newspaper rack, breathing heavily. She was seeing tiny stars in her peripheral vision. People were staring at her and whispering. Her phone started to ring and she grappled with her bag to pull it out.

It was a number she didn't recognise. 'Hello?'

'Ruby Wetherspoon? This is Frank Barnes from *Celebrity News*. We'd like to interview you.'

'How did you get this number? This is a private number.'

'We'd like to know about your relationship with the Prince Regent and the recent photos that have been taken of the two of you together. We understand that you're working together. But it looks a whole lot more personal than that. Would you like to do an exclusive with us?'

Every word sent a chill down her body. For a few seconds she couldn't even speak. Then, 'No. Don't phone again.'

She disconnected the call and looked around her. Alex. She had to talk to Alex.

Her phone started to ring again. Another unknown number. She pressed the button at the top, switching the whole thing off.

She put her head down and her legs on automatic pilot, walking back to the palace. She resisted the temptation to break into a run.

The warm sun was usually pleasant, but her face felt flushed and she could feel the sweat running down her back. The usually enticing smells from the delicatessen, the baker and chocolatier made her stomach flip over.

All she wanted to do was talk to someone—talk to Alex. Talk to Polly. Talk to anyone—anyone but a journalist.

Her legs were burning. The warm air didn't seem to be fully filling her lungs. There it was in the distance—the pink palace. She reached the gates and crossed the gardens quickly. The driveway had never seemed so long.

When she finally reached the palace entrance the doorman barely glanced at her. Was that a sign of something?

As she stepped into the hallway she was aware of the absolute silence. Usually there was always noise from somewhere—talking servants, discussions between visitors, footsteps from people going about their daily business.

Today the whole palace seemed silent.

She turned on her heel and headed for the library. If she'd had an ounce of common sense about her she would have purchased one of those newspapers. Instead she was reduced to doing an internet search.

The amount of hits made her cringe. *How many?*

Her eyes widened as she read, and tears formed in her eyes as a horrible feeling of dread crept over her skin.

Pictures really did speak a thousand words.

If Alex had any doubt about how she felt about him, once he'd glanced at these pictures he—and the world—would know for sure.

If she was an ordinary girl, in an ordinary world, this might seem quite nice. The looks and glances in the pictures were reciprocal. She wasn't just fawning over him. Their gazes were locked together—as if, for that second, they were the only two people on the planet.

Little moments, captured in time.

Tears started to roll down her cheeks. She'd tried to be so careful. She'd tried to be guarded. She didn't want the whole world to know that she'd loved Alex de Castellane for the last ten years. It had taken her long enough to admit that to herself.

Things were good between them right now. Things were great. Annabelle was showing real signs of improvement. And Alex...

He was showing real signs of moving on. *Really* moving on.

Last night had been wonderful.

She clicked on another link. This time it was a red-top newspaper from England. It carried the same photographs as the others. But the text took her breath away.

Vitriol. Libel.

Ruby Wetherspoon had been plotting to get her hands on Alex de Castellane for years. She'd come to Euronia purely with the purpose of trapping the world's most eligible bachelor into marriage. She was a devious woman with money on her mind.

No mention of Annabelle. No mention of her job.

She clicked on the next link. An exclusive from Maria Cochette, telling of how Ruby Wetherspoon had laughed at the way she'd tricked Alex into giving her his mother's

diamond earrings and said it was only a matter of time before she got a whole lot more. Apparently Maria had known
right from the start what kind of woman she was—and
Alex was still heartbroken after the death of his wife…
he was vulnerable.

Ruby retched. Any minute now she was going to be sick.

This was all her own fault. She should never have
crossed Maria Cochette last night. Of *course* someone like
her would have newspaper contacts. The truth was Ruby
had no idea how to handle people like that. She was unprepared for what she was up against—and it showed. She
just wasn't equipped to be part of this world.

The tiny little bit of backbone she'd shown last night
had backfired spectacularly.

How many times had she picked up a newspaper or
a glossy magazine and devoured all the headline news?
She'd read about affairs, arguments, secret children, kid-
napping, celebrity diets and drunken parties. Although
she was sure it was sometimes blown out of proportion,
she'd never really given much thought as to how much of
it was actually lies.

She'd never given *any* thought to the fact that some of
those people might be hurt by what was being written about
them. She'd never considered it at all.

Not until now.

It seemed some of the papers had gone to extremes.
One had tracked down an ex-boyfriend for a whole range
of quotes about her that had been blown out of proportion.

She cringed. Luke wasn't that kind of guy. He wasn't
malicious and she knew that. He'd just been blind-sided.
But the words *'I always knew she wouldn't stay with me'*
still hurt.

The truth was Luke had never really stood a chance
against the memory of a guy he knew nothing about. None
of her exes ever had.

She was feeling swamped. Overwhelmed. No one mentioned the kiss. No one mentioned the fact that Alex had kissed her in front of everyone and made it clear how he felt about her.

Maria Cochette claimed she'd hung over Alex all night—apparently her conduct had been 'desperate and embarrassing'.

Other reports said the King and Queen of Leruna had been 'horrified' by her presence and had seemingly reacted with shock at the thought of Princess Ruby replacing their daughter.

Was this true? Had she maybe misread the whole situation?

Right now she didn't know what was right and what was wrong.

Her eyes swam with tears. Reaction was overwhelming her, swamping her with emotions she didn't know how to control.

Today should be a happy day. Today should be the start of a new kind of relationship with Alex.

Instead it was turning into the worst day of her life, with the world thinking she was some kind of sad, desperate woman who wanted to trap a prince.

Not a girl whose heart was filled with joy because she'd finally connected with the man she'd loved for ten years.

There was a noise behind her. Alex. His face was almost grey and the warm eyes she'd expected to see were clouded with worry. Rufus and another advisor were at his back.

'There you are, Ruby.' He walked across the library in long strides. 'We need to talk.'

Today wasn't supposed to be like this. He was supposed to be smiling. Taking her in his arms and telling her that he loved her.

But Alex looked distant.

She could almost see all her hopes and dreams disintegrating in front of her.

This was all her nightmares come true.

* * *

For a few seconds that morning everything had been perfect—right up until he'd woken up and found his bed empty.

Ruby was gone. He'd expected her still to be in his arms, expected to touch her soft hair and stroke her silky skin. Instead there had been a little dip in the bed where she'd lain.

He hadn't had much time to think after that, because Rufus and the other advisors had arrived, their faces grim.

It had been more than bad news. Ruby had been painted as a villain across the world's media. He guessed that jealous Maria Cochette had phoned most of her contacts to give the most skewed and inaccurate view of the evening.

His worst fears. People had painted his marriage to Sophia as a fairytale. No woman could live up to the aftermath of that. It was what he'd always feared and tried to protect Ruby from.

In his head, he knew exactly what he should have done. He should have introduced Ruby gradually to the world's press. He should have made it clear she was no longer an employee. She was a friend. A family friend.

But his heart hadn't been able to keep the slow pace required. He'd already waited ten years for Ruby. He didn't want to wait for the media to catch up with him. He didn't want to waste a tiny second. But his impatience had probably cost him everything.

This was all his fault. Totally his fault.

He should have spoken to Ruby about this. He should have spoken to his advisors. He should have prepared her, taken his time, treated her with the respect and love that she was due.

He was unworthy of Ruby. He'd failed her completely.

And from the look on her face she thought that too.

'I went to the shops…I went to buy us breakfast,' her words faltered. 'I know that they have everything in the kitchen, but I wanted to get something special—for us.'

Her voice was shaky and her eyes were strangely blank, as if she was disengaged. As if she couldn't really comprehend what was happening in the world around her. His heart twisted in his chest. She'd walked into the city. She'd found out about this on her own.

There were tear trails down her cheeks, glinting in the morning sun. He ignored the advisors in his ears and knelt next to her chair, staring at the computer screen in front of her.

'I'm sorry, Ruby. I should have prepared you for this.'

Her eyes widened in clear disbelief. 'You can prepare people for *this*? For these lies? This complete invasion of privacy?' She shook her head. 'They phoned me. Someone phoned me this morning, wanting an interview—'

'What did you say?' butted in Rufus.

Alex held up his hand to silence him.

She was still shaking her head. 'I hung up. How did they get my number?'

Alex took a deep breath. 'It's not hard, Ruby. They do things like this all the time. You get used to it.'

'You get used to *this*? How?'

He reached out and took her hand. It was icy cold and that shot a little fear into his heart. He could see the hopes and dreams for the way all this should go begin to crumble all around him.

It was her face. The expression on her face. She was devastated. Beyond devastated. And he was the one who'd exposed her to this.

She pulled her hand backwards. 'What about Annabelle, Alex? How will you keep Annabelle from this? Is this the kind of life she'll have? Every teenage kiss, every hand-hold, every party plastered across the press?' She was shaking her head and tears were flowing freely now. 'How on earth will you keep her safe from all this?'

Safe. The word struck fear inside. Ruby didn't feel safe. But something else had resonated with him. Even now she was thinking about Annabelle in the future. She was raising the issue of trying to protect his daughter.

'We have rules in Euronia, Ruby. Photographers are not allowed to take unofficial pictures of any members of the royal family. We're strict about these things. They know they have to respect our privacy.'

'Really?' She spun the laptop around to face him again. 'So what happened here, then?'

It was one of the photos from the newspapers. A picture from months ago, when he'd first taken her to the café in front of the casino.

'What happened to respecting your privacy? What happened to respecting *my* privacy. This was when I first got here—how many more private pictures do they have of me, Alex?'

Her breaths were ragged, the pain on her face sending shards through his heart. This was exactly what he hadn't wanted to happen. But these last few days his feelings for Ruby had just started to overwhelm him.

She'd been in his mind and his thoughts for ten years. Having her under his palace roof had taken every single element of his self-control. She'd opened his world again—asked him the right questions, made him question his own thoughts and feelings. She'd influenced his relationship with his daughter. It had improved beyond all recognition.

It was almost as if she'd taught him how to be a parent. How to love every part of Annabelle and, more importantly, how to communicate with a little girl who wouldn't talk to him. Before he'd been confused and felt guilty. Now he took each day as it came. His time devoted to Annabelle was never compromised.

Ruby was still crying, the tears slowly trickling down her cheeks. He reached out and touched her cheek but she flinched.

'I'm not the person they say I am,' she whispered. 'I don't want people to write things like that about me.'

His heart was breaking for her. 'Ruby, I'm sorry. I should never have invited you to the ball. I should have waited. *We* should have waited. If we'd introduced you slowly the press would have been easier. My advisors could have told you how to act, what to say. This is my fault.' He shook his head, 'I just didn't want to wait any longer, Ruby. I wanted you to be part of my world—part of Annabelle's world.'

Right now he couldn't care who else was in the room. Right now he was only interested in Ruby. The pain on her face was tearing him apart. More than anything he wanted her to look at him and tell him that was what she wanted too. To be part of his world. But even though she was looking at him it was as if she'd switched off.

She shook her head. 'But that's just it, Alex. I don't *want* someone to tell me how to act and what to say.' She pressed her hand against her chest. 'What's wrong with just me—Ruby Wetherspoon?'

He took both her hands in his. 'Nothing—nothing at all. We can make this better, Ruby. I promise. *I* can make this better. We can work together. We can find a way to deal with the press. I'll find the photographer who took those pictures of us and he or she will never be allowed in Euronia again. This isn't as bad as you think.'

There was a noise behind him. The tiniest clearing of a throat...the squeak of a shoe. Ruby's eyes darted to the advisors behind him. He winced. He didn't need to turn around to know what the expressions on their faces must look like. He'd heard them talk incessantly since they'd knocked on his bedroom door this morning.

Their solution was simple: Ruby must go. The good name of Euronia must be protected and if the Prince Regent wanted to date then it must be handled by the press team.

He hated this. He hated all of this. For the first time in his life he wished he was free of all this. Free of the responsibility. Free of the ties. He wanted to be free to love

the woman he'd loved for the last ten years. He wanted to
be free to tell the world that. He didn't need to ask their
permission.

'Ruby, talk to me. Tell me what you're thinking. Whatever it is you're worried about—we can fix it. We can make
this work. You and I can be together. I love you, Ruby. I'm
not going to lose you twice.'

She sucked in a deep breath. It was the first time he'd
told her how he really felt about her. But this wasn't the
way he'd wanted to do that. Telling someone you loved
them should be for sunsets and fireworks—not bright li-
braries, with three other people listening to every word.

Ruby pushed herself up from the chair and walked over
to the window, looking out over the gardens. It was almost
as if she hadn't heard his words.

'I need to go, Alex. I need to get away from all this.
I can't think straight.' She reached out and touched one
of the ornate curtains at the window. 'I need to get away
from here. This isn't my place. This isn't my home.' She
spun around to face him. 'I need to get away from *you*,
Alex.'

It was like a wave of cold water washing over him. She
hadn't reacted to his words. She hadn't even acknowledged
that he'd said he loved her.

Doubts flooded through him. Maybe he'd been wrong
all along. Maybe she didn't feel the same way as he did.
Maybe this was her way of letting him down gently.

He felt his professional face fall into place—his Prince
Regent face—the one he'd never had to use around Ruby.

'Where will you go?' He couldn't help it, his words
were stumbling.

This time her eyes seemed more focused. 'I'd always
planned on visiting my mum and dad at Christmas. I'll
go now. They're in France. I can get there in a few hours.'

Her shoulders straightened. He watched her suck in another deep breath and look his advisors square in the eyes.

She was determined. It was almost as if now she'd made a decision nothing would get in her way. She started to walk forward.

He tried to be rational. He tried to think logically. 'I'll arrange for the jet to take you.'

She gave him the briefest nod and walked straight out of the door. Not a single hesitation or backward glance.

His advisors all started talking at once. But Alex couldn't hear them. All he could focus on was the stillness of Ruby's skirts as she walked along the corridor. The spark and joy he'd felt around her last night had vanished. Even the sway in her steps had been curtailed.

His Princess Ruby was vanishing before his eyes.

She couldn't breathe. An elephant was currently sitting on her chest, squeezing every single breath from her lungs.

Her legs burned as she climbed the stairs and strode along the corridor to her room.

Alex had told her that he loved her.

Alex had told her that he loved her.

Her heart should be singing. Instead it felt as if it had been broken in two.

All those conversations. All those questions about whether she was sure, whether she was ready.

The cold, hard truth was that she wasn't. Right now she doubted she ever would be. Waking up to see people she didn't know telling lies about her, people the world over reading and believing those lies, was like being dunked in an icy-cold bath.

Was this what her life would become?

She opened the cupboard and pulled out her suitcase, leaving it open on the bed. She started yanking clothes from their hangers, not bothering to fold anything.

Then she stopped, her fingers coming into contact with some of the more delicate fabrics. Some of the more beautiful designs.

Were these clothes even hers?

Should she even take them?

Confused, she walked into the bathroom and emptied the area around the sink with one sweep of her hand into her toiletries bag.

There was a movement to the side of her eye. She sighed. Alex. She needed some space.

Except it wasn't Alex. It was Annabelle, her eyes wide as she looked at the disarray in the room.

Ruby was shocked. She dropped to her knees and put her hands on Annabelle's shoulders. The little girl's bottom lip was trembling.

'Oh, honey,' she said. 'I'm sorry. But I need to go away for a little while. I need to leave.'

Annabelle shook her head. Her mouth opened and she scowled fiercely.

'No.'

It was one word. It was a tiny word—fuelled by emotion. But it was the biggest step in the world.

She flung her arms around the little girl. She hadn't thought it was possible for her heart to break any more. But she hadn't counted on this.

She cradled the blonde curls in her fingers and whispered in Annabelle's ear. 'I love you, honey. And I'm so proud of you for saying that word. You are such a clever little girl.' She pulled back and held Annabelle's face in her hands. 'That's the best word I've ever heard.'

'No.'

Annabelle said it again, and pointed to the case. There was another movement to the side. This time it *was* Alex. His face was pale.

'Ruby?'

She nodded. 'Yes. She spoke to me.'

She kissed Annabelle on the forehead, then lifted her and handed her to Alex as she continued to pack her case.

Alex was the parent here—not her. It was his job to be

by his daughter's side. She doubted she could ever fulfil her professional role again. Loving both Alex and Annabelle had wrecked her perspective. Becoming emotionally attached would make leaving harder for them all. She had to draw a line in the sand.

Alex's face was racked with confusion. 'And you're still going to go?'

She nodded. She had to.

Everything was too much right now. She didn't just love Alex. She loved his little girl too. If she didn't leave now she didn't know how her heart could ever recover.

She jammed the last thing into the case and closed it. Picking it up, she turned to face him.

He was clutching his daughter and shaking his head. 'How can you? How can you go now?'

'Because I have to. Because this is the right thing to do.' She stepped up close to him. 'Because if I stay this will only get worse. You think I didn't see the panic on your advisors' faces? You think I don't know that every single action you take could affect the people in this country— your trade agreements, your business? I'm not so stupid as to want to destroy the country that you've built. I'm not that stupid and I'm not that selfish.'

'But what about us?' He glanced down towards Annabelle, who had cuddled into his chest. 'How can you leave us now?' He was getting angry. He was getting frustrated. 'Don't you have a heart?'

She flinched. But it was exactly what she'd needed to hear. It made it so much easier.

'I left my heart in Paris ten years ago, Alex. You should know.'

And she held up her head and walked out of the room before her shaking legs could stop her.

CHAPTER TWELVE

IT WAS STRANGE, spending Christmas in France. The weather was unseasonably warm. Ruby was used to Christmases in England, with freezing temperatures and snow.

Her mother appeared at the door. She had a pale cream envelope in her hand. 'This came for you. I had to sign for it.' She turned it over and over in her hands.

Ruby sighed. 'Is it from Alex?'

She stared at her desk. It was already littered with A4 envelopes—some from Alex, and some from his advisors. All full of details on how to deal with 'the situation'. Pages and pages of plans for dealing with the press.

A plan for how often she could be seen. A plan for how much time they could spend together. A plan for when Alex could eventually put an arm around her. Followed by detailed protocols and information on the history of Euronia and Leruna. It was like studying for a university degree all over again. But this wasn't a qualification. This was a plan for a life. *Her* life.

And she just didn't know if she was strong enough.

In amongst the plans were little handwritten cards from Alex. He'd sent one every day, his pleading words increasing in intensity with each card.

'You'll have to speak to him sooner or later,' her mother said. 'He phones three times a day. I'm beginning to feel like he's part of the family already.'

The words twisted inside her. 'I can't speak to him, Mum, you know that. I need some time.'

Her mother sighed and sat down next to her. 'Why do you need time away from the man and the little girl that you obviously love?'

Ruby was shocked. She'd never used those words to her mother. She hadn't said those words out loud to anyone.

'What? You think I didn't know?' Her mother waved her hand. 'It's been written all over your face from the second you got here. I've never seen you so miserable. It was a few lousy newspaper articles. You know what your dad says—today's news, tomorrow's chip paper.' She gave a half-shrug. 'You only made two lines today in the British press.'

Ruby gave a half-smile. Her father had been surprisingly good-natured.

She stared at the letter. 'I don't think I can read anything else from Alex.'

Her mother shook her head. 'It's not from Alex. It's from Leruna. Who would be writing to you from there?'

Her skin prickled. She couldn't have—could she?

She took the heavy envelope in her hand and opened it, sliding the paper out. There was no doubt. The royal mark was in the top corner. Queen Isabelle.

She blinked. 'Give me a minute, Mum, will you please?'

Her mother nodded and disappeared out through the door. Ruby unfolded the letter on her desk. No typing. This letter was full of beautifully crafted handwriting.

Dear Ruby

I hope this letter finds you well. It was a pleasure to meet you at the Ball and I was delighted to see your obvious affection for Annabelle and your commitment to her.

I understand that you are upset over the recent media coverage. Please be assured that this is a cross

*we all have to bear. I only hope that a little time will
give you the strength and courage of your convictions to fight for the love and family that you deserve.*

*Alex and Annabelle have blossomed in these last
few months. I have no doubt who is responsible for
the transformation of their relationship. The press
can be cruel to us all, but I hope that you won't allow
others to impact on the life you could have.*

*My granddaughter misses you terribly. The spar-
kle that had returned to her eyes has gone again.*

*My beloved Sophia is gone. She was a kind-
hearted girl with a much wilder spirit than she was
credited for. I believe that she would have wanted
both Alex and Annabelle to be loved with the passion that they deserve.*

*I want you to know that you will always be wel-
come as my guest in Leruna. You have our full support.*

Good grace and wishes,

*Her Majesty Isabella DeGrundall, Queen of
Leruna*

Ruby's head was swimming. She could never have expected this. It wasn't even the words that Queen Isabella
had used. It was all the unwritten things in between. She
was giving Ruby her blessing. She was acknowledging
her presence in Alex and Annabelle's life. The invitation
was clear.

'Ruby?'

Her mother was hovering around the door again.

'The car that brought the letter…it's still there. It's waiting for you.'

'Waiting for me?' She glanced outside.

Her mother smiled. 'It seems there's a celebration for
New Year's Eve tonight in Euronia.' There was a rustle

and she held up a clothes hanger and a shimmering dress. 'Apparently your attendance is non-negotiable.'

The flight took less than an hour. The stewardess helped Ruby into the dress and escorted her down to the waiting car.

Her eyes were squeezed shut for most of the drive as her stomach turned over and over.

So many thoughts and questions spun around in her brain. Although having some space had served her well, reading over the plans for her gradual romance had been mind-boggling.

She didn't want to live her life to a plan. But rational thoughts were starting to creep in. She loved Alex. She loved Annabelle. They weren't your average family. And if Ruby wanted this life she was going to have to work for it.

Was it really so unreasonable for her to learn how to handle the press? Would learning about a new country and its customs really be so different from gaining the professional degree and qualifications she already had?

She knew she had the ability to learn. She knew she had the ability to adapt to different situations—she'd been doing it for years in the health service.

She was thinking with her heart instead of her head. If she thought with her head this all seemed rational—practical. It seemed like something she could actually do.

The car turned down the driveway towards the palace and she gasped. The pink palace was outlined in dozens of white lights. It was spectacular. People from the city were within the grounds. It seemed the party had already started.

The car pulled up in front of the palace doors and a guard opened the door and held out a hand to help her out.

She glanced at her watch. Eleven o'clock on New Year's Eve. Eleven years ago she'd been in Paris. Eleven years ago she'd met Alex for the first time. Eleven years ago they'd shared their first kiss.

Alex. He was standing at the top of the steps waiting for her.

She'd thought she'd hesitate when she saw him again—she'd thought she'd waver.

But she didn't. She moved away from the car and took her first step towards him.

Her dress was shimmering silver, crying out to be touched, but he kept his hands firmly at his sides as she climbed the steps towards him.

The designer who'd made it had assured him it would look perfect on her. But 'perfect' wasn't close enough to how it actually looked.

The silver beads sparkled in the white lights around the palace. If Annabelle were watching she'd think that Ruby was some kind of fairy. It was almost as if a movie spotlight were shining on her.

She stopped just a few steps away, her hair curled around one shoulder, brown eyes fixed on his and her red lips inviting his kiss.

He held out his hand towards her. 'I'm so glad you came, Ruby. I was worried you would never come back to Euronia.'

'I wasn't sure if I wanted to.'

He could see the uncertainty on her face. She still hadn't decided what she wanted to do. This was it. This was his final chance to convince her to stay.

'I don't want to be part of someone's plan, Alex. I appreciate the work that your staff has done. But I don't think I can live my life like that.' She gave a sorry smile and a little shake of her head. 'I can't wait to love you, Alex. I can't wait to love Annabelle. But I don't have royal blood. I haven't been brought up in the same circumstances as you.' She held out her hands. 'I think we both need to face facts. I just don't fit in around here.'

Her dress shimmered some more, reflecting light back

up onto her face. She'd never looked so beautiful. She'd never looked so radiant. And he couldn't bear not to touch her for a second longer. His heart was filling with joy and breaking at the same time. She'd told him that she couldn't wait to love him. She couldn't wait to love Annabelle. But it was too hard. There were a million obstacles in their way.

But all that mattered to Alex was the fact that Ruby loved him and his daughter just as much as they loved her.

At the end of the day, what more did he need?

He would do anything to make this work.

He wrapped his arms around her waist and pulled her close.

'Eleven years ago in Paris I met the woman of my dreams. Eleven years ago I met the woman I was destined to be with for ever. Fate tried to get in the way. Life tried to get in the way. But from the first time I met you—from the first time I kissed you—I knew, Ruby. I just *knew*. I think that you did too.'

The palms of her hands were resting against his chest. Her bottom lip was trembling.

He smiled at her. 'Ruby, I don't ever want to let you go. You are the only woman I want by my side. But more than anything I want you to be happy. You are the best woman I've ever known. I love you, Ruby. Annabelle loves you too. I'd love to tell you I don't care what the media says— but that wouldn't be true.'

She flinched and he pressed on, moving one hand from her waist and pressing it above her heart.

'I care because *you* care. I don't want anyone to hurt you. I don't want anyone to upset you. I want you to be happy. I want you to be safe. I want to love you, cherish you and keep you for ever. I want you by my side whatever I do.'

'But what about me, Alex? What about my work? I'm not a stay-at-home kind of girl.'

Even as she said the words she wondered how true they were. She'd already been thinking of changing her role at work and trying to find a less stressful kind of job. She loved her patients. She just didn't love the bureaucracy.

He smiled. 'I want what you want. I want to support you in any work you want to do. What is it you want to do, Ruby? Can you do it Euronia?'

She nodded slowly. 'I want to work with people, Alex.'

'Then you can. We have a hospital here. You can be the people's Princess Ruby. If you want to work there—you can.'

'Really?' Things were starting to seem more real. More possible. More within her grasp.

'I want you to be the person I turn to when I need guidance. I want you to be the person Annabelle comes to when she cuts her knee, quarrels with her friends and...' he grimaced '...needs boyfriend advice. I want you to be the person holding my hand and squeezing it when Annabelle says her first sentence. When she starts school. When she's crowned Queen of Leruna.'

Her voice trembled. 'That's a whole lot of wants, Alex. Some parts even sounded like wedding vows.'

He nodded slowly. 'They did—didn't they?' He reached up and tangled his fingers in her hair. 'Here's another one, then. I *want* to make this work. I want to make this work for you and me.'

Tears were forming in her eyes. 'I want this to work too, Alex. I've missed you, and I've missed Annabelle these last few days. I felt as if I'd left part of me behind. But I still want to be normal too, Alex. I'll let you down. I'm not cut out for this kind of life. I'm just Ruby Wetherspoon from Lewisham.' She gave the slightest shake of her head. 'I can't be Princess Ruby.'

One tear slid down her cheek. He pulled her closer and whispered in her ear. 'I think you can. I think you and I can figure this out together. There's no one else for me, Ruby. It's just you. Tonight is our anniversary. Tonight, eleven years ago, someone was smiling down from up above and telling me to reach into the crowd and pull the girl in the red coat up next to me. And that was it.'

He pulled back and pressed his hand over his heart.

'That was it for me, Ruby. Our defining moment. Everything in between has been just smoke and mirrors. Everything that's happened has brought us to here and now.' He held out his hand over the palace grounds. 'This is where we're supposed to be right now. This is what we're supposed to be doing.'

'Paris was a fairytale, Alex. Every girl knows that fairytales don't come true.'

He smiled and slipped an arm around her shoulders, turning her to look out over the crowds. 'But fairytales are magic, Ruby—don't you know that? Every girl doesn't get a prince. Just like every guy doesn't get a princess. But I'm hoping that tonight my fairytale comes true.'

The fireworks started immediately.

The crowd in the gardens all turned towards them. They were spectacular. White and gold Catherine wheels streaking across the black sky. Flashes of blue and red confetti cannons. Roman candles and rockets firing into the sky and exploding in a cascade of brilliant lights. The effects were dazzling.

Multi-coloured waterfall fireworks came at the end of the display, mirroring the fireworks in Paris eleven years ago. They'd been put there at Alex's special request. Would Ruby remember them?

Of course she did. She turned and smiled at him.

'It's almost identical.' Her voice was low and hoarse. 'I haven't watched a firework display since then, Alex. I didn't want anything to spoil the memories I had of Paris.'

His heart lifted. She felt the same as he did. 'Ruby, I love you. I want you to stay with me in Euronia. I don't want you to be Annabelle's speech therapist. I don't want you to be an employee. I don't want you to be waiting in the wings. I'm ready, Ruby. I'm ready to tell the world that I love you and I want you by my side.'

He held his hand up to the fireworks.

'This is for us, Ruby, and I'll recreate these fireworks every year for us. Eleven years ago was the start. I wish we'd had a chance to continue from there. And while I wish my friend Sophia hadn't died I couldn't ever wish my daughter Annabelle wasn't here. Maybe it was always destined that our two countries would be united. But what I know in my heart is that I was always destined for you.'

He knelt down on one knee and pulled the ring he'd had made out of his pocket.

'I love you, Ruby Wetherspoon. Will you do me the honour of agreeing to become my wife? I promise to love and cherish you for ever. I promise to be by your side no matter what happens. Whatever you want to do, you will have my full support. And I hope I will have yours. What do you think, Ruby? Can we create our own fairytale here, in Euronia?'

The fireworks continued to explode behind her. The shimmering silver dress reflected every one of them in the dark night. The colours lit up Ruby's face and there it was—the sparkle in her eyes again. The thing he'd longed for and hoped to see for the last two weeks.

She reached down and pulled him up. She was smiling. 'Don't kneel for me, Alex. That's not where I want you.' She slipped the custom-made ruby and diamond ring on to her finger. 'I want you right by my side.'

He slipped his arms around her. 'Is that a yes?'

She slid her arms around his neck and tipped her lips towards his. 'That's definitely a yes.'

And he kissed her as the fireworks lit up the sky behind them.

Princess Ruby was here to stay.

EPILOGUE

RUBY ADJUSTED HER veil nervously while Polly fussed around her.

'How long *is* this train?'

They were currently all enveloped in the back of the car by mounds and mounds of jewelled pale cream satin. She practically couldn't even see her father at this point.

'Twenty-five feet.' She smiled, even though she was afraid to move. 'Apparently it's a tradition.'

'It's a tradition, all right. Can you even walk with this thing?'

Ruby nodded. 'I've been practising.'

Polly's eyes widened. 'You have? When?'

She smiled again. 'At night. Rufus—Alex's private secretary—has helped me for the last few nights. We've practised up and down the main staircase and out through the main doors.'

'Wow.' Polly handed Ruby her red flowers and lifted her hands to straighten the ruby and diamond tiara on Ruby's head. 'Seems like someone has introduced a few traditions of their own.'

'Ooby—look!' Annabelle was practically standing on one of the other seats, waving at the crowds as they passed, her short red bridesmaid dress bouncing around her.

Ruby stretched over. 'Come here.' She gave Annabelle a hug. 'You look beautiful, Annabelle. You're going to be the most gorgeous girl anyone has ever seen.'

The little girl couldn't stop smiling. Her speech was improving every day. Simple words...

The car pulled up outside the church and Ruby couldn't wipe the smile from her face. *This was it.*

It seemed to take for ever for Polly and her father to unwind her dress and the train from the car. Then there was a nod as Polly took Annabelle's hand and led her ahead.

She waved to the crowds and headed to the church door, the heavy train hampering her steps. If she had her way she'd be running down the aisle to meet Alex.

The crowd in the church was hushed. Queen Isabelle turned from the front pew and gave her the tiniest nod of her head. But Ruby's eyes were fixed on Alex.

There was no tradition here. Her groom would never stand facing the front, waiting for her to appear.

Alex had turned around to face her, his bright blue eyes fixed firmly on hers, smiling from ear to ear. He'd never looked more handsome. She'd never been so sure.

Ruby's father took her arm. 'Ready?'

She nodded. 'Always,' she said, and took the first steps that would start her new life.

* * * * *

LET'S TALK
Romance

For exclusive extracts, competitions
and special offers, find us online:

f facebook.com/millsandboon

🐦 @MillsandBoon

📷 @MillsandBoonUK

Get in touch on 01413 063232

For all the latest titles coming soon, visit
millsandboon.co.uk/nextmonth

JOIN US ON SOCIAL MEDIA!

Stay up to date with our latest releases, author
news and gossip, special offers and discounts, and
all the behind-the-scenes action
from Mills & Boon...

 millsandboon

 millsandboonuk

 millsandboon

It might just be true love...

MILLS & BOON
MEDICAL
Pulse-Racing Passion

Set your pulse racing with dedicated, delectable doctors in the high-pressure world of medicine, where emotions run high and passion, comfort and love are the best medicine.